Cross Talk

Caught Dead in Wyoming series

Sign Off
Left Hanging
Shoot First
Last Ditch
Look Live
Back Story
Cold Open
Hot Roll
Reaction Shot
Body Brace
Cross Talk
Air Ready
Holiday Bullets
Cue Up

"While the mystery itself is twisty-turny and thoroughly engaging, it's the smart and witty writing that I loved the best."
—*Diane Chamberlain, New York Times bestselling author*

More mystery from Patricia McLinn

Secret Sleuth series

Death on the Diversion
Death on Torrid Avenue
Death on Beguiling Way
Death on Covert Circle
Death on Shady Bridge
Death on Carrion Lane
Death on ZigZag Trail
Death on Puzzle Place

The Innocence Trilogy

Proof of Innocence
Price of Innocence
Premise of Innocence

Storm clouds at KWMT

The Caught Dead in Wyoming mystery series is reaching a vital turning point. *Cross Talk* picks up where *Body Brace* left off, as Elizabeth and her cohorts work to unravel the truth behind the death of a woman described as Thurston Fine's top fan. But there is more going on in Elizabeth's life. A resolution is coming for her romantic relationship(s), but Elizabeth, and Mike and Tom—or is it Tom and Mike?—must change through the course of the series to reach the point that there could be a happy beginning.

CROSS TALK

Caught Dead in Wyoming, Book 11

Patricia McLinn

Cover design: Art by Karri
Cover image: Nicolaus Wegner

DAY ONE

MONDAY

Chapter One

IF YOU'VE SEEN movies where a soldier carrying his flag in battle is shot and one of his brethren picks up the staff and carries it forward, you get the general idea of what happens when a major cog in a daily newscast goes down.

In this case, the cog was Thurston Fine.

He's the anchor at KWMT-TV in Sherman, Wyoming, where I also work. E.M Danniher, "Helping Out!" consumer affairs reporter, that's me.

Despite Thurston's lack of ability—rare among anchors—he is, by definition, a major cog.

He refuses to share anchor duties, so there's no co-anchor to take up the slack as at most semi-sane news operations. (None is totally sane.)

In sports, the theory is called *Next Man Up*, the expectation that if one player goes down, another will move into position and carry the flag, so to speak. That's how former NFL player and KWMT-TV alum Michael Paycik explained it to me.

I asked what happened if there was no one left who played that position. He said I was harping on details when the concept mattered.

I argued details counted, including in football. Great game plan with no execution meant your team was a goner.

You'd think, with no co-anchor and with our supposed news director being Les Haeburn, that KWMT-TV also was a goner. We certainly had no game plan. What we did have—

But I'm getting ahead of myself.

Let me tell you how I learned Thurston Fine wasn't available for Monday's five and ten p.m. newscasts.

After working long hours on a special that aired Saturday night, I arrived Monday just before noon, planning to make an appearance, then take off the rest of the day to attend a funeral.

Before I reached my desk, I picked up an airborne buzz of something big happening.

I dropped my belongings and headed for the coffeemaker, both for caffeine and to discover the source of the buzz.

This buzz didn't come from something identifiable like excited voices or lots of activity. Because no one occupied any other desks in the bullpen.

Instead, what I picked up on was an effervescence in the atmosphere, residual adrenaline from major happenings past that newsrooms—even KWMT-TV's—emit when there's a big story afoot.

Audrey Adams, the day's assignment editor, turned the corner from the back hallway and gave a muffled sound.

"*Elizabeth.*" She hurried at me. "Have you heard? Do you know?"

I kept moving toward the widened area in the hallway serving as a break room. Toward the coffee pot, specifically, despite knowing what awaited me there.

Jennifer Lawton, a news aide by title and salary, but far more than that to the station, zoomed toward me from the direction of the still-swinging door to the ladies' room.

She cut directly to the news bulletin.

"Thurston's the prime suspect in a murder."

"*Thurston?*" I repeated. Then asked, "*Another* one?"

Not another time the anchor of KWMT-TV was a prime suspect in a murder, but another murder.

The special we'd aired Saturday night had been about one, too. That one solved. For which I can take some credit, along with Jennifer and several of our investigating colleagues.

"This one didn't take place here in the county," Audrey said.

That would be a relief to my friends—using the term loosely—in the Cottonwood County Sheriff's Department, some of whom pointed to a jump in their murder rate since my arrival. I pointed to an even higher jump in their cases-solved rate.

"We don't know it didn't take place here. All we know is the body wasn't *found* in Cottonwood County." Jennifer was showing off a little. I liked it. The young woman had been a huge help in several investigations since I landed in Wyoming a year and a half ago, and she'd learned a lot.

"What's the connection to Thurston?"

"We don't know that, either. Except he went to the sheriff's department a few minutes ago—"

Jennifer hijacked Audrey's words to follow her own path. "So we haven't had time to organize the celebration and order champagne."

"A banner's certainly in order," I said.

"Knock off the comedy routine you two," Audrey ordered. "Or I'm not telling you anything else."

Impressive.

Audrey's first sentence reflected her efforts at being more authoritative as she aspired to move to larger markets and better operations than KWMT—most newsrooms are both.

The second sentence demonstrated an even more important skill—knowing what makes the people she supervised fold. And fast.

Cutting off a source to answers to my curiosity sure did it for me.

I raised one hand in half a surrender. The other hand opened a cabinet for a coffee cup. I needed caffeine.

Under ordinary circumstances I needed caffeine. Under these circumstances, I *really* needed it.

"Okay, so you think Thurston's a murder suspect because...?"

"Because," Audrey said with emphasis, "sheriff's deputies came here, demanded to talk to him, took him away, and said not to expect him back soon."

That ratcheted up my attention, qualifying the events as quite different from *went to the sheriff's department a few minutes ago.*

From the standpoint of producing newscasts today, it also created a crisis.

In my share of newsroom crises, I've seen people freeze, I've seen people get tunnel vision, I've seen people act before they had the information needed to make good decisions.

The trick was getting enough to prioritize, but not waiting to know everything before acting on the most pressing issues.

Questions were the answer.

"Was he in handcuffs?"

"No… But they woke him up and insisted he go with them right away. He wasn't happy."

He seldom was. Especially not when awakened from his post-lunch nap. The guy came in late, took lunch early enough to be on East Coast time instead of Mountain, then settled in for a long nap in his office. Real tough schedule.

"It wasn't only Cottonwood County deputies, either," Jennifer continued. "The Horse Creek County deputies seemed to be in charge. I'm surprised you didn't see them leaving."

As I poured coffee from the pot kept going from the newsroom's first arrival to the last departure, I shook my head, confirming I hadn't seen law enforcement vehicles as I drove in. "Was Les here then? Is he here now?"

Les Haeburn's door with the legend "News Director" on it was closed, which was standard and not indicative of his absence.

"No and no."

"Did Thurston say anything as he left?"

"To *us*?" Jennifer's disbelief was at my thinking I needed to ask. Thurston mostly talked to a handful of acolytes and Les. That excluded most of the newsroom, including the three of us.

"To anybody. Like *call my lawyer*?"

Looking at each other, Jennifer and Audrey shook their heads. Tentatively at first, then more firmly as they faced me.

I sipped. And grimaced. I should have raised both hands in surrender and skipped the coffee. Whoever made this pot must have been really unhappy about being at the station.

"Was anybody else here?"

"No."

We all meant in the newsroom area. A spattering of non-newsroom people would be elsewhere in the building.

I put down the coffee cup and took out my phone.

"Who are you calling?" Jennifer asked.

"James Longbaugh."

The lawyer's assistant answered immediately. I identified myself and asked to speak to James.

"For *Thurston?* Why get a lawyer for Thurston?" Jennifer demanded.

Audrey took another angle. "We don't have time for that, Elizabeth. We have to have a newscast in a few hours, and then *another* one at ten. We need you to anchor—"

I held up an index finger commanding her to wait.

"Yes, hello James. Thank you for taking my call." In a couple sentences I told him what I knew of the situation, finishing with "…and I doubt he'll think to ask for, much less call, a lawyer. If you need a retainer—"

"The station has me on a retainer. I can stretch it to see what's going on. But not until after Sally's funeral."

"Thank you."

Sally's funeral. I'd almost forgotten.

With whatever measure of human kindness or professional consideration I owed a colleague—even this stinker colleague—paid out in full, I could concentrate on the next major issue.

Making sure that flag got picked up.

In other words, that we had newscasts on air at five and ten.

As soon as I clicked off, Audrey resumed. "We need you to anchor, Elizabeth. Without Thurston—I can't believe I'm worried about not having Thurston, but with so little warning… You have to do it, Elizabeth. We can't do this without you."

Although reporting floated my boat a lot higher than intro-ing and outro-ing other people's stories, I have anchored. Including in major markets, though mostly on weekends. That was all before being drop-kicked out of that career and life to Sherman, Wyoming.

Still, anchoring was comfortably in my skillset.

"Of course, you can do it, Audrey. What's the hardest part of a newscast with Thurston anchoring?"

"Making it Thurston-proof." She added ruefully, "Trying to. He once read a story about someone being tried in absentia and ad-libbed that he didn't know what part of the state it was in. Like *absentia* was a town."

I hadn't heard the story before, but it fit. "So, you gain all sorts of time from not having to Thurston-proof the copy. Besides, your local packages are in progress."

"Oh." Her gaze shot to her computer screen. She couldn't see details from here, but she had all the assignments in her head anyway. "We can get in held pieces—" Because Thurston insisted on room for his pet puff pieces on his cronies. "—and maybe more non-local news."

"Exactly. But, first, call Leona."

Leona D'Amato was the part-timer who had covered what passed for society in Cottonwood County, Wyoming, and its county seat, Sherman, since the station opened. She knew everyone, everyone knew her, she loved that job, and hated anchoring.

The last point was why Thurston approved of her as his substitute. She'd never try to take his job.

Audrey wilted a bit after her momentary cheer. "She hates hard news. She'll hate me for making her do it."

But I saw it as another good sign that she said *making* Leona anchor, not *asking* her.

"She's a pro and she'll do it. Besides, she'll be familiar to viewers."

"Right, like when she fills in when Thurston's gone for a long weekend," Jennifer said. "But you're wrong about one thing, Elizabeth. Not all the stories are in progress. What about the one on Thurston being arrested?"

Chapter Two

"OH, **G**OD**," A**UDREY groaned.

"You said he wasn't handcuffed. Very unlikely he was arrested." I spoke automatically over Audrey's groans. "He's cooperating with law enforcement in looking into this tragedy."

"That's it," the assignment editor said with abrupt intensity. "That's *exactly* the sort of phrasing we need. You have to do the story, Elizabeth. You know what we can say and what we shouldn't. The rest of us—I guess we can pull together everything else. But *that* story? You have to do it. You have to anchor."

Jennifer nodded her support.

"Absolutely not."

Audrey wilted.

Jennifer switched to head-tilted interest. "Oh, because if Thurston gets out of this murder charge, he'd try to kill you and be right back in jail. Right? But he wouldn't succeed, you know," she said, reassuringly.

She was probably right he'd try to kill me and land in jail. I hoped she was right about him not succeeding.

The other possibility was he'd die of apoplexy, but I didn't raise that. No sense getting her hopes up.

"Leona's the only appropriate person to anchor. Make the story the A block lead, deal with it right off the top, then briskly get on with the rest of the news. I'll help write the copy if we can't find Les— Where *is* Les?"

It was telling that we'd all moved so easily past his absence. In a good news operation—even most not-good news operations—the news director would lead the charge in a situation like this.

He or she might not pick up the flag from the fallen anchor, but he or she sure as heck would order someone else to.

"I don't know. He went out for an early lunch, even earlier than usual, like about ten-thirty, and not with Thurston. He hasn't been back. Should I try to call him? But I don't think the number I have works anymore. Because he said he was getting a new one and he wasn't telling anyone the new number. Ever. He said he was changing it after someone called him over lunch after he said we should never, ever call him over lunch for any reason and—"

"Slow down, Audrey. Take things in order."

She sucked in a breath. "Okay. Yes. First…"

She ground to a stop, her face blank.

I said, "No working number for Les settles the issue of whether you should call him. We'll work on the newscasts. If he shows up, fine. If he doesn't, we'll worry about that later. But, first, call Leona."

"Right, right. Okay." She hurried off to her desk.

I looked at Jennifer, who'd gone quiet and oddly interested in the ceiling.

The KWMT-TV newsroom's walls aren't interesting, much less its ceilings.

"What?" I asked her.

"I have his number if you want it."

"You have Les Haeburn's super-secret phone number he doesn't want anyone to know much less use?"

"Uh-huh. Remember he had me program a special ringtone?"

"*Ding-Dong! The Witch Is Dead.*" That stuck with me, since he used it for Val Heatherton, the station owner, no less. A person I'd yet to meet in more than a year here. "That was for email alerts."

"Also his ringtone for her. Thurston heard it and had me do his ringtone with music about Valkyries for Val Heatherton. Anyway, when Les got this new phone, he had me program it with the same ringtone. I, uh, happened to note the number on the phone. In case."

"Okay." I slowly nodded. "In fact, great. But let's see how this develops. Would hate to use up our really-need-it opportunity and then need it later."

"Because if we called him, he'd get another new phone."

"Exactly. Now—"

"How do we know when we really need it?"

"We keep going without using it until it's the only possible avenue of attack left."

"Okay. But you know even if he didn't have me program a ring-tone, I could get—?"

Audrey turned back toward us and called from her computer, "Leona had a few choice words, but she's coming straight from the funeral. Now what?"

I checked the time. I could still make the funeral.

"Adjust your blocks for the Five and Ten as you need to. Call the folks out in the field on daily stories to adjust. If you need to cut—"

"Cut? More like we'll be short. Because the first thing I'll do is trash two puff pieces Thurston insisted on." She smiled for the first time. "In fact, I can cut more padding because he insists on those long on-camera intros and Leona won't."

"Hah. Well, if you're short, run one of my backlogged 'Helping Out!' pieces." My supposedly regularly-scheduled consumer affairs pieces were the first things held. As a result, I had enough stored up to coast for years. "I have one on scams involving fake celebrities that—"

"Or more regional news."

"Already breaking reporters' hearts. You're made for this job."

Audrey ignored my piteous plaint. "Plus, we'll need time for the story about Thurston being arrested. Or not arrested," she amended quickly.

WITH THE ANCHORING situation sorted, our coverage of Thurston Fine's absence became the outstanding issue for tonight's two newscasts.

That brought attention back to why deputies knocked on Thurston's office door during his nap.

"What do we know about this person who died and the circumstances?"

I was going straight to heaven for not giving in to the temptation to say *This person Thurston's suspected of murdering.* I would never use that language on-air, but not using it in newsroom exchanges? Definitely straight to heaven.

Jennifer looked toward Audrey, letting her take the lead. A vote—probably unconscious—for Audrey's strides in leadership.

"All we know is female, mid-to-late thirties, who lives—lived—in Sherman. But they found her body in Horse Creek County."

That was an eyebrow-raiser, though it did explain why their deputies were involved in waking Thurston.

Horse Creek County is not to be confused with an unincorporated area in the southeast corner of the state also called Horse Creek.

I consider that part of Wyoming's ongoing efforts to deflect invaders.

It's not the first location with that goal, as I learned during my time in Washington, D.C. In its core, diagonal state-name streets overlay a grid of east-west alphabet streets and north-south number streets. The diagonal intersections of Pierre L'Enfant's plan result in circles or squares to baffle and delay the British if they invaded again after burning the city during the War of 1812.

The layout still baffles and delays tourists.

Wyoming doesn't have big enough cities for that, so it employs other tactics.

For example, neither Fort Laramie nor Laramie—which are not near each other—are in Laramie County, but rather Goshen and Albany counties respectively. While Horse Creek is in Laramie County, not in Horse Creek County.

Actually, not much is in Horse Creek County.

It is east of Cottonwood County and one of the smallest counties in a state favoring giant, economy-sizes.

KWMT-TV reached Horse Creek County viewers, but never covered news there during my tenure here. I did not know if that was because nothing happened or the station had a policy of not covering it.

If there was such a policy, we would make an exception for finding a dead body, especially one of a Cottonwood County resident. More accurately, former resident.

"How do you know about the body. The location? Where she lived? ID? When was she found—?"

"This morning," Audrey said with the air of someone jumping onto a moving train. "We don't know exactly when. A bulletin came over the wire during the morning meeting that the Horse Creek County Sheriff's Department had responded to a scene, without any details.

"After Les, then Thurston left, Jennifer caught something saying Horse Creek's sheriff's department had found a body, they had an ID on the body, and an address here in Sherman."

I nodded approval at Jennifer for staying on top of events.

She picked up the tale. "I called the Horse Creek County Sheriff's Department. They said *they* had an ID, but weren't telling us. Amateurs. Cottonwood County wouldn't have admitted having an ID. Anyway, since I could follow the two departments' communications—" She hurried on and I pretended I hadn't recognized she didn't want to detail *how* she managed that. "—I heard them say our deputies were meeting theirs at a location in Cottonwood County. Very cagey. No address given. It was like they'd figured out I was listening and were purposefully not saying much. But definitely Sherman. So, I told Audrey."

The assignment editor said, "I was trying to figure out how big a deal it was and who to pull off what story if we needed more—Oh! I never said. I'd already sent Diana—"

The station's best photographer and my good friend.

"—and Walt—"

A veteran reporter.

"—to the neighborhood based on what Jennifer heard. Before the deputies came for Thurston, Walt messaged that law enforcement vehicles were around, but it wasn't clear which house was involved. I have to let them know about Thurston and—"

"Do that. Get them up to speed." They'd get what there was to get. Especially if they knew the story had grown. "Jennifer will tell me the rest of what happened."

Audrey hurried off and Jennifer resumed reporting.

"It wasn't long after I'd told Audrey the intersection for Walt and Diana to focus on, when deputies walked right into the newsroom and said they needed to talk to Thurston. Guys from Horse Creek County, along with a couple from Cottonwood County—including Sergeant Shelton. Audrey said Thurston couldn't be disturbed, like we're supposed to, but they weren't taking no for an answer. Then—"

"Wait." In years in this business, I'd learned speed was good, but rushing rarely paid off. Especially rushing past important details. "How does Thurston's timeline today fit into this?"

She frowned in concentration. "When Thurston came in from lunch, I'd connected the earlier stuff about a body being found in Horse Creek County with chatter about arriving at a residence in Sherman."

"Did you say anything to him about the events?"

"*Thurston?* No way."

It was the answer I expected, but better to ask the question than assume the answer. "Go on."

"He went to his office for his nap, as usual."

"How long after did deputies come?"

She turned and looked at her computer, as if recreating what she'd done during that span. "Twenty minutes. Tops."

Drive time isn't much in Sherman, but still left the law enforcement types only ten, maybe fifteen, minutes at the dead woman's house to encounter something connecting her to Thurston.

Something with the power to bring them straight to the TV station, pick him up, and persuade him to accompany them to the sheriff's department.

Not handcuffed, but also not a quick chat in his office.

"What are you thinking, Elizabeth?"

"Not thinking a thing. Except about what we need for the story tonight. The circumstances, where the body was found—"

"Not a lot of detail, but a Horse Creek County deputy found her this morning. Audrey sent Jenks to shoot that scene, figuring law enforcement will still be working it, so there should be good video. He called just before you came in and says it looks like the body was in a vehicle on an unused road."

Raising the question of why a deputy was on an unused road.

I didn't ask. I didn't want to stop Jennifer's flow of what she did know with something she probably didn't.

"Oh," she added, "also right before you came in, I heard one deputy tell someone else the victim was thirty-seven. Not mid-to-late thirties, but specifically thirty-seven."

Knowing the dead woman's age made it far more likely law enforcement had a complete identification. Identification associated with the vehicle was a good bet. Possibly her personal ID.

As for why they weren't releasing the name, possibly as benign as ensuring they notified next of kin before it hit the news or as not-so-benign as wanting to spring a trap on … someone.

"We have to find out this woman's identity."

"We don't have the exact address, but from where deputies were parking, it's a couple blocks from the bed and breakfast, in that area of old houses north of the courthouse."

The Wild Horses Bed and Breakfast opened last year as part of a neighborhood resurgence and was well-known in town, since it offered only the third option for lodging. It was particularly well-known to KWMT-TV staffers because the couple who owned it included Krista Seger, the niece of the station's owner.

"The neighborhood where she lived," Jennifer continued, "and her age should be enough to confirm—once I have a possible name."

"Anything else?" From her expression, I thought there was.

She grinned. "They mentioned her car. A VW Beetle."

"Ah." Not the most common vehicle in Cottonwood County, Wyoming. "Checking every female of the right age associated with a VW Beetle—and keeping in mind the possibility that it could have been borrowed—might be a tedious route to a name," I warned.

"I hadn't thought about it being borrowed. Still, not so bad. Not like a Chevy pickup around here. I'll find her."

"Jennifer—"

"I'm not hacking. I'm using human capital."

"Something you learned while you were visiting Mike in Chicago?"

Michael Paycik, our former colleague—and integral part of our previous investigations—had taken a TV sports job at a major station in Chicago and Jennifer recently returned from visiting him. Her trip also resulted in her being offered a spot in a Northwestern University program starting after the first of the year.

"Nah. Learned a fancy term for what I was already doing." Ah. *The guys.* Her online buddies with skills rivaling her own. Though I worried their ethics didn't fit into my comfort zone. "I told them no hacking."

I grinned briefly in acknowledgment of her mind-reading, "Before you get back to overseeing your human capital, finish telling me what happened with Thurston and the deputies."

She lifted one shoulder. "They knocked on his office door. He bellowed. They knocked again and said they were from the Horse Creek County Sheriff's Department. He snatched open the door, his hair sticking up on one side and bellowing how he'd get anyone who disturbed him fired—then stopped mid-bellow when he saw their uniforms.

"They all went in, except one burly guy from Horse Creek, who stood outside with his arms crossed over his chest like we'd storm the door. As if I couldn't have listened in if I'd wanted to."

"Don't tell me how. Just don't tell me."

"Okay, I won't," she said cheerfully. "So, after about fifteen minutes, they all came out—Thurston was *not* in handcuffs. He said in that lofty voice like he's ordering servants around, that he was going to the sheriff's department to clear up a misunderstanding for them, like he was doing them a favor. Audrey asked when he'd be back—you could tell she was thinking about the Five—and a deputy from Horse Creek County mumbled something about taking as long as it took. As he went by, Shelton said, low, not to expect Thurston back today.

"I think he was trying to be nice. Sort of. But it knocked Audrey sideways. Gotta admit, it surprised me, too. Sure glad to see you coming in the door."

Chapter Three

I KNEW WHAT I had to do.

I'd known it almost from the minute Audrey and Jennifer started telling me what happened.

There's nothing like a crisis to focus your thinking.

Mine focused on getting two newscasts on-air for KWMT-TV in the next few hours. Ones that included adequate coverage of the news would be nice.

But before I did that, I had a funeral to attend. Not for the benefit of the deceased, a woman named Sally Tipton. But for Emmaline Parens, who had arranged the funeral and for whom I had great regard.

Audrey objected. I stood firm.

As it was, I arrived at the small church after the service started and slipped unobtrusively into a seat at the back.

The readings were uplifting, the music simple and compelling, the speakers brief and to the point.

I heard about twenty-five percent of any of it, with my mind on what came next at KWMT.

The minister and Mrs. P, accompanied by Gisella Decker, her neighbor, ally, and rival, and rancher Thomas David Burrell, exited directly into a covered side entry area where they would form the compact reception line.

Having attended other funerals in Cottonwood County, I knew I had an opening and I took it, walking New York speed down the side aisle while the rest of the attendees were slowed by exchanging greetings with those in nearby pews.

Even so, I caught a number of questioning looks from people who clearly had already heard about Thurston and wondered about my reaction. Most of those looks also held a measure of concern for me, which I was sure I'd find warming if I weren't moving so fast.

The look from Leona D'Amato held no such concern, but, instead, comradely irritation. I totally understood.

My strategy put me fifth in line to greet the receivers, behind three women and a man of Mrs. P's generation. They must have been in the other front pew to have gotten here ahead of me.

Over their heads, I briefly met the gaze of Tom Burrell, who stood behind and to the side of Mrs. Parens—not in the reception line, but clearly in support.

He lifted one brow at me in a subtle version of the others' questioning concern. Something I saw because he had not yet put his cowboy hat back on.

Things are complicated between Tom and me. Part—but not the biggest part—of that stems from things being complicated between Mike Paycik and me.

Things are not awkward between Mike and me. They have been awkward between Tom and me, but we've made progress in that area recently.

Nothing is complicated or awkward between Tom and Mike. At all. Which can be downright annoying.

I gave Tom a micro grimace in reply to his lifted brow to convey that, at the moment, the things going to hell had wildly overflowed the handbasket, but that I would cope.

"Elizabeth." Gisella enfolded me in a hug, which I returned fully. "How good of you to come under the circumstances."

"I wouldn't have missed supporting you and Mrs. Parens, Aunt Gee," I said, for she was Mike Paycik's aunt and extended the relationship to his friends. "Diana sends her regrets. She was called out on a last-second assignment."

"Of course. She's very pleased you're here." Aunt Gee's conspiratorial eye-shift indicated Emmaline Parens, who turned to me at that moment.

I extended both hands and she took hold of them. "Mrs. Parens, you all created a wonderful farewell for Sally. She could not possibly have asked for a better one."

I avoided any mention of what the woman had deserved, because she had surely gotten more consideration and care from Emmaline Parens over a lifetime than she had deserved.

"Thank you, Elizabeth. In addition to the vital service you rendered Sally in her life, it was most considerate of you to attend today, when I am aware there are unexpected and urgent calls on your time and expertise. We shall miss you, but understand that you cannot attend the graveside service nor the reception."

That was as clear a dismissal as the end-of-school bell she'd heard thousands of times in her career as a teacher and principal.

"Yes, ma'am."

The minister cleared his throat, masking a chuckle. A glint of amusement showed in Mrs. P's eyes as she introduced us. I said something mundane to him, then impulsively reached back to hug Mrs. P.

Not waiting to see any reactions, I employed another burst of New York speed to reach my SUV, exchange the funeral shoes for a workday pair I kept on hand, then zip back to KWMT-TV.

It was a good thing Cottonwood County deputies were involved with the case of a dead body and not patrolling the roads right then.

WHICH BROUGHT ME back to what I had to do.

I'd put it off as long as I could, after checking in again with Audrey to make sure she had prep for the Five in hand. She wanted to go over everything she'd done so far.

She'd wasted no time pulling in more news to the rundown, including a regional story on changing approaches to water usage—always a hot topic. Thurston would have run it ... never.

Everybody out on daily stories cooperated and most rose to the occasion. Then she called Bruce, Thurston's pet producer, which did not go well.

When Audrey hung up, she sighed. "I might have to produce the newscasts."

"You've done that before. It's hard doing double duty, but you'll handle it. And you know who you can rely on."

She perked up.

The studio camera operator and floor director, Jerry, was a professional and no fan of Thurston's. He'd do his job and support Audrey. The director was about as old as the equipment he babied along and which he liked a lot better than people. He'd do his job. Along with Leona, that should keep the newscasts on the rails.

As long as I did a decent job of writing the report on the dead woman and Thurston.

Driving my SUV out of the KWMT-TV parking lot, I waved to Leona, driving in. I wouldn't have minded a little chat. But that was pure delaying tactic.

That left me to wend my way into downtown Sherman, turn left alongside the imposing courthouse, and pull into the parking area behind it.

The lot served both the courthouse and the county buildings at the back of the block. Those buildings housed the tiny Sherman Police Department, offices for the fire department, the county jail, and (taking up the largest portion) the Cottonwood County Sheriff's Department.

I'd been to the sheriff's department many times since divorce skulduggery by my network exec ex zip-lined me from New York City to Sherman, Wyoming.

Most times I rather enjoyed the dance of wits involved in getting information from the denizens of these offices.

This time was different.

Chapter Four

DEPUTY FERRANTE WAS behind the front counter when I walked into the office, hurried along by a push in the back from a playful wind gust.

That wasn't unusual.

Neither the push from the wind, nor Ferrante behind the counter.

Still, I'd hoped for better—regarding the presence behind the counter, not the wind, though it was not as cold as last night's, thank heavens.

You could say Deputy Ferrante hadn't taken a shine to me.

Or anyone else as far as I could tell, though his wife—in one of those how-on-earth-did-these-opposites-attract? pairings—was a friendly and upbeat personality.

"I'm not telling you anything, E.M. Danniher," Ferrante declared as I entered. "You turn around and get out of here. Same as I told Needham Bender."

I withstood the temptation to say that telling me the owner, publisher, and editor of the Sherman *Independence* had been here *was* telling me something.

Declining to batter my head against the brick wall Ferrante constantly tried to erect in front of me, I sidestepped.

"When was Needham here?"

Needham and his wife had been among the concerned-questioning lookers at the church.

"Left about fifteen minutes before you came sashaying in here. Left empty-handed, the way you will."

"Sashaying?"

Before I could do more than subtly raise the question of his word choice with that echo, the door behind me opened to let in Sergeant Wayne Shelton and Deputy Richard Alvaro.

Darn.

Ferrante tried to erect a wall, Shelton succeeded. In fact, he could make the builders of the Great Wall of China look like the little pig who opted for straw.

Coming in this door, rather than a side door convenient to their parking area, could mean they'd been at the courthouse, probably in the offices of the county attorney. One possible reason to use that office was to have their confab—as yet a product of my educated conjectures—away from the ears of any Horse Creek County deputies still around.

They likely were around because I suspected Thurston was, too. I'd tried calling him on my way here. He hadn't answered. Neither had James Longbaugh.

Those thoughts proved I was on the job. Another indication was I didn't turn my back to the annoyance that is Deputy Ferrante when the newcomers arrived, but positioned myself so I could keep an eye on him, yet see the two newcomers.

"Not telling you anything, Danniher," Shelton said immediately. It seemed to be a theme with the Cottonwood County Sheriff's Department.

"All I'm here for is the official statement. Sheriff Conrad is far too professional not to have one available for the media, especially after a joint operation with the Horse Creek County Sheriff's Department. I bet Deputy Ferrante has one right there behind the counter. Though, if he doesn't have one, we'll have to go with the account from the Horse Creek County Sheriff's Department."

That oblique threat didn't unsettle Shelton a bit. He probably knew no such account by Horse Creek County existed. But I heard Ferrante's feet shuffling.

"That's all you want, an official statement." Shelton phrased it not so much as a question as an invitation to sell my soul.

"That's all I want."

And that is why I had not wanted to make this trip.

It wasn't my usual approach to a news story, not at any point while I worked my way from Dayton to St. Louis to Washington, D.C., to New York. Also not since I got my bearings after landing here.

But this was what KWMT-TV needed from me right now.

Quick in and out. Get the facts. Get back to the station. Write the story. Let the investigative chips fall where they may.

Habits are hard to break, however.

"Of course," I added, "if you choose to tell me if Thurston Fine is in custody or—"

"No." Shelton's favorite word.

"Isn't in custody?"

"I don't choose to tell you."

"Is he still here talking to authorities?"

"No comment."

"Did Thurston know the victim?"

"No comment."

"If he didn't, what made you decide it was urgent to talk to him right after you'd arrived at the victim's home? Must have been something there."

Shelton didn't even flicker an eyelash.

Neither did Richard Alvaro, who—from a journalist's point of view—had been learning all the wrong things by hanging around Shelton.

But my peripheral vision picked up Ferrante's frowning dart of a look toward the sergeant.

As if Shelton had given it away, when Ferrante was the one who confirmed my hypothesis that something in the victim's house led them to Thurston.

Based on the timing, the *something* in the victim's house was not hidden.

"No comment. Ferrante, give her the release." Shelton spoke faster than usual, probably trying to mask what was already revealed by Ferrante's reaction. "Could've gotten it electronically. Didn't have to come here."

"But, Sergeant, then I wouldn't have had the pleasure of seeing you and Richard and Deputy Ferrante." Shelton remained deadpan, Richard flushed, Ferrante scowled.

To further cement my position that I was interested only in the release, I started to skim it.

"This doesn't give time of death."

"Ask Horse Creek County."

Shelton, with Alvaro right behind, strode toward the hallway that led to offices, a break room, and interview rooms that might even now contain Thurston.

The sergeant and deputy were so in sync that when Shelton abruptly stopped, Alvaro didn't even bump into him.

"I suppose," Shelton said over his shoulder toward me, "that we have you to thank for James Longbaugh showing up."

I smiled beatifically at him. "No comment."

Chapter Five

BACK IN MY SUV, I traded the release for my phone.

First, I read a message from Mike Paycik saying Jennifer had told him what was happening. *Anything I can do?*

I texted back, *Want to write Leona's copy for the Five?*

Then I hit a phone number, which was answered immediately.

"Walt? It's Elizabeth Danniher. Anything new?"

"No official ID, if that's what you're hoping for. Gave Jennifer a specific house address based on activity, along with what the neighbors say about who lived there. Her name is Melissa Oxley, she drives a VW Beetle, and the age fits. If Jennifer confirms it from real estate sources, maybe we could use the name—"

"Nope."

Not until law enforcement released the name.

With a staff member being questioned, we would tread carefully.

"I know. It's just frustrating." He sighed. "Looks like a single-family home, not as big as the others, but original. Neighbors say she lived there alone. No family in town. So it could take a while. Doubt official ID will come tonight, for sure. Shelton and Alvaro have gone. The scientists are busy doing their stuff. Certainly not taking time to talk to a reporter. Otherwise, a single Cottonwood County deputy left to move traffic, along with three Horse Creek County representatives, which must leave most of their county unprotected."

"Have you picked up anything about a connection between Thurston and the victim?"

"Nope. Law enforcement's being entirely closemouthed. About to start deeper on neighbors. But I won't mention his name. Don't want to muddy the waters. See if they bring him up when I ask about visitors, friends, associates."

"Perfect. I'll send you the release. Not much there, but you'll have the official language, including *unexplained death*."

"Anything about Thurston—?"

"No. They're not saying much, which almost certainly means not charged. Yet."

He whistled through his teeth. "Surreal. The whole thing. I was remembering when he started. Had the intro for a piece a young intern—when we had such people—had done with a child behavior specialist about thumb-sucking. Only Thurston said that term wasn't *dignified* enough for him. He insisted on referring to it as finger-sucking."

I might have made a sound.

"Yeah, you can see where this is going. He said it right the first two times, then switched the first letters, as he tossed it to the intern for her live set-up. She was horrified, but you could also hear her crew—we had a whole crew out with the reporter in those days—laughing their asses off.

"She got through it. Barely. Had herself in hand for the toss back to Thurston … until he said it again. *Singer f*—Well, you get the idea."

"That might be among the top five Thurston screwups. I hadn't heard it before." Though I had witnessed my share.

"But you didn't call about Thurston stories."

"No, I didn't. Not enough time in the day for all of those. Audrey gave you the timeline of the deputies getting to the victim's house, then almost immediately leaving? There's definitely something in that. Confirmed here at the sheriff's department, though not specifically what it was that sent them hot-footing to Thurston. Probably something in the house and not subtle. Maybe the neighbors will know."

"Maybe. But I'm getting a lot of hardly-knew-her vibe. Fair number of these folks have bought recently and this woman—assuming we have the right ID—was away a dozen or more years before moving back earlier this year. Not an open-door kind of person, either. And not active in the community."

"Darn."

"You sure it's something in the house? Because they're not saying anything here."

"Nothing was said here, either, but there *was* a reaction."

He considered a moment. "Not Shelton. Probably not Alvaro. Ferrante? Something he picked up from the guys returning earlier from the scene?"

"Yep. And probably."

"Gotcha. Okay. I'll push it with the neighbors I talk to from now on, see what we get."

THE BOILERPLATE RELEASE was as sparse as expected.

But it did give that the victim's body was found in western Horse Creek County at approximately eight-twenty this morning. Also that she was in her thirties—less specific than what Jennifer picked up— and not a Native American. Sadly, that last detail was added because so many Native American women had gone missing or been killed. It had become its own category of crime.

With those few firm details, and weaving in a fair number of "according to the Horse Creek County Sheriff's Department" or "the Cottonwood County Sheriff's Department said," or "the two departments, working in cooperation, indicated," it sounded like we had more than we did.

A story about finding a body in these circumstances guaranteed an attention-grabbing headline. But rarely did you have the answers to the who, what, when, where, how, and—especially—why, that listeners wanted in the next breath.

The criminal justice system contends with the CSI effect, when juries expect the level of detail—especially physical evidence—that is presented on TV dramas of the ilk of the CSI franchise. Juries also expect cases to be resolved in less than an hour, since trials don't have advertising timeouts.

I feel for prosecutors. On the other hand, the media has experienced the impatience of the public forever. They want all elements, neatly packaged, along with eye-catching video, while we're scrambling to get to the scene.

Social media compounds the problem, including a segment of the population making up their own answers, not bothering with fact-gathering or multiple sources. Or any sources. They jump to conclusions, then shore up those shaky edifices with selected—or made-up—information.

Bad enough that some people indulge in the activity. Truly scary that others believe them.

I suppose the gullibility of mankind is job security for me as a consumer affairs reporter. I'd happily give it up for a higher rate of critical thinking.

None of those insights made it into the five o'clock report, of course.

✦   ✦   ✦   ✦

IN ADDITION TO Walt's live standup in the vicinity of a house he described as "a focus of law enforcement activity," we had video by Jenks from where the vehicle was found.

The blue VW Beetle was identifiable in some of Jenks' footage, but not in what we aired, for the same reason we didn't identify the victim.

It meant we'd have to wait to use an evocative shot of the vehicle sitting isolated in a semicircle of official vehicles from Horse Creek County, with a narrow band of deteriorating pavement forming a straight stroke through the brush, scrub, and rock that stretched endlessly under a dome of blue sky.

What we used wasn't bad, but it hurt not to be able to use that footage.

One of the most noticeable differences from the usual KWMT-TV fare was the cross talk—that's on-air conversation between the anchor and on-site reporter. In this case, Leona and Walt.

Leona's questions and interest elevated their cross talk beyond anything our viewers would have seen in the rare times Thurston deigned to participate—he did his best to avoid sharing the screen or audio with anyone.

Though, I had heard a couple stories about Thurston's early years here when his technical ineptitude contributed to another kind of cross talk—a voice from one microphone unintentionally bleeding into another.

After those incidents, the view was that the less desirable cross talk anyone asked Thurston to do, the less chance for the undesirable tech glitch variety.

Jenks came into the newsroom during the Five.

That was notable, though not as notable as it would have been eighteen months ago.

He had the quaint notion that even journalists should be home for supper with family. He'd managed it most of his time at KWMT-TV by aligning with Thurston, who didn't believe journalists—or, more accurately, he—should work much at all.

When I'd arrived in Sherman, Jenks had been Thurston's pet shooter.

That relationship deteriorated as Jenks' journalistic instincts roused from hibernation. Now part of the general pool of camera operators, he didn't always get home for supper, but he maximized his opportunities.

He was not alone in showing up at the station. After Walt's live bit, he and Diana came in and joined another half dozen staffers, who stood, looking up at Leona's stalwart presence on monitors hung near the ceiling. No one spoke.

I've been in newsrooms when monumental national and international stories broke. Every time there'd been a moment like this.

A breath between the first rush and the long haul, a brief nod, acknowledging that shift and absorbing the import of what had changed in the world.

These KWMT staffers would be caught up again in the rush—shortly, with the prep for the Ten, or tomorrow. But for this breath, they stood. Individually, yet somehow together.

Chapter Six

"I'VE GOT NEW footage," Jenks announced generally.

Leona and the production crew had just come into the newsroom, receiving congratulations on the newscast. Now most of the lingerers headed out.

The rest of us turned our thoughts to the Ten.

"Let's see it," Audrey said.

As she moved to lead the way to an editing booth, Diana and I exchanged a glance, signaling our mutual satisfaction at her taking charge.

We followed them and our satisfaction shifted to what was on-screen when Jenks ran his video.

If you listed the elements in what aired on the Five and in this video, they'd be nearly identical.

The effects were not.

The earlier video was fact. This was … more than fact.

The sky's brilliant blue had faded and grayed. Across it, clouds could have been drawn by a grubby-handed toddler creating dots and dashes. Jenks shot from lower and closer this time, shifting the perspective and making the unidentifiable slice of a civilian vehicle solitary, dwarfed by the vastness. The road became a foreground stripe of rubble.

"Jenks, this is … this is amazing," Audrey said. "It's *haunting*."

He went deadpan. "You can thank Diana."

"Me? This is all you. I wasn't there."

"No, but a while back when I was griping about an assignment sending me to a scene with nothing but space in it, you said to make the space the shot. I remembered after I sent the usual stuff in for the Five. So I waited a while and moved around. Deputies and the scientists thought I was nuts. Took some doing to get an angle that caught the clouds, enough of the Beetle without the make being obvious, and none of the other vehicles."

"Audrey—"

She cut me off. "I know. Change the stack for the Ten. Lead with this. Set the scene, then do the rundown. I'm on it. Can you rewrite Leona's intro, Elizabeth?"

"Sure. After sustenance."

"Dale should be back soon with the order from Hamburger Heaven. Jenks, send the full and—"

Diana and I slipped out.

Walt caught us in the hall.

"Was looking for you. After Jerry resets, I'm going to do my bit for the Ten, edit the package, and then head home to make calls. If I get anything hot…" He lived close enough to come back to go live. But we knew the chances were slim. "Want the little I got from the neighbors?"

"Absolutely."

We settled in around my desk so I could take notes.

"The family's been there in one form or another since the house was built. It was Melissa Oxley's mother's family. It's not the biggest or fanciest house, but it never fell into absolute ruin like some.

"The neighbors knew the mother, a widow for a good chunk of time. Didn't talk to anyone who knew the first husband."

I glanced toward Diana, but she didn't return it and said nothing.

"They had one child—Melissa, the one we think was found dead today. She moved out post-college, like normal kids do, which is the highest aspiration I currently have for my son. The mother—Barbara—married again a couple years after Melissa went to college.

"Unfortunately for us, the new husband wasn't chatty with the neighbors. They said he'd wave and say hello but that was about it. Their main contact was with the mother, who died at the end of last year. There is one tidbit—the second husband moved out and the daughter back in shortly after the funeral."

"Huh."

"Nobody I talked to knew details. They say the daughter's the same as her stepfather—wave and say hello. None of them mentioned Thurston or any connection there. I nudged a bit, you know, asking about boyfriends. Nothing. But there is one possible thread for you to follow up."

"Me? Why not you? It's your story."

"For all I got, it's not much of a story."

"You did fine on the Five."

"Glad you think so, because everyone'll hear about the same thing at ten. Anyway, I was talking to Krista Seger, who owns that bed and breakfast." He waggled his eyebrows, reminding us she was the niece of the station's owner, Val Heatherton. "It's a block and a half down from where Melissa Oxley lived. Didn't have anything more for me than anybody else, but at the end she asked why you weren't there. I got a vibe she might be more forthcoming with you."

"Interesting," Diana said.

I wasn't as enthusiastic. Krista was grateful we hadn't dragged the B&B into the spotlight on an earlier situation. She seemed to feel she needed to say it every time we saw each other.

Walt headed to the studio to do his update for the Ten.

Diana and I remained at my desk in the bullpen.

In my case to be closer to the door when the news aide returned with our takeout dinner orders.

It also gave us time for a replay of the Five.

A critical viewer might have spotted arm-waving to retain our balance, but I do believe we successfully negotiated the big-story-not-much-info tightrope.

Before restringing the tightrope for the Ten, we had this brief respite.

I called my next-door neighbors, Iris and Zeb Undlin, asking if they'd look in on my dog, Shadow, because I'd be home late. They said it would be their pleasure. It would also be Shadow's pleasure, because he'd probably get a meal cooked specially for him instead of kibble.

Diana called her children, Jessica and Gary Junior, who had schedules of academics, extracurricular activities, and social lives that spilled over the lines of any ordinary calendar. Neither was supposed to be home for dinner and Diana would only stay at the station another hour or so to help go through video, but she liked to check in with them to make sure nothing had arisen.

Nothing had.

I suspected this was a respite of sorts for all of them, too.

Amid the wrap-up of our previous investigation, there'd been some turmoil with the kids, Diana, and her love interest, Sheriff Russ Conrad.

"Not going to call Russ?" My question was a tiny bit of mild needling.

"Already talked to him. He completely understands about my schedule changing, because his did, too."

"Did he have anything interesting to say?" As sheriff, he frequently came down on the opposite side of free and open access for the media. If he'd mentioned anything about the news story of the day...

"Interesting to me, yes. To you, no."

I inhaled to continue the jousting, but put the oxygen intake to better use to say, "Dinner's here," at the sight of lanky news aide Dale returning with bags and bags from Hamburger Heaven.

We'd finished eating when a call came in on my phone. Identifying the caller as Needham Bender—first for myself, then aloud to Diana, I figured I'd soon learn if my assessment of our balancing act during the Five was justified.

He greeted me with a grumble. "It would happen when I'd just closed up the edition."

No question of what *it* was.

Coming out three times a week, the *Independence* that he owned and edited sometimes struggled to get in breaking news that KWMT could with twice daily newscasts. On the other hand, it had the advantage over KWMT of time, space, and Needham to produce thoughtful and probing coverage.

"But you got something in anyway."

"Barely. But you guys… Nice job on the fly, Elizabeth. Real nice job. More news than's usually in three or four episodes of the Thurston Fine Show. Can't wait for the Ten."

"Be sure you catch the opening with new video from Jenks. As for the Five, that was Audrey Adams, who handled the assignment editor job she was scheduled for, and now producer for both newscasts because Thurston's pet had a meltdown."

"Good for her. With you the power behind the throne, I'm betting. You sure you're not a newspaperman?"

I chuckled in response to his compliment—it definitely was a compliment.

"Leona sounded like the hardest of the hard-news junkies," he added.

"Don't tell her that."

"Not a chance. I'm not stupid. Though it wasn't quite as exciting as waiting to hear what Thurston would say."

"Thurston Fine, the greatest living practitioner of churnalism."

"Hah." Needham barked out a laugh. "Great term for churning press releases into a poor substitute for news. Don't know about him being the greatest, but certainly the most prolific. I remember watching his first newscast here and having déjà vu. Didn't make sense. Only thing I could think of was I must have seen him before. On a trip or something.

"When I got home, I asked Thelma if she'd recognized him. She hadn't paid close attention, so I made her concentrate on the late news. At the end, she said she was sure she'd never heard or seen him before and she'd remember, because he was awful. So the familiarity wasn't from stumbling across him before.

"Next day's early news, having the same déjà vu, a phrase caught me. Started digging through press releases—"

"*News* releases, please. *Press* releases refer to print, so applies only to you ink-stained wretches."

"We're the only ones who count, which is why I was pawing through *press* releases … and there was everything Thurston said. Word for word."

"I am steeled against the degradations he has imposed on journalism. I will not groan or cry."

"We'll see about that."

It was a good thing I liked him.

"Never will forget him following up a story about protests by doing his version of cross talk—with himself—and he speculated about why the incendiary devices the protestors threw were called *mazel tov* cocktails."

"*Mazel tov*—?"

He laughed briefly. "Yeah. That old Soviet politician and all-around buzzard Molotov would be real sorry to lose his namesake. Though he'd still get credit for Molotov's Bread Baskets. That's what the Finns called the Soviet bombs in 1939 when the Soviets invaded, while Molotov said on the radio they weren't *bombing*, oh, no, not them, only *dropping food parcels* to the Finns."

"I'd heard of Molotov, but not the rest. The Finns developed them?"

"No. Gave them the name, but borrowed the idea of relatively easy-to-make and surprisingly effective incendiary devices used in the Spanish Civil War. You know that was all contemporary history for me."

My mental math rebelled. "Baloney."

He grunted. "You're right, but it's getting so people look at me and think I was around for the American Revolution. Anyway, I talked to a bunch of people who did live that history."

A momentary pause had me suspecting Needham was remembering those conversations and that history.

Then he asked, "What next?" proving, he wasn't only looking back.

"Rinse and repeat for the Ten and for tomorrow. Hope Les Haeburn takes hold of himself—" And returned to the station. Though I wasn't prepared to feed that tidbit to a media rival, even Needham. "—and makes plans so the station can handle it, whether this is long-term or short-term."

"I meant what next with the murder."

"Don't know it *is* a murder."

He snorted. "Suspicious death for print. Murder between friends."

"Not sure even between friends. They seem tied to unexplained death, which includes the possibility of suicide." Unexplained also backed down several rungs on the ladder from suspicious death and well down the hierarchy from murder.

"Shot herself in the head? Possible, sure. But in the back seat of her car? What? She wanted to get more comfortable, have more elbow room and less legroom?"

"Back seat?" I asked before I could stop myself.

Shot in the head or overdose ranked as top candidates for my guesses at cause of death, but the victim—Melissa Oxley—being found in the back seat of her VW bug? *That* I wouldn't have guessed.

He chuckled. "Like you didn't already know."

I should have. Would I have known if I'd asked Shelton more questions? Or if I'd gone to the scene where she was found and—

Needham continued, "A more likely setup would be someone else in the back seat with her."

"Not in a VW Beetle."

"So you *do* admit knowing that, huh? Officially, it's a four-seater, so someone could've been back there with her. Or leaning over from the front or in from outside to pull the trigger."

"Is that the official cause of death?" I asked, as if teasing.

"As if they'd share official COD when they're still futzing around with identification. But it's true nonetheless. She was shot in the head in the back seat of her vehicle, most likely by someone else who—"

"Or by her own hand after a disappointment." That came out without my thinking.

His satisfied grunt told me I should have thought first. "Oh-ho. That's what you're thinking about Thurston's involvement? That's the direction you're following with your investigation?"

I was at a real disadvantage, since I hadn't realized the thought was anywhere in my brain until it blurted out of my mouth. I hadn't been careful, because I'd been sure I wasn't thinking about this from any aspect other than KWMT's coverage.

I tried to recover, if not retreat.

"Not at all. There is no direction, because there's no investigation. I'm sure Thurston is tangential to this whole matter. We—KWMT— will cover the investigation, of course, but the sheriff's department isn't being particularly cooperative. Can't entirely blame them, since the body wasn't found in their jurisdiction and they appear to still be thrashing that out with Horse Creek County."

He chuckled. After a moment of my silence, it faded out. "You're serious?"

"Yes."

"You're just going to report it, not investigate it?"

"It's not my story, but, yes."

"Really?" I heard not only skepticism, but a suddenly deepened interest. Not what I'd been going for. "Why? Do you think Fine did this?"

"I have no idea. I'm leaving it to the law enforcement professionals."

"Elizabeth—"

"I've gotta go. Another newscast to get ready."

Chapter Seven

Diana snorted from where she still sat at the next desk, sunk down in the chair, with her crossed ankles resting on the edge of the desk's dinged surface.

In case I didn't interpret that snort, her tone conveyed scoffing disbelief. "You're *leaving it to the law enforcement professionals?*"

"Yes. We don't look into every murder—and especially not every death."

"You're thinking it's suicide?"

"That's certainly a reasonable explanation, and one that would not involve Thurston being a clever murdering mastermind."

"If he did murder her, it sure didn't reach mastermind status, considering law enforcement is talking to him the day the body's found."

True. Though beside the point—beside *my* point, anyway. "Either way, this situation doesn't call for our talents. Law enforcement appears to have a handle on it."

"What if they think it's murder and it's really suicide."

"I'd expect you to have more confidence in Sheriff Conrad and his people getting to the truth."

She certainly had confidence in Russell Conrad in other areas, not only her heart, but opening the relationship to her teenage children.

She'd taken that process slowly and carefully ... until he recently used the L-word in front of the kids, apparently for the first time.

Men.

"I have all the confidence in Russ. On the other hand, with a different department spearheading the investigation and the possibility that said different department could land on Thurston as the killer when he wasn't…"

"Doubtful. Besides, maybe he is. *If* it's murder."

"But you're prepared to sit back and wait? That's not like you, Elizabeth."

Enough hedging. "Are you accusing me of something, Diana?"

"Like disliking Thurston enough to send him to the proverbial gallows by your lack of action even if he doesn't deserve it? No—"

"You need to tell Conrad—because his department *is* involved—you think they couldn't separate a murder from a suicide and would rush to judgment to convict someone you seem positive is innocent."

"And you need to stop deflecting. As I started to say, no, I don't think you'd do that. But would you avoid helping Thurston for another reason? Like, maybe, you're feeling easily bruised with Mike in Chicago, Jennifer heading the same direction after the first of the year, and Tom keeping his distance."

"I am not some hothouse flower who—"

"No. You're human. And it would be hard not to feel the holes in your life from those—well, call them departures. Especially when something like this comes up, hitting closer to home, while also crying out for an investigation—"

"Crying out for? You do know I'm memorizing all this to repeat to our illustrious sheriff."

"—and immediately after the previous one with all its reminders of who was gone and who would be soon."

"Balderdash."

"*Really? Balderdash?*"

"It's a good word."

She swung her feet down from the desk and stood. "If you say so. You certainly know how to use words." She side-eyed me. "Especially to avoid acknowledging to yourself what's going on."

✦ ✦ ✦ ✦

BEFORE SHE COULD expand or I had to respond, we turned at the sound of the outer doors being opened.

"Oh, my God," Audrey said, not quietly.

Les Haeburn.

His need to wrestle closed the wind-driven outer doors and get the inner doors opened gave us time to exchange looks across the bullpen.

"You," Audrey said to me.

No mistaking what she meant. I wanted to say that as assignment editor and de facto producer for both newscasts, she had the official honor of informing the news director of what was happening, now that he'd shown up.

But the woman had been swimming as fast as she could in the deep end all day. No sense hitting her with a tsunami-like wave, too, when I could handle it.

I charted a path to intersect his in the hallway outside his office. Diana followed me and Audrey met us. Leona, with Jennifer behind her, stood a couple feet away, where the hall turned to head back toward the studio.

"Les."

He'd intended to walk past us without making eye contact, but my voice—backed by stepping in front of him—brought him up short. Fumbling with his phone in his pocket, still not saying anything.

"There's something you need to know."

I tried—hard—to keep out of my voice the subtext that he should have damned well been here. What the you-know-what had he been doing all day? And a couple more you-know-whats could possibly explain his failing to contact the newsroom?

"Sheriff's deputies came to the station to talk to Thurston about the death of a woman. The deputies asked Thurston to go with them to the sheriff's office."

I waited.

For an exclamation.

For a demand to know if I was kidding.

For amazement.

For shock.

He continued to look down at his phone. I saw a string of unan-swered calls from the same number starting with our 307 area code, but not long enough to get the rest of the digits.

Could Thurston have tried to reach him? Could that mean—?

"Did you already know about this, Les?"

"No. First I've heard. No connection all day."

I wanted to ask where he'd been. I wanted to ask why he hadn't been in touch with the newsroom all day.

But, in fairness, we'd never asked before when this happened now and then. We'd taken the gift horse without a glance in his mouth.

It wasn't reasonable to fault him for not being here today because something major happened when we'd celebrated the other occasions.

"Thurston hasn't been back since he left with the deputies. We haven't heard anything from him. Audrey adjusted the stack and called in Leona to anchor. We're working the story of the woman's death. No official ID, though we have strong indications of who it was. She lived here in Sherman."

I emphasized that fact hoping it would trigger the all-news-is-local instincts that had to be in him somewhere.

"We used a short, factual statement about Thurston in the coverage for the Five. We can get you the tape and fill you in on the blocks for the Ten to look over—"

"No." After the single, sharp word, he appeared to have trouble swallowing.

"Had you already heard? Did you see the Five?"

"Told you, no," he said. "I have calls to make."

"For Thurston? Elizabeth already—"

I interrupted Audrey. "The station's lawyer went to the sheriff's department to connect with Thurston hours ago. James Longbaugh will give Thurston whatever help he needs."

If Thurston listened to sense. Not a given.

Apparently, I shouldn't have bothered with the reassurance. Les didn't appear to hear anything we'd said.

"A woman died in Horse Creek County. I have calls to make," he repeated. "Keep on with what you're doing."

He scuttled into his office and slammed the door behind him. We heard a muffled sound from inside I couldn't identify. Could he possibly be in there sobbing? Over Thurston?

"A woman died in Horse Creek County? So we shouldn't cover it?" Jennifer demanded. "Did he not hear the part about her being from Sherman?"

Then, from inside the office, we heard the distinct ringtone of *Ding-Dong! The Witch Is Dead.*

The owner of the station was calling the news director.

Before we could react, much less scatter, his office door jerked open and he pushed past us on the way to the outside doors.

He had been summoned.

And he left.

For a second there, I'd thought it might be like an ordinary station, with ownership chewing on the news director's tail about coverage and the news director taking hold and turning up the heat under the staff and…

I cleared my throat. "Okay, let's get back to it. We have another newscast to put together."

Chapter Eight

THE TEN WAS done.

At least as good as the Five, maybe better for having been tightened and polished.

The viewers wouldn't know what hit them, since it was a newscast packed with something they only received sporadically from KWMT—news.

A minute ago, Leona had passed me on her way outside for a well-deserved night of rest.

Everyone—even the usually wordless types from the control room—had said what a great job she did.

She'd known it, too. She'd been pleased with herself, but also exhausted. Hating to do a job didn't mean not having the self-respect—and respect for co-workers and viewers—to do it well.

There were people—like me—on whom breaking news and/or newsroom disasters had the same impact as mainlining adrenaline. It was the high of all highs. Hard to come down from, and when it was past leaving a faint wistfulness to get back to it, along with a jazzed recognition that eventually you'd be tired.

Others—like Leona—marshalled their resources to do the job, but it sucked the energy out of them.

She'd definitely been dragging when she muttered good night on her way past.

I barely clamped my teeth on my bottom lip to stop from hitting her with a litany of ideas about tomorrow. What we'd do differently, what we'd expand, what we'd trim. All that swirled through my brain in anticipation of a conversation with Audrey as soon as she returned from a trip home to feed her cat, which she had not taken the time to do before the Ten.

Poor cat. Deadline collateral damage.

Turning away from the deeply disappointing offerings of the break room, I started toward my desk, which I knew held a package of Pepperidge Farm Double Dark Chocolate Milano Cookies. Actually, multiple packages.

It was important to have reliable go-tos in times of need.

But I forgot about the cookies when I looked down the hallway to where it ended in two sets of glass doors separating KWMT-TV's block structure from the great outdoors.

Or the not-so-great outdoors, since the doors opened onto the parking lot, lit harshly, but not well, at this hour of the night.

Possibly once paved, either the pavement broke up or someone gave in to the inevitable and dumped gravel on it. Either way, it produced a steady supply of dust, which Wyoming's surfeit of wind deposited both on parked vehicles and the building, including a coating on the outside of the outer doors and not much less on the outside of the inner doors.

With that through-a-glass-dustily effect, I couldn't see detail, but what I did see had me sprinting toward the doors.

Someone in the parking lot appeared to be yelling at and towering over a second someone. A second someone who wore the raspberry-colored blazer over jeans that Leona D'Amato had on when she passed me on her way outside a minute ago.

"*Hey!*" I shouted as I pushed out the outer doors.

Leona D'Amato is a redoubtable woman, but she was dwarfed by a young Amazon with a poor sense of personal space and a definite mad on.

The young woman with mousy brown hair down to an impressive pair of shoulders nearly bumped Leona—who did not back away.

For all her stalwartness, Leona couldn't do much about being significantly shorter and four-plus decades older than the Amazon looming over her. Not to mention Leona's exhaustion.

"—and you can't do that. Nobody can. We won't allow it. No matter—" The younger woman was screaming.

"*Hey*," I shouted again, charging up to them.

Facing the other woman, I wedged my shoulder between her and Leona, followed up with my hip, then moved forward.

My maneuver displaced the Amazon about as much as it would have a tank.

Fortunately, she was more distractible than a tank.

Or maybe not fortunately, I decided when she swung toward me from about six inches away.

The young woman was outraged. Yet there was also real sorrow in her staring, reddened eyes.

That didn't have time to stir sympathy in me—if it would have succeeded with all the time in the world, considering how she was acting—because in the next breath she directed the roar at me.

"I know who *you* are, too. *And* what you're up to."

"I'm Elizabeth Margaret Danniher and I have no idea what you're talking about."

"And I know all about you and how you've been after his job ever since you came here."

My position between the other two began to erode. Not because of the Amazon, who hadn't budged, but because of Leona wrapping her hands around my left arm and yanking back, trying to get me out of her way.

"Make up your mind." Leona's order came out with plenty of snap, but might have been more impressive if she'd delivered the words without anything or anyone between her and her confronter. With our height differential and my determination to not let her push me out of the way, she said it while looking around my shoulder. "I thought *I* was the one after somebody's job, though whose—"

"You *both* are. You're horrible. You're evil. You're … you're *harpies*. That's what she said and she told me what it means and she was right. Old and pathetic and—"

"If we were pathetic," I said, "you wouldn't be worrying about us doing whatever it is you're worried about us doing."

Have you ever noticed logic can enflame some people? Particularly those not inclined to use it themselves.

The Amazon's face turned dark red.

"It's jealousy. All jealousy. It would be laughable if it weren't so evil. And if it weren't aimed at such a wonderful person."

As angry as she was, there was a hesitation in her words, like an actor repeating a script not quite memorized.

"She told him and told him he shouldn't be so tolerant of your schemes, but she said he's such a magneti—No, no. That's wrong. Magnanimous." She pronounced it with care. "She said magnanimous. And that's why he hasn't swatted you like insects."

"You're talking about somebody who works here?" Leona demanded.

"*Works* here? If it weren't for him, this whole place would fall apart. There wouldn't be a TV station. It's only because of Thurston Fine. He's—"

"*Thurston?*" Leona and I chorused, our harmony ragged, but the dumbfounded sentiment heartfelt.

The young woman couldn't have recognized our astonishment or she wouldn't have said, "Oh, *now* you know who I'm talking about. As if you haven't been stabbing him in the back and trying to push his body aside to climb over him to the top for *ages*. That's—"

"You think I want Thurston's job? You are—"

"—what she always said would happen and now it has. And to do it—"

"Who said?" I asked.

She might not have heard me because Leona hadn't stopped talking. "—out of your head. Completely—"

More likely the young woman didn't hear my question because she wasn't listening.

"—you had to climb over her body first. Her *dead* body. Oh, my God. *Dead!* She's *dead.* How can she be dead? I can't believe—"

"Whose body?"

"—and totally out of your head," Leona declared.

"—you've done this. It's so evil. So wicked and—"

I got as much into her face as I could and repeated loudly, "*Whose body?*"

"Melissa's. I should have protected her. I let her down, but I won't let you—"

"Melissa who?" I roared. I was not going to put words in her mouth she could try to deny later.

She blinked. "Melissa Oxley."

"You're saying Melissa Oxley said someone was after Thurston? When? Who?"

"As if you didn't know. You—" She jabbed a forefinger the size of a tree limb into my chest, then a second jab over my shoulder toward Leona. "—*both* of you or one of you, but even if it was one of you, you're both guilty—"

Preoccupied with trying to unravel the implications of her inventive viewpoint on what had happened, I almost missed the vehicle coming at us from the entrance to the parking lot.

It might not have hit us. But I took no chances on *might*. I used my left arm to keep Leona behind me and sort of hooked it around her, while grasping the Amazon's jacket front and tugging her toward the station doors, hoping it put all of us out of the vehicle's path.

The driver—Audrey, I saw—rammed the heel of her hand into the horn.

The Amazon tugged her jacket from my hold without much effort, then clapped both hands over her ears as she lumbered toward a pickup that had been blue before the rust took over.

"Wait." I started after her. "What's your name? You knew Melissa Oxley? I'd like to talk to—"

Audrey clasped her arms around me, impeding my progress. I still called after the Amazon, but she'd shown no inclination to heed my words when I'd been just behind her. She sure didn't now, with the gap between us expanding.

"*Ma'am? Ma'am?*" came a disembodied voice.

"Dammit, Audrey—" came from my body, still restrained by her.

The pickup backed up, tried for a three-point turn, but needed several extra points to get headed in the right direction to rumble away.

Audrey released me, apparently satisfied I wouldn't run after the vehicle like a barking dog ... though my SUV was right there in the lot...

Unfortunately, my keys were in my purse in my desk.

"Leona, are you okay?" Audrey grasped her shoulder, turning her toward the light.

Leona jerked away. "Of course I'm okay. I was handling it before you and Elizabeth butted in."

Audrey snapped back. "Let's get inside before you both take me apart for ruining your fun."

"She was a foot and a half taller than you and—"

The disembodied voice interrupted my assessment. *"Ma'am? Ma'am? Is anyone hurt?"*

Audrey looked around for a second before focusing on the phone she still clutched in one hand, explaining the disembodied voice.

"Oh. Hi. Sorry. I'm here," Audrey said into the phone. "No, no one's hurt, but it was still an attack, no matter what some people— Anyway, the assailant has left, but please get someone here right away."

"Sheriff's department is here." I tipped my head toward an approaching vehicle topped by strobing lights. It came at a significantly more sedate pace than Audrey had. "Hang up."

She wasn't fast enough for me, taking time to thank the dispatcher and probably invite her to Sunday brunch.

"Hang up now."

She did with a bit of a huff. There was no time for that, either.

"Do either of you know who that woman was?"

"No." Audrey gained points for brevity, even if it was the result of being peeved at me.

"I can guess she's connected to the woman found dead—"

I cut off Leona. "No guesses. Understand? We tell them only what we know for a fact about what happened. Got it?"

"But—"

"Got it," Leona said.

The driver's door of the sheriff's department vehicle opened. One short leg emerged.

Sergeant Wayne Shelton.

"We do not include our visitor mentioning the name Melissa Oxley," I added.

Audrey's eyes went wide, but Leona nodded crisply.

Chapter Nine

"**YOU HAVE NOTHING** better to do a few hours after the body of a young woman who lives in your county was found than to come check out an altercation in a parking lot? Not even at a bar? Just a mundane TV station?"

Shelton did not rise to my bait.

"The dead woman's not in our county and—"

"She was a resident here."

"—not our case. When I hear about an altercation at the TV station, I'm not going to miss that."

"You did miss it, Sergeant. It's all over."

"How did whatever's over start?"

"You'd have to ask Leona. I—"

"I will. I'm asking you now."

"—saw something going on out in the parking lot through the doors."

"What was going on?"

"I couldn't see clearly." I gestured toward the doors. "Very dusty."

"Saw well enough to make you go outside."

"I recognized the color of Leona's jacket. That was enough. I was concerned."

"What did you see when you came out?"

"A tall young woman I didn't know looming over Leona and yelling at her."

"Saying what?"

"Really, Sergeant, she was incoherent. I couldn't make sense of what she said, much less remember it."

He didn't believe me.

I didn't believe me.

I was usually better at dissembling. And why was I bothering?

It had been pure instinct to tell the others to limit ourselves to what we knew for a fact. But why, when we were leaving the investigating to law enforcement?

On the other hand, I'd given the order. I couldn't leave Leona and Audrey high and dry now by going beyond the few hard facts we had. That wouldn't be right.

"Did she touch Leona?" he asked.

"Not that I saw. I got between them. She poked me."

"Poked?"

"With her finger."

"Uh-huh. Hurt?" He sounded hopeful.

"Some."

"Break the skin?"

"No." I hadn't checked. But right now, it could be gushing blood and I wouldn't have told him.

"Name?"

"No idea."

"Description?"

"Quite tall—maybe a little over six-foot. Medium brown hair. Broad shoulders."

He snorted dismissal of my descriptive powers.

I added, "I don't think she came to the station intending to hurt Leona, me, or anybody else."

"How'd you come to that conclusion? Mind-reading?"

I gave Shelton a cool, level stare. "She would not have pulled into a parking spot with a pickup that steered like a tank. It took her five or six painful wheel cranks to get headed in the direction of her getaway. Anyone with an iota of sense and planning to do harm would have backed into the parking spot."

He stared at me for another beat. "Get the tag number?"

That was small-minded. Instead of lauding my reasoning skills, he tried to undermine my observational abilities.

"Wyoming," I shot back. "Last two digits were 47."

He grunted. "Don't go anywhere."

He strode off to where a young deputy I'd only seen a couple times stood with Leona and Audrey, apparently prepared to tackle them if they talked to each other.

That deputy also had barked, "Stay inside," when Dale, the news aide, started to exit. Poor guy, stuck at the station despite his shift having ended.

I, on the other hand, was feeling significantly more cheerful, since I'd memorized all of the vehicle tag on the Amazon's truck.

It was reflex. So was not sharing completely with Shelton.

I hadn't lied. I'd given him the less helpful portion of what I knew.

Maybe I would call him in the morning and give him the whole license plate.

Since we were leaving this to law enforcement.

Chapter Ten

LEONA STOOD AT the doors, watching outside, while Audrey and I slumped in chairs by her computer.

Headlights of a turning vehicle flashed across the glass.

Leona exhaled with satisfaction. "Finally, they're gone." She started toward us.

As invested in the establishment of Cottonwood County as Leona D'Amato was, she had a streak of distrust of law enforcement that made me wonder if she had an interesting past.

"You'd think it was the crime of the century," she grumbled.

"Oh, Leona, when I came into the parking lot and saw you and Elizabeth being attacked—" Audrey choked with tears.

She jumped out of her chair and wrapped the older woman in a hug.

Leona looked at me with comical dismay.

To cover any potential reaction of my own—toss-up if I'd cry with Audrey or laugh with Leona—I got up and turned it into a group hug.

A voice beyond us coughed, and we all turned to Dale, who'd been in a nearby chair all along.

"Dale, what are you doing here? You should have gone home ages ago," Audrey said, as we three huggers each took a chair.

"Deputy said to stay until he said I could go."

Then forgot he was waiting. Poor kid.

"You're going to investigate all about this death, Elizabeth?" Was Dale interested, excited, or worried?

The last would be about Jennifer.

His adoration of her was such that he did anything she asked. Mostly picking up shifts and tasks, which allowed her to participate in our inquiries. At the same time, he appeared to worry about her.

"No," I reassured him. "Not this time."

I became aware of scrutiny from the two women and returned it with a pointed, "What?"

"Nothing." Audrey looked away.

Leona didn't. "After you said not to give Shelton anything beyond name, rank, and serial number?"

"Knee-jerk reaction that it's better to tell him too little than too much."

"She knew the dead woman is Melissa Oxley," Leona pointed out.

"This is a small town. Word could have gotten out."

"You're not curious?"

"There's more than enough to do right now with keeping the news on-air at KWMT."

"That's the truth."

Leona ignored Audrey's endorsement of my position. "You must want to know about this person who attacked us," she insisted.

"You said you didn't know her."

"No. I said I could guess she was connected to the woman found dead. And I don't *know* her. But I do know her name is Fawn Raglettley. She played basketball for the high school. Mike will know more."

"I'm sure we don't need to bother Mike," I said.

"But Fawn coming here was connected to Melissa Oxley's death. You heard what she said."

"Sergeant Shelton will assess whether or not her coming here fits into their—or Horse Creek County's—investigation."

"Not after we didn't tell him anything." Leona narrowed her eyes at me. "You're not going to look into a young woman being found dead and Thurston being questioned?"

I loved that Leona considered thirty-seven a young woman, but stuck to the point. "It could be seen as a conflict of interest if KWMT staffers poke around."

She scoffed with an emphatic expulsion of breath. "Wouldn't stop you if you wanted to poke around."

Before I could fall into the trap of saying anything along the lines of *Maybe I don't want to*, I foresaw her follow up.

Instead, I said, "Once they announce the identification, it will likely be—sadly—a routine matter of a woman who took her own life."

"And Thurston?"

"Law enforcement is in the best position to determine what, if any, role Thurston played."

"If I had my eyes closed, I wouldn't believe that was E.M. Danniher saying those words." She pressed her hands to her thighs as she stood. "I'm going home. I'm tired. And there's more of this nightmare tomorrow."

We had Dale follow Leona home.

"Make sure no one else is following her and go with her to the door," I added.

"That's ridiculous," she protested. "This isn't a crime-ridden city—"

"Go with her to the door and don't leave until she's checked all over the house," I elaborated. "And if she won't check, then you do it. Closets, too."

"Good grief. Fine, fine. I give up—before you make the kid stay until a SWAT squad clears the place."

He messaged us that Leona was safely in her house with no sign of any disturbance or of anyone following her.

Fueled by satisfaction at that state of affairs, along with my stash of cookies, Audrey and I got down to sketching out a framework for the next several days.

THERE WERE TOO many unknown variables to map out much detail, but the time was well spent because Audrey's confidence rose as we worked.

Neither of us said it, but it seemed she was the de facto person in charge. At least for now. Others—like Les and Thurston's pet producer—had the titles, but no inclination to lead. In the vacuum left,

Audrey had already stepped up impressively.

I'd seen this before in newsrooms.

As in many workplaces, those who talked a good game, especially about themselves, got the attention and the titles. But failed to rise to the occasion of an emergency, while the untitled pulled irons out of the fire, getting little recognition except from other people doing the work.

I'd known one guy who turned every event into drama and trauma. In retrospect I saw it was so he could claim credit for handling the D-and-T. When real crises hit, he was out of his depth.

Unfortunately, by the time I recognized this, I'd been married to him long enough that I felt I owed him loyalty despite flaws of character and crisis management.

On that cheery note, I turned into my street, looking forward to the consoling company of my dog, Shadow.

Several houses away from my driveway, I recognized, from the presence of a familiar pickup truck, that I had other company. Whether it would prove to be consoling was unlikely.

Thomas David Burrell more often riled me—in more ways than one—than soothed me.

Especially when he showed up like this, which meant he had something to say to me he didn't think I'd want to hear—things I wanted to hear he pretty much figured I'd cover myself—and he thought he was the one to say it, because he didn't pass off dirty jobs to others.

I respected that. Also found it annoying.

Chapter Eleven

HE'D PARKED IN the far lane of the double drive, which let me remotely open the garage door on the near side and pull in. The other half of the garage held considerably less stuff than it had when I moved in earlier this year, but still more than would allow a second vehicle inside.

Except, possibly, a Volkswagen Beetle.

Since Jennifer left the station, had she or her *guys* tracked down ownership of all VW Beetles in Sherman?

We needed to hit that ID hard tomorrow. Preferably officially, but, maybe, if we built enough proof and the sheriff's departments dragged their feet…

As I exited the garage by the open overhead door, then hit the remote on my keychain to close it behind me, my path approached where Tom rested his backside against the front right corner of his truck.

As was his custom, he didn't start the conversation—except by showing up here—so I said, "We've got to stop meeting like this."

"You mean I need to stop showing up like this?"

"I didn't say that." Wasn't going to say I was glad to see him, either. Which might have been the reason I said what I said.

Not an issue I needed to sort out, considering how things stood.

Which, as I said before, was complicated.

After an extremely rocky start to our acquaintance—though I never *really* thought he would kill me—he'd helped, often reluctantly, with inquiries.

And there'd been something else between him and me. Something related to, yet beyond, the steamy kisses we'd shared.

Until he'd called an end to whatever was between us, because it confused his young daughter, Tamantha.

Called an end to it when it hadn't truly begun. Not in the physical sense, not beyond those kisses that stoked rather than satisfied. In the non-physical sense? Who the heck knows?

Tamantha wasn't alone in being confused.

I'd also shared hot kisses with Mike … before his departure for fame and advancement in Chicago.

And I didn't know how I felt about any of it, except that I missed spending time with both men.

I missed it a lot.

…you're feeling easily bruised with Mike in Chicago, Jennifer heading the same direction after the first of the year, and Tom keeping his distance.

I cleared my throat. "Rest of the funeral?"

"Fine."

"Good. I'm going to let Shadow out."

And that wasn't only for the sake of his bladder. He liked Tom nearly as much as he liked Tamantha.

With Shadow at the top of the agenda, we walked to the backyard. I unlocked the back door. Shadow looked past me, alert. Then he relaxed, woofed softly, and made eye contact with me in the dim light from a kitchen under-cabinet light.

"Okay," I told Shadow.

He beelined for Tom.

The rough and tough rancher murmured things I mostly couldn't hear, but the tone was pure mush. He also rubbed and stroked Shadow's ears in a way that had the dog's bottom wriggling in delight.

"If you're coming to see my dog, we could probably set up a visitation schedule, especially if you bring Tamantha."

His fourth-grade daughter was the delight of Tom's life. And Shadow's. A good chunk of mine, too.

"Might do that," he said. "She'd like it."

"She could come visit Shadow and me. Any time."

He grunted, acknowledging the who-the-heck-knows complexity between us, while also shifting toward neutrality.

Bundled in our jackets, we sat on chairs I hadn't yet taken in for the season. I better do it soon, because Wyoming didn't lollygag in switching from summer to winter.

Shadow industriously explored the edges of his domain.

"I considered intercepting you at the station." That's how Tom introduced the business portion of this meeting.

I slanted a look toward him. "It was a little busy tonight. It's also gossip central."

He confirmed with a single dip of his head. "So I came here."

"Message, email, phone, letter," I proposed.

"Too easy for you to ignore. Too hard to read your reaction."

"My reaction to what?"

He shifted his head toward me. There wasn't much light back here, only a few patches tossed out from the back windows of the house. Under the brim of his cowboy hat all but his considerable jaw blended into black.

"What happened at the station when the deputies talked to Thurston?"

"I wasn't there, but I'm told deputies from both counties came and said they wanted to talk to him at the sheriff's department. Presumably about the woman whose body was found in Horse Creek County. Did you know her?"

"Leona said on the news no ID's been released."

"Like that would matter. You seem to know everybody and every-thing. Cottonwood County's answer to the great and all-powerful Oz."

"Not even close." I heard the crooked grin in his voice. "Tried to get folks to wear green glasses. Nobody fell for it."

I sucked the insides of my cheeks to guard against any answering amusement.

After a long moment, he spoke again. "Do you think he did this— Thurston? Murdered that girl?"

"Woman. And I don't know. How could I?"

"You know him."

"Only to the point of knowing he's vain, self-centered, and the single worst journalist I've ever imagined much less encountered. I've made a point of *not* knowing him. Law enforcement professionals appear to think he might have insight or information on her death."

"On her death," he repeated slowly. "You're thinking it could be a suicide."

"I don't know. Can't possibly know, while they *should* know. That's their job."

"When has it being the sheriff's department's job ever stopped you?"

"A lot. Look at the data, Burrell. The number of cases the sheriff's department handles in a year and the number we've looked into. Minuscule percentage." I slid away from data. "Why would you care? Are you harboring a secret fondness for Thurston Fine that I never knew about?"

"No. I'm harboring a ... *fondness* for you that you do know about."

"That makes no sense." Especially when he'd decided *fondness* was off the agenda. Considering that, I let *cranky* have its way with those words.

"Can't say it does. Or—" The shadows above his jaw shifted slightly. A faint grin to match the rueful tone. "—do you mean my advocating for you to look into this matter doesn't make sense?"

I sidestepped the other implications. "You've disapproved of the investigating I and the others have been involved in—including you when you'd get off your high horse. Why—"

"I've mostly come around."

"—would you *advocate* for me to look into this for Thurston's sake?"

"Not for his sake. For yours."

I flapped my hands up, then dropped them to my lap. Shadow turned from snuffling a section of the back fence where a particularly porky squirrel liked to hang out.

He regarded us a long moment. Then, apparently satisfied, returned to his inspection.

"It *is* for your sake," Tom said, unshaken by my hand-flapping.

"You need to know what happened. The truth. You always do. And nobody's better at it than you. You know Diana will help. Jennifer. Mike, as much as he can from Chicago. I'll help, too, if you want me to."

"If I want you…?" To get away from that phrase, I jumped into a fire of another sort. "I didn't ask the cause of death."

He turned toward me. "Didn't hear a cause was released."

"It wasn't. That's not the point. I didn't ask. I *didn't ask*. The only reason I know she was shot in the head was because Needham said it because he thought I already knew."

He sat with that in silence for a long moment. "Okay. So, you think that means you're no longer capable of figuring these things out? Is that what you're saying? That's why you're not investigating?"

"I'm not saying that." And something in me sure didn't like him saying it, even as a question. "But there are two divergent tasks here— keeping KWMT running and investigating the death of this girl."

"Woman."

I growled. "I can only handle one. With Les AWOL, Thurston sidelined, Audrey stepping up but inexperienced…"

"Got it."

He said nothing more for a full minute.

"Thing is," he added then, "you don't really believe you can handle only one."

"Yes, I do. I just told you—"

"You are already investigating, no matter what you said to yourself or anybody else. You made up your mind to do it almost right away."

"I'm not and I didn't. That—"

"You did it the instant you refused to anchor. With your background and experience, you were the obvious choice. But you wouldn't have time to investigate if you were anchor. You immediately went for the option that would let you investigate, along with helping keep the newscasts going."

Was he right?

Without an answer to that, another potential angle hit me.

If I'd slid into Thurston's job, that truly could have been seen as a conflict of interest with poking into whether he was involved in a … death. Had I avoided that subconsciously by declining to anchor?

After a long silence, I turned toward him, peering into the face shadow despite knowing I'd see nothing. "Did Diana call you about this? I know Jennifer didn't. She's too busy skipping around the newsroom and singing her version of *Jeremiah was a bullfrog*, with lots of emphasis on the *Joy to you and me* part."

"Diana did not call me. I called her," he said.

I wanted to say *Oh, ho!* Like I'd caught him out at something. But what when he'd admitted it flat out?

"After Needham called me," he added.

Et tu, Needham?

Into the silence that settled around us, he eventually said, "Okay then." He shifted as if to stand up.

"I *will* make you help."

"Said I would."

"And I get to see Tamantha."

"You don't need to blackmail me into that. Not ever. You should know that since the two of you and Mrs. Parens are planning that trip to Buffalo and Fort Phil Kearny."

"I figured you approved of an educational field trip solely because of Mrs. P."

He didn't address that accusation directly. "Tamantha told me what you said to her about being friends with her first and that what's between the two of you isn't ever going away. Thank you."

"Didn't say it for you."

"I know. You said it because it's the truth. I'm grateful it is. And I'm grateful you expressed it in a way Tamantha understood and believed."

After several more beats of silence—at least from the humans, while the sounds from the night and the roaming dog stepped up to center stage—he stood.

Then he remained there.

From this angle, a patch of light from a back window sliced diagonally across his face.

"You think we can get past this?" he asked.

I didn't pretend he meant the discussion of investigating or Ta-mantha.

"To the point of being friends? Yes."

Without moving his head, he shifted his eyes to look at me. But he didn't ask another question.

The question.

He dropped his head to tip his hat. Murmured, "Night," and was gone.

Shadow and I remained there for a while. I didn't pay attention to how long.

DAY TWO

TUESDAY

Chapter Twelve

I **DIDN'T GET** out of bed right away in the morning.

There'd been a comfort yesterday in saying I wasn't going to investigate.

I sent one message. Before I could think too much about giving up yesterday's single focus.

Then I checked the station's website.

It occurred to me that if I looked at this situation from the outside, without any knowledge of Thurston, that was one of the first steps I'd take.

It hadn't been updated in years. Possibly not since Thurston arrived. That should have meant the write-up relied heavily on his background. Instead, with no details, it presented him as a full-blown demigod who'd shown up in Sherman and weren't we all lucky to have him.

I'd lost my appetite for breakfast.

❖   ❖   ❖   ❖

IN THE SMALLEST of the editing booths, I sneezed, possibly in response to the residual despair of its previous occupants. Then I sipped the coffee that was bad even though—as the first newsroom arrival—I'd made it the same way I made coffee at home.

Must be the pot.

"I thought you liked my other footage better," Jenks said to me from the doorway, holding a coffee cup.

I'd known—in theory—that he liked to come in early so he could get off early. Since I rarely came in early, I hadn't known how early, though.

I might have preferred to keep this viewing to myself, but it wasn't a big deal. I'd wanted to see it again on this screen, which had better resolution than the one on my desk—better, not good. All the equipment at KWMT appeared to have been bought at a fire sale decades ago.

Besides, it might be useful to have Jenks here.

"I do like the second video better—I like it a lot. For atmosphere, for story-telling. But what you shot earlier in the day has details not as apparent in that later video. Sorry the coffee's awful."

"Details like what?" He lifted the cup and sipped. "I've had worse."

He was on his own with the coffee. I'd given fair warning. I was more interested in our other topic.

"The seat position."

He leaned toward the screen. "Driver's seat looks about right. You mean the front passenger seat being all the way back? That could be from when she'd had a passenger, getting more legroom."

"But she died in the back seat. If she drove, she had to get into the back seat."

"She got out and climbed in back."

"Ah. The footage you got when you first arrived shows evidence techs taking a whole lot of photos around the vehicle. Was there anything there visible in person that doesn't show up on the video?"

"Not that I remember. Why?"

"Because then they were taking photos of nothing. Why would they do that unless it was significant? Did you shoot the other side of the car?"

"No. Sorry."

"So, it's possible she shifted from the driver's seat to the passenger seat and got out that side to get in back. Or, *maybe*, someone with a lot of wriggling, flexibility, and a small frame could maneuver between the two front seats to get back there. But why? It was cold Sunday night, but not bone-chilling. Surely not enough to keep someone from getting out of the driver's seat to get in the back seat. Especially not someone intending to kill herself."

"Somebody else drove her there and she got out the passenger side to get in back. And the techs took photos of her footprints on that side."

"Then what happened to the driver?"

"You got me." He was mildly intrigued, but Jenks would not be joining our investigating group. "Anything else?"

I didn't want to put words in his mouth. "Anything strike you about the location?"

He tipped his head. "Lonely as hell. No, I take that back. It *looks* lonely as hell, but it isn't the absolute back of beyond. It's not real far from Colter."

"Colter?" That sounded familiar, but I couldn't place a location.

There could be several reasons for that.

First, it hadn't taken me long to recognize that *not real far* was Wyoming speak for near. Took a little longer to realize that Wyomingites' idea of near and mine did not match. So, Colter could be on the other side of the state or in another state altogether and still earn *not real far.*

Second, Colter could be a railroad crossing, a ranch, a park, a mountain, or a hundred other geographic features.

"County seat, about the only place that qualifies as a town in Horse Creek County."

"How far a drive is this—" I gestured toward the screen. "—from Colter?"

"Let's see, you go down that road a few miles to where it connects with an access road, then you follow that about four or five miles to the highway. It's maybe five, eight miles down the highway."

"That's *not real far?*"

"Uh-huh. Is that what you were after?"

"Anything else strike you about the spot?"

"Isolated, even for being not real far from Colter." Okay, now he was rubbing it in. "The sort of place nobody'd have reason to go by."

Putting aside *not real far*, I looked from the screen to him. "Then how was the car spotted?"

"One of the Horse Creek deputies saw a flash of color when he was driving the highway. Decided to check it out—I suppose he didn't have anything else going on. Lucky, because if that car had been a little farther off the far side of the road, it would have been down the dip enough to not be seen."

"The dip?"

"Yeah. That road's low on the northbound side, low on the south-bound side, with a rounded mound in the middle. It's like driving on the back of a snake. But that dip's what let me get the angle for the later video. Is that what you're getting at?"

"Honestly? No. But it's interesting. Anything else strike you about the road?"

"Nope. Give an old guy a break and tell me what you're thinking, Elizabeth."

"It's paved. Or it was at one time or another." The video didn't reveal that level of detail, nor whether footprints showed or not. "Someone cared enough and took the time and expense to pave it. There are roads around here generally considered next-best to main thoroughfares that aren't paved, yet a stretch of road that's not used *is* paved."

"Oh, that. That's because it's the old Shangri-La Mine Road."

"Shangri-La? Really?"

"Yeah, they didn't want to go with an obvious name like Bonan-za," he said dryly. "It was supposed to be the grand entry to a major development. That was when Horse Creek County expected to have a boom."

"A boom? What kind of energy?"

Wyoming's had booms and busts in many forms of energy—coal, oil, gas, solar, wind. In fact, multiple booms and busts in each.

"Gold."

That raised my eyebrows. "I thought Wyoming gold rushes ended more than a century ago and weren't that much to start, certainly not like California, Alaska, Montana."

"That's pretty much right. What happened with the Shangri-La wasn't a legit boom. Some guys basically salted a couple spots with gold, started a rush, which took off at warp speed compared to the old days.

"Instead of miners in denim streaming in, they had supposed scientists, developers, and guys dressed in flashy suits and shiny boots, crawling all over Horse Creek County and spilling into Cottonwood. They showed off test results, economic projections, and a lot of references. All fake.

"Thing is, the locals didn't fall for it except one or two. Needham did a series on it in the *Independence*."

"Sounds like a great story." I experienced a sudden itch between my shoulder blades. I couldn't claim infallibility for my itches. They did not always turn up a story I could use. But the majority were interesting. Slowly, I added, "I need to work that into a 'Helping Out!' segment."

"Pretty old news. As you can tell by that piece of road it happened … geez, must be thirty years ago." Jenks stood. "Gotta get to an assignment."

And he was gone, with no indication he'd recognized his words had set off an itch I did not have time to scratch.

JENNIFER AND AUDREY burst into the editing booth in a reprise of yesterday's greeting, except being here instead of the newsroom meant none of us had room to breathe, much less move.

Audrey got to the headline first this time. "Jennifer's confirmed the ID. It's Melissa Oxley, like Jennifer thought."

"Narrowed the car registration down to her. I know we can't use the ID on-air, but it was definitely her car, so that's enough for *us*, for investigating."

She handed me a printout of a driver's license photo.

Melissa Oxley had an oval face with eyes that looked straight at the viewer, but with little expression. Her mouth seemed slightly compressed. Her medium-brown hair fell straight from a side part. Her statistics indicated unremarkable height and weight.

"All right," I said.

"Just all right?" Jennifer complained. "You said we couldn't do anything until we had the ID. Now we do."

I'd also said I wasn't going to look into this death. Apparently, she hadn't believed it. And she'd been proven correct. Darn it.

"Good that we've confirmed the victim is Melissa Oxley. Now, what do we know about her?"

"She lived alone in that house built by her ancestor," Audrey said.

"She has that crazy friend. Fawn Raglettley. Oh. That license number you messaged me this morning came back to Isaac Raglettley. Could be her father by the age. Speaking of age, I thought it was a typo when I saw what year that truck's from. It's older than me. It's older than Fawn. It's—" She faltered as her math told her it wasn't older than me. "Anyway, it's really old."

"Good thing it moved slow in its old age, because that's how I memorized the number. As for Melissa Oxley, we need a lot more. Starting with, how is she connected to Thurston?"

"Jennifer found that out, too. She found social media accounts Melissa Oxley ran, all about Thurston," Audrey said. "They said Melissa was Thurston Fine's biggest fan and president of his fan club."

"Thurston has a fan club? Wait. You said Melissa Oxley identified herself as his *biggest* fan, so he must have more than one—in fact, more than two if the statement is grammatically correct, because otherwise she would have been his *bigger* fan."

Jennifer groaned. We'd had a few discussions about how *-er* is for comparing two, while *-est* requires more than two.

But she abruptly cheered up. "Couldn't she be his biggest fan and be the only one? Also his littlest fan and—"

"Audrey!" someone shouted from the newsroom. "Phone."

She hopped up. "Jennifer, I'm going to need you. Elizabeth, we'll talk later about the follow story you're going to write."

"Wait, have you heard from Les? Thurston?"

"Not a word." She left with an authoritative stride.

It boggled my mind that the news director had gone radio silence under these circumstances. Thurston? Not as hard to imagine.

And yet … it didn't *surprise* me about either man.

Jennifer stood, but lingered. "We've got to get more about what Melissa had to do with Thurston. To prove he—"

"Jennifer!" Audrey called to her.

The younger woman—youngest, if you counted all three of us who'd been in the room—rolled her eyes and said to me, "Later."

Chapter Thirteen

NOT TEN MINUTES later, Diana stood in the doorway.

It was just as well I had another interruption. I'd been running Jenks' video over and over, as if the blue VW Beetle would tell me something definitive.

It didn't.

Unlike Jennifer and Audrey, Diana did not try to come in—the wisdom of her long experience with KWMT-TV's pocket-sized editing facilities.

She also didn't say anything.

"Hey," I said. "When you were out there yesterday, shooting neighbor reaction stuff, did you get any more than Walt said?"

"You're asking me that now?"

I looked around at her. She sounded like she had a point that I didn't exactly follow. "Yeah."

"You didn't ask last night."

"No."

"Even when I stuck around and gave you the chance to ask anything you wanted after the Five. When I could have cut loose and gone home."

"You stuck around to help Audrey and Leona."

"I also stuck around to let you pick my brain."

Ah. Now I got it. "I wasn't in the brain-picking business last night. If you'd had anything I could have used for the on-air report, you'd have told me."

I left a pause, inviting her to fill it with the obvious answer that now she had something that couldn't have been used for the on-air report. She did not oblige.

I sighed. "Okay, okay. I am now in the brain-picking business."

"Because?"

"Because I thought about what you said and decided you were right."

She snorted her disbelief. "I know Tom went to talk to you. And I know you know I know."

"More like he talked at me. You could have warned me."

"He was nearly to your place when he called. But I wouldn't have warned you anyway."

"Thanks a lot. Let me walk into a surprise attack."

"You're welcome. Only way to get through to you sometimes."

I scowled, but didn't dispute directly. "Still, a true friend would have warned me he was coming."

"A true friend knows this was better for you. Not as much time to build a wall and let the mortar set. You're going to do it? And don't ask *do what.*"

"I wasn't going to."

She wanted her pound of flesh and an admission of error.

Hard to tell which would hurt more.

"All right. I was wrong. You were right. Last night, Tom—and you—made compelling arguments and, starting today, I am prepared to look into this death, including Thurston's possible involvement in it."

"Including the possibility he had no involvement *and* that it might have been a suicide or accident?"

"If you bring that up to Jennifer, she'll grind her teeth enough to do real damage. But I'll just say, *yes.*"

"I'll take that. What do you want to know?"

I kept all impatience out of my voice. "Did you pick up anything more than Walt told us last night while talking with Melissa Oxley's neighbors?"

Signaling the ceasefire that marked her complete victory, Diana slid her hip onto the edge of the chair back that theoretically meant another person could fit in here. "Yes. I called Walt from home and filled him in. Nothing definitive, nothing in a sound bite, and nothing dazzling enough to include on-air."

I gave her time to sort out what she intended to say.

"First, when I asked what kind of car she drove, they all said a blue VW bug. Only two neighbors have lived there since Melissa Oxley was a little girl. One knew more than she said and the other less—a lot of guesses in his info. Neither came right out and said it, but the sense was that everything changed for the family when Melissa's father suddenly made serious money."

"How? When?"

"They were very cagey about how. I'd give the guesser a pass, believing he didn't know or maybe didn't remember. The other? Her name's Faye Nafus and I think she knew and wasn't sharing. As for when the change in fortunes happened, it sounded like Melissa was in early grade school.

"Faye Nafus lives two doors down and she's been there fifty years. She said that until the change in fortunes, Melissa was a normal little girl, part of the neighborhood, going to school, playing with kids, going to birthday parties. Pretty quickly after, she wasn't."

"Parents pulled her back or other folks cut her off?"

Diana shrugged and shook her head. "I didn't press. Anyway, another shift happened when her father died a few years later. Faye said Melissa was a real daddy's girl. But his death brought Melissa and her mother closer together. Had the usual teenage issues, but otherwise a close relationship.

"Melissa went to college back East, came home for a while after graduation, then moved to Cody to work at a bookstore. One thing Faye said really struck me. She said Melissa didn't move easily through the world."

I *huh'd* my understanding of why Diana noted the phrase. It conveyed a lot.

She continued. "The unifying theme among all the neighbors was that her mother's death hit Melissa Oxley hard. Probably didn't help that her mother's instructions in her will specifically said to kick out her second husband after she died."

"Whoa. If they were still married, why didn't Mom kick him out herself if she didn't want him there?"

Diana shrugged. "No idea. And it turned out to be a mess for Melissa to handle. Her stepfather did not want to go. Pretty much refused to go. Melissa had to get the sheriff's department involved and there was a scene in the front yard with him shouting at Melissa and basically being dragged away.

"I think the neighbors rather enjoyed that part. None were fans of the mother's second husband—his name's Magnus Boesch. They all said how much they preferred Melissa and several speculated glumly that now he'd probably be back. Despite the benefit to them of having Melissa instead of Boesch, a couple neighbors indicated they thought it was a mistake for her to move back into that house all by herself."

"Lonely? That could argue for suicide."

"I don't know about that," she said. "Only one said she seemed lonely. Others talked about her keeping herself very busy—coming and going, lights burning every night as she watched and rewatched KWMT's newscasts. She could repeat everything Thurston said the night before by the next morning."

"Yikes. Did you hear—?"

"The fan club? Yeah, Jennifer told me. A couple neighbors, including the long-term one, talked about a tall young woman who came to the house."

"Leona's friend from last night? Fawn Raglettley?" I assumed Diana had heard about that because that's how newsrooms are, not to mention that's how Cottonwood County was. I wouldn't be surprised if Penny Czylinski at the Sherman Supermarket knew about it before Fawn left the parking lot last night.

The head checker made modern news media look like paper and pencil. As for KWMT-TV, she made it look like stone and chisel.

"Your friend, too, from what I hear."

"Leona was her prime target. Being on-air instead of Thurston and all. I was secondary. What about the last time the neighbors saw Melissa?"

"Several on Saturday. Two said they thought they saw her Sunday. One had her in a dress coat around noon and the other in jeans and a jacket about seven p.m. Also said her lights were burning when the neighbor went to bed, but were out Monday morning."

"Good detail. I've been thinking about something Jennifer said."

"Everything I've heard her say has been along the lines that the legal system should skip all preliminaries and sentence him tomorrow."

I sighed. "It's going to be uncomfortable for her if or *when* he comes back. His supporters have dwindled in the newsroom, but a few will gladly tell him what she or anyone else says."

"She knows. She said it didn't matter, even if she got fired, since she's leaving at the first of the year."

"Bad enough I'll have to break someone new in. I don't want her gone early."

"Poor Elizabeth." She patted me on the shoulder. "Empty nest syndrome."

"Right back atcha. Your actual nest will be empty in not too many years."

"I'm aware. We'll be empty nesters together. But what was it Jennifer said that got you thinking, since it doesn't seem to be her gleeful declarations that Thurston must be guilty?"

"It's not. Jennifer said if I anchored and Thurston got out of jail, he'd try to murder me, but not to worry because he couldn't pull it off."

She tipped her head. "Innocence by reason of ineptitude?"

"It makes you stop and think, doesn't it? If Thurston *is* guilty, I'll have to accept I misjudged his eptitude, although—"

"*Eptitude* being the antonym of *ineptitude*."

That was so obvious I didn't feel a need to confirm. "—with the major upside that he'd be going to prison."

I expected that to get a response. It didn't.

"Diana?"

"I'm still trying to get over you changing your mind."

With great dignity and generosity, I said, "I thought about it overnight and you were persuasive."

"About you feeling vulnerable because things are changing."

"No. About my knowing how to use words. And realizing I hadn't let myself consider the more interesting elements because digging into it would—*will*—mean talking to Thurston."

Her lips parted. She was a breath away from disagreeing. Then her expression changed. "You know, that's a good point."

"I do know. And realizing that's what's ahead almost had me changing my mind back. There is no way around needing to talk to him."

She was trying not to grin. "There isn't. Yet you're still going ahead. That's noble of you."

"I'm glad you think so, because you'll understand how I couldn't possibly deny my dear friend—that's you—the opportunity to be ennobled by such a sacrifice. You're coming with me when the time comes. It's all cleared with Audrey, who seems to feel she owes me a few favors."

DIANA HAD AN assignment to get to.

I left the editing booth with her, then stopped at my desk to get my things.

That caught Jennifer's attention.

"Elizabeth, Diana, where are you going? I can't get away—"

"I know. Audrey needs your help. Both yours and Diana's."

"Yours, too. You told Audrey you'd write the follow-up story for Leona."

"I'll be back in plenty of time. As long as you all gather material for me. While you're doing that, I'm going to Cody."

"Why?" Jennifer asked.

"That's where Melissa Oxley lived before she moved back to her family home after her mother's death." Diana turned from Jennifer to me. "Aren't there a lot of things we need to know about her that we can find out here?"

"Yes. But it's what makes sense to do now. First, I'm the only one free right now. Second, we'd have to fight off other people trying to get the same information—from Needham to Shelton to the Horse Creek County Sheriff's Department. Cody's the one place we can get in first. Especially if Jennifer can find out where Melissa Oxley lived and worked in Cody while I drive there."

"On it."

"Want me to go back and ask that long-time neighbor for more details?" Volunteering that displayed Diana was well past her pique with me.

"Not yet. If she's that much of a sharer, let's not give her our intentions to explore Cody to share, too."

Chapter Fourteen

MOST OF MY experience with Cody was about the same as a tourist might have—good restaurants, cute shops, enticing hairstylists, and the impressive Buffalo Bill Center of the West, which comprised five individual museums.

This trip showed me a different aspect of the town.

Not exactly the bowels, but a more practical Cody, where residents fulfilled the necessities and some of the pleasures of life.

Saying she was still working on where Melissa worked, Jennifer messaged me an address that turned out to be a ten-unit apartment building—five small units on the first floor, five more on the second floor. With ten parking spots in front, each with a first initial and last name on it.

A reminder that Cody and Wyoming were not always the same as other places I'd lived, where names were not associated with apartment numbers or doors for all sorts of security reasons.

So far, I'd knocked on eight of the ten doors. Three were answered by a self-identified bartender and two waitresses. All had worked the night before. None were enthusiastic about answering the door before ten a.m. I couldn't blame them.

But they were awake now, so I asked my questions.

The bartender and one waitress had no answers for me. They'd moved here after Melissa Oxley left and hadn't heard of her. In a no-stone-unturned habit, I gave them my contact information.

I hoped they could fall back asleep easily.

At the moment, I stood in front of the other waitress—the one who'd opened Door 8—who went from three-quarters asleep to at least half awake at the name I asked about.

When I identified myself, she responded with, "Kit."

A flowy robe with giant pink blooms across its polyester failed to cover the men's white muscle shirt and drooping pajama bottoms she wore, despite her clasping the edges of the robe's opening to a bosom inclined to leak out either side of the shirt's straps.

Lusterless black hair contrasted with both the white roots at her hairline and the pallor of her skin, highlighted by the morning sun.

"I heard a rumor last night that was her found in Horse Creek County," Kit said. "That's weird. Thought she left here to move back to Sherman. Would've sworn she'd never leave the house some great-great something of hers built in Sherman. Horse Creek County? *Why?* Cottonwood's bad enough."

"There are a lot of uncertainties." My job was to ask questions, not answer hers. "You lived here when she did?"

"Yeah. She lived two doors down—Unit J, last one on the right."

"Were you friends?" My phone hummed with an incoming message.

"Nah. Said hello when we saw each other was all."

"Do you know where she worked?"

She frowned in an exercise of memory, but came out with another, "Nah. Weekdays, though. Regular hours. Not nights like me."

If that was a jab at me for waking her up, she'd have to do better to get through my journalist-knocking-on-doors thick skin. "What about a boyfriend?"

"Her? Not that I ever noticed."

"Other friends, visitors?"

She hitched a shoulder. "Nothing out of the ordinary. She'd be gone a lot of weekends, because my boyfriend could use her parking spot and that was a lot more convenient. None of the people here now ever leave."

She sounded aggrieved.

"How about a tall young woman? Over six-foot. Brown hair."

She shook her head, not interested.

"Anything else you remember?"

"Pretty quiet. That's about it."

I thanked her, gave the spiel about contacting me if she thought of anything else, and left her my info.

Which was sadder, the loss of a person mourned deeply by many or the loss of a person who hadn't had that in life? I'd encountered plenty of both in my reporting career. Both were sad.

To check my phone, I moved away so I wouldn't be visible from Kit's windows in case she opted for observation over sleep. I would have in her position, but that's why I became a journalist.

Jennifer came through again.

Melissa Oxley had worked at Legends Bookstore on Sheridan Avenue in Cody.

I messaged back my thanks, but didn't leave right away. I had two more doors to knock on, including the one where Melissa had lived.

Some might say to skip it since there couldn't have been overlap, but sometimes—rare, but sometimes—new residents picked up interesting tidbits about previous residents. Gossip from mutual neighbors, hints from mail still being delivered, an item or two left behind.

But no one answered at Units H or J.

I headed downtown toward Legends Bookstore.

If I were desperate, I could come back here after business hours to try again to talk to the other residents.

THE CENTER WINDOW at Legends Bookstore featured a silhouette image of a cowboy-hatted figure tipped back on a chair with its front legs raised, possibly rocked into that position by his reaction to the open book he read.

I liked to think so, anyway.

I hung back, waiting for a moment when one of the booksellers wasn't helping a customer. That was only right considering the customers were here to spend money and I was here to gather information.

In the meantime, there were books to look at.

It seemed to me that from inside, the reading figure in the window appeared more relaxed. Maybe that was the soothing influence of all the books around.

The moment came when I could identify myself to a young woman bookseller and ask if she had worked here when Melissa Oxley did.

"Oh, yes, I've been here almost since it opened, but… I don't want to be on TV."

"I understand. I'm here strictly for background. No camera, see?" From my empty hands, so completely unthreatening, I smiled up to her.

She smiled back, but demurred, "I didn't know her well."

"When did you start working here?"

With easy questions about her working experience at Legends Bookstore, we slid toward Melissa.

She was chattier now, telling me Melissa had been a good worker. Reliable, on time, diligent. But reading between the lines and with the help of her unconscious expressions, I also gathered Melissa had been better with books than customers.

"She was quiet, you know? Unless she got started on something that really interested her, and then she didn't realize it didn't interest someone else as much as it did her. I don't mean…"

"I know exactly what you mean," I told her. "That fits what other people have said."

Often, if you can assure someone they're not the sole source for certain information, they'll give you more.

"I didn't know her well," she said again.

"Did you do things together outside working hours?"

"Staff lunches. But if you mean separate from work, no. Most of what I do is with my family, and Melissa certainly wasn't interested in soccer or dance recitals."

She smiled slightly. I mirrored it.

"What was she interested in?"

"Hmm." Her forehead bunched. "Regional history, for sure. Her family was around not long after Sherman was founded. She found a picture of her family home in a book with photographs from the 1800s. She was excited about that and showed it to me. She talked about how the family was just her and her mom—that, of course, was before her mom died—and it made her sad the family would end with her. I said she had plenty of time to continue the family, but she seemed certain she wouldn't."

She exhaled. "Poor thing was right. Other than that..."

From being about to tell me she couldn't help me more, she abruptly brightened.

"Movies. She was interested in movies. And the actors. Plus TV series. Mostly whatever was hot. That started after she met—Oh. Of *course*. I should have told you this at the start. You need to talk to Joanne Sheidenstricker.

"She's a regular customer—mostly for entertainment magazines and bios. She and Melissa met here, got started talking, then they did things together with a bigger group outside of work. They all seemed to have a good time together. Come to think of it, when she met Joanne was when Melissa started being interested in movies and celebrities and such. I'd say they were best friends for the last four or five years before Melissa's mom died and she moved back to Sherman."

For the first time, I took out my notebook and pen to get the spelling on the name, where she worked, and anything else about the woman who'd been Melissa Oxley's best friend.

Yes, I picked up a few books before I left. A spy thriller by a former colleague and what I thought of as a grown-up coming of age book about a woman going home again and healing decades' old scars.

Chapter Fifteen

Joanne Sheidenstricker had surprisingly pale skin for Wyoming. She worked in a small office behind a boot store that I reached by way of a side street. But the place did have windows, so that didn't explain her skin.

I barely got my name and identification out before she started talking.

She told me her boss was on a weeklong check of real estate holdings and she'd been here alone the whole time and it was so quiet she'd been sure the phone was broken and with him gone she couldn't even get to the bookstore except for a few minutes at the end of her lunch hour, because he called the second she was supposed to be back and if she'd taken sixty-one minutes instead of sixty, she'd hear about it, so she was glad to have my company.

Finishing my intro with the same spiel I'd given at Legends Bookstore about gathering background on Melissa Oxley, I hoped Joanne also received the message that I had not shown up in her office for the sole purpose of relieving her isolation.

"Melissa? Poor, poor Melissa. I couldn't believe it when I heard."

Clearly the lack of official identification had not slowed the grapevine.

"Could. Not. Believe. It," she emphasized. "Why she would do such a thing I can't imagine. Especially without talking to me first."

Surely she didn't intend that to mean that talking to her would have pushed Melissa toward suicide faster.

"You're surprised Melissa might have committed suicide?"

"Oh, well, surprised. That's harder to say."

I could have sworn that's what she just *had* said.

"Melissa kept things inside, you know? Didn't let her feelings out. Let stress build up inside of her. I told her and told her it wasn't healthy. That she needed to be more open, to talk out her issues the way I do. Like when I had surgery and…"

I didn't interrupt, but half tuned out, counting on half my attention to pick up anything vital or interesting while the other half took in the surroundings, further assessed the woman across from me, wondered about her boss, reminded myself to pick up dog food for Shadow, started to mentally put together the follow-up piece for the Five, and reminded myself that being a broadcast journalist was all glitz and glamor.

"…the surgeon said nobody he'd ever operated on before healed as quickly, so he felt confident in letting me stop checkup appointments way ahead of most people." Or had selfish motivations prompted the surgeon to cut short post-op checkups? "And all because I didn't bottle up stress and anxiety."

I dove back in. "Telling Melissa your experience must have helped her tremendously. When—?"

"Did I tell Melissa about that? I'm not sure I did. Because that surgery was well before we met. Though I certainly shared other instances in my life when not bottling up stress and anxiety benefited me and everyone else. One time—"

"When *did* you meet?"

I was a strong believer in letting talkers talk in hopes of gems hidden among the dross. On the other side of that coin, the dross could bury you if you weren't careful. At the moment, my airways felt in imminent danger of closing permanently from dross dust.

"Let's see. That was well after our group started. I know that for sure. See, a couple of us first got acquainted from running into each other at Legends Bookstore.

"We started talking about movies made from the books, then other movies, and I had the idea we should go to movies together. *Some* people were real snobs about only reading the books, but enough of the others joined me going to movies to make it real fun. And a few brought in another friend, like someone from work."

She laughed sharply. "I don't have that opportunity, obviously. I'd started the group, but then others, what with bringing in their friends, started wanting to vote to change this and that.

"Then I met Melissa—at Legends Bookstore, not at work, though it was *her* work, not a customer like the rest of us. I'd go in there looking for my favorite magazines. I mean, some people try to stay up to date with TV or the internet, but I find a good article in a magazine gives you the depth and perspective you can't get otherwise."

Optimism almost triggered me into an enthusiastic discussion of how journalistic endeavors varied based on media ... when I realized she was talking about celebrity magazines, celebrity TV shows, and celebrity websites.

"Melissa asked if I needed any help and we started talking. She had *so* much to learn. She didn't know much at all about movies or TV or the stars, like the rest of us. She didn't even have favorites to start. She would soak up everything I said, barely saying a word."

Making her the perfect addition to the group from Joanne's perspective.

"What all does your group do?"

"We go to the movies together, of course, every other week or so. Wednesday nights. Then we'd go out for ice cream."

"Sounds like fun."

"It is." She sniffled, surprising me. "We hardly know what to do this Wednesday. We had it all set to see a comedy. But what with Melissa, it doesn't seem right to go to a fun movie then have ice cream. But maybe if we go to a *serious* movie ..."

And eat serious ice cream?

"How long was Melissa part of the group?"

"Gosh. I don't know exactly how long. A few years. Certainly not the first time I talked to her. You know, we're a little careful, because we've had people who seemed fine at first, but then they turned out weird or worse. But Melissa wasn't like that," she added quickly. "She had her own ways, but she was nice and she stayed in the group until she moved back to Sherman after her mom died and she inherited that house."

"Help me get a clearer picture of what she was like. You said she was nice and had her own ways. What kind of ways?"

"Oh, well… Like I said, she was quiet. Didn't talk about herself, her family like the rest of us."

"Uh-huh." That was filler. Silence can get people to talk in a lot of circumstances, by using people's discomfort with silence to pull words out of them. But with someone as talkative as Joanne, it can feel antagonistic. I wanted to keep her comfortable, to keep rolling along.

"Something else she was different about, we'd talk about the people in the movie afterward. The actors. Who we'd heard things about, who we liked best. You know, in real life."

Real life.

"Uh-huh," I muttered again.

"And she'd pick some actor who wasn't even important and get all interested in him. It wasn't even like she could find information on him, not in the magazines or TV, not even on the internet, because *nobody* wrote about him. We'd tell her over and over that she should find somebody important to get interested in, but she never did."

Great training for becoming a fan of Thurston Fine.

"And I'll tell you something else, she'd go back to Sherman a lot to see her mother. A *lot*. I mean, way, way more than everybody else in the group put together and some of us have family right in town. But time after time when we'd want to do something on the weekend, she said no because she was going *home*. Like this wasn't home."

Was the draw the mother she'd been so close to according to their neighbors, the house that had been in her family so long, or…

"Was she a fan of Thurston Fine when she lived here?"

"Who?"

"He's the anchor on the Sherman TV station's news."

"Oh, that guy. She mentioned him one time when she came back to see us all after she'd moved. Showed us a picture of them together. Like a selfie you'd take with a *real* celebrity. I told her he looked like a half-melted Ken doll from retro Barbie stuff."

Harsh, though not entirely inaccurate.

"I mean he's sure not young, is he? And he's not getting older in an interesting way. Yet she was all wound up about him."

"What did she say about him?"

She looked blank. "I don't remember details. She talked like he was important, when all he does is read the news on TV in Sherman. You'd sure never find him in a magazine at Legends Bookstore."

Not unless he was charged with Melissa Oxley's murder. Then a news anchor at the smallest market in TV-dom might be quirky enough to draw attention. Perhaps a lot of attention.

"When did she talk to you about him?"

"Gosh, I don't know. No, wait. It was the beginning of summer, because I had on a new pair of espadrilles and the dust was awful." She paused. "You know, I think it was the last time she came back here. At first, after she moved, she came back for most of our Wednesday nights, for the movie and for the ice cream, though she'd be one of the first to leave. Then she'd skip the ice cream and leave right after the movie. Then she came less often. And then not at all. Guess she decided the trip was too long."

"Did you ever go to see her in Sherman?"

"Nah."

It clearly didn't penetrate that Melissa might not have come back because her former friends mocked her obsession and couldn't be bothered to make the trip to see her.

Would that send someone toward suicide?

Before I drove back to Sherman, I did what I know best to do—I looked for someone to ask questions, preferably someone who would have good answers.

I called Mrs. Parens and Aunt Gee for recommendations. When the same name cropped up among each of their first two suggestions, I called.

She answered on the second ring.

After identifying myself, I added, "Emmaline Parens and Gisella Decker suggested I call you for background on suicide in this area."

"You're doing a story on TV about suicide?"

I hated to deflate her obvious hope, but honesty compelled me. "Not at this time. But I hoped for any insight you—"

"I don't have much time. We're sitting in the part of this country where the suicide rates are the highest across the groups."

That startled me. "Wyoming?"

"Wyoming's part of it, but not alone. The highest suicide rate is for middle-aged white men in the mountain west."

"Why?"

"That's the question, isn't it? The lone ranger ethos probably figures in. Fewer and/or spread-out services contribute. Access to guns, which increases lethality of an impulse, and likely a dozen other factors."

"Would they apply to a woman who—?"

"Yes, these elements apply to women—higher rates in this region, for instance. Though the rate's about four times higher for men."

"Women here use guns to commit sui—?"

"Sure. Most common method among Wyoming women, but nowhere near as prevalent as with men—say, less than half of women, while two-thirds of the men. Poisoning's not far behind as a method for women. But here's the other factor, women are four times as likely to do self-harm as they are to commit suicide."

"Four times?"

"Men, on the other hand, are about twice as likely to commit suicide as self-harm. I've got to go. Call me back if you're going to get something on TV."

I was promising her I would when she hung up.

WHEN I RETURNED to KWMT, Diana was out on another assignment. Jennifer was on break. Audrey, in a reprise as assignment editor and producer for both newscasts, was holding her head above water by paddling like mad.

Still no word from Thurston or Les.

Was I tempted to get that phone number for Les from Jennifer and tell him to get his derriere in here and be a news director?

Not anymore than I was tempted to call Thurston to come in and anchor.

Mostly, I couldn't believe our good fortune.

James Longbaugh might be advising Val Heatherton or Craig Morningside or both that Thurston not be on-air for now. Les could be part of those discussions, though I didn't see a reason for James to tell him to stay away.

Unless…

But even if they had reason to think Thurston was guilty of the worst, why keep Les away? And why would none of them contact the newsroom?

Those were all fleeting, curious thoughts. But mostly I was grateful.

Nobody had anything new on Melissa Oxley, who officially remained unidentified.

I set to work drafting a second-day story for the Five.

Second-day stories are among the tougher jobs in the biz.

Though, these days, they should be renamed second-minute stories.

If the previous day's breaking news generates new information, it's a news story, not a second-day. By definition, the second-day has no news. You're reworking what you reported the day before, while needing to mask that none of the questions have been answered.

Certain words or phrases signal second-day stories. *Returned* or *headed back*, as in law enforcement returned/headed back to the crime scene, looking for more evidence. *Again*, as in we asked officials again for an official ID. *Yet*, as in they haven't provided one yet. *Still*, as in still no answers/law enforcement still doesn't know, etc.

Yeah. Scintillating copy.

So, we try to avoid those words and phrases … while conveying we still don't have anything new yet except law enforcement headed back to the scene again.

Ideally, the second-day story adds context, depth, even without new facts. My favorite kind of second-day story is what my hometown newspaper editor called a *reax*. That's newspaper for reaction.

Trouble was, we'd used the best usable reaction video yesterday. In the rest of the footage, interviewees skated too close to the uncon-firmed ID. We could edit, sure, but it was risky.

It almost felt like the two sheriff's departments dragged their feet to make my life more difficult.

Okay, and maybe to find next of kin.

I sucked in air, hoping it contained second-day inspiration.

"Elizabeth!" Audrey called. "Jenks found out the deputy who found the body is going to be back at the scene in twenty minutes. If you hustle, you can get there in time to talk to him."

Perfect fodder for a second-day story and with fresh video. But—

"Twenty minutes? It takes twice as long to get there."

"Diana could make it."

"Diana could get to Iowa in twenty minutes. Never mind, I'm going, I'm going." I grabbed my pre-stocked bag—including cookies—and was out the door.

Chapter Sixteen

"**DEPUTY ITSON, HOW** nice to meet you. I understand your sharp eyes were responsible for spotting the victim's car. May we have a few moments of your time for the viewers of KWMT-TV?"

It took more than that and my winsome smile to get him in front of the camera and microphone, but with his county getting minimal coverage—especially positive coverage—I didn't expect it to be impossible.

It nearly was.

I stuck with it, though, even going as far as suggesting we call his sheriff to determine if he should make a statement on camera.

From his reaction, I knew I had him.

Greg Itson was fiercely clean cut with the stubble of a buzz cut visible under his hat.

He'd taken the standard law enforcement stance, with feet wider than usual, one foot advanced, which also brought that shoulder closer. The farther away side held his gun.

Considering how many deputies I encountered professionally, perhaps it was the standard-issue haircut and stance making him feel vaguely familiar.

"Would you mind taking off your sunglasses?" I asked.

The compression of his lips said yes, but he removed them.

"And your hat? Shadow's bad," Jenks said.

The top of Itson's head sported slightly longer fuzz than the sides.

As if in compensation for the sunglasses and hat, he said, "I can't answer anything about an ongoing investigation."

"I completely understand. If a question oversteps, say you're not answering. And I apologize in advance."

"I will tell you Thurston Fine has stated he did not know the victim."

His greatest fan. Wonderful.

But Itson didn't tell us that on-camera. The stinker.

"Did you ask Thurston about the victim by name?"

"Not going to answer that."

"Do you have further information on a confirmed identity?"

"No. Also," he said, "you can't film the car."

I suppressed a grimace.

If we told this guy we already had video of the Beetle, he'd try to confiscate it, not bothering with the detail that we'd used our judgment not to run it.

Better to let him think he was calling the shots. I glanced back at Jenks, who shifted around to where it was blatant the deputy's backdrop was his official vehicle and an angle of police tape to his side.

This spot was nearly as isolated as Jenks' video had indicated, though it hadn't taken me as long to get here once I left the highway as I'd feared.

I gestured to Jenks to start filming. Wasn't taking the time to do an intro now in case Itson reconsidered.

"Deputy Itson, tell us how you came to spot the victim's vehicle here yesterday."

"Not much to it. Keeping my eyes open while I'm patrolling, like always. Looking for—you know—something that doesn't fit. That's what I thought when a flash of blue caught my eye. *That doesn't fit.* Not that color, this time of year. Went by it, but looked back and it stood out for sure. Metallic like, too. So I got off the next exit, went to where the Shangri-La Mine Road starts and came along here to about where I thought I'd seen the color. Wasn't sure it was on the Shangri-La Mine Road, but it was a good place to start. Thought if it wasn't on the road, I could see it from there. But it was there."

Too much detail. Too much boring detail. And he was doing it on purpose.

"Called it in," he continued. "Approached the vehicle with caution. Only there was no need, because that poor woman's not going to cause anyone any problem ever again."

Genuine sympathy came through his words and expression. I warmed to Deputy Itson.

I also wondered, considering what my suicide source said, how many times this young man—by Leona's standards—had come on similar scenes. Could not be an easy part of the job.

"What was the victim wearing?"

He hesitated slightly, before saying, "Not going to answer that."

"What were your first impressions of the scene?"

"Not going to answer that."

I'd hoped by letting him say his piece about how he'd found Melissa's vehicle he might have forgotten the out I'd given him.

"Really? Impressions? You could answer anything you wanted."

"Not going to answer that."

Deputy Itson was smarter than he looked or, possibly, as dogged as he looked. Either way, he didn't respond to the subtle goading.

"But I'll tell you something," he added. "It was meant to be that I find that poor woman. If that vehicle had been a little farther north or a little farther south or even a little farther west, I wouldn't have spotted any flash of blue from the highway and she could still be sitting there. Could go on sitting there for a good long while."

Not new information for me, since Jenks had said something similar. But this had the major advantage of being a piece of video we could use.

"It must have been a horrifying scene."

"Unnecessary loss of life is always horrifying."

"Do you have an indication of how long the vehicle had been there?"

"Not very long."

"Less than a week?"

He narrowed his eyes, slightly. Possibly thinking, I suspected, about how easily we could—as, in fact, Diana and Walt already had— find out when neighbors last saw Melissa Oxley.

"Yes."

"More than a day?"

"I'm not going to answer that."

"Do you have experience investigating deaths, Deputy Itson?"

"Some." He relented slightly. "Still, a dead body's quite a thing around here. Not like the murders in Cottonwood County, where you got folks killing each other left and right lately. Always hearing about murders over there."

"Bet you'd find more murders if you investigated as carefully as the Cottonwood County Sheriff's Department does."

Good Lord. Where had that knee-jerk defense of Cottonwood County come from?

He *huh'd* disbelief without putting it into words.

"Can't answer a hypothetical." A glint came into his eyes. Uh-oh. "But what I can say is the crime I'd been working on before finding that woman's body was a bicycle left leaning outside a house the night before and not there in the morning.

"The bicycle owner didn't realize it wasn't there, because he's not one for early rising to take a bike ride. But Monday morning it was found leaning up against a side wall outside a bar. The bar owner called us about the bike being left there."

Great, he got all expansive about a stolen bicycle of no interest to our viewers.

But if he wanted to dangle this like a piece of yarn in front of a cat, I'd bat at it and see if it led anywhere.

"Had it been stolen? Or ridden there by the owner or someone near and dear and left there in a haze?"

The glint remained, but amusement lightened his eyes slightly. We weren't buds, but he appreciated my recognizing the bike's possibilities. "No knowing."

The lightening disappeared.

"I was driving back to town from talking to its owner when I spotted the victim's car."

That could make a humanizing sound bite, if I introduced it right with a phrase about the stolen bike—juxtaposing the mundane against a woman's death, which his tone and solemnity conveyed.

He shifted his weight in a clear signal this interview was about over.

"Deputy Itson, there were no footprints around the car except yours. What do you make of that?"

"How——? Not going to answer that."

Maybe he'd have asked how I knew. But he hadn't. Plus, my statement was not provable by Jenks' video. Maybe it was provable one way or the other by their evidence, but he wasn't sharing.

I ran down the acrobatic possibilities of how there could be no footprints if Melissa drove her car there. "But someone else being there is far more likely. Someone who wiped out his or her footprints——"

"Then disappeared in a puff of smoke," he sneered.

"——and got Melissa's at the same time. Making this more likely murder than suicide."

"Or suicide and somebody didn't want to get in trouble."

He clamped his mouth shut on those not very revealing words. "You can't use that."

"Not even tempted."

He did not look reassured.

My time had run out with Deputy Itson.

I took a stab with one more question.

"Have you learned anything further about the victim or the circumstances of her death that you can share with the viewers of KWMT-TV in Horse Creek County and Cottonwood County?"

"Not going to answer that."

DIANA STUCK HER head in the editing booth where I worked, though this one had room for a bit more than that. "What are you doing?"

"Tearing my hair out trying to piece together something usable and interesting. I'd say this deputy was Shelton's clone except he's taller, younger, and possibly even more closemouthed."

"Ah. I heard you'd interviewed Greg Itson."

"You know him?"

"Just to nod to. The Itsons are pretty well-thought-of. Family's been around for generations. Not as long as the Caswells in Cottonwood County, because Horse Creek County was settled later, after irrigation came in big. Nowhere near as well-to-do, either."

I counted Linda Caswell, the current family leader, as a friend.

"I've heard the extended Itson family's having a hard time right now. The deputy's mother's got early onset-Alzheimer's," Diana continued. "They have her in a nice place in Cody, but costs keep rising, the government help isn't keeping up, and their money's running out."

"All he'd talk to me about was a damned stolen bicycle."

"You'll get enough—or write around what you don't have on film. You're great at that. I'm off to another assignment. Jennifer's shift ended and she went home to do mysterious research she wasn't telling me about. She said to call her if we get together to compare notes."

"Notes? My notes are big, fat blanks."

She clicked her tongue. "Finish this piece, eat cookies, and you'll feel better."

She was right.

Chapter Seventeen

AFTER THE FIVE, I volunteered to make the takeout run.

The bit with Deputy Itson looked better than it had any right to. I'd even saved one clip to be fresh on the Ten. And Audrey ran my "Helping Out!" segment on the fake celebrities, so that was good news.

I would pick up our order after a stop at the Sherman Supermarket to buy dog food for Shadow, even if he did prefer Iris Undlin's cooking.

The Sherman Supermarket is such a community hub that smart politicians should declare his or her candidacy there, rather than on the courthouse steps.

The parking lot isn't as video-friendly a background as the stone courthouse, but the familiar front of the supermarket would draw the attention of everyone in the county. They all eat, while not all have dealings at the courthouse.

More important, though, the Sherman Supermarket has Penny Czylinski.

Penny hears all, knows all, understands all.

She also talks. Constantly. The trouble is—from my perspective anyway—her comments are … let's say non-linear. Putting the pieces together is more of a challenge than the all black, round jigsaw puzzle my sadistic brother, Rob, got a few years back when it was his turn to purchase the annual Danniher Christmas vacation puzzle.

Succeeding is all the more satisfying for the challenge, he'd declared. We banned him from the next year's puzzle for a good twenty minutes.

I'd completed shopping and was heading toward checkout when my phone rang.

With the behemoth cart even less steerable because of the massive dog-food bag's weight, I fought momentum for a wheel-squeaking stop to reach the phone.

Shadow was a stray when I took him in last year—or, he let me take him in. I'd lured him with food and I wasn't about to trim the supply now, even though he'd replaced the gaunt, hollow look of a supermodel with the sleek shine of good health.

In the basket part of the cart, I had four packages of Pepperidge Farm Double Dark Chocolate Milano Cookies for me.

Recent events depleted my work supply. Nor did the need for such supplies look like it would let up. Nothing worse than pushing hard toward a newscast and discovering you're out of the optimal fuel.

The phone rang again.

I answered the video call from Mike Paycik in Chicago, happy to see his face—and struck anew by how appealing it was, all the more for not being *too* handsome.

Somehow, he looked like what he was. A smart, funny, Wyoming native with ranching experience, former NFL player but not of the glamorous ilk, who'd returned home to Sherman to start his broadcasting career, then leapfrogged to the Chicago market, where he was thriving.

"Jen brought me—"

"Jennifer," I corrected.

"—up to date, but I want to hear your take. I don't have to call her Jennifer if she can't hear me."

"You're going to get caught." She'd outlawed nicknames a while back, declaring people didn't take her seriously.

"Probably. But I like the name Jen. Anyway, I didn't use Jenny, which she *really* doesn't like. Now, tell me what you think."

"I think you should be working. Don't you have a big-time sports job to keep?"

"I told you, the equipment here is so great, I can do twice the work in half the time it took in Sherman, so I can help you investigate." He leaned in closer to the screen. "Where are you?"

"The supermarket." We'd had a few of our pivotal encounters in this supermarket, including when he first tried to lure me into investigating a Cottonwood County deputy's disappearance.

"Ah." His syllable exuded nostalgia, but not for our encounters.

"I'm about to check out."

"You could detour down the snacks aisle for old-time's sake."

Since I was in the cookie aisle, that wasn't much of a detour.

The store was almost empty, so I shared the snack aisle choices with him—as if the man were marooned on a snack-less island instead of in a Chicago metropolitan area replete with snacks, not to mention pizza and steak—without anyone staring at me as if I were nuts.

Though maybe I didn't mind doing this for him. Did missing someone make you a little nuts?

In between, I impressed on him that this might not be one of our full-bore investigations.

"Do you mean because it's suicide or because Thurston lacks the intelligence to commit murder? Hey—how many ounces in the big package of pretzels? You wouldn't believe the dinky ones they try to pass off as party size here."

"Go to a real grocery store, not the places around the corner from your apartment or the station."

"Yeah, yeah, I know. But I can't ever find parking. Not like there."

The Sherman Supermarket spread its arms wide to about an acre of parking spaces never fully occupied, despite the brisk business and high percentage of mega-pickup trucks it attracted.

"Pick up or get delivery. You can afford it." He'd saved and invested his NFL earnings, topped off by his current impressive salary.

I skipped pickup or delivery except for emergencies because I would miss Penny Czylinski's checkout aisle, an experience like those puzzle pieces I mentioned shooting out from a pitching machine set for fastballs, only they were from a dozen different puzzles, and you didn't know what any of the puzzles looked like.

To make it more challenging today, my exposure to the pitching machine's missiles would be limited because my few items would take no time under Penny's ministrations.

"Leave me on," Mike ordered.

"Only if you're quiet or I'll mute."

"Fine. Though—"

"Shh."

I'd reached the entry to Penny's aisle.

"Well, hi there, Elizabeth. Poor girl—"

After a flick of surprise, I decided that was likely for Melissa Oxley, not me.

Though whether she knew the victim was Melissa Oxley…

"—sad, sad to go that way. Going any way at all at her age—"

She knew the age and it sounded like she might know the identity.

"—but also real sad when it wasn't going to turn out anyway. But bad ideas real common with girls that age. Told Billy it wasn't a good idea for his birthday. Opening—"

Billy? She so rarely used clear pronouns, much less names, it startled me. Not that the name helped me, since there was no Billy involved in what I wanted to know about.

Penny leaned over, aimed her handheld scanner, and caught the price code on the dog food bag without my needing to remove it. I'd counted on it giving me an extra minute with her.

"—a can of worms never is and they can call them strands and give them fancy letters all they want, but worms is what they look like, worms is what they are, first, last, and always. But she didn't listen. *Fun*, she said. *No secrets*, she said. Like there's ever such a thing. She didn't listen to me, either. Wish I'd—"

"Do you know who—?"

"—been clearer. Like with getting rich. Never quick unless you're—"

I held back the last two packages of cookies to slow this down. "—the woman they found is? You—"

"—getting poorer. *That* goes fast enough. As that old fool should have known." She glanced at the two cookie packages still in my grasp, hit a button twice on the register and they joined the others on my bill.

"Not rolled the mess over to the next generation and the next, even if it was meant well. Gold mine's a hole in the ground with a liar on top."

"Great line—"

"Mark Twain. Could have said a hole in the ground with a liar on top and a hundred fools lining up to dig in the hole. Uncle of mine used to say there's gold in every mountain range in Wyoming and his wife said right back there were even more snakes than gold and some on two feet."

A roundabout way of saying she considered someone a snake? Someone she had mentioned? With her casual sprinkling of pronouns that didn't narrow it much.

I gave in to the inevitable and paid my bill, still trying, "Did anyone say anything about considering suicide or—"

Before I could expand, I heard the irrevocable door-closing phrase, "Bye, now."

I gently placed my bag of cookies in the basket and shifted the phone to a more secure grip so I could grasp the handle of the dog-food-heavy cart, as Penny said to the person behind me, "Well, hello there, Johnny. Looks like you're planning quite the party."

I turned back, looking past Mike's face on the screen, to see a guy I'd have said was in middle school—which probably meant he was in college—with a pile of condoms sliding their way toward Penny on the conveyer belt.

Instinctively, I mashed the button to turn the phone's focus so Mike could see what I saw.

Then I had to scramble to mute his hoot.

Out in the parking lot, once more face-to-face with Mike on the screen, I said, "Poor kid. It must hurt to turn that red that fast."

"He'll be even redder when his girlfriend's father finds out. Anyone with a lick of sense knows you go to another county, not the local grocery store. Rank amateur move."

"How would you know? You said at his age you studied, played football, worked, and nothing else."

"I was. I'm *still* living a life of monastic purity."

"Right."

"Glad you agree, since you're the reason."

"Mike—"

"Now, the reason I called. What are you thinking about this situation, now that you've gotten over not investigating?"

I could only be grateful he'd changed the subject. "It's still secondary to keeping the newscasts on track, helping out Audrey, and preserving Leona's sanity."

He dismissed those worthy objectives with a scoffing sound. "Tell me everything Jen doesn't know yet."

"I'll only talk as long as it takes to pick up the dinner order and get back to the station." I shared what little I'd added to our knowledge today, then warned him, "I'm pulling into KWMT's parking lot."

"Two more questions. Is Thurston in the clear?"

"I wouldn't say that. There's whatever sent the deputies rushing after Thurston right after arriving at Melissa Oxley's house. Probably her fandom, but we don't know for sure. He's not back at the station, which *could* mean the Horse Creek people are still talking to him."

"You think Les told him to stay away until this is cleared up?"

"I can't imagine Les doing that on his own initiative. If the general manager or owner ordered him to, I suppose, but that would be the first time either's exerted any command or control over the newsroom. No, I suspect someone else with a logical mind and a good dose of realism. James Longbaugh."

"How's he involved?"

One area Jennifer hadn't updated him on. I did, finishing with, "And that was your third question. I'm going in—"

"No, no. Those were sub-questions of the Thurston question. The second real question is, do you think it was a suicide?"

"I don't know. It seems to be the direction the officials are leaning."

He expelled a breath. "Jen—Jennifer will be sorely disappointed."

✧   ✧   ✧   ✧

"I'VE TOLD JERRY and the control room to go," Audrey said as she and the cameraman emerged from the hall to the studio after the second newscast.

The Ten had clicked along well. At least to my biased eyes, it certainly looked more professional than KWMT-TV's usual offerings.

Adrenaline pulled off yesterday's newscasts. Today's productions promised well for the future.

"Good idea. Keep them fresh."

"I'm always fresh." Jerry got the laugh he wanted.

"I can stick around," I offered Audrey.

"No. Tonight, we'll all walk out together. Safer. Besides, it's gone well." She immediately backtracked on her certainty. "Don't you think it's gone well?"

"I do."

"Okay, then. We know where we're picking up tomorrow and we could all use extra rest tonight."

"Damned straight," Leona said.

Audrey hugged her shoulders. "You've been amazing, Leona. I can't thank you enough."

"Just because I don't like hard news doesn't mean I don't have a brain. Speaking of hard news and the reporting of it, I am leaving before I have to do more tonight. But I'll be back at it tomorrow, because we're all in this together."

"Hear, hear," I contributed.

Jerry beamed at her.

"Aw, shucks. You'll make me blush. Just don't ask me to do it forever."

Chapter Eighteen

MY CHANCE OF extra rest evaporated at the sight of two vehicles in my driveway.

Neither belonged to Tom Burrell.

As I pulled in, Diana and Jennifer emerged from Diana's, with Jennifer's parked behind her.

"We picked up a few things," Jennifer said, hoisting two shopping bags.

"And invited ourselves to your house. Surprised?"

"No. But you could have let yourselves in." Each of them had a key. "Jennifer, two bags are overkill. Without Mike or—Without guys, we won't consume as many snacks."

"Wanna bet? And if we don't today, there's always tomorrow."

I groaned as I opened the door.

Shadow greeted them with pleasure.

While I tended to Shadow, Diana put out snacks, and Jennifer set up her device to connect with Mike.

"…and we have great snacks," she told him as I came in with Shadow.

"Hey. That's not fair. What kind—?"

"Forget the snacks, let's get started. I want to get some sleep."

"All right, all right, but next time, I'm going to have Chicago style pizza. Maybe hot dogs. Fannie May Mint Meltaways."

"Oh, those *are* good."

"Don't encourage him, Jennifer. They'll have to roll Mike into his studio chair. And we don't have time for this."

"Sorry. And I do have something I was thinking about after we talked earlier, Elizabeth."

"When did you talk? Something about the investigation?" Jennifer asked.

Mike reported our conversation with—actually, our listening to—Penny.

I contributed my questions about whether there were marks around the car.

Everyone was caught up on everything.

"Which is pretty sad," I said, "because it means we haven't made progress."

"Mike said he had a thought," Diana invited.

"A suicide note."

After a beat of silence, Jennifer said, "Is there one?"

"Don't know. But a suicide note could be an answer to what took law enforcement so quickly from Melissa Oxley's house to the station to round up Thurston."

"That's good, Mike. It could," Diana said. "Although if she had things visible that indicated being his biggest fan…"

Jennifer clicked her tongue in disgust. "A Thurston groupie. That woman couldn't have been mentally stable."

"You need to set aside your prejudices. We all do. We can't think less of this woman because she was obsessed with Thurston."

"All right, all right. I get it."

"Good, then remind me when I need it."

She grinned at me.

I grinned back, then sobered. "Mike's thought about a suicide note is a good one. Let's see what we can find out about that. Diana, if you could test the temperature of the gossip on that and anything else of interest. Jennifer, keep that in mind as you listen to any conversations between the sheriff's departments."

"Yep," they each said. Jennifer didn't even complain about leading away from Thurston as a murderer.

"Another question to consider," I said. "The location of Melissa Oxley's death is interesting. Why there?"

"Lonely," Jennifer said.

"Isolated," Diana agreed.

Mike took a different angle. "A place where nobody would interfere with a suicide attempt."

"Lonely, isolated, nobody to interfere. All true. But, still, why there and not any of the places in Cottonwood County that fit that bill.

"Why not go into the Absaroka Mountains? Mike, you told me when I first came here that there are plenty of places in the mountains where someone could never be found. Why go to another county? And to the one spot where a vehicle can be spotted from the highway. Parking on the sort of crest of the road."

"People in Wyoming do drive in the middle when there's nobody coming on," Mike said.

"Because that's where the pavement's best," Diana added.

"Do they also park in the middle when they're going to shoot themself?" I waved that off. Even ignoring the car being in the middle of the road, it was in the one spot forward or back where it could be spotted from the highway. Jenks said that and so did Deputy Itson."

"That is interesting. But you can't totally discount the possibility it was a fluke," Mike said.

"Can't discount it wasn't, either. Which should narrow the timeline. Could the car have been sitting there Sunday afternoon and not be seen? Doesn't sound like it. Seems most likely she drove there after dark Sunday."

"That's probably true. But even if the location was chosen for that purpose, it doesn't add to the argument that she was murdered," Diana said. "Melissa could have wanted to be found quickly. But—"

"Less likely to be eaten by animals," Mike said. "What? It's true."

"Let's not get sidetracked. But what, Diana?"

"But why would a murderer want his or her victim found sooner?"

"That's worth keeping in mind."

"Isn't everything?" Jennifer asked with genuine curiosity.

The others chuckled. I joined in. "Pretty much. I've got plenty of questions. But one of them you guys might know the answer to. What the heck is up with the station's website? I went on there for basic background on Thurston and—"

Mike sighed. "Now you've done it."

Diana said, "Uh-oh."

Jennifer growled. "What's up with the website is it sucks. It's an embarrassment to the station and everyone who works here."

I suspected her embarrassment cut deepest.

"My first day, I said something had to be done about it right away," she seethed. "I said I'd do it in addition to my shifts at way, way less than my usual rate. And do you know what happened?"

"Les said no."

"Les said *no*. Didn't even think about it. And Thurston said it was unimportant and a waste of money. Instead, he got a new fridge for his office. Nothing has been done to it. *Noth-thing*. It sits there shaming us all."

"Also not providing basic information on staff, which I need you to dig up, please."

I thought Mike's mutter was *Good diversion*.

If so, Jennifer didn't catch it, because she would have let him know. Instead, she said, "What information?"

"Thurston's background before he came here. It doesn't even list his past stations or education."

"Do you know something that has you thinking—?"

I interrupted Diana. "Not a darn thing. Just covering the basics. Like victimology."

"Suspectology," Mike said.

"Speaking of victimology," Jennifer said, "Diana told me about what the neighbors said about Melissa Oxley and her family. I have more details.

"Her mother's name was Barbara and her will was registered—it's out in public. Like she wanted everyone to know she'd cut her husband—Magnus Boesch—out of it.

"She *says* in the will that's because the house and money should go to Melissa because the house came down through her family— Barbara's family, the Fyalls—and the money came from Melissa's father, Dodd Oxley. But at the end she adds it's her express wish that

Melissa not let Magnus Boesch continue to reside in the house. And she says flat out it's because Boesch had started out okay, but turned out to be a terrible husband."

"Wow. Those words?" Mike asked.

"That's the gist. I'll send you each a copy. So, another thing I found was Dodd—Melissa's father—died when she was not quite eleven years old. Found an obituary from the *Independence*, with stuff like him being from back East and they met in college and married after graduation, then moved here, into the Fyall family home. And he helped restore the house to its former glory. Which sounds like a good thing, only I got the feeling… Maybe it was the photo that ran. There's only about a half-dozen people at the burial. And you know how Cottonwood County usually turns out for a funeral. Guess he wasn't well-liked."

"Well-observed, Grasshopper," Mike said.

"Are you quoting that old TV show?"

"The original, the classic, the only true *Kung Fu*."

Jennifer grimaced, but he didn't seem to notice. "So, what next?" he asked me.

"Despite my spectacular lack of success in Cody, I think we follow the same theory of going where the others—especially law enforcement—aren't."

"Is that an excuse to not talk to Thurston because law enforcement is talking to him?"

"No." I drew it out to a couple of insulted syllables the way my nephew used to when asked if he was two years old after he'd turned three. "It's saying what I think comes next."

"You are going to have to talk to Thurston at some point," Diana said.

"Along with you."

"Yeah, fine. Audrey confirmed you'd cut that deal—bargaining me away without my having any say."

"What's the point of talking to Thurston? He'll lie and try to make himself look good," Jennifer said.

"He will," Mike agreed. "But Elizabeth can pick up good stuff from people's lies. So, if not Thurston next, then what, Elizabeth?"

"Fawn Raglettley."

"Why on earth Fawn Raglettley?" Mike's eyebrows rose along with his voice.

"Didn't Jennifer tell you about the encounter Leona and I had last night?"

"Yeah, but—that was Fawn? I can't believe Fawn accosted you and Leona. Not to mention she must have pulled her punches or you'd have real damage."

I wasn't discussing finger pokes, suspecting a similar reaction to Shelton's.

"What do you know about her, Mike?" Diana asked.

"When she was under the basket for Cottonwood County High School nobody was getting past her to score. And rebounding? It was like the ball was the last morsel of food on earth. She started as a freshman and the team was great all four years she was on it."

"Anything a little less basketbally?" Diana asked.

"She has a mean right hook. Saw her use it on the court, though not during a game. Some guy, drunk out of his skull, was manhandling an opposing player after a game, yelling at her about all the things she'd done wrong and yanking her around by her arm. Supposed to be her boyfriend," he said with disgust. "Her coach stepped in, told him to back off. Instead, the guy pushed the coach, who stumbled and fell, then the guy took hold of the girl's hair and started to drag her toward the door.

"There was a surge from players, coaches, spectators, officials all going after him—"

"Media?" Diana asked.

"Yeah, I was with the others, but Fawn got to him first. As I said, a mean right hook. Dropped him right there. When he came to, he was arrested."

"And Fawn?"

"Definitely not arrested. Wouldn't say it made her popular. She was still awkward, uncomfortable with people. But players—her own team and others—appreciated her. Might have been a little wary of her, too."

"That couldn't have been easy on a teenage girl," I said.

"Doubt Fawn's had much easy in her life. Her mother died when she was little. I suppose her father tried to do the best way he knew. He's an itinerant ranch hand. Does good work, but scratchy kind of guy, usually runs up against authority or a fellow hand before long and moves on. He'd take Fawn with him. I remember her as a kid when her dad worked for Jack Delahunt."

Jack Delahunt was the long-time foreman of a major ranch near the Montana border. Mike worked on his crew off and on through high school and college as school and football allowed. I suspected Jack had been a role model and mentor to Mike.

Now that Mike was an adult, the like and respect appeared mutual.

"Isaac Raglettley swung south for a while, but when they returned to this area, with Fawn somewhere in early grade school and already taller than any of the other kids, it turned out he hadn't put her in school at all their stops. Mrs. P got Isaac by the ear and said she didn't care how many jobs he quit, they were all going to be in Cottonwood County and Fawn was staying in school from then on.

"And he did. He's even stuck after she graduated high school. Last I knew they had a trailer way on the low side, near the Horse Creek County line. They both worked for an old couple running a small spread nearby right after Fawn graduated—word is she's a real good hand. Isaac got in a squawk with somebody like always and moved on, but Fawn stuck and lives in that trailer. She still works for them. Isaac lives there when he's working close enough."

"Otherwise she's all alone?"

"I'm not sure she's not better off without Isaac's company," Mike said dryly. Abruptly, he added, "What's the matter, Elizabeth?"

"Matter?"

"You're scowling at your hands."

"Was I?" I searched backward along the path of my thoughts. "Something tickled a memory, but I can't remember what."

"It'll come back to you if it's important. That's what my grandma says, and she forgets all sorts of stuff these days," Jennifer told me kindly. "But I guess she always has."

Diana morphed a chuckle into a cough behind her hand.

"When do you leave for Northwestern?" I asked Jennifer with assumed sweetness.

My effort at a poke to say putting me in her grandmother's demographic was not welcomed backfired.

"You don't remember that, either?" she asked with a measure of pity. "Right after the first of the year."

DAY THREE
WEDNESDAY

Chapter Nineteen

ONE OF THE major downsides of living in the Mountain time zone is people in the Eastern and Central time zones get a head start on the news each morning. And they call to pump or lecture you about it before you're fully awake.

At least they call to pump or lecture me before I'm fully awake. Especially after an early morning the previous day.

I was out of bed, showered, and almost dressed when my phone rang.

"What?" I growled into it.

"It's Dell," he said, as if there must have been a mistake in my answering any of his calls with anything other than joyous alacrity.

"I know." Caller ID had warbled Wardell Yardley at me. It hadn't expanded that into his being the White House correspondent for a major network. "It's eight a.m. here and I haven't had any coffee."

"No coffee. That's bad." No shred of sympathy surfaced in his voice. "What are you waiting around for? Walk and talk, girl. Walk and talk—right to the coffeemaker."

I growled again.

He didn't hear or he didn't care. Toss-up which. "What are your people getting up to out there in the Wild West, Danny?"

If he meant the nickname to soften my mood, he didn't succeed.

Well, maybe a little. Or perhaps it was going down the stairs from bedroom to kitchen—and thus closer to the pre-set coffeemaker putting out its life-source scents—that lifted my gloom slightly.

"Working hard, living clean. Unlike you Washington, D.C., elitists."

"I take issue with that characterization. Not about my being elite. That is most certainly true. It's the working hard and living clean for your fellow Cottonwood County residents I take exception to. Did you not think an item about Thurston Fine, anchor of KWMT-TV in Sherman, Wyoming, being interviewed by law enforcement in connection with the death of a local woman would leap out at me?"

"How big an item?"

"I just quoted you most of it. Few will notice it. Then again, few have the perspicacity of Wardell Yardley."

More like few in Washington, D.C., would have any reason to note something happening in Sherman, Wyoming. Dell not only had me as a connection, but also the curator of the local history museum.

They'd, ahem, connected when he'd been out here last year, covering a story about gold coins and becoming a reporter of the people, according to an exec at his network. To my surprise, they had stayed in touch. That's Dell and Clara, the curator. Not Dell and the exec.

"You owe me for the times I've helped you with your investigations. Now tell me everything," he ordered. "Is it true? Is it murder? Did Thurston do it?"

"Why don't you ask Clara? Especially why don't you ask her or anybody other than me at this hour of the morning?"

"The hour wouldn't bother her in the least." Which meant they had talked at this hour. In my universe that would've meant my long-distance suitor had a death wish. But for Clara and Dell, who knew? "But she's working with the severe disadvantage of only having KWMT's reporting as a source. Now when Needham gets the next edition of the *Independence* out..."

"Ha. Ha. Ha." Though I shared his assessment of Needham as a journalist.

Forcing myself not to gulp the coffee, I let Shadow out as I told Dell the events of the previous two days that made the answer to his first question *yes, it's true* and the answers to the next two *to be determined if it's murder and what Thurston's involvement is or isn't.*

When I got to the part about Les not being around and Audrey stepping up, he whistled. "The news director AWOL? That's crazy. Though I suppose it matches the ownership and station manager. Must be nice. It's enough to make me consider moving out there."

"Right. You giving up D.C. for Wyoming. But you're right, this is the weirdest setup I've ever seen."

I told Dell my observation about newsroom title-holders often not being the ones who led well—or at all—in an emergency. "Because they got promoted based on day-to-day performance. But—"

"Plus schmoozing and brown-nosing abilities."

"—different skills are required when the fan starts spreading manure in all directions and at top speed."

"Well observed, Ms. Danniher. It reminds me of something this great old guy I interviewed a while back said. He was on one of those Honor Flights for World War II veterans coming to D.C. to see the sights."

"I saw that piece, Dell. Great reminder to people you aren't limited to hard news. A deft touch."

"Of course. Anyway, we got talking—beyond the interview—and he said the U.S. military was real different in battle from how it was in peace and different types rise to the top. In battle, you needed people who could think on their own. Ad lib. In peacetime that's frowned upon. As he said, he was a good soldier in war, but he'd've been a lousy peacetime soldier."

"Similar with newsrooms. The cream that rises to the top in an emergency are the independent types. They're not in favor with the folks handing out promotions, though, under ordinary circumstances."

I exhaled. "That's completely believable, and it stinks. Because it means Audrey won't be rewarded the way she should be for holding things together here."

"With your guidance."

"With help from me among many."

"You truly need to attend the Wardell Yardley School of Accepting—Nay—Inviting Compliments. Possibly the remedial session. But putting that aside, you're right. She won't be rewarded unless one of two things happens. Either she moves on to another shop—"

"That's exactly my point. She does a great job, shows she's capable of so much more than she's been allowed to do—so much more than the people supposedly her supervisors have done—and to benefit from what she's put into this station, she has to leave it. Which also stinks for the station, losing talented people who actually do step up, while keeping the not-talented who don't."

"It's the way of the world, Young Danniher." At least he didn't call me Grasshopper.

"I don't like it. What's the other thing that could happen so she'd be rewarded?"

"You'll like that even less because it hardly ever happens—in our biz or others. That's having the people handing out promotions change. Either the ones in place finally learn to disregard those who suck up to them and recognize the value of those who step up when needed or they're replaced by people who do. The latter is exceedingly rare. The former is not possible based on my extensive and insightful observations of the world for more decades than anyone looking at me would believe."

"Gee, thanks, that's cheered me up no end. I've gotta get going, Dell."

"Chasing a lead?"

"Getting to the station. I'm not sure there are any leads to chase. Except Thurston as a suspect."

"And that would mean talking to him, which you don't want to do." He knew me well. "Going to have to at some point. Beyond that, do what you folks usually do in these circumstances."

IN THE SHORT drive, I considered his advice.

What *did* we usually do?

Ask questions.

That's what I did in most circumstances.

When we were looking into a mur—an unexplained death, we

asked even more.

Especially about the victim.

These past two days, with the demands on Jennifer, Diana, and me of the daily newscasts, as well as the absence of Mike, we hadn't dug deep.

Yet.

With luck, the newscasts should get a little easier as everyone adjusted to new roles.

Which was why I dug into drafting copy for today's newscasts as soon as I got to the office.

Even if what I wrote was overrun by events, in other words wiped out by news between now and the newscast, it helped to have a framework—something to change instead of a blank.

Having that in hand gave me time to snag Leona when she arrived, escorting her to my desk while Audrey was out of sight.

Chapter Twenty

JENNIFER ALSO TOOK advantage of Audrey's absence to hustle over to join us.

"What's this?" Leona asked, looking pointedly at my hold on her elbow.

I released it and used that hand to gesture her to a chair I pulled up from a nearby, empty desk. A few other desks were occupied by people who all showed interest in what we were doing.

Jennifer snagged another chair and drew it close enough to bring all our knees together.

"Just a few questions I'm confident you can help us with from your vast knowledge of Cottonwood County and its people."

"A few questions?" Leona scoffed. "I have more work than there is time to do it in order to sound halfway intelligent when I deliver the news by knowing the background—"

"Thurston never knows what he's talking about," Jennifer mumbled.

Leona's gaze shifted toward her as she finished her thought. "—on events." Then back to me. "Oh, fine. Go ahead and ask a question. *A* question. *One.*"

"Tell us everything you know about Melissa Oxley," I said.

Jennifer's hoot drew the attention of anyone who hadn't previously tuned in.

"Thought you weren't looking into this," Leona said.

"Oh, that changed yesterday," Jennifer said cheerfully. "We're on the case now."

Surprise and speculation jostled for precedence in Leona's expression. Speculation won.

"To clear Thurston? To get a story?"

"Neither, though either could happen. To find out the truth."

"And a special for KWMT," she bargained.

"While keeping an open mind about doing a special report, as we've done before."

In tacit acceptance, Leona said, "Not sure I know much at all, not beyond what we've reported. I might have met her a few times but I don't remember ever talking to her." She tipped her head. "Unless it was at the bookstore in Cody where she worked, without realizing she was the daughter of Barbara and Dodd Oxley. Either way, not an encounter that stuck."

"You *did* know her parents?"

"A little. Barbara's parents kept a presence in the community. Not splashy, but steady. That was sort of the way the Fyalls had aways been. Built that house back before the turn of the Twentieth Century, not the biggest, not the fanciest, but a nice house in the best area. Then they plugged along, generation following generation. Nobody making a big splash, but always holding onto the house.

"Barbara's father was a Fyall and inherited the house. It's where she grew up. Times were tougher for them, but they had enough left in a trust to send her to college back East. I imagine the plan was for her to marry money. Didn't work out that way, not to start. The parents were disappointed when she came home married to Dodd Oxley and didn't hide it.

"But he got the last laugh... After a few false starts, he did real well for himself financially. He was never a bum. He'd worked for the Heathertons—"

"Really?"

"Not connected to KWMT. Another part of their business. And why Barbara's parents didn't approve when the father worked for them, too, I never figured out. But when an investment came in for Dodd, he quit, and his money put the house back to rights after a long decline under Barbara's parents' watch. And they saw it happen before they passed away. Never sure which they felt more strongly, pleasure at the house being fixed up or pain that their son-in-law did it.

"And I do mean he did it—not just paid for it. Organized it, oversaw the work, real involved. Good thing, because Barbara Fyall was the type to sit back and fan herself. A misplaced magnolia in the depths of Wyoming and without any steel."

"Was Melissa like that, too?" Jennifer asked.

"Like I said, I didn't know her. I do know that when her father died, when she still was a kid, there was even more money. Big insurance payout."

"Anything in that?" I asked.

Leona rolled her eyes. "You're thinking major fraud and he's not really dead and came back to life as Magnus Boesch?"

"That's not bad," Jennifer said.

"It's a soap opera plot for heaven's sake," Leona said. "If that's what you're thinking, Elizabeth—"

"It's not."

"Thank heavens you still have some sense. For the record, I'll say there was never anything even hinted at about Dodd Oxley's death. To all appearances, both Barbara and Melissa were devastated. But it was real obvious they never wanted for anything material."

"How'd that play out with family, friends, and neighbors?"

"Not much family. Barbara's parents had died by then, the year before Dodd. That left her and Melissa the only direct descendants of Hiram Fyall, who built the house. Huh." She pulled in a deep breath. "Hadn't thought of that until now, but with Melissa's death, it's the end of that line. Sad to see another old family gone."

She expelled the last of the breath in a final spurt.

"Anyway, Barbara wasn't one to take hold of herself and deal with the practicalities. It was a good thing the one relative she had around here—an older cousin from her mother's side, so not a Fyall—looked after her financial affairs after Dodd's death. Made a nice living off of her, but he did look out for her and Melissa. Kept safe what she got from Dodd, inheritance and insurance, even built it up. Took care of running the house and their lives."

"A woman who let other people take care of her?" I said.

"No *let* about it. Barbara Fyall Oxley Boesch was one of those women who thought she *deserved* to be taken care of. She had been all her life, after all. She didn't make decisions. Other people did that for her, leaving her vulnerable to Magnus Boesch's brand of flattery and purported guidance. He'd been the bookkeeper for the family for years. First when Dodd was—"

"He cooked the books?" Jennifer asked.

"Not that I've ever heard. No one ever said Dodd Oxley wasn't sharp. It would have taken a brave—and brazen—man to try to cook his books. Besides, James Longbaugh would have spotted anything hinky after Dodd died. So would that cousin, and he kept Magnus on. When he died, well… Magnus would have been familiar and Barbara felt she could trust him. Magnus caught her at a vulnerable time. And maybe I'm not being entirely fair to Barbara. Yeah, she had other people take care of her and she didn't like conflict—preferred to withdraw than confront—but she was not a complete fool. Look no further than her will for evidence of that."

Jennifer pulled in a breath. I gave her a look, hoping it conveyed that she shouldn't stop Leona's flow by bringing up what she'd already found out about the will.

Either she understood the look or had reached the same conclusion herself, because she said, "That's right, you guys said Fawn said something about Melissa's inheritance the other night when she, uh, accosted you."

Leona snorted. "Good word for it. Better than attacked, which is the wild rumor going around. Anyway, the girl got that right, even though she was wrong about everything else. Melissa inherited nearly everything Barbara had to leave, except a stipend to Magnus Boesch. What went to Melissa included the Fyall family home, which was where Barbara and Magnus were living until she died. Melissa had moved out after her mother's second marriage."

"A mother-daughter break?" I asked.

"From what I've heard, they had conflicts—normal teenager stuff. Some carried over to when she came back from college. Melissa thinks she's grown up. Barbara thinks she's still a kid. Nothing out of the ordinary."

The same gist as the long-time neighbor.

"Do you know Faye Nafus?"

"As a matter of fact, I do. Why?"

"Did you talk to her these past two days?"

"No. I've been otherwise occupied. What are you driving at, Elizabeth?"

"She gave Diana a similar precis of the mother-daughter relationship Monday. The fact she told you that before Melissa died adds to its credibility."

For a moment, I thought she'd take umbrage at my assessing the credibility of something she'd relayed. Then the journalist in her took charge, and she nodded.

"Never heard of a split. No sign of a falling out over Barbara's marriage, for instance. In fact, Melissa and Magnus seemed to rub along fine. Until the will.

"Melissa moved back into the house and declined to go against her mother's express wishes that Magnus not live there. Surprised some, though Faye said Melissa had a wide streak of determination from Dodd. What with Barbara more inclined to let others make decisions, she might have let Melissa run things."

"So maybe it wasn't that Melissa thought she was grown up and Barbara didn't," I mused. "Maybe Melissa was tired of taking care of her mother."

"Possible. Or, Magnus took over the role. It was after Melissa went to college he started, uh, courting Barbara. They married a couple years later.

"As for the will, Faye said it served Magnus right. According to her, he started off all right, but after Melissa moved to Cody and he had a clear field, so to speak, he wasn't as willing to fill the taking-care-of-Barbara role. He griped all the time about that house, resented money spent on its upkeep. Then, after the will was read, suddenly he only wanted to be a good steward of the *heritage*. Hah. Like he could change the will.

"Had no shame, either. Even as he was being removed from the property, he kept shouting, begging, saying they could work this out."

"What happens to the inheritance now?" I asked.

"Magnus Boesch gets some through a trust Barbara set up to take effect in the event Melissa died without children. I don't know about the disposal of what Melissa inherited outright, like the house."

"How much was the original stipend Magnus got?"

"Enough to keep him from starving or living on the streets, but not a lot more. He had to get a job again. He's working in the back office of the country club. Used to swan around there like he owned the place."

Leona was not a member, but her contacts kept her updated.

"Did he know Thurston?"

"Oh, yeah. They were buddies when Magnus was on Barbara's dime. Once Barbara died and Magnus sank in the social hierarchy, he ceased to exist for Thurston. You know how he doesn't see anything but his own wonderfulness."

"Will the added amount now that Melissa's dead restore him to his former way of life?"

She gave me another sharp look. "Motive? What I heard from people who should know is it won't be enough for Magnus to quit, but he will have a bigger cushion. Now, if he's named in Melissa's will or if she doesn't have one and he snags money as a sort of relative…"

"I'll find out."

Leona smiled at Jennifer's certainty. I did not.

Meeting my gaze, she wrinkled her nose in a *no, I won't hack* message. Though I was never a hundred percent certain her message meant *no, I won't hack at all* or *no, I won't hack so anyone can catch me.*

Leona shifted, catching sight of the time writ large across my computer's screen saver.

That's useful on deadline. Not so useful now.

"I have to go. You got me talking and now I'll have to scramble."

✧ ✧ ✧ ✧

I FINISHED DRAFTS for both the Five and the Ten.

Being squashed flat by fast-moving news was the best fate I could hope for them. In the meantime, they provided the security of having an if-all-else-fails backup.

I'd also followed up on Jenks' comments and dipped into Needham Bender's series in the *Independence* from several years back on the Shangri-La mine scam.

It was an indulgence to scratch my itch even that much, but I justified it to myself that it gave me background on the road where Melissa Oxley was found.

Yeah, pretty weak.

On the other hand, it wasn't a waste of time, because I couldn't go out and do interviews anyway. After last night's confidence, Audrey relapsed and asked my opinion of things she'd handled on her own long before deputies escorted Thurston out of the building.

In between her advice-seeking, I called the sheriff's departments in Cottonwood and Horse Creek counties for updates.

They were united in not telling E.M. Danniher a thing.

Ditto for James Longbaugh when I called and asked for an update on Thurston's legal situation. But at least he chuckled pleasantly.

He suggested I call Thurston for an update.

I took that as another bit of humor, but asked, "That's confirmation he hasn't been arrested?"

"Ask the sheriff's department."

The guy should do standup.

As far as I knew, no one had heard from Les. Nor had anyone tried to contact him.

Diana was on assignments. Mike called in for an update, which I wrapped up with "…in other words nothing."

I'd found satellite images on the Internet of the road where Melissa Oxley's body was found—a poor supplement to Jenks' video, but since I couldn't go out there it satisfied a fringe element of the itch—when I was called into action.

Chapter Twenty-One

"ELIZABETH!" JENNIFER SHOUTED. "Come here. Right away."

I did the six-desk dash that got me to where she and Audrey worked side by side in record time.

Audrey stared at the station phone on her desk and mumbled, "Oh, my God, oh, my God, oh, my God."

"It's Thurston," Jennifer explained.

"Answer it," I told Audrey. She started to shake her head. More firmly, I said, "If you don't, he might drive here."

"Answer it," Jennifer said. As Audrey reached toward the handset, she added, "On speakerphone."

Jennifer turned to the remaining three people in the bullpen and made a palms-down, dampening sign for them to keep quiet.

Audrey hit the speakerphone button, then froze.

Jennifer looked at me. I shook my head sharply and pointed to her.

"KWMT-TV newsroom, Audrey Adams' phone."

Thurston's practiced voice came on. "Audrey, I have bad—"

"No. This is Audrey Adams' phone. Hold for Audrey."

Audrey gawked at her. Jennifer couldn't reach the hold button, but held up one finger, pantomiming for Audrey to wait.

After a lengthy pause, she pointed to Audrey to go ahead.

"Audrey Adams." From a shaky start, she ended strong.

The sound of the outside doors opening, pulled everyone except Audrey around to them.

Diana walked in.

She must have been surprised to be greeted by a silent newsroom with most of its occupants holding a *be-quiet* finger to lips and madly mouthing *Thurston*. On the other hand, she's the mother of teenagers, so maybe not surprised at anything.

"It's about time," Thurston grumbled. "What do you think you're doing making me hold—?"

"Who is this calling?"

Jennifer rocked back in her chair in ecstasy, silently clapping. Diana joined us by Audrey's phone.

"Thurston, of course." He wasn't irked so much as stunned that such ignorance was possible.

"Oh, hello. Where are you?"

"At home. The station's lawyer says I need to stay here, which sounds remarkably stupid, but he's persuaded the rest of them—"

An apparent reference to the station owner, general manager, and—possibly—news director, which put him on a par with them.

And typical of Thurston to assume everyone knew what he referred to, because if it was in his world, it had to be of prime interest to everyone else.

Okay, this time he was right that everyone knew what was going on, but assuming it was still irksome.

"—it's the best move for my career. He also says it could permanently damage my career to go on-air until the idiot sheriff straightens out this ridiculous mess that has resulted from his department's incompetence."

If I'd had James Longbaugh in front of me, I would have kissed him on the lips. Or at least given him a big hug. Not only had he established that Thurston shouldn't be on-air, but he'd done it with a reason Thurston would listen to—his self-interest.

Diana looked slightly less pleased, likely because she doesn't appreciate her honey, the sheriff, referred to that way.

Thurston added, "You'll have to get Leona to anchor."

Jaws hitting the floor around the room should have been audible.

Thurston could not have watched the KWMT-TV news the past two days or he'd know Leona had filled the anchor chair.

Did he think the station hadn't done a newscast these past two days because he wasn't around? Left static for the Five and Ten? Sat here paralyzed without him? Waiting for his call?

He probably did.

"Leona," Audrey started in a strangled voice.

"Of course, Leona," he snapped. "Not anybody else. You hear me? Not *anybody* else."

Every eye came to me.

I pasted on a smile and did a royal wave.

Chuckles sprang up.

Quickly, Audrey said, "Leona," again, loud enough to mask the chuckles.

"I'll call after the Five and tell you what you've done wrong."

"Good-bye, Thurston."

She sounded strong and she clicked off the phone without hesitation, before he did.

She received a cheer—not particularly rousing, since there were only six of us to cheer her, but heartfelt.

As the bullpen occupants got back to work, however, Audrey slumped.

"This is awful. Absolutely awful. I think I'd fooled myself into thinking he'd gone away for good. Like he wouldn't ever come back, but now—This is awful."

"This is *good* news, Audrey." She gawked at me. "You know what's going on instead of pretending. First, you know the station's lawyer has told him to stay off the air *and* to stay put at home until further notice. That means, he's not going to suddenly show up expecting to anchor. He's not even going to show up to take a nap in his office. He's not going to show up, period."

"But he's going to call…."

"I wonder if we could bribe James Longbaugh to order him to stay off the phone, too," Jennifer said.

"I don't think he's bribable. Besides, this saves us having to pool money for a bribe. I'm betting this means James first persuaded Val Heatherton and Craig Morningside—or whatever mythical ownership people he's talking to—that it's in the station's best interest to keep

Thurston off the air. That makes it firmer than relying on Thurston demonstrating enough good sense to follow James Longbaugh's advice.

"All you have to do, Audrey, is answer Thurston's call, let him drivel on, say *uh-huh* a few times while you continue with whatever you were doing, and then ignore everything he says."

"But he'll notice we didn't change things for the Ten."

We all stared at her for a couple beats.

Audrey interpreted our message correctly and agreed with it. "He won't notice."

"He might not even call," Diana said. "Or remember to watch."

Audrey's eyes widened in remembered shock. "When he said I'd have to get Leona to *start* anchoring... That has to mean he hasn't watched, doesn't it?"

"Yup. That's what it means."

"Why was I ever afraid of that idiot?"

I TOOK ADVANTAGE of Audrey's new-found confidence to say I was leaving to do an interview.

It didn't hurt that she was accustomed to me keeping my own schedule and not being one of the too-few-pieces she moved around on the assignment editor's schedule, trying to hide gaping staff shortages.

Jennifer overheard me, jumped up from her chair, and disappeared.

As I opened the door to the parking lot, having gathered my jacket and go-bag from my desk, Jennifer caught up with me, already wearing her jacket.

"I'm coming with," she announced.

"But Audrey—"

"Dale's covering for me. Besides, she's riding the crest of being a Thurston-slayer. Where are we going?"

When Jennifer revealed insights like that, it reminded me she'd grown up a lot in the time I'd known her. She might view me as a mentor, but that didn't mean the mentee was a kid anymore.

"To talk to Fawn Raglettley."

She sighed. "I used up a favor from Dale for her? I sure hope she has something good to say."

"You have an endless supply of favors from Dale."

"That's true."

That perked her up for the rest of the drive to the eastern edge of Cottonwood County, while I kept returning to the thought that I, too, hoped Fawn had something good to say.

What with filling the pesky needs of KWMT-TV, we had not gotten traction on this so far.

Chapter Twenty-Two

SINCE WE'D LEFT Sherman, the mountains that marched in ragged formation down the west side of Cottonwood County had receded in the rearview mirror.

Water from snow pack in the mountains made what was called the High Side of the county far more fertile than the Low Side, which required irrigation … at a minimum.

As we neared the eastern edge of the county, the land in front of us recalled the flatness—though not the rich, black soil—of my native Illinois. It struck me that raising cattle was a good use of this land. There was only so much even intensive irrigation could do.

This was the low of the low side.

"This is the place," Jennifer said.

I squinted a moment before recognizing what she'd seen—a subtle change in the fencing, which indicated we'd left one ranch and reached another.

As I turned north into a dirt entry road by the sign that said Baxters, she pointed out her side window to the east. "Horse Creek County starts where the crossroad comes in. They need even more irrigation over there. I swear it gets dustier when you cross the county line."

"That would be impressive, since there's enough dust here to rival a haboob."

"A what?"

"Haboob. It's from Arabic, a term for sand or dust storms, often associated with a microburst."

"Have you been in one?"

"Yes."

"Wow. You've done such exciting things."

I laughed. "Being in a haboob was not one of them. I ate sand for a week and had sand in parts of my body that do not benefit from sand."

"Ouch."

"Exactly." I coasted to a stop and tooted the horn to let any dogs or residents of the weathered house know visitors had arrived. A barn stood nearby, stripped bare of paint.

A woman with short, curly gray hair, wearing a man's jacket to her knees and jeans that ended halfway up her boots, came out the house's side door. As she approached, she clapped on a cowboy hat worn to near floppiness.

A mid-sized mottled gray and black dog ambled toward us from the barn.

"Hi, Mrs. Baxter?" We'd pinned down who Fawn worked for in order to figure out where to find her. "I'm Elizabeth Margaret Danniher from KWMT-TV and this is my colleague, Jennifer Lawton."

"Call me Shelley. Colleague, is it?" She peered at us, then addressed Jennifer. "You're Faith and Kent's girl?"

"Yes, ma'am."

"Barely done being kids themselves. As for you—" She swung toward me. "—heard you've got Mike Paycik and Tom Burrell tied up in knots."

"I—I—"

Jennifer's snicker covered my stutter. Shelley Baxter waved off any response.

"Now that I see you in person, I imagine you're tied up in knots yourself. TV hides that. Must be the makeup. What do you want?"

The starkness of a question I've been asked often in my career put me back on my metaphorical feet.

"We're here to talk to Fawn Raglettley."

"Does she know you were coming?"

"No." Not a chance I'd try to get around this woman with finesse.

She grunted.

Turning to watch us every couple steps, as if playing the old game of Mother, May I? she went onto the house's porch, to a huge bell mounted by the side door. She yanked the pull several times.

The sound was loud, carrying, yet surprisingly melodious.

"That'll get 'em. Fawn's been real upset since she heard the news Monday night. Didn't know how to be sad, so she found something to be mad at. Tried to talk her out of going to the TV station, but she wasn't listening at all. Was even more upset when she got back, but we've calmed her down since. You do know you can't hold her accountable for scaring anybody?"

"She didn't scare anybody, ma'am. We're not here about Monday night."

"Well, you two might as well come in while you wait. I've got last bits and bobs from the garden to can still, what with Fawn building a cover for it."

The kitchen's counters, cabinets, table, appliances, and accoutrements had slid past dated toward vintage. A variety pack of vegetables lined up for canning, with a phalanx of pickles in jars at the far end.

"You two are tall. Put these jars up on that top shelf in there—" She gestured to a hallway narrowed by shelves deep enough for a single row of canning jars on each side. "Keeps Glenn from going through them all by Christmas, but Fawn can get them down as we need them."

The opening of the back door found an assembly line of Shelley Baxter to Jennifer to me. We loaded the last two jars as the new arrivals shed their footwear inside the door.

Fawn looked toward us, dropping her head before any eye contact.

"What is it, woman?" Glenn asked his wife with mock irritation. "Did you call us in for coffee?"

He had hair on either side of his head, but a bald swath from his forehead, over the crown, and down to the back of his neck.

She took the hint and poured them mugs, holding the pot up in invitation to Jennifer and me. She said no, thanks, I said yes, please, while Shelley answered Glenn's first question.

"These two from the TV station want to talk to Fawn."

The married couple exchanged looks.

He shifted so he could slide his feet back into his boots. "We'll leave you to talk, Fawn. Give you privacy."

Fawn looked around at him in dismay.

"No. I'll come back out with you. I don't want—" She interrupted herself, focusing on me. "You. I know you."

I'd have skipped our first meeting if I could, since it did not represent the pro-E.M. Danniher mindset I wanted her in. But better to get it out in the open now than have it crop up later.

"Yes. We, ah, talked the night before last outside the TV station."

Her frown persisted. "Yeah. But that's not it."

"Of course you know her," Jennifer said impatiently. "She's Elizabeth Margaret Danniher. She's been on the news here for a year and a half. Did an important special report on—"

"I don't watch news."

I couldn't resist. "Not even Thurston Fine?"

"I watch him for him, not for news."

"Good thing," Jennifer muttered.

Fawn didn't get the insult to her idol, didn't care, or didn't have time to acknowledge it, because her concentration had laser focused on me.

"You did that thing about fake celebrities."

"That was on last night, for Pete's sake."

Jennifer's comment drew a disapproving scowl from Mrs. Baxter.

Putting together this exchange with Fawn's reactions Monday and now, I concluded her manner stemmed from more enduring issues than distress over her friend's death.

I said to her, "Yes, I reported that piece."

I'd completed the "Helping Out!" piece Audrey ran last night in the summer, after a viewer wrote in, saying he'd been sending money to Jennifer Lopez for months and he was beginning to think something wasn't right.

It was, in fact, all wrong.

As you might have guessed J-Lo was not corresponding with a trucker from Wyoming. Nor asking him to send her money.

He'd posted a comment on a legit Jennifer Lopez social media account and had been over the moon when "she" responded by direct message. Thus began a messaging relationship that didn't take long to develop into I-love-you-please-send-money.

The piece pointed out that cybercriminals create social media accounts to mirror celebrities' legit sites as well as haunt legit sites for potential victims.

"You said you didn't watch the news for news and Thurston wasn't on last night," Jennifer said.

I added my pointed look to Mrs. Baxter's. Jennifer appeared to get the message this time.

Fawn gave no sign of following the byplay. "It's a kind of habit to watch. Melissa said I should watch every night Thurston was on. It felt sort of like I had to do it for her. Keep it up, even though he wasn't… And she isn't…"

She slid off the conversational rails in a mix of confusion and unhappiness.

Then, with startling abruptness, a wide smile took over her face.

"But that wasn't news, what you did," she said to me. "That was about what happens with actors and celebrities and stuff. It was great."

"I'm glad you found it useful."

"It was. It made everything so clear and I finally understood why Tom stopped writing to me. I knew it wasn't because of the height thing, no matter what Melissa said."

"Height thing?"

"Even if he really is five-seven, it wouldn't bother him that I'm six-one. He's not like that. And, anyway, I think they have that wrong, the magazines and shows and stuff. He said they did." She scowled. "Unless that was after the fake one took over. The one who asked for money."

"It was *always* the fake one. That was the point of Elizabeth's package." So maybe Jennifer hadn't received the entire message.

"Not always," Fawn insisted. "You don't know what Tom's like."

"Real celebrities aren't on social media all the time chatting to normal people. Forget that."

"You're like Melissa. She said I wasn't ever talking to Tom. She said that's why she wanted someone who lived nearby. So she could connect, face-to-face. But I know it was Tom at the start. It was later the fake one took over, like you said."

She nodded toward me, but didn't take a breath.

"Besides, I started to think what she said about Tom was because she didn't want me distracted from Thurston's fan club. And she's right about it being exciting when you can see him in, like, real life. Track him down, you know. Watch him, even talk to him."

There was a lot to follow-up in that response. Don't ask me why I started with "Tom who?"

"Tom Holland."

Jennifer expanded with the air of one helping a little old lady across the street, "Actor. Spider-Man."

"Spider-Man? Tobey Maguire's my favorite."

Fawn and Jennifer rolled their eyes at me and exchanged a look of momentary solidarity at the wayward ignorance of an older demographic.

Chapter Twenty-Three

WITH THE DIGNITY earned along with my aged status, I moved on to take advantage of Fawn's favorable view of my reporting. "How did Melissa come to start the fan club for Thurston Fine? Had she met him? Or…" I trailed off enticingly.

She ignored the enticement. "Don't know."

"But you and Melissa did meet Thurston in person after you joined the club?"

"Oh, yeah. I mean, I met him then. Of course, Melissa already knew him. They were together, but I met him a lot, too."

"What do you mean Melissa and Thurston were together?"

"You don't know that *either?*"

I kept my gaze on Fawn despite a sort of gurgling noise from Jennifer.

"I want to know what you mean by it, Fawn, so there's no confusion."

"I meant they were…" She seemed to hunt for words. Not successfully. "…*together.*"

In this instance, I had to risk putting words in the interviewee's mouth or be stopped at this impasse. "A couple? Dating regularly? Exclusively? An item? Serious about each other?"

"Yeah. That stuff. She went to his house. He went to her house—not when I was there, of course, but other times."

"Did they go on trips together?"

She hesitated, looking down at her hands, which she tightened around the coffee mug. "You mean when he went to Denver? She always drove him to the airport in Cody for his trips and picked him up."

We'd all heard about his going to Denver to get his hair cut. Otherwise, Thurston didn't leave much.

I know talent who are wary of being off-air for any stretch, for fear of someone better, younger, cheaper taking their place in the hearts of the viewership or ownership.

Most were paranoid. In Thurston's case, it was justified.

Exposed to anyone competent for any time, the viewers wouldn't want to watch Thurston. The ownership here, however, was a mystery.

"Did Melissa's routine change if he went out of town?"

She shook her head.

"Who else was in this fan club?"

"She said a bunch of people she knew in Cody were, but they became sort of a sub-group of the club and met there because it was hard to get everybody together."

"Was there anyone else in it from Sherman?"

"You mean, besides Melissa? Because I don't live in Sherman."

"That's right. So anyone else who, say, lives in Cottonwood County, besides you and Melissa?"

She considered for three slow breaths. "No."

"How did you and Melissa meet?"

"At the library."

I smiled encouragingly. "I like the library, too."

"Go on, Fawn," Shelley said. "Tell her about meeting your friend."

"I was reading a magazine. You know, a newer one I couldn't check out. I always look through the older ones with stories about celebrities—the ones you *can* check out—to see if I missed anything. If I wait until I can check them out, I can take my time. Go slow and be sure I get it all. But I can't stand to wait. I look at the new ones in the library.

"Anyway, Melissa saw me reading it, and she started talking. She told me she had a group of friends in Cody she got together with all the time and they go to movies—not just watch on TV, but go to the real movies—and read the magazines and talk about the people."

"When was this, Fawn?"

"Last spring. I'd been working real hard, what with calving. Shelley and Glenn don't have a lot of head, but enough to make it busy because they don't do as much as they used to. We were down to two calves still to come—an experienced mama and a heifer, but the heifer still had a while to go. Shelley said I should take that Saturday off and have a rest."

She looked at the older woman.

"Probably the second week of May," Shelley supplied.

"But I didn't want to rest. It had been months since I'd been to the library and I wanted to catch up, so I got cleaned up and got there early, so I'd have lots of time. And I'm really glad I did or I wouldn't have met Melissa.

"After Melissa and I talked and talked at the library, we went to Hamburger Heaven and sat in a booth and we talked and talked more. It was... I'd never talked with somebody like that. I mean, my teammates on the basketball team a few years ago, but it was about the games. But Melissa'd worked in a store over in Cody where they had racks and racks of magazines, with *only* the newest ones, so she *knew* things. Things I'd never read about. But she still asked me questions. About what I knew from the magazines and stuff and who I liked. It was... It was a great day."

She'd found a friend.

Each of them had.

"Did you join the fan club for Thurston?"

"Not then. She wanted me to come back the next day, but I couldn't with work and all. She gave me her phone number and I called when calving finished and I knew I could take a day now and then. Even before that, she messaged me. Stuff about Thurston, mostly, but sometimes about the stars.

"And then she invited me to her house and that's when we set up club rules and a schedule for meetings and such, and she showed me Thurston's shows for the first time."

"What did you do at your meetings?"

"Watch the shows with Thurston. Her favorites. She had all of them."

Jennifer choked back a sound.

"It sounds like you and Melissa got along well."

"We did. That's why I know she wouldn't have done what they're saying—what the woman in Thurston's chair on TV said she did. She *wouldn't*. She had *everything* to live for."

"That woman didn't say *she* believed Melissa committed suicide. She reported that the law enforcement officials are considering that as a possibility as they try to piece together what happened and why. I'm sure nobody wants to know that more than you do, because you were such good friends."

Fawn looked even more troubled.

"What is it, Fawn?"

"Go on, tell them," Shelley urged her.

"We did get along, like I said, but she got angry at me not long ago—real angry. We made up," she said quickly. "She called me and I went over to the house and we talked and talked and talked. It was good. Like we'd always been—even better than we'd always been, because she asked what I thought."

"What about?"

"About Thurston. About their relationship. About how he treated her. Like how to make him change and treat her better. I … I couldn't believe she asked me. It was kind of scary. I don't know anything about that sort of thing."

"You have a good head on your shoulders," Shelley said.

That eased Fawn's frown.

"How *did* he treat her?"

She looked away. "She said he treated her great. Well, until the last couple months, anyway. She talked about what a gentleman he was and how he could talk and talk and talk without demanding anything of her."

Except letting him talk and talk and talk.

"She used to say she was in awe of him, of how many people he knew in the county and how important he was, shaping the opinions of leaders and the populace alike."

That sounded like a quote from Thurston, transmitted via Melissa.

"And not just in Cottonwood County, either. He went to Denver a *lot*. He *flew* there. Melissa used to say how she'd drive him to the airport, leave him there, then drive a little way away and watch his plane take off and she'd feel empty. And the only thing that made her feel better was he'd be coming home soon and she'd pick him up at the airport, practically the second he landed."

And Thurston got free and convenient rides to and from the airport.

"She even let me be there and watch."

"Let you be there?"

"At the airport. As long as I stayed out of sight, she said it was okay."

"You didn't drive with them?"

"Oh, no." The idea scandalized her. "I drove my truck. He didn't know I was there. Sometimes, after he left, we'd meet up and Melissa and I would have lunch. In *Cody*. I liked that, but she was usually pretty sad. The only thing that made her feel better those times was showing me the pictures."

"Pictures?" I asked mildly.

"She has a website—not the one for the fan club anybody can see, but another one with a password and everything—where she kept all the pictures she took of him. Others, too, but lots and lots of pictures at the airport. Every time he left and every time he came back. Except…"

She let it hang so long, I asked, "Except what, Fawn?"

She startled at the slight nudge. "Nothing. Really, nothing."

Jennifer came to her rescue. "You said Melissa had a password-protected website? What's the URL?"

"Thurston and Melissa."

"*And* spelled out?"

"I, uh… Yeah, I think so, but… You can't look at it. That's Melissa's and nobody else has the password. Unless maybe Thurston—"

"That's okay."

That clearly reassured Fawn. It didn't have the same effect on me.

Putting aside my uneasiness for now, I aimed to take Fawn back to familiar and comfortable territory. "You said Melissa talked about Thurston a certain way until the past few months. How did she talk about him more recently?"

"She just said things, you know? Like he was taking her for granted. Even—she said this one time—he'd *used* her. That surprised me, because that wasn't the way things were between them at all. But…"

"But?"

"Nothing. Nothing, really. I have to go now. I have to help with the work."

My aim at familiar and comfortable totally missed the mark.

"Just a minute, Fawn. Monday night you said you didn't believe Melissa killed herself…"

"She didn't. She wouldn't. I know she wouldn't. She'd inherited that whole house and all the money she needed to run it and never work again." She looked down at her hardened hands. "Her mom left her all that. They talked all the time and her mother taught her things about clothes and shopping, and then left her a *lot*. Her mom really loved her. Melissa wouldn't have committed suicide. She wouldn't. She had her house and all that money and Thurston."

"But if she felt she didn't have Thurston anymore, if they had a fight…"

"She said she'd fix it. She knew how, and she was going to. Besides…"

"Besides, what, Fawn?"

"She wouldn't have done it. She wouldn't have left me all alone again. Not on purpose."

I stood, taking my cup to the sink. Also standing between Fawn and Shelley.

It was time for the big question.

"How did you know Melissa was the person whose body was found in Horse Creek County, Fawn?"

Her mouth sagged slightly.

"It was on TV—" Shelley started from behind me.

"No, it wasn't. But you were sure Monday night that it was Melissa. Why?"

"Because… because… She told me."

Chapter Twenty-Four

I HAD TO shuffle sideways to stay in front of Shelley. Awkward, but dignity came in a distant second to keeping Fawn's answers unpolluted by Shelley's protective input.

"What did she tell you, Fawn?"

"She told me she was going to the old mine road."

"When?"

"Saturday. She told me I couldn't come over like sometimes I did. Even though she'd said earlier I could."

"She told you that or said she was going to that road on Saturday?"

"Wh… I don't…" She tried to look around my shoulder to Shelley.

I drew in a breath. That was my fault. Combining questions because I was rushing.

"What day were you talking?"

"Saturday."

"Was she saying you couldn't come over that day—Saturday?"

"Uh-huh."

"Because she was going to that road on Saturday?"

She frowned. "No. She was going Sunday. She said she'd go Sunday night and had to get ready. So I shouldn't come over then, either. But after that I could."

Because Melissa expected to be back at her house? Or because Melissa expected to be dead and wouldn't have to deal with the consequences of putting off Fawn?

"Did she say why you couldn't see her Saturday?"

Her frown cleared. "Oh, because she was getting ready. She needed time to get ready. Then Sunday night she was going there."

"What was she going to do at the old mine road?"

"She didn't say. But she said it would fix everything, and then I could come over again, because it would be even better than before, and then she'd tell me all about it."

"Did you go to the mine road, Fawn?"

"Me?" She appeared shocked by the idea. "Melissa didn't say I should go there."

"But after you heard the news about someone being found dead on the Shangri-La Mine Road, did you go there?"

"No. I went to the TV station."

From behind me, Shelley said, "She only heard about it on the ten o'clock news."

She circled the work table, not only eluding my blockade, but reaching Fawn and gripping her forearm meaningfully.

"She and Glenn were out working all day. We had supper around six-thirty. Fawn helped me in the kitchen, then we all sat down to watch a show, followed by the news before we went to bed. When that story came on about the woman found dead on the Shangri-La Mine Road, she lit out of here before either of us could stop her.

"I'll swear to it in any court of law. She didn't know a thing about it before she heard it on your TV show."

"Sunday—?"

"No." Shelley cut me off. "She was here all day and all night. And Saturday she had a call with Melissa, then went right back to work like always. I'll swear to it in any court of law, too."

"DO YOU BELIEVE her?" Jennifer asked as we drove away.

Shelley and Fawn stood on the porch, watching us go, Shelley with her arm around Fawn's waist. It was as protective a gesture as an arm around the younger woman's shoulders would have been if their respective heights allowed.

"That Shelley would swear in a court of law to Fawn having an alibi, absolutely."

"But not so much that it's the truth?"

"She's one source. Even enlisting Glenn, it's really one source. A biased one. Not the best to rely on."

"What about Fawn? She doesn't seem like she's... You know. Does that mean she can't lie?"

"Something else that's not the best to rely on."

"It seems like she doesn't... Well, I kind of felt sorry for Melissa, for her isolation, especially after the death of her mother. But Fawn saw her as fortunate and that made me feel even sorrier for *her.*"

"That's perceptive, Jennifer, and your empathy does you credit. But you also can't let that sway your judgment, especially about her mental abilities, because one doesn't wipe out the other. If she's not lying, Fawn put together what Melissa said and the report about a woman found dead and came up with the right answer."

"That's true." She didn't sound particularly happy about it. "Where to next?"

I'd been thinking about that. "Needham Bender."

"Why?" I don't think she enjoyed our deep dives into journalism tales and trivia.

"I want to know what he knows."

"He won't tell you."

"No. And I won't ask." I grinned.

"That's weird."

Chapter Twenty-Five

AT HER REQUEST, I dropped Jennifer at the station—I did not chance going inside and discovering Audrey in needy mode—and drove into town to the offices of the *Independence*.

The brick building housing the *Independence* since the 1890s was all a newspaper office should be to my mind. Storefront windows, old wood floors, a historic hand press on display, a constantly going coffee pot available to all comers with good coffee, and often with a cluster of residents around it, presided over by Needham.

I'd texted him on the way back from talking to Fawn, and he'd said to come to his office whenever I arrived.

Having spotted me through glass walls that let him survey his kingdom—and spot potential competitive spies—he shut off his computer screen as I entered.

"Got something hot?" I asked.

"Read it in the *Independence*. And in the meantime, go work your own story. That is what you're here for, right? To pump me about the death of Melissa Oxley?"

I didn't take that amiss. It had been true plenty of times.

And he'd returned the favor.

It was journalists behaving normally, and we both understood that. It not only didn't strain our friendship, it made it stronger.

"How'd you get the name?"

"Same way you did. Logic and working a few sources."

"Not from rumor around town?"

"I am a journalist." He descended from that lofty pronouncement to add, "If Penny's got the name—which she probably does—she isn't sharing yet. If that's all you came for…"

"It's not. I read your series on the Shangri-La gold mine scam in Horse Creek County from thirty years ago and wanted to talk to you about it."

His bushy eyebrows rose. "You don't have anything else to do at the moment?"

"Maybe I need a break."

He eyed me. "Uh-huh. What about it interested you?"

That threw me off momentarily. I expected to fend off a few pointed remarks about the dead woman being found on a road associated with the scam. But I'd take the free pass.

"It's a damned good story. Scams interest me, of course. And this one has the twist that the locals didn't get taken."

He snorted. "Locals knew the porphyry copper-silver around here with gold in it was already worked where it was reachable. That leaves what's not reachable. There are downstream placers, but those are for tourists."

"That still happens? People try to strike it rich on their vacation?"

"Sure. Like people go to Las Vegas. Only you get fresh air and sunshine while looking for gold. That business isn't as strong around here as elsewhere in Wyoming and beyond, but, yeah. Used to be a cottage industry around here. One family in particular copied out maps, making them look hand-made, then they'd cozy up to someone, slowly let them in on the *fact* they had a family heirloom map. Hate to give it up, but times are so tough, need food for the kiddies or whatever their current sob story. And pretty soon the mark had them begging to take their money."

"Good heavens. Cottonwood County's answer to the Nigerian prince scam?"

"With the addition of a lost gold mine. And they tended to take cash, not identities. Not that they wouldn't've grabbed identities, too, if they'd been operating now. You know one of the last of the family. Hiram Poppinger."

I gaped at him. "I'm trying to stretch my imagination to Hiram

Poppinger cozying up to somebody. He'd sooner shoot a stranger than cozy up to them. Not to mention any outsider who bought anything from him in any context had to be nuts."

"Now, sure, but I've seen pictures, he was a downright adorable kid. And he could cry on cue. Not big, gulping sobs, but a trickle like he was trying to hold it back and be brave—got them every time. Then his parents, aunts, uncles, grandparents fleeced the mark and all was happiness and light. Until Shelton's father busted them. Somehow, it stuck in Hiram's mind as a kid that the strangers were responsible for his family's woes. Surely not the Poppingers, of course."

He tipped his head, considering.

"Suppose he could have blamed the older Shelton. Maybe even our current one. That happens often enough. But he didn't. The Sheltons—father and son—have been the most successful at curbing Hiram Poppinger's worst tendencies toward self-destruction, along with other-destruction."

"The Sheltons and Yvette," I muttered, naming Hiram Poppinger's recent love interest, who claimed to have driven Elvis to such distraction that he'd faked his death.

"Remains to be seen if she leads him away from self-destruction or just toward crazy."

"Getting back to the Shangri-La gold scam, I read most locals steered clear. But a rancher in Horse Creek County went for the supposed jackpot. When the scam burst open, he got most of his land back, but he'd sold his stock and equipment on the cheap and never could return to where he'd been."

"Yup. On the flip side, there was Dodd Oxley."

"Melissa Oxley's father?"

My itch collided with today's news.

That explained Needham's earlier restraint. He'd not only seen this coming, he'd thought I did, too.

"As if that isn't why you're here. Yep, Melissa's father. He went in at the start, backing the Shangri-La."

That was his investment that made good? Why hadn't Leona mentioned this?

Because she hadn't known I knew about the Shangri-La mine, much less might be interested.

"But if it was a scam, how did he come out with money?"

"Ah-ha, so you admit to knowing that." Pleased to think he'd caught me, he mellowed into story-telling mode. "As I said, he got in early, but he also got out early. You know how in a Ponzi scheme the early investors can do well if they get out fast enough?"

While other people weren't so lucky, even if almost all of those were far from Horse Creek County, Wyoming.

"Did he get out at the right time because of inside information?"

"Never proven. Swore his money didn't come from the mine at all."

"But?" I prompted based on his expression.

"But the Fyall house—Barbara's family's house—here in town got fixed up all of a sudden. Quit his job. They had newer vehicles, nicer clothes."

"That had to raise eyebrows."

"Eyebrows and ire. The people behind the scam … well, a couple died in unclear circumstances. Others high-tailed it out of the area. Not Dodd Oxley. He stuck—wasn't likely Barbara would have left anyway—and brazened it out. But weren't too many crying eyes when he keeled over from a heart attack in his late forties. After, nobody much held it against his widow or the girl. Almost nobody."

"*Almost* nobody," I repeated. "The rancher whose ranch never returned to what it had been, what was his name? You didn't name him in the series."

"No sense rubbing it in. Poor man had died by then. His name was Terence Itson."

"*Itson?* Related to Deputy Greg Itson?"

"His grandfather. Not something you already knew, huh?"

"I didn't." And wished I *had* known it yesterday when I'd talked to the deputy. "And now Dodd Oxley's daughter is dead and the person who found her is Terence Itson's grandson."

"I'd caution you against getting led down one path because people from the same families involved in a matter back then are involved with a different matter now. Weren't many families around here to pick from back then and if they didn't die out or move, the chances are good they'll be involved in things—good and bad—now."

"Makes sense." A reminder that sometimes an itch was just an itch. Not the solution to a murder.

"Also, let me tell you, Horse Creek County won't thank you for bringing up the Shangri-La mine. I got all sorts of blowback for that series. It's a sore spot. Still. Rival sports teams chant about gold to taunt Horse Creek County." His expression turned thoughtful. "One time it riled up their football team but good and they upset Cotton-wood County, kept us out of the playoffs."

From experience, I knew a comment like that could lead into de-tailed reminiscences of Cottonwood County sporting events.

I jumped back to the scam.

"Are there any vestiges of the Shangri-La mine around, besides the road where Melissa Oxley was found?"

"Nope."

"I hear it's not far from Colter."

"I guess, if you're willing to follow an antelope track that connects to the road about half a mile past where her vehicle was found. Now, I've told you all sorts of stuff, tell me what's going on there at the station."

"Strictly off the record. Just between us."

"Spoil sport. But I've gotta know. Just between us," he pledged. "And Thelma."

I okayed the inclusion of his wife.

Then I gave him nearly the same rundown I'd given Wardell Yard-ley, though without asides to identify the players or provide history, since Needham knew them better than I did.

He whistled softly. "Has Les shown up today?"

"No. And I can't say he's missed. Spineless weasel. He kowtows to Thurston, for heaven's sake. He kowtows to Val Heatherton and Craig Morningside, who have to be the most hands-off ownership I have ever heard of, much less worked for."

"A little kowtowing's understandable. They are responsible for his livelihood," Needham said mildly.

"It's not a little. And I don't understand them, either, letting the station limp along like not-quite-dead road kill. But ownership's one thing. It's almost expected they don't care about the news. A news director is supposed to be our advocate to the business interests."

"Journalism and business have been necessary bedfellows since the start. Need the business side to keep the presses rolling—or the pixels flowing. You know about Bill Nye, right?"

"Bill Nye the science guy?"

He scowled. "No. Bill Nye, the newspaperman and humorist. In all your talks with Emmaline Parens, she hasn't told you about—? Well. I'll have to address your ignorance. Full name Edgar Wilson Nye, but used Bill in pieces he submitted to papers in Laramie. Passed the bar there, in the mid-1870s. After a few other jobs, he founded the *Laramie Boomerang.*"

"*Boomerang?*"

"The *News* or *Times* or *Post* or even the *Independence* would have been too staid for him. Story goes he was out drumming up ads for the *Boomerang* and a merchant named Wagner said no thanks, claiming advertising did no good.

"Nye noticed Wagner's reduced the price on pants in his store. He went back to the paper and put in a *breaking news* piece saying *Wagner's Pants Are Down*. Pants sold out. Wagner took ads. In fact, became an investor in the paper."

I laughed. "That's pretty good, but if that's your proof of business needing to come before journalism…"

"Not before. Not above or below, either. Beside. As I said, keep the presses rolling and—"

"The pixels flowing. Both of which imply adherence to the principles of journalism. Thurston and Les want to run KWMT like it's the mouthpiece for their pals."

"There's history of that, too. Publishers cozy with politicians or moguls. Even in Wyoming. Ever hear of Caroline Lockhart? No, well, you should have.

"Editor and owner of the top paper in Cody in the early 1920s. At the same time, she was instrumental in keeping up Buffalo Bill's image—this was after he'd died, when his renown could have faded away—and that let her and others build up Cody. Hear of the Cody Stampede?"

I acknowledged familiarity with that pro rodeo event.

"And the sculpture of Buffalo Bill outside the historical center?

"Of course."

"Caroline Lockhart was behind starting the Stampede and she's the one who talked Gertrude Vanderbilt Whitney into creating that sculpture. Dedicated in 1924, while Lockhart still ran the paper."

"Vanderbilt as in...?"

"Yup. Also Whitney as in the museum of western art at the historical center. Some museum in New York, too, I hear."

I smiled, as he'd meant me to. "The Whitney Museum of American Art?"

"Yeah, that's the one." He never broke his deadpan. "Gertrude was quite a sculptor, which is why Lockhart went after her. But well before Caroline Lockhart, came the Huntington sisters, Gertrude and Laura."

"You're going to tell me Gertrude and Laura sold their souls for newspaper ads."

"That would have gravely disturbed their father, who was a minister. The sisters, in their twenties, purchased the weekly *Platte Valley Lyre.*"

"A newspaper called the *Lyre?*"

"Yes. No accident, either, though it wasn't the idea of the Huntington sisters. That was the name when they bought it in the late 1800s. Gertrude was the editor and Laura the business manager. They certainly were boosters for their community."

"I see what you're doing, Needham. Mouthpiece journalists elsewhere went for power or money or both. In Wyoming, they built community. But," I argued, "Les Haeburn has no such excuse. You could argue Thurston's a booster for Sherman, though it's really pandering to what he sees as power. But Les sure isn't."

"Nah, I'm not making excuses for Haeburn. You have him right. He's a spineless weasel."

Chapter Twenty-Six

I HAD A message from Jennifer when I left Needham.

Call with everybody set as soon as you're available.

Ready, I messaged back, sitting in my SUV, parked two doors down from the *Independence,* in one of the angled on-street spots that are so easy to use they should be included in all promotional material for Sherman. I know people who would flock here to see them.

The video call came through in seconds.

I saw Mike in a posh conference room at his Chicago station, Jennifer in the off-hours quiet of the KWMT-TV studio, Diana in the Newsmobile—a disreputable van, famed for a goat-like ability to climb sheer inclines.

"What are you doing downtown?" Mike asked me as soon as the hellos ended.

"Visiting with Needham."

"Don't you have an investigation going on?"

"Yes," Jennifer said emphatically. "And we need to talk about what we've found out before I have to get back to work. Did you guys know Thurston and Les didn't come here at the same time? Found that out this morning before we went to talk to Fawn."

"Fawn?" Mike asked. "You two talked to Fawn without me?"

"We can't wait around for you to visit from Chicago, if you ever do," Jennifer said.

"Could have used a video call like this."

"Probably would have freaked her out—she doesn't seem tech savvy—and that's if we could have gotten a signal where they are."

"What did she say?" Mike asked, not disputing Jennifer's assessment.

"First, I want to hear what Jennifer found," I said.

"Me, too." Diana smiled slightly. "Although, I was here when Les arrived first, then Thurston. Why are you surprised they arrived at different times, Jennifer?"

"They were both here when I started and joined at the hip and it seemed like they must've always been that way."

"Joined at the hip?" I repeated. It didn't sound like a phrase she'd use.

"Yeah, it means like Siamese twins or something, never apart or on their own. My grandma uses it about a friend of hers who wants to do everything with her."

I nodded wisely, keeping a straight face. I turned quickly to Diana. "Were they any different at the start?"

"Thurston? No. Les? Yes, I think he was."

"You think?"

"He came after I'd transitioned from receptionist to shooter, so I didn't have much other experience and didn't work under him long before Thurston came.

"That was a hard time. This place was in shock after Artie died. He'd been the news director from day one. Quite the character. Ruled the roost. I've always thought he was a large part of Val Heatherton being so hands-off. Artie wouldn't stand for interference from mere ownership.

"He's the reason I'm a shooter. It surprised people that someone who'd been around as long as he had was open to a woman shooter— especially one without experience—but he caught me sneaking a camera back in after unofficial practice, insisted on looking at what I'd shot, then invited me to apply for a position. I fought hard to get through that door, but Artie opened it."

"Your hard work and talent opened that door."

She grinned. "Thanks, pal. But, truly, Artie was a good guy. Ask Leona about him. When he died everyone was heartsick. Then Les came in as a shock hire. Nobody expected it. All we heard was Val

Heatherton came back from a national broadcasters' conference and announced she'd hired a news director. Bam. No warning. No one else met him ahead of time. No other candidates considered. The No. 2 guy—who would have been Artie's choice—left and is doing great in Arizona, last I heard. Anyway, Les showed up. All drive and ambition and—"

"Really?" Jennifer's incredulity reflected my reaction.

"Yep. Didn't bother trying to win over hearts and minds. Then he brought in Thurston. Over the next year, the last of the folks who weren't tied to Sherman were gone. And Les morphed into what we know and don't love."

"That's a lot more interesting than what I found, which was a lot of dates and places. Like Thurston came from a station in Ohio. Zanesville. Only place he'd worked before here. Les hopped around, lots of different stations, each one bigger. Last place before here was in Michigan."

"Zanesville is south and east of the center of Ohio, so not cozied up to Michigan. Certainly not in overlapping or neighboring markets, which makes it less likely they met that way and prompted Les to hire Thurston here," I said.

Jennifer shrugged. "I'll send you places and dates."

"Great. Now tell us about Fawn," Mike said.

When we got to the part where Jennifer asked for the URL of Melissa's password-protected photo storage, Mike hooted. "You got into it and found the photos, didn't you, Jennifer?"

"It wasn't that hard." But she looked pleased. "I started thinking about what Fawn said about Melissa taking all those photos when she took him to the airport for his Denver haircuts and picked him up, as if no one here is worthy of taking scissors to his locks. I'd like to take scissors to more than his locks." Jennifer avoided any reprimand for bloodthirstiness by quickly adding, "But it's more than that."

Diana pointed to her through the screen. "You're sounding more like Elizabeth every day and—"

"How nice," I said.

"—it's scary. Probably a good thing you're going to Illinois."

"Hey. I'm a good influence."

"You're an influence all right. We can debate the *good* another time. *What's* more than that, Jennifer?"

"He goes to Denver for more than a haircut."

"How do you know?"

"Well, I don't *know*. But it's logical. I was looking through the photos Melissa Oxley took of him. Why would a man take two big suitcases with him to be away for a couple days to get his hair cut?"

"Costume party?" Mike suggested. "Appearing in a play and he has to provide his own costumes?"

Jennifer tipped her head. Then shook it. "Maybe once, but not every time he went."

"He took two big suitcases *every* time? Can you pull up those photos?" I asked.

"Yeah. I'll share my screen."

She tapped away. An image appeared of Thurston Fine with two rolling suitcases, neither of which would qualify as carry-on for any plane I'd ever been on.

"That's the most recent," Jennifer said. A date amid identifying metadata at the top margin of the screen confirmed it was two and a half weeks ago.

A swipe and another photo appeared.

"The month before," she said. Swipe. "And the one before." Swipe. "Before that." Swipe. "And even before that. Goes back to January."

"Go through those again, will you?" Diana asked.

"Same order or backward?"

"Either way."

She went backward.

"Same suitcases every time," Diana said. "So he's not leaving them there. Though he might be leaving the contents."

"Moving bit by bit by suitcase?" It was rhetorical. "What about when he returns? Did Melissa have photos of that?"

"Oh, yeah." Jennifer kept talking, but absently, with her focus on what she was tapping and typing. "I swear she had photos of about every time he appeared in public, and some when he wasn't in public. If you know what I mean."

"I sure hope I don't know what you mean."

"Then you do. Looks like she had a camera set up in her bedroom." Jennifer interrupted herself. "Here we go. We'll take the returns in the same order as I showed you the departures the first time."

She swiped through the photos at a steady pace that let us see them, but not study them. Three times, before she switched away from the shared screen and we all stared at each other instead.

"Confirms he brought back the same suitcases, which we knew, or he wouldn't have had them available on the next trip," Diana mused. "Hard to tell if they're heavier or lighter, because he's rolling them."

"Drugs?" Jennifer didn't believe her own suggestion.

"*Thurston?*" Diana asked.

"I know. And with that volume, he'd have to be going into business. Unless he was hiding them in among a lot of other stuff thinking nobody would ever find them? But wouldn't making regular trips with big suitcases attract attention?"

"It would," Mike said. "Somebody *must* have checked them, maybe several times."

"So drugs are unlikely," Jennifer said. "But then … why?"

I said, "Can you show us the photos again, pairing up departure and return?"

"Sure." More tapping and typing. "But why?"

"It's the old journalism saying, if at first you don't see a pattern, keep shuffling in hopes you will."

"I bet Edward R. Murrow said that every night before he went to sleep," Mike muttered.

"My favorite of his is *Just because your voice reaches halfway around the world doesn't mean you are wiser than when it reached only to the end of the bar.*"

"Sounds like he foresaw social media."

"Yup. Wonder what he'd—"

Jennifer interrupted my dreadfully insightful musings with, "Here we go."

She swiped through the photos working from recent to old, then from old to recent.

"Wait a minute."

"Elizabeth's spotted something," Jennifer said gleefully. "Mike says you always say *wait a minute* when you spot something."

"Not yet I haven't. Not for sure. Go through again. Slowly."

She complied, while commenting, "She doesn't take pictures between the leaving and returning shots, like there's nothing worth photographing with Thurston out of town. That's disgusting. She—"

"Stop. There. You're right. She never took pictures in all those months while he was out of town until—see it? Every other time, the ID numbers are right after each other. But this most recent time, there are forty-seven numbers between when he left and when he came back."

"Why would she suddenly—? Oh. I know. She went there. To Denver," Jennifer said. "She followed him because she couldn't stand not knowing what he was doing and she took pictures there. Which means she knew what he was doing and had photos, but she took them off her camera and out of her archive because she was blackmailing him about whatever he's doing in Denver and he killed her and—"

"Wait. You've leapt from a toe in the water into the middle of the lake. Take this step by step. All we know is she took photos between the time he left for Denver and returned."

"And those photos likely were of Thurston," Diana said.

Jennifer jumped on that. "Exactly. Because that's all she ever took pictures of. Those missing pictures aren't in her storage or archive, but if they were deleted, I might be able to get to them."

"SINCE WE DON'T know why Thurston would take those suitcases, why not ask him," Mike asked with would-be innocence.

"If I have to, I will, but first I want to talk to Magnus Boesch, Melissa's stepfather." I sketched out what Leona had told us, adding what Needham said about the will and family dynamic.

"A stepfather passed over by his wife, not only in her will, but if her daughter died? Doesn't seem likely as a motive to kill his step-daughter," Diana said.

"What's likely and what Magnus *thought* would happen might be two different things. We need to find out what he thought he'd get if Melissa died."

"I'll ask around," Diana volunteered. "See what the popular view is about his expectations."

I told them about reading the Shangri-La mine series in the *Independence*, my conversation with Needham, and the connections from that scam to Melissa Oxley and the deputy who found her.

"South Pass is best for gold now," Mike said.

"You're an expert?"

"No, but most Wyoming kids look for gold growing up. You hear stories, so you keep your eyes open riding fence line or moving cattle. Heard lots about gold, including the Shangri-La mine, in the summers I worked for Jack Delahunt. Then I read up, to improve my chances. Didn't work."

"What I don't get," I said, "is why they set the scam in Horse Creek County instead of where there are lots of creeks."

"Ah, that was ingenious. Creek beds change all the time. You get a lot of snow one year, the melt comes fast, the water pushes out of its banks into another route. Over a hundred years, you could have ten, twenty, fifty changes in the course of one creek. Not to mention creeks that don't exist anymore. All that's true. Shangri-La sold the marks thirty years ago on a belief that once upon a time an area outside Colter was a creek teaming with gold, the creek dried up, soil and debris covered the gold, but it remained—for those brilliant folks who knew to look there."

"People just believed…?" Jennifer asked.

"Nope. Needham's series makes it clear the investors had samples tested and certified before they put in their money."

"But, if tests showed there *was* gold…"

"The gold didn't come from there originally. They spread a little gold around, make it look like it's going to be a real profitable venture and the sky's the limit."

She frowned.

"It's called salting a mine," I clarified.

Her frown didn't go away. "But they had to buy gold first? Wouldn't that be expensive?"

"Sure, there's expense setting up the scam. You show some gold around, put more in samples taken to test what the mine could be expected to produce. The prospective buyer finds X amount of gold, multiplies it by the area of the mine and comes up with a figure of what it could make over time. That's where the con men make their score. Buy land, plant gold so it looks like the enterprise will be— excuse the expression—a gold mine, and sell."

"Exactly," Mike said. "A guy down in Leadville, Colorado, during the silver rush named Chicken Bill Lovell stole the silver to salt a mine. But then the guy who bought it went deeper and there really was silver. I wrote a paper about it. You should ask Mrs. P. She'll probably slip in chemistry stuff, too. Something about chlorine. How'd you miss that, Jennifer?"

"I had Mr. Grubinowski for History of the West."

"If you want to come along, you can make up for that, because Mrs. P is my next stop," I said. "Although if you're still working…"

"You're not going to see Magnus Boesch next?" Diana asked.

"I'd like to get Mrs. P's background first. And that gives you a chance to—"

"Run right out and get answers."

"Exactly."

"What does any of this gold mine stuff have to do with Thurston killing Melissa Oxley?" As I started to respond, Jennifer hurriedly amended, "Or possibly not killing Melissa Oxley. I suppose I can go with Elizabeth to Mrs. P's."

Chapter Twenty-Seven

Jennifer hid her reluctance well when we arrived at Mrs. Parens' home in O'Hara Hill, which is the second-largest town in Cottonwood County.

Outside of Wyoming, no one would associate this town with the word *large*.

We both glanced toward the right. That's where Mike's Aunt Gee—Gisella Decker—lived.

No car in that driveway said Gee wasn't home. Possibly at her job as head dispatcher for the county's sheriff's department substation.

No car in Mrs. P's driveway told us nothing. She didn't drive. Besides, we'd called before we left Sherman, so she was expecting us.

She welcomed us to a room that would be the envy of many museums—if they concentrated on the education system and history of Cottonwood County. Photos and maps covered most of the walls, with the well-stocked bookcases only a hint of her collection.

I knew the way to Mrs. Parens' heart. More important, the sometimes way to her mouth.

"Needham was telling me about the history of Wyoming newspapers, including a couple of sisters in the 1890s."

"Ah. The Huntingtons."

"Indeed. Gertrude and Laura." She regarded me closely, perhaps looking for signs of smart ass. "The daughters of a minister."

"That is correct. Gertrude and Laura were the oldest of nine siblings. They ran the newspaper for a dozen years, though a younger sister became business manager when Laura married in 1898."

Of course, Mrs. P knew the exact year.

"I see your expression, Elizabeth, you are mistaken in this instance. Yes, Laura left the newspaper when she married and she nursed her husband during a lengthy illness, but neither she nor Gertrude, when she married in 1905, retired from active life.

"In addition to being editor of the *Lyre*, Gertrude was the elected superintendent of her county's schools for eight years. After selling the paper, she worked in the law office of the man she married. After his death, she ran the insurance business they started. She headed the local American Red Cross from its establishment to her death.

"After her husband's death, Laura worked in civic offices, including completing the term of the treasurer. In addition, she ran the insurance business after Gertrude's death. She lived into her nineties.

"In conclusion, these women ran businesses, worked in professional capacities, held offices, and married. It was not a binary choice more than a century ago, nor is it now."

"They sound remarkable."

"I do not presume to know Needham's intention in telling you about the Huntington sisters. However, mine is not to make them sound remarkable. Certainly, they were not remarkable enough for much of history to *mark* them. One might justifiably argue that history has an exceedingly narrow and blurry lens, even when it ventures away from battles, royalty, and conquerors.

"Rather, my intention is to introduce young minds to women who lived their lives with vigor and purpose, as it is incumbent on all of us to do. As you do, Elizabeth."

I got her message that there were many more women—and men—whose lives were worth marking than history bothered with. That lives and events not in books or timelines or biopics provided the foundation for history and—more importantly—for now and the future.

Marriage and women's lives, then and now, represented a new theme.

"Needham also talked about other early Wyoming journalists," I ventured. "Bill Nye and Caroline Lockhart."

"In addition, Nye passed the bar, wrote books and succeeded on the lecture circuit. Caroline Lockhart worked as a reporter in Boston and Philadelphia, including jumping into fire nets and donning a dive suit, before arriving in Cody. She wrote novels of the Old West, with several made into movies. In 1920, she bought and edited what became the *Cody Enterprise*."

"And used it to launch the Cody Stampede. Conflict of interest."

"She was not deterred by disapproval. I doubt she would be stirred by yours. She did use the platform of the newspaper to promote the town. Both editorially and in practice, she expressed disapproval of Prohibition, which the majority of Cody's citizens backed. When she sold the paper, she started a ranch in Montana. As she accomplished all this, she never lacked for male companionship. She refused many offers of marriage and when she gave up ranch life, she moved back to Cody with her then-boyfriend, both of them well into their seventies."

I'd thought her point about the Huntington sisters was that a woman could marry and still be independent and achieve. But Caroline Lockhart remained adamantly single … though apparently not maiden-like.

Asking for clarity wouldn't get me anywhere. The glint in her eye said she'd enjoy my journey to nowhere.

Mrs. P intended me to puzzle out what she'd presented. Didn't mean I had to.

I smiled broadly.

"Thank you, Mrs. Parens. As always, your trips into Wyoming history are fascinating. And you are right, you presented aspects Needham didn't mention in our discussion about journalism and the business of media."

"You are welcome, Elizabeth. I hope for Jennifer's sake—"

Jennifer stopped squirming instantly.

"—you are now prepared to inform me of the real reason for your visit today."

Busted.

Still, didn't mean caving and blurting out my core questions would serve my purposes.

"The other thing Needham told me about was the Shangri-La mine scam. I read his series in the *Independence* from the twenty-fifth anniversary. I'd had no idea gold fever hit this area, especially so recently."

"Wyoming has not proven immune to that particular malady, nor its relations."

Jennifer jumped in. "Mike knew lots about the old mine scams—way before the one in Horse Creek County. Mr. Grubinowski didn't include fun stuff like the guy named Chicken Bill when he taught History of the West."

Mrs. P assumed an expression of mild disapproval. Not sure I believed it.

"Mr. Grubinowski covers substantively the same course material as I did. The *fun stuff* to which you refer was covered, however Michael ventured deeply into the topic, including submitting a report on William Lovell, commonly known as Chicken Bill. Michael was inordinately entertained by Mr. Lovell's crude methods, including stealing ore from a successful mine and dumping it into his as-yet-unproductive exploration, then selling his stake on that basis.

"However, as the engineers and investors became more knowledgeable, such methods no longer sufficed to dupe them. Those bent on swindling adopted other ploys. For example, they used gold chloride—"

A possible explanation for Mike's comment about a chemistry lesson.

"—to paint the rock face, going so far as to insert it in crevices with syringes. They loaded shotgun shells with filings from gold coins to shoot from close range, embedding the metal into the rock.

"They also bribed workers to smuggle gold in to salt the samples. They used syringes to inject gold chloride into sample sacks or dusted gold into the sacks' seams. Assayers and their equipment could also be corrupted."

Before she took us too deep into the weeds of precious metal scams, I steered her back toward current events.

"I was interested because the woman who was found dead in her car—you heard about that?—"

She nodded.

"—was found on Shangri-La Mine Road. Melissa Oxley."

She didn't respond to the name.

I knew she had strongly held views against gossiping. I suspected the main reason she told us anything was that her views on murder were even stronger. Still, she generally limited assessments she'd shared with us to academic records.

In that moment I decided to reach Melissa by way of Fawn.

"Law enforcement seems to lean toward suicide as the manner of death, but Melissa's best friend, Fawn Raglettley, says she's certain Melissa wouldn't have committed suicide. Do you know Fawn? Was she a student of yours? Can you give me any insight into how much credence we should give her?"

"You spoke with Fawn and you are an observant woman, Elizabeth. I should think your insight would be more valuable to your needs than mine."

She wasn't getting out of answering that easily. I broke down the questions. "Did you have her in class?"

"Yes, though not for an entire academic year."

"Why?"

Her mouth pursed, followed quickly by a shift in her gaze that made me think she calculated the answer was either public information or widely known and she preferred to get her presentation of it into the hopper first.

"Fawn Raglettley came into Cottonwood County schools in the middle of an academic year. I assessed her in the classroom for several weeks before assigning her to track."

"Remedial?"

She grimaced at the word, which was still a lot better than other terms used. "Fawn faced academic challenges throughout her time in Cottonwood County schools. She also faced challenges in her homelife."

"Mike told us," Jennifer said. "He knew her from when she played basketball for the high school."

"Participating in sports can become a major distraction for some students, while providing motivation for others. For Fawn, basketball provided structure, connections, and a place where she was valued."

"You know she works for an older couple named Baxter with a place on the eastern edge of the county?"

"I do."

"They seem quite fond of her. Do they have children?"

"A great-nephew, I believe, lives in the Los Angeles area. He has never been here."

Our gazes held. "They might like to make ... arrangements to help her out after, well, they're no longer employing her, but aren't aware of how. And not open to interference from an outsider."

"I believe you have assessed their situation accurately, Elizabeth."

Jennifer gusted out a breath. "So Elizabeth's going to figure out how the Baxters should set it up to help Fawn after they're dead and Mrs. Parens will talk them into accepting whatever Elizabeth finds. Unless it turns out Fawn killed Melissa. Can we get back to the case now?"

Mrs. Parens fought to keep a neutral expression. I grimaced.

"I sure hope you learn subtlety at Northwestern," I said.

"I don't. Not if it takes up this much time."

"Fine. You want direct? Mrs. Parens, was Melissa Oxley a student of yours?"

"I did not have her in class."

"What do you know about her academic career?"

Often, that was all she would tell us.

"Melissa started her education in the Cottonwood County school system and showed herself to possess a bright and curious mind. She became somewhat more withdrawn socially after second grade. Whether that changed afterward I cannot say, for her mother removed her from school before Melissa would have entered fourth grade."

"When her father died," I guessed. "*Because* her father died?"

"I cannot speculate as to the reason behind the decision. I can state the facts that I know."

"Did Barbara Fyall Oxley send her daughter away to school?" That didn't match with the close relationship the neighbors talked about.

"Melissa was homeschooled." No disapproval leaked into her tone or expression, yet I knew she did not approve.

"Were you familiar with Barbara's academic background?"

"To the extent of having had her in class twice during her time in the Cottonwood County school system."

"What kind of student was she?"

"She could have achieved more than she did, however, she was satisfied with adequate."

"But she went on to college."

"She did, at a college with which her family had a long association."

"A legacy student?"

"I do not know the ins and outs of Barbara Fyall's admission to that college, nor her academic achievements at it."

I knew Mrs. Parens wasn't a fan of homeschooling, but there'd been a bit beyond broad disapproval in her tone.

"Did Barbara have a background in education?" I asked.

"She did not. However, if I am correct in discerning the direction of your questioning, she did not take direct responsibility for Melissa's education, but rather she hired tutors."

"Tutors, plural?"

"They were employed serially."

"Did you know any of them?"

"Danielle Pruiting, the young woman Barbara Oxley, as she was then, employed as Melissa's final tutor had been an excellent student in the Cottonwood County school system before obtaining her undergraduate degree. With her earnings from the year of tutoring, as well as other financial help, she returned for her master's degree in education. She has been a teacher at the high school since that time."

In other words, Mrs. P knew her as student, alum, and teacher, and more than likely had been a mentor to her throughout.

"She's still in Cottonwood County? Great. I'll track her down and see if she's willing to talk to us."

"There is no need to, as you termed it, track her down. I will call her. If she's willing to talk with you, I will share with you her contact details."

"Thanks." And if the woman didn't want to talk to me, I'd track her down. "Leona said it was sad to see another old family line end, considering Melissa was the last direct descendant of Hiram Fyall."

"I do not doubt the veracity of your report, yet I acknowledge surprise that Leona expressed such a sentiment. She knows as well as anyone that the family lines twist, twine, fray, and sputter long before they officially die out. At the same time, new families, whether wide-ranging or narrowly focused, contribute greatly to the county, state, region."

I fought muscles trying to raise my eyebrows. I also kept my voice neutral. "You're not a fan of the first families of Cottonwood County? I thought you were interested in all the history."

"I am not, as you say, a *fan*. Nor am I not a *fan*. The lives and ac-complishments of individuals, whatever surname he or she might carry, create history that does, indeed, interest me."

"Whatever surname?" No hope of fighting the grinning muscles now. "Are you saying what I think you're saying about the various families and individuals in the history of Cottonwood County sticking to their marital beds?"

"You're far too wise and too old, Elizabeth to view such realities as fodder for an outbreak of the giggles."

Ouch. "No giggling from me."

"Very well," she conceded. "As for what I was saying, you are fully competent to ascribe accurate meaning to my words."

Chapter Twenty-Eight

AT TIMES, EMMALINE Parens could be subtle to the point of inscrutability. For example, leaving me to puzzle out if she was warning me to stay away from family scandals or to explore them.

But now that she'd escorted us to her front door, it became clear this was not one of her inscrutable moments.

Tom Burrell's truck sat in front of the house. He was out of it, walking toward the front door and regarding my vehicle with an expression that indicated he might be having the same thoughts about Mrs. Parens as I was, as I walked down her front steps.

"Jennifer," she said from the open door. "Come back inside for a moment. I need help returning a box to a shelf."

I turned around to say I'd help her—in the unlikely event she truly did need help—but she'd already snagged Jennifer, drawn her inside, and closed the door.

"That was subtle." I said it to the door.

"Might be my fault."

That brought me around to face Tom. "Oh?"

"Not intentionally. Tamantha told Mrs. Parens this morning that I hoped to talk to you soon. When she called and asked me to come over to help her with—"

"Let me guess, returning a box to a shelf."

Either the shadow under his hat brim was lighter than usual, or a brief frown shifted to a grin.

"—returning a box to a shelf, I should have suspected something."

"No worries." I closed the door on Mrs. Parens' machinations and exactly what she had in mind. "As it happens, I have something to ask you. Do you know Greg Itson, a deputy from Horse Creek County?"

He paused. "Met him now and again, wouldn't say I know him well. Why?"

"What's your assessment of him?"

"My assessment? You interviewed him—saw that on TV. Nice job, too. He's not the most talkative."

"Yeah, I've encountered a few of that type around here." For an instant, we smiled at each other. We both looked away. "He was on guard with me. He wouldn't have been on guard with you, when you encountered him. Besides, you know the history, the area."

"I know his grandfather's history, a little about his father."

"You mean about the Shangri-La mine."

"Yeah. His grandfather gambled big-time and lost."

"Tell me more."

"Terence Itson was long-time chairman of the Horse Creek County commissioners. He was also in a world of hurt. His daughter, the younger sister of Greg's father, had leukemia. Bad. They've made a lot of progress, but that was thirty years ago. The family used up a lot of their resources getting her treatment. There was another treatment, but to get her in..."

"They needed money."

He declined his head in confirmation. "They'd stretched the ranch's resources thinner trying to have a baby—that's Terence's son and daughter-in-law. All sorts of treatments. Didn't work."

"But Greg—Adopted?"

"Yeah. And couldn't have been more loved and wanted from top to bottom in the Itson family. Ranch was starting to bounce back when the girl, Terence's daughter, got sick. What I heard was he went all in on the Shangri-La mine. People tried to talk him out of it. Wouldn't listen. Maybe he couldn't. No other options."

I knew Tom imagined himself if Tamantha's chances of a cure hung in the balance, and empathized.

"He sold all his cattle?"

"And a chunk of the family land. It shut down his and his son's work. All to get shares in the mine. Then it went bust. The girl went into a different clinical trial. She didn't make it. It broke him. Broke the rest of them, too. Greg's father put himself back together fairly well with major help from Greg's mother. Terence… He stayed broken, withdrew from the community, from just about everything."

I looked off to the top of the trees. "Greg was a kid, watching this?"

"Pretty much. Idolized Terence, who died not long after the daughter, but not before he'd lost his family ranch, the inheritance he'd been grooming Greg to take over. That family got hit with a lot in a short time. After, they pretty much stayed to themselves."

I remembered Diana saying the deputy's mother had early onset Alzheimer's. The hits hadn't stopped.

"He said he played football."

"Yeah. I saw him play against Cottonwood, other games. I can tell you he had good football sense. Beyond that? Nope."

"Still, with all the people you know, you'd've heard things about his … character. What sort of man he is?"

In an uncharacteristic move, he thumbed the brim of his hat back, letting more light cross his face.

"I'd take your observations and knowledge of people over what I might pick up every day of the week and twice on Sundays."

Mrs. P had touted my ability to read people a few minutes ago, too. But I suspected she'd done it partially to deflect questions.

This wasn't the same thing at all.

I was flattered. Touched. And doing my best not to show it. "That might hold true for people outside of Wyoming, but here, totally different matter," I joked.

He didn't crack a smile. "Anywhere. Anytime. Anyone. You once told me you doubted your judgment because you'd loved that ass you divorced."

I knew exactly when and where he meant. A year ago, in the parking lot of a bar called the Kicking Cowboy, when we'd touched on confidence, judgment, and the damage to both done by divorce.

In that same parking lot conversation, he'd pointed out his ex-wife—Tamantha's mother—would have let him be held responsible for murder.

That topped—or bottomed—my experience with my ex.

"Don't doubt, Elizabeth. You know you're past it. Questioning yourself can get to be a habit. You can do as much damage that way as by going straight ahead and making a mistake."

I was over the divorce.

Was I over the doubt?

Was he?

"I won't if you won't." I made it teasing, dry.

"Deal." He resettled his hat to the more familiar shadow-casting angle. "As for Greg Itson, if you want me to speculate from a few encounters, I'd say he's a man who feels things strongly, doesn't reveal much, has a real sense of right and wrong, though it might not align a hundred percent with the general notions of those."

That echoed my impressions. "Thanks, Tom. That does help."

I made a move toward passing him and going to my SUV to wait for Mrs. P to release Jennifer from the bogus task. No, probably not bogus, knowing Mrs. P. She'd have set up something real. Make it an unnecessary task.

"Elizabeth."

I turned to Tom, who hadn't moved.

"I said I'd help you with this—"

"And you did."

"Not much. There's something else I—we—might be able to do to help. I know you're working a lot of extra hours, to keep the daily newscasts on, plus investigating…"

"If you have a talent for producing news segments you never happened to mention before now, I might fall on your neck."

One side of his mouth lifted in a familiar half grin. "No. But Tamantha and I could stop by and take Shadow for a good walk every day. I know Zeb and Iris are feeding him, but he might not be getting his usual exercise."

I blinked, only then realizing this sting in my eyes was from incipient tears. Over someone offering to walk my dog. I am a total sap.

"That—" I cleared my throat. "—would be helpful. Not to mention keeping my dog from becoming a sausage from all the goodies the Undlins give him. Thank you—both of you."

"No need for thanks. Tamantha will love it and I'll earn points with her for making it happen."

"I guess you need a—" I tried hard to not stumble over the final word, with its import of developments and connections that this most certainly was not. "—key."

What flashed through his eyes was gone too soon to interpret. "We'll work it out with Iris and Zeb. The idea is to give you less to worry about, not more."

The front door opened to Jennifer and Mrs. Parens.

The former said *hey* to Tom as she jogged down the steps and past him.

The latter's eyes glinted with satisfaction, likely from finding Tom and me smiling at each other.

Then the back door of the house next door opened and Gisella Decker emerged.

"Oh." She gave an Oscar-worthy start. "Imagine you all being here."

"Yes," I said, "we hoped to say hello, but with your car not in the driveway, I was certain you were working."

"Car's in the shop. They're bringing it by any minute. I came out so they wouldn't have to wait for me."

Mrs. P emitted a soft sound that in a less genteel personage might have been a snort.

It was chilly out today, with a sharp wind—think knives when a Wyoming wind turns sharp. Not to mention, Gee was fully aware of what was due her dignity. She'd more likely expect—and get—white glove service from the *shop*, than wait outside in the cold.

Tom's gaze, filled with wry amusement, met mine.

Mrs. Parens saw that, too, and her satisfaction returned in full glint. Which Aunt Gee saw.

Quickly, I said, "This gives me a chance to thank you both for the contact about Wyoming suicide information. She was very informative."

"We've both had cause to interact with her."

At Gee's grimness it struck me, as it should have earlier, that both she, as a dispatcher, and Mrs. P, as a teacher and principal, would have encountered the ravages of suicide.

"I suppose that was wanting background on the death of Melissa Oxley, though it has not been officially ruled a suicide. Or not a suicide. I was talking with Michael," Gee said, "and told him what I felt appropriate to share. It's complicated with Horse Creek County leading the case and not being as forthcoming and collegial as one would hope—"

She snapped that off in apparent recognition that her pique might lead to saying more than she'd intended.

"They're giving our folks fits." I said with a sympathetic—and leading—shake of my head. The *our* was a nice touch. "Have to wonder if Deputy Itson is up to the job."

"He seems to be an upstanding law enforcement officer," she said carefully, then turned the conversational wheel sharply. "Mike told me he's working with you from Chicago to sort out what happened."

"He hasn't done much. But I suppose he wouldn't have if he were here, either, since he can't write copy for Leona like Elizabeth has to. It's taking up a lot of her time," Jennifer said in disapproval. "Although he could have talked to Fawn. That—"

I started to explain to Gee who Fawn was, but saw from her expression that she not only knew that, but also of Fawn's Monday night activities outside KWMT-TV. What she didn't hear from official channels, she would have found out from her web of connections.

"—might have helped."

"Michael has a *very* important job in Chicago," Gee said repressively.

Unrepressed and unimpressed, Jennifer said, "He could still do more." She shifted her gaze to Tom. "So could you."

"I'm not the investigator you all are. But if I can help with auxiliary support, let me know."

"I will. C'mon, let's go, Elizabeth."

As we pulled out with good-bye waves, Gee's vehicle came sailing majestically down the street, piloted by a middle-aged man being extremely careful.

✧ ✧ ✧ ✧

I ANSWERED DIANA'S call with a wink toward Jennifer.

"Cutting it awfully close. We're almost back to town."

"Ingrate," she said without heat. "Magnus Boesch apparently told neighbors of Melissa's—the woman from two doors down and people across the street—that he'd be back in the house before long."

"Before or after her death?"

"Hah. If he said it before, that would wrap things up quickly, wouldn't it. It was this morning. He was at the house—outside. Apparently, the authorities wouldn't let him go in, which irked him, according to both sets of neighbors.

"I also asked Leona to tap her country club connections, and they said he made comments when the news came of Melissa's death that he wouldn't be working there much longer—things would return to the way they *should* be. That was the quote. Sounds like he thinks he's going to inherit."

"It does. And he's wasting no time talking about it. It's also interesting he was at the house today when the ID has not been officially released. Did the authorities tell him he was next of kin?"

"No. In fact, Faye Nafus, the lady from two doors down, was rather huffy about his being there and questioned him. He acknowledged not being next of kin, but said of course he came, as soon as he heard a blue Beetle was found at the scene—so that much has leaked out, anyway. I'll see if I can find anything more concrete than *He said.* What are you two up to?"

I gave a one-minute recap of the visit with Mrs. P, skipping mention of Aunt Gee and Tom. Because the focus was on the death of Melissa Oxley. Nothing else.

"Now that we have context, I think we'll try Magnus."

"I've got his address," Jennifer said. "Got addresses and contact info for as many of the people as I could."

"Good. We'll try his home first and if he's not there, the country club. I'd like to talk to him before everybody else does, though if Magnus is blabbing to neighbors and country club pals…"

"Yeah, he doesn't sound like a model of reticence," Diana said. "Jennifer's going with you? Audrey was asking about her."

I glanced at my passenger. "You said you were off."

"I am. Uh, informally. While Dale fills in."

Diana and I t'ched at her simultaneously.

But I did not take her back to KWMT. And before going to Magnus Boesch's address, we drove past Melissa Oxley's home, to get a visual.

Chapter Twenty-Nine

MAGNUS BOESCH LIVED in a one-bedroom apartment complex on the west side of Sherman.

By complex, I meant five buildings, each with four units. The sign out front bragged of a playground and parking. When you highlight parking in Manhattan, that's a true perk. When you highlight parking in Wyoming, that's a stretch.

Still, they weren't awful.

If I'd known about the place when I arrived in Sherman, I would have jumped at it over the house I rented sight-unseen and unaffectionately called the Hovel.

These apartments had a vaguely redwood appearance with stonescapes in front instead of lawn. Magnus Boesch's unit was on the second floor. He opened the door after one knock.

He had straight hair that flopped over his forehead and must have made him look boyish long after he was. He maintained a marked chin, but with jowls descending on their side of it.

He smiled at us.

An automatic response, I suspected, to two presentable females. I also suspected he considered it a boyish grin.

I introduced us, making no mention of Melissa Oxley.

He invited us in without hesitation.

From the entryway, we could see the whole unit, including the bedroom and bathroom through their open doors, and out the small balcony to a view of the parking.

As I said, not awful. Yet quite a come-down from the Fyall House we'd driven past.

That building was a clay-colored brick cottage with a second story tucked under a sharply slanted roof—not cottage as in Newport, Rhode Island's mansions, but not a seaside shack, either. A wrap-around porch added to its presence but didn't hide it was significantly smaller than its neighbors, which ranged from Italianate to Queen Anne to a few Colonial Revivals.

That neighborhood was far more interesting than this.

"Has the news been announced about Melissa—?" His eagerness slid out unattractively.

"If you mean is identification official, no. Which is why we're here to talk to you unofficially." And without a camera. "We're hoping for the insight and background only you can give so that when law enforcement does officially release the identity, we can give our viewers a full picture of her."

He considered for half a second. Under the hunk of hair on his forehead, his eyes took on a calculating sheen. "The sheriff's depart-ment said not to tell anyone, but since you already know it's Melissa…"

"Exactly."

He gestured to the would-be leather sofa, while he took the chair opposite. All new, but not good quality.

Before I needed to ask anything, he said, "I had no idea she was that unhappy, but she wasn't a real steady person, you know?"

"I—I'm not sure." The falter in my voice was artistic, if I said so myself.

"She was always a little … well, backward might be too strong—"
She didn't move easily through the world.

"—but she didn't know how to get on with people. Awkward, like. Not comfortable. Her mother didn't see it, always went on and on about how marvelous her memory was, knew all the movies, the stars, the news. But she was … wasn't one for, you know, having a guy come after her and them getting married. Out of step. Her and that real tall girl. What's her name? Dawn? Raggedy—something like that."

I didn't fill in the correct name. No sense undoing my artistic falter by revealing now that I knew anything.

"I thought I'd heard something about her, uh, involvement with somebody…"

"That TV guy? Don't you believe it. I don't. No matter what she said. He's a weird duck himself—but it didn't have anything to do with Melissa. Though maybe if she'd had illusions about him and then she realized it wasn't real, that could have driven home to her that she had nothing to live for."

Same person, same circumstances. Fawn saw her as having everything to live for. Magnus saw her as having nothing to live for … or so he said.

I wasn't ready to take the gloves off completely, but maybe peel the cuffs back a bit.

"She did inherit that lovely home in a great neighborhood along with the means to support herself from her mother."

He leaned forward, dipping his head a bit to stir the floppy section of hair, and looking earnest. "Something like this makes me realize I'm better off for having had to make my own way all my life—"

Except for when he was spending his wife's money.

That wasn't the objection I said aloud. "Didn't Melissa support herself while she worked in Cody?"

"—and how I appreciate what I have more. Plus, the satisfaction of having earned what I have and not having it handed to me." He used one hand to push back his hair, but let it flop forward again immediately, but not before it revealed a large patch of gray not showing elsewhere. "Oh, she worked *some*, sure. But she got gifts all the time from her mother."

Gifts from mom might mean any number of things from big infusions of cash to a pair of cute socks. I received a steady influx of them—mostly of the cute socks variety—while supporting myself since I graduated from college.

"And then she inherited everything."

"Not everything. Barbara knew I could take care of myself, but she left me a little."

Far too little in his estimation from what he'd told others.

"It's only natural it bothered you that when your wife died, she left her daughter the house. The house where you'd been living. And you had to move out—" I left a slight pause to let him know we knew about the sheriff's department pulling him away from the house. "—and leave your comfortable life behind."

"No problem for me. Never liked that place. Ask anybody." All of whom would likely confirm Leona's take that he'd hated the work associated with it and resented the money spent on it. "Besides, Melissa grew up there. It was in her family for generations. The Fyall family built it back at the beginning of time. Made complete sense that it go to Melissa, to stay in the family."

"Plenty of room for both of you to live there."

He laughed raucously. "She was a little off, but she wasn't weird enough to want to live with her stepfather. And I don't blame her. That would put a crink in both our styles, if you know what I mean. Mine more than hers to be totally open and honest about it. But we got along okay."

"She'd moved out of the family home after you married her mother."

"She was a grown woman. Of course, she did."

"Come now, Magnus, as you said, let's be open and honest—" Neither of which I associated with him. "—you were happy enough to ignore Melissa and vice versa until after the will was read. Then you began a campaign to win her over, to claim ties of affection and family, to work on her to give you a portion of the estate when her mother had left you very little."

His mouth stretched wide in what he clearly intended to be a smile.

"Yeah, I can guess who told you that. Weird how those two *girls* hung around together so much. Said it was over that guy on TV, but you got to wonder if they weren't hiding something. Besides, shows how much *she* knows. Melissa and I agreed on everything last week. Even went to a lawyer to start the process to get it finalized."

"Which lawyer?"

He hesitated a slice of a beat then smirked. "He can't tell you anything, because I'm his client."

"You could tell him to tell us everything."

"No thanks. Even with my heart breaking at the death of someone who was like a daughter to me, I have to be practical about these things. Figure out what Melissa's death does to our agreement and ... everything."

"Why bother with pursuing the enforceability of a deal never completed when you might inherit her mother's entire estate now?"

This slice of a beat of hesitation wasn't pleasant at all. "Inherit it all? Gee, hadn't even thought of that possibility."

"WHAT DID YOU think of what he said about Melissa and Fawn?" Jennifer asked as I drove toward KWMT.

"Trying to sling mud."

"I know. But even if that was his reason for saying it, maybe there could be something in it. Fawn was awfully upset. And if there was something romantic between them..."

Ah. "An additional motive for Thurston?"

"Well, if he thought they were drooling after him and instead found out they were, you know, *together*, that would be a big whack to his ego. You know how he is."

"Seems more like him to try to re-write reality by ignoring anything he doesn't like."

She slumped "That's true."

To assuage her dejection—and also because we shouldn't ignore any possible angles—I said, "But you're right. We shouldn't ignore it because the person who gave us information was trying to redirect away from himself."

Chapter Thirty

WE SLIPPED INTO the station with as little notice as possible, though Jennifer received a wide, adoring smile from Dale as she gestured for him to clear out of the top news aide's computer and return to his lowlier post.

Audrey acknowledged the change with a look, but without taking Jennifer to task.

Some of her calm leaked away, but that was natural as daily deadlines came closer.

At my desk, I checked for updates that would change my drafts and found none. Then went through email and messages. No breakthroughs there, either.

I'd checked top national and international news sites and opened the wire for a quick skim, when a stir around Audrey caught my attention.

"The Cottonwood County Sheriff's Department issued a statement confirming the victim is Melissa Oxley," she said.

"Did they give a reason for the delay?"

"Not directly. Implied it was only because of difficulty finding next of kin when they said they'd now found a second or third cousin or something like that in Pennsylvania—All-eek-pa?"

"Aliquippa. Near Pittsburgh," I said absently, as I considered whether there could have been another reason for the delay.

"Al-ah-*quip*-pa?" Audrey repeated the pronunciation carefully. "How do you know that?"

"I knew somebody from there. One of those places that changed drastically after the local steel mill closed down."

"Well, this whatever-cousin is a dentist in Aliquippa. What matters is now we have the name for the Five."

And I had real news for redrafting the lead story for the Five.

"It doesn't help with the investigation." Jennifer didn't mask her priorities. "We already knew who was dead."

"Don't despair," I told her. "Sometimes having the name opens floodgates of people who knew the victim, had a meaningful conversation with her, saw something suspicious."

"Oh, the investigation's wrapped up. It's suicide," Audrey said.

My surprise jumped out. "They said that?"

But what surprised me more—she hadn't said that first or law enforcement landed on suicide?

"The sheriff's department's scheduled a news conference for six-thirty. That's got to be what they're going to say."

"Which department?" Jennifer asked.

"It's here, but Horse Creek County put out the notice, which is weird. Anyway, when they say it's suicide, we'll have a new lead for the Ten."

Audrey hurried off toward the editing booth where Leona had hidden herself away.

Jennifer grumbled, "She's not going to be so perky when she realizes suicide means Thurston'll be back soon."

THOSE FLOODGATES I'D mentioned to Jennifer remained stubbornly closed as we tried to advance the story past having Melissa Oxley's name.

New Orleans could have used floodgates that staunch during Hurricane Katrina.

On the other hand, my copy rewrote itself with the new lead and condensed my original drafts into B matter at the end.

Having the official ID also meant we could use film of the neighbors from the first day.

Audrey's level of frazzle rose with the breaking news, but she still had it under control.

Communicating by message and raised eyebrows, Jennifer and I even coordinated to get outside to my SUV, unseen, and she initiated a video call.

"Just Mike, first," she said.

She briskly filled him in on the trip to O'Hara Hill to talk to Mrs. P, then added Diana to the call.

"I don't have much time," Mike started.

"Us, either," Jennifer said. "You're not the only one working."

"I didn't mean—"

I cut across them both. "Add Diana to the call."

Diana was waiting for a reporter named Iverton to interview a man who claimed he had irrefutable proof that Dewey actually did defeat Truman in the 1948 presidential election.

"That would make the *Chicago Tribune* happy," Mike said. It ran the famous erroneous headline, leading to the equally famous photo of Truman holding up an early edition, grinning broadly.

"It's kind of late, isn't it?" Jennifer asked.

Diana had the final word. "It is. And so is Iverton. In the meantime, what's up?"

I said, "The identity of the victim's been confirmed as Melissa Oxley by the two sheriff's departments."

"They found next of kin?"

"Not very next. A cousin of some kind in Aliquippa, Pennsylvania."

"Aliquippa!" Mike said in apparent delight.

"You know somebody from there, too?" Jennifer asked him.

"Know *of*, sure. Mike Ditka."

The silence from the others had me filling in, "Former NFL player and coach, including for the Chicago Bears." Mike Paycik had played for the Bears, though well after Ditka's connection to the team.

"And Tony Dorsett, Cowboys running back," he said.

"Dallas," I added under my breath.

"Hall of Famers for college and the NFL. I have so much to teach you when you get here in January," Mike said.

Jennifer rolled her eyes.

Perhaps to turn the subject, Diana said, "Do you think disillusionment with Thurston could have been enough to push Melissa to suicide?"

"You mean discovering that not only his feet, but also his head and everything in between were made of clay?" I asked. "On the one hand, I have a hard time imagining anyone being so dense they didn't see it from the start. On the other hand, Melissa Oxley lived a pretty sheltered life. Isolated."

"Sure would like to see any suicide note—if the sheriff happens to have one." I eyed Diana significantly.

She ignored the significance. "A note involving Thurston could explain the deputies going right to the station to talk to him. As for what else it can tell us, we can't know unless we can see it."

Before I could mention a couple ideas about how we could see the assumed suicide note, both of which involved Diana and her romance with the sheriff, Mike asked, "You're doubting the suicide explanation, Elizabeth?"

"I don't know."

Jennifer came out of her slump. "It could still be murder?"

"I don't know that, either. We can't close any doors. Which reminds me of your theory about Thurston's trips to Denver not being for haircuts, Jennifer. Though, wouldn't we have noticed if he went for haircuts and didn't come back with his hair cut?"

Diana spoke for all of us. "I never looked at him that closely. We could check shows, before and after his trips."

Jennifer groaned.

"Hey, I'll do it," Mike volunteered. "I could use a few laughs."

"I'll send them to you. That's easy."

"Iverton's here," Diana announced. "So tell me fast, what's next, Elizabeth?"

"The Five, the news conference, then…"

"Then?" she nudged.

"Thurston."

Chapter Thirty-One

"Making progress?"

In response to my mild question, Richard Alvaro eyed me with distrust from the desk in Sergeant Shelton's office, where he appeared to be writing reports. No sign of Shelton anywhere.

I didn't deserve the distrust. Truly, I didn't. I pretended his baleful expression arose solely from lack of progress and had nothing to do with me.

"It can't be that bad. You've got the ID, right?"

"You know we do. Leona announced it on the five o'clock news. Interesting to have something like that reported without hearing the same phrases from the news release. Kind of weird."

"That's how it's supposed to sound. Like news."

"I guess."

He was not volunteering more. So I poked a bit.

"How is it working with Horse Creek County?" And, because he'd given me that side-eye, I repaid him by adding, "Working *for* them, since they're running the death investigation."

He rolled his eyes, as if he knew exactly what I'd intended. "Not the easiest. Pushed off the grunt work on the ID on us. Said we had resources they didn't—hah! They didn't want to do the unglamorous scut work."

I eyed him. "You found the cousin in Aliquippa?"

That explained why the release of the ID from the Cottonwood County Sheriff's Department and the soon-to-happen news conference weren't combined.

"Yeah. Finally."

"If it makes you feel any better, Aliquippa produced at least two football Hall of Famers—Mike Ditka and Tony Dorsett." He actually did brighten slightly. "Call Mike and ask him about that. It'll make his day. Maybe his week."

He relented into a grin. "Wouldn't mind saying hello to him, see how he's doing."

"I'm sure he'd love to hear from you."

"Yeah? Are you two staying in touch?"

There was so much subtext, the question nearly sank under it.

"Of course. I keep in touch with a lot of former colleagues," I said lightly. "Do you have his number?"

He did.

"Who pushed off making the official ID on you guys? Deputy Itson, or someone else?"

Deputy Ferrante appeared in the doorway, glaring at me. He spoke to Richard. "News conference is about to start."

NEWS CONFERENCE TURNED out to be an overly formal designation for a gathering of two members of law enforcement and five members of the media. Walt and Jenks, officially representing KWMT-TV, a reporter named Cagen from the *Independence* who also carried a camera, a stringer who told everyone he was working for a Cody outlet, and me.

Horse Creek County Deputy Greg Itson stood in front of the sheriff's desk, with Deputy Richard Alvaro off to the side, apparently as a visual representation of Cottonwood County's tangential involvement in the case.

Also as a visual representation of how Cottonwood County's Sheriff's Department ranked the case. Not the sheriff, not Sergeant Shelton, but a well thought of, but decidedly young deputy.

The interesting thing was holding it in Sherman instead of Colter.

Maybe they thought the turnout would have been even lower for Colter, since Horse Creek County didn't have any media outlets and it would have been farther for the Cody stringer.

After the standard introductory material on who was talking, who represented which department, and who to contact for more information—which would not be forthcoming no matter whom you contacted, not for the kind of information I wanted—Deputy Greg Itson got to the meat of the matter.

He sprinkled in a few caveats about pending findings before saying, "…investigators from both our departments are satisfied that Ms. Oxley committed suicide."

No wonder being here to represent Cottonwood County had been passed down the totem pole to the young guy. None of the rest wanted to be associated with announcing anything until every possible caveat was dealt with.

I looked toward Richard.

He stared over the heads of everyone in the room, looking uncomfortable.

"In addition to a communication in which she declared her intentions, we found considerable evidence that supports this finding.

"Although the final confirmation will come from the state crime laboratory, preliminary findings by the Horse Creek County Sheriff's Department on fingerprints found at the scene and on the weapon used are those of Ms. Oxley."

Most jurisdictions would keep quiet until the state lab weighed in. Was it Horse Creek County's inexperience that had them releasing preliminary findings? Or something else?

Deputy Itson repeated that he had found her body at approximately eight-twenty Monday morning. "Preliminary findings set the time of death at one to five a.m."

He was also giving us *preliminary* findings on the medical findings? I thought Richard was going to keel over.

Watching for signs of teetering had to be why it took an extra beat for me to process that the time of death was largely useless, even if it held up through the final report.

One to five a.m. was home in bed asleep time. Thurston, Magnus, and Fawn each lived alone. No alibis, nobody eliminated.

Itson then went into more details on the identification, including background on Melissa Oxley—address, education, former employer. He even mentioned the death of her mother within the past year.

Could that have been a motive for suicide mentioned in the note?

Boy, I'd like to see that note.

He continued with a few pro forma thanks to the Cottonwood County department and state lab, along with a phrase or two of praise for his own department, which included the name of the sheriff in every one of them.

When Itson finished and asked for questions, Cagen—well-trained by Needham—immediately asked if they'd be releasing the note.

"No."

"What is the other evidence you mentioned?" Walt asked.

"We are not disclosing that at this time."

"What motives for suicide did the note—?"

He cut me off. "We are not disclosing that at this time."

"How do you know the gun at the scene is her gun?" I asked.

"Evidence."

As if I hadn't heard him, I continued, "Even if you found a holder that fit it, that doesn't mean the gun you found at the scene is the one that shot her. Even if it had been shot recently. Could have been swapped out. Plus, since Wyoming doesn't require registration, what proof do you have for the statement that it was Melissa Oxley's or—"

"There was a receipt. Recent. In her name. Like someone who'd been thinking about suicide went out to buy the means, then followed through in a couple days."

That slowed me, but didn't stop me.

Especially since everyone else in the room shifted, as if all hearing the siren whisper, *Supposition.*

"Owning a gun is not a surefire guarantee of attempting suicide or there would be a significantly lower population in the United States." Especially Wyoming.

His jaw had clamped tight.

"Did you confirm that the person who received that receipt was Melissa Oxley? Or possibly someone else, who—"

"Thank you all for coming."

Deputy Itson walked out on me mid-question.

Not the first.

✧ ✧ ✧ ✧

AS I LEFT the sheriff's office after not answering a few questions myself, since they came from the Cody stringer who apparently wanted me to report the story for him, I heard voices down the hall in the break room.

I took a couple steps to see Richard Alvaro pouring coffee for Greg Itson.

Alvaro said to the visiting deputy, "Don't let her get you talking. Best policy is to say nothing."

He once was such a nice guy. Until Wayne Shelton got ahold of him.

Chapter Thirty-Two

THE OUTSIDE OF Thurston Fine's house matched the wood and rock mold of the others in this neighborhood that grew up around the country club.

Like the Fyall House's neighborhood, it had once been the most desired in town. Time and new neighborhoods had passed it by. None of these houses had slid down as far as the worst around the Fyall House, but none had been renovated, either.

The inside of Thurston Fine's house belonged in Las Vegas … several decades ago. All it needed was orange shag carpet and avocado appliances.

All he needed was…

I surveyed his pullover sweater and creased pants after he'd opened the door to me.

… white shoes to be Pat Boone. Or was I confusing Boone with a cast member on the *Lawrence Welk Show*? My siblings and I had a babysitter who'd watch those reruns ad infinitum.

"What are you two doing here?"

"We need to talk, Thurston."

"I have no idea what you could want to talk to me about."

Want? Neither could I.

Need? Yeah, I was stuck. Unless…

However, he not only didn't close the door in our faces—my secret hope—he let the door swing wide open.

"You must have heard from the sheriff's department when they collected you at the station yesterday that the young woman from

Sherman found dead in Horse Creek County was named Melissa Oxley." I slathered on the sarcasm.

It didn't penetrate.

He walked down two steps from the entry, into a living area suited to a Rat Pack wannabe.

Somewhere I'd heard Dean Martin quoted as saying he once shook hands with Pat Boone and his whole right side sobered up. Count on Thurston for the unlikely mix.

He took a seat, arms spread across the top of the cushions. "So?"

"That's why they talked to you." I sat across from him. Not getting comfortable because I didn't intend to stay long.

Diana sank into a low chair shaped like an X that had the advantage of being off to the side.

Seeming to forget about her, he huffed, "That is a leap, even for you. I have reported any number of stories about bodies found—"

"Because you knew her personally."

"—in this area. Wyoming is unforgiving to those who are not prepared for its rigors."

So sayeth the great outdoorsman Thurston Fine.

"She wasn't hiking in the wilderness or in a national park or forest. She was in the back of a small car—her own—on the side of a road."

"Carbon monoxide," he said wisely.

"Not carbon monoxide. A bullet to the head."

He paled, but not being someone to abandon a bad position when stubbornly holding onto it could do more harm, he said, "Obviously suicide. She was depressed."

The way he said it, I was sure he hadn't heard about the news conference yet.

"How do you know she was depressed?"

"Because she committed suicide," he said triumphantly.

"That is begging the question."

He would say it didn't make him beg to ask the question. Because of the many people who weren't aware *begging the question* was a term that meant using the premise as proof of the premise—"smoking cigarettes can kill you because they're deadly"—no way was Thurston an exception.

I was right about that, but was still wrong in my prediction.

He asked, "What question?"

I ignored that and hit him with the same point with slightly different wording. "You said you thought she was depressed, so you must have known her."

Instead of sticking with his denial, he hedged. "I barely knew her to say hello."

"Is that what you told the sheriff's department?"

"Of course. I am a strong supporter of our men in law enforcement. And women."

Huffy *and* adding women as an obvious after-thought. Gee, why had I not looked forward to this conversation?

"Then they know you lied to them."

"How dare you—"

"Cut it out, Thurston. This is not about your affronted ego or self-image. This is about whether you go to prison for the rest of your life."

His mouth opened and closed, but no words came out. That was enough for me.

"Melissa Oxley ran your benighted fan club. She certainly knew you. More important from the point of view of the deputies from Horse Creek County investigating her death, they'll find out she took you to the airport regularly and picked you up regularly. Not only will there be human witnesses, there are security cameras. It's worse than pointless to deny that you *did* know her."

"Not well." It came out sulky, but at least he acknowledged knowing her.

"We'll deal with that qualifier later. When was the last time you saw her?"

"I don't remember."

"Another useless lie. Do you remember the last time you had a hair appointment in Denver?"

He looked slightly uncomfortable with that question. Usually he bragged about going to Denver.

"So what that she drove me to the airport," he scoffed. "That makes every car service, taxi, or rideshare the basis of a relationship in your world."

"Oh? Did you pay her?"

"No. She *wanted* to drive me to the airport."

"So, *not* like a car service, taxi, or rideshare."

"I used those examples to convey the casualness of the interaction."

"Casual, huh. The head of your fan club. When did that start?"

"She contacted me at the beginning of this year saying she'd established the group and asked my blessing for using my image and name at their meetings and such, which I gave. She wrote a recap twice a month of my stories she found most notable, as well as my off-air activities. If my schedule allowed, I would add a comment or two. Behind the scenes tidbits, she called them. She said they were popular as a reward for my fans."

He had no idea it had been only her and Fawn. No, wait, Fawn didn't join until May, so it was only Melissa.

"That sounds more devoted than casual."

"It is both," he said. "You won't understand that, not having fans yourself. But it is the fans' pleasure to do things for you, to serve you."

I thought of the people who'd been scammed by fake celebrities. The scammers taking advantage of exactly that dynamic. In this case, it was the real person—I could *not* think of him as a celebrity—taking advantage.

"What did she want in return?"

"Nothing." Testy Thurston reappeared. "I told you, it was her pleasure to do things for me. Little things, like give me the occasional ride to the airport."

"Regular rides to the airport. And how about going to Denver with you?"

"Going to… *With* me? Never. She drove me to the airport, she picked me up on my return, she most certainly did not go *with* me."

Thurston was fully capable of lying about this—or anything else. On the other hand, I thought his pitying attitude indicated he was quite confident he was right and I was the misinformed party.

Yet there was that gap in Melissa's photo-taking.

"Did you ever encounter her in Denver? Whether a planned meeting or bumping into each other by seeming accident. Or saw someone you thought resembled her?"

"I told you—"

"Answer the question."

"No. Why on earth would I?"

"It wouldn't be unusual for two people in a relationship to go away together for a few days."

"A relationship? *Relationship?* We were not in a relationship."

"Other people said you were." Apparently including Melissa Oxley. Or did she? We only had Fawn's word for it. In the face of Thurston's outraged denial, even with him being a serial denier when it came to anything to do with the dead woman, we needed a second source.

"That's ridiculous."

"Did she ever stay overnight here? Did you ever stay overnight at her house?"

"How dare you?"

"Oh, for heaven's sake, Thurston, drop the outraged Victorian virgin act. Did she? Did you?"

"Absolutely not."

He was lying.

Stupidity? Or guilt?

I expelled a breath through my teeth, then slowly pulled in replacement oxygen before leaning forward.

"Thurston, you know a group of us have solved a few murders lately. I'm telling you now that we're looking into Melissa Oxley's death and—"

"It's suicide."

"—we'll do our best to find the truth. We won't protect you. You—"

"You think you're so smart. You think you're better—"

"No. But I think we have a chance of figuring this out, based on our track record. And I do think you're foolish to lie. You would be well-advised to go to law enforcement and tell them the whole truth right now."

Diana rose before I did.

He looked toward her, but did not meet her gaze.

We did not wait for him to escort us to the door.

I DIDN'T TURN on my SUV right away.

Staring straight ahead, I said, "I honestly don't know if, in the darkest reaches of my soul, I hope Thurston's guilty to get rid of him. What kind of person would do that?"

"Not the kind of person you are," Diana said staunchly.

"You thought I might be. That's why you bugged me about not investigating."

"I bugged you about it because you were wasting time by fooling yourself."

"*Tom* thinks I might be. That's why he pushed me into this when I would have sat on the sidelines."

"Bull. All around. You wouldn't have sat on the sidelines and he didn't think you would."

"That's why he came to my house Monday night and *said*—"

"What he says, what you say—You're both idiots. And so is Mike Paycik. All of you. Twisted into knots."

"But Tom—"

"Forget Tom. Forget Mike. Forget yourself. Be quiet and let your brain—the part of your brain that's so good at this—work without all this chatter. Close your eyes."

"Diana—"

"Do it. Close your eyes. Pretend you're playing Free Cell. Game after game after game of Free Cell. Nothing else is in your mind. No thoughts. Not feelings. Only Free Cell. You're moving the cards, creating order…"

It was weird, but I felt everything slow and calm around me. Like someone turned off a blender I was inside and the contents—including me—gradually settled to stillness.

"Now," Diana's voice said from outside the now-silent blender, "did Melissa Oxley commit suicide?"

"No." I said it again, stronger, "No. And it's not because I want to get rid of Thurston by having him convicted of murder."

I opened my eyes.

"But I'm not sure my *feeling* certain gets us any farther."

"Sure it does," Diana said. "We stop wasting time wondering."

Chapter Thirty-Three

THE PHONE RANG in the newsroom while Jennifer and I sat watching Leona introduce the final story in the A block.

"Thurston," Jennifer announced.

"Took him longer than I thought," I said. The report of the news conference stating that Melissa committed suicide had been the lead item. He'd waited through nine more stories before calling.

"Probably didn't understand it the first time. Had to replay it to get the big words. Should I answer?"

"No. The folks in the studio—" Leona and Jerry in the studio, plus Audrey and the others in the control room. "—should be in on the fun, too. Don't want to keep it to ourselves."

Jennifer muted the phone and we watched the rest of the Ten in peace.

As soon as Audrey and the others appeared, I nodded to her. She unmuted the phone and it immediately rang.

Jennifer looked at it as if she needed to find out who was calling.

"Thurston," she announced again.

Several people swore. Barry scuttled out the front exit, a couple more people disappeared toward the back, leaving Jennifer, Audrey, Leona, Jerry, and me.

Jennifer gestured that she was putting the call on speakerphone, then answered, "KWMT-TV."

"It's about time. What have you idiots been doing? I've been calling and calling."

"We're sorry you've had to wait, sir. But we've been busy with the newscast. How may I direct your call?"

"How may you direct—? Do you know who this is? I will have your job—"

"Who's calling, please?"

"Who's calling? Who's *calling?* This is Thurston Fine, you idiot."

"Oh. How may I direct your call, Mr. Fine?"

"Get me the person in charge—the person who thinks they're in charge and if nobody else is there, I'll talk to Leona."

Audrey reached for the phone. Jennifer swatted her hand away.

"Everyone else has left, Mr. Fine. I can send you to voicemail or—"

"*Voicemail?* I demand to speak to someone now. Give me Leona's personal phone number."

"I'm sorry, sir, we're not allowed to give out personal phone numbers."

"This is *Thurston Fine!*"

"Yes, sir. I heard that before. I have very good hearing and there is no need to shout."

From the sound of his breathing, he might be hyperventilating.

Good thing, because even though his audience around Jennifer's desk had hands over their mouths, that didn't muffle all the amusement.

Jennifer drew in a deep breath to steady her voice. "I can take a message if you like, sir."

"You tell Leona to tell the others that I will be back as soon as I straighten out the ownership. Now that those cretins in the sheriff's department have finally realized it was suicide, as I told them all along, they can't make any more excuses about—"

"Cretins is really rude," Jennifer said.

"Cretins, morons. Those deputies deserve that and more."

Thurston had to be part spider. Considering how often he put his foot in his mouth, then chomped down, he needed a spider's ability to regrow legs—and feet—or he'd have run out a long time ago.

Jennifer didn't relent. "Cretin is from a medical syndrome. Moron is also rude. You shouldn't disparage people who can't help it."

It did not penetrate Thurston's self-absorption. "I've always supported law enforcement—"

When it suited him.

"—but they must be held accountable. If this county still had a strong county attorney—"

A low-voiced groan rose at the reference to one of Thurston's departed pals.

"—there wouldn't be those people telling me not to leave the county. As if I *would* leave. I have newscasts to anchor. The mess you people have made of it left to your own devices, totally disregarding the needs of the important people in this community by leaving out stories—"

"Our own devices? What about our news director?"

"Les?" His voice skidded up, well out of mellifluous Anchor Voice range. "*He* ran today's newscasts?"

"No. But I still ask, what about him?"

"If it weren't for this ridiculous lawyer having the ear of the ownership, I'd be back on-air now. They can't keep me off forever because some stupid woman killed herself."

He clicked off the phone.

"IT WAS FUN while it lasted," Audrey said. "Now that it's been declared a suicide, Thurston's going to get back on-air, and that's that."

She started to turn away, but Leona grasped her arm. "Not so fast. If I'm any good at reading expressions—and I am—Elizabeth Margaret Danniher is not satisfied it *was* suicide."

Audrey looked over her shoulder at me. "You're not?"

"Don't ask me," I said rather testily, "Leona's the one claiming mind-reading ability."

She scoffed with *huh*.

"Why?" Audrey asked.

Jennifer interrupted. "If it's not suicide, that could still mean Thurston's a murderer." A thought that clearly made her day.

Jerry masked a splutter of laughter with fake sneezes—more original than coughing.

"What about an accident?" Audrey asked with an air of someone who dared not dream too much.

"Nah," Jennifer said. "Why would she get in the back seat of her own car by herself and hold a gun to her head? Who does that? But she would have to do that to set up an accident."

Slowly, I turned to her. "That is an excellent question, Jennifer. Why would Melissa Oxley get in the back seat of her own car by herself and hold a gun to her head?"

"Well, I'd say she wouldn't, because I say she was murdered," Jennifer said.

"But the fingerprints—they said they were consistent with hers," Audrey said.

Jennifer dismissed that with, "Preliminary. From Horse Creek County. Wait for the state lab to say."

"How do you know that?" I asked her.

"I live streamed the news conference."

"Does the sheriff's department know?"

"The microphone was on the lectern, labeled Live Stream."

In other words, no, they didn't.

"Did you record it?" I asked.

"Of course. I'll send you a copy. Diana and Mike, too."

"And me," Audrey said.

"Me, too." We all looked at Leona. "What? I read mysteries, too. Besides, if it *was* her gun, her fingerprints *should* be on it. That doesn't prove anything."

"Good point, Leona."

THE NIGHT BELONGED to Shadow.

I smiled at that notion as we walked silently through my neighborhood.

A note on the kitchen counter told me Tom and Tamantha had walked my dog earlier in the day, so we were not out for his needed exercise.

We were walking because of my restlessness.

Shadow hadn't objected to accompanying me on a one a.m. ramble.

The dogs we'd had when I was growing up had been pals with all us kids, playing, chasing, wrestling, running, gamboling.

Shadow is not a gamboler.

Nor did he seem to crave games or excessive exercise. He'd been turned out by a hard-hearted person who was supposed to be his mainstay. I knew how that felt. Though I never went hungry or slept without shelter. However, for a time, while I adjusted to my new reality, my grooming left something to be desired, too.

At this stage in our relationship, I'd say Shadow was a companion. An equal.

He certainly qualified as neighborhood watch.

He picked up every sound, every sight, every scent. He was acutely aware of everything around us. And I had the notion it was beyond those things in this moment, but from earlier in the day, maybe longer ago. He didn't take a snapshot of the moment, but rendered a 3D sensory recreation.

Me? I walked beside him.

I had questions—too many of them—in my mind. I let them tumble over each other, in and out of focus, like clothes appearing and disappearing in a dryer. Not trying to give them order or importance, just watching them roll, mix, separate.

But deeper than the mental dryer fluffing up my questions, I felt something else.

Tranquility.

Not something I had ever sought or craved, not something I ever felt I'd be good at.

Yet, I did achieve a measure of something very like tranquility when driven to these late-night walks with Shadow.

Even better, I think he felt the same.

DAY FOUR

THURSDAY

Chapter Thirty-Four

"HEAR YOU HAVE interesting news out there."

Matt Lester's voice on the phone was welcomed, even if it was still morning. At least he didn't call as early as Dell.

Also in his favor, he'd known me longer—since journalism grad school—and he was more tactful.

Also, I'd had coffee.

"You, too, angling for news? This isn't anything that'll interest newspaper readers in Philly."

"You never know. Who else?"

"Dell—Wardell Yardley."

"Ah. So you've had your fill of dishing?"

"More like there's nothing to dish."

"At least you should be happy that Thurston Fine's off the air."

"The newscasts are so much better, Matt. You wouldn't believe it. Not sure it's all Thurston, either." I told him about the conversation— brief as it was—with Les Haeburn.

"Obviously not part of the solution. Is he part of the problem?"

"Definitely. What surprises me is he started off with a string of awards, moved around fast, stepping up in job, or market, or both. Then he came here and *pffft.*"

"Technical term, huh?"

"Concise and evocative. You just wish you could use it in print."

"Fair. So, how and why did he go *pffft?*"

"I fear I'd have to dig into his psyche for why—and I do mean fear. As for how, for starters he hired Thurston Fine and gave him free rein. Actually, that covers starters and finishers."

"Why hire Thurston? And why give him free rein?"

"Delusions. He saw Thurston's looks, heard his voice, and thought he was going somewhere, once he'd hitched his wagon to that supposed star, he was stuck. And management ... well, with this the worst market in the country, Val Heatherton and Craig Morningside clearly don't have much in the way of expectations."

"Who?"

"Owner and her son-in-law, the general manager, who never shows up at the station. I haven't met either one."

"They were smart enough to sign you to a new contract."

"I suspect Mel did some sort of Mel magic to persuade them." Mel Welch was a Chicago lawyer who qualified as both a distant relative and friend of the family. When my divorce also cost me my agent, Mel stepped in. "Probably knew somebody who knew somebody they wanted to keep happy."

"Uh-huh. Blackmail as a negotiating strategy with TV news ownership, who don't appreciate their workers."

"Newspapers are no better. When was the last time you saw a newspaper listed among the best places to work?"

"Never." He sighed deeply. "It gets discouraging, the view that anyone can do our job by posting a guess online. Not letting facts interfere with their opinions. *Crowd-sourcing?* More like mob mentality."

"Yeah. It's not pretty when there's only one source pushing out what a dictator wants, whether that's political or ownership."

"I'm betting part of your happiness in Wyoming is from *not* having contact with the owners."

"You're probably right. To be honest, it might contribute to their happiness, too. A friend said Val Heatherton is rich enough to not attend charity events because she writes a check that overcomes the multiplier effect of attendance. In other words, she uses her money to avoid people. Although... Anyway, this ownership and management appear content to let KWMT bump along at the bottom."

"That's logical and boring. What I want to know is, *although* what? You dangled that out there."

"Oh. That. Although Haeburn spends a good amount of time schmoozing with Val Heatherton. Probably the son-in-law, too."

Matt laughed. "Well, that's normal—a manager sucking up to higher management."

"I suppose I should count my blessings—no ownership around, no general manager around, no news director around."

"And no Thurston Fine around. Unless you clear him, of course."

"It's not like I'd hide evidence that he wasn't guilty or somebody else was to keep him off the air."

"Tempting as that might be," Matt elaborated.

"Overcoming temptation is the signature of maturity."

He laughed. So did I.

MRS. P HAD left me a voicemail with the contact information for Danielle Pruiting, Melissa Oxley's last tutor.

IN THE STRENGTHENING morning sun, Faye Nafus was pulling out plants from a bed beside the front steps when I entered her yard.

"Hi. Those are healthy looking. Lucky they weren't caught by frost yet, huh?"

She straightened slowly, looking directly at me. "They are thistles. A weed. I know who you are."

"E.M. Danniher with KWMT-TV. I do the 'Helping Out!' segment."

If she thought I was here about consumer affairs, her demeanor might soften enough to return my smile.

It didn't.

"You're sure not a gardener. You do that piece on the TV when people get cheated, though sometimes it's more like they're inviting people to cheat them, the stupid things they do."

I wished I'd brought Diana with. Better yet, I wished I'd left this to Diana. With her long-time roots in the area, she often had better success than I did with the core of Cottonwood County.

Or maybe it wasn't her roots.

I dropped the interested gardener approach and went with my strength.

"I understand Melissa Oxley was close to her mother when she was growing up."

"Hmm."

"Some of Melissa's friends from Cody said that when she was living there, she'd still come home here to see her mom most week-ends."

"Friends," she repeated, calling into doubt their right to that title.

I waited a beat, but that didn't break through her reserve.

I kept casting. If more recent history didn't work, try longer ago.

"You must have known Melissa well when she was a little girl, since she didn't go to school." She didn't respond, so I added, "I understand she was homeschooled, by tutors."

"Those *tutors*. That's what they *called* them. A whole line of them."

Who knew the tutors would be the key to unlocking her?

"The few normal ones among them, Barbara kept at arm's length. The rest of them she should have kept a lot farther away from Melissa." She shook her head. "What that girl got was a parade of crazies. It was no wonder she held onto her mother so tight. And I'm not sure that was an accident on Barbara's part.

"She and Dodd closed ranks after, uh, well, after he made a lot of money."

In the Shangri-La mine scam. Or, at the very least, adjacent to it.

Did Faye Nafus know which it was?

But I was not about to interrupt this stream now that it was finally flowing.

"Drew in Melissa, too, and closed out most everybody else. After Dodd died, it was even worse. You can say all Melissa had was her mother, but that's true the other way around, too. And her mother was the one hiring those tutors."

Her mouth shifted into a slight, grim smile.

"Until Emmaline Parens slipped one in at the end. Danielle Pruiting is a nice girl. If it hadn't been for her, I wondered if Melissa would go off to college at all. But, between Danielle and the *family tradition*, Melissa did get away for college. Gave her a chance to be a person herself."

"Family tradition?"

That question felt justified. First, repeating something the other person said often doesn't feel like an interruption to them. It also emphasized her position as the knower of things and mine as not the knower of things. Besides, I was curious.

"The first Mrs. Fyall, back in the 1800s insisted each of the girls go back East for a period of time. At first it was more of a finishing school. About a hundred years ago, it shifted to them going to college. Small school in New England.

"No matter how small it was, it had to open up that girl's world a whole lot because it didn't include Barbara from sunup to sundown. Melissa came home a fair amount the first year, but by her second, she was more on her own."

Faye gusted a sigh.

"Just shows how smart I am, because I thought that was all to the good. Only that was when Barbara started casting around for more company herself. First, Magnus comes around with that wobbly old cousin of Barbara's, then he comes around on his own. Then that old fool ups and dies and there's Barbara, all ripe and plump on the vine.

"*Plop*, she drops right into his hands and they're married before anybody can say boo."

"That must have been a jolt for Melissa," I slid in smoothly.

"Melissa? A jolt? Not so you'd notice. She said she was happy her mother was happy. And I do believe it was the truth. She finished school, came back home a bit, then moved to Cody. But, like you said, came back to visit regular. No sign she or her mother saw anything but good in Magnus Boesch, either. Got along fine.

"That's why, when Barbara died and the will came out—oh, my. That was something. Magnus got more than a few surprises, that's for sure. Never expected Melissa to stand up to him the way she did. Don't know if Barbara knew Melissa would and that's why she left it to the will to do what she should have done herself or if Barbara didn't know, but didn't want to face the consequences of what she'd done in marrying Magnus Boesch.

"The one thing Melissa said to me was her mother should have dealt with it when she still had a chance to change the man. Only time I ever heard her criticize her mother. And over that, of all things. Like any man ever changes." She tipped her head in contemplation. "Or grows up, for that matter. Still, they're useful for some things.

"A regular boyfriend would have smoothed out a lot of things for her. Wouldn't have gotten so wound up about that fellow on the news for starters. And whatever's going on with the big, tall girl."

"She's another fan of Thurston Fine—the man on TV news," I said.

"I suppose she'd have to be, wouldn't she. Walk in Melissa's house and you're about hit over the head about the fellow. Pictures all over, life-size cutout, running the TV night and day with him on it."

It certainly must have hit the deputies over the head when they walked into Melissa's house. No wonder they went right to Thurston.

"Told the girl with the TV camera how Melissa would tape every news show and memorize his parts about word for word. Yeah. that big, tall girl would certainly have to be a fan, too, to spend any time in that house or spend any time with Melissa. She talked about that fellow all the time. Him or her family. That was it.

"She wasn't always like that. Guess she'd dated when she was in college. But the one she brought home to visit for a week only lasted a weekend. Don't know if it was Barbara driving him off or him fleeing. If Melissa dated any in Cody, she never brought them here."

I thought we'd reached a stage where I could venture a tangential shift, but carefully.

"Since she moved back after Barbara's death did she have other visitors to the house? Or people she socialized with?"

"She went back to Cody pretty regular at first, but that died out. She told me she didn't have time—she was too busy with more important things. Suspect she meant that fellow from the news."

She shook her head again.

"I said she didn't have a regular boyfriend, but there were men by now and then. Not many around a second time. Except one. Saw them together two—no, three times. At the house. And then, of course, he came back with the others. After."

"Others? After?"

"After she died, of course. He came back with the other law enforcement fellas. One of those from Horse Creek County. He was the one talking most with Wayne Shelton. In fact, he seemed to be giving Wayne orders, even though he was a lot younger."

Deputy Greg Itson.

"And you saw him at Melissa's house before she died? How often? When?"

"Good heavens, I don't know. Not like I kept notes or anything. Two, three times, I suppose, over the past couple months.

"But nothing like as often as that tall girl—Dawn?"

"Fawn."

"Huh. Okay. Fawn—who's been coming around since spring. Or that TV guy, with his overnight stays."

Chapter Thirty-Five

I COULDN'T TELL if my heart jerking around in my chest was from pleasure at being right that he'd lied, amazement that he truly was that stupid, horror that he might be a murderer, or a bit of vicarious thrill for Jennifer.

I did my best to keep all of that out of my voice.

"Thurston Fine."

"Yeah, him." She shook her head. "And for all her smart words about where her mother went wrong, there she was, practically rolling out the red carpet for the man, the way Barbara did for Magnus early on."

"He was here a lot?"

"Not a lot. Saw him going in or coming out two, three times. Maybe that many again when I spotted that red Buick of his parked around the corner. Not far, because apparently he didn't want to walk much. Like nobody'd recognize it.

"Saw him one time, scurrying up the walk like he didn't want to be seen, and there she's standing, with the door wide open to him, smiling like he was Prince Charming in the flesh.

"That's not all. She had pictures of that guy on her phone, more than you can imagine. Not exciting pictures, either. Just him walking, standing, staring, blowing his nose for Pete's sake. I asked her, didn't she at least have nudes of him or shots of him wearing ladies' underwear?

"See, you think it's funny. She didn't see the joke. Got huffy about how their relationship was beautiful and everlasting." She streamed out a breath. "Girl needed a sexual outlet and she wasn't getting much of one with that piece of soft rope, that's for sure."

I cleared my throat. "You mentioned her friend, Fawn Raglettley?"

"Friend? I guess. Melissa bossed her around a lot. Got real heated not long ago. Was wishing I hadn't turned off the outside water, thinking I could have turned the hose on them to stop their squabbling. But that tall one turned and walked away. Melissa yelling after her about she didn't deserve to be in his presence—suppose that was about the TV guy. Didn't seem smart to keep after her when she was so much bigger and stronger, but Melissa had things her own way so much from a young age she didn't ever get that things could go any other way.

"Real shame, too. She was a real nice little girl. Wasn't awful when she got older, either. Someone else, someone who wasn't nice at the core, would have been a terror. As it was, she did drive away a lot of people."

It was insightful and sad.

"But if she killed herself over that man—" Tears came into Faye's eyes, possibly surprising her as much as they did me. "—all I have to say is shame on her. Shame on her for wasting her life over him or anyone else. It was *her* life and she should have lived it."

I'D TOUCHED BASE with Audrey, who handled the morning meeting like a pro. She was doing so well, I didn't want to cramp her style in the newsroom, so I sat in my SUV to wait for a call with the others.

Leona tapped on the passenger door window, then got in at my welcoming wave.

She gusted out a sigh as she sat. "A couple more days of this and I'll need the makeup shoveled on to be ready for air. So, what are you doing staring into space, Elizabeth? Solving all the major mysteries of the universe?"

"Not even the small ones right in front of us." She did look tired. Remembering something Diana had said, I invited, "Tell me about Artie, Leona."

"Artie… Ah, Artie. Quite the throwback. Got his start in radio. I swear he was on hand when they flipped the switch on the first TV news broadcast. Worked all over, covered presidents and popes and wars. But he'd been raised here and he circled back. Said it was for his winding down years—then he kicked ass and took names across the county for decades."

She looked less tired now. And softer.

"He died at his desk and with his boots on. In fact, with his boots on his desk. I still miss the old bastard."

"Quite a change to go from someone like that to Les Haeburn."

"Would have been hard for anybody to come in after Artie. Those weren't shoes that could be filled. He had a knack for spotting and developing talent. He also had cronies at every top J-School in this country and several others. That gave us a steady source of right out of school, green but talented kids who worked here a while to get their first experience, then moved on. Benefited them, benefited us. Balanced the crew of old-timers who weren't—aren't—ever going anywhere else, like me."

"Diana mentioned some people quit after Les came in. The green but talented kids?"

"Yup. And we never got a resupply. That died with Artie. But at the start, everybody thought Les would follow the pattern. He was touted as the fresh, young genius. A rising star who'd quickly outgrow us, but we'd be better off for his having graced us with his leadership. Yeah, right."

She sounded downright snarky.

"I heard Artie kept the ownership at a distance and ran the show. How was it with Les when he started? Surely, he didn't have the same kind of sway as Artie."

She looked off to the right side, away from me. "No, he didn't have the same kind of sway." No snark, but something else edged her tone. Then she continued and it was gone. "But the owners let him run the show, including bringing in Thurston. Kept on letting him, even as pretty much everything at KWMT slid farther and farther from being a legitimate news station. In fact, the first exception that comes to mind is bringing you in. That came down from on high. Thurston was beside himself, but Les didn't—couldn't—stop it from happening. That was fun to watch." She grinned at me. "It's been even more fun to watch since you got here. Well, better get inside. See what torture's in store for me today."

✧ ✧ ✧ ✧

"WHY ARE YOU frowning?"

That was Mike's greeting when we were the first two on the scheduled video call. Any minute now, Diana should be here in person and Jennifer by phone from home.

"Something I was talking to my pal from Philly about is nagging at me."

"What were you talking about?"

"Journalism, money, management styles, and how there was no pressure from ownership to improve KWMT."

"Yeah," he said, like he wondered what my point was.

"You might think it's normal, but it's weird. Something you're going to learn fast enough in Chicago, if you haven't already, is most ownership wants to increase viewership so they can raise ad prices to make more money, all without increasing expenses like equipment and salaries. Considering KWMT's viewership, ads must be bargain basement prices."

"No, they're not," he said. "Val Heatherton rakes in money from the ads."

"You're kidding. How did you never mention this to me?"

"Everybody knows. Val—"

"*I* didn't."

"—Heatherton wouldn't hold onto the station if it weren't a money-maker. She—Oh, Jennifer's signing on. Talk to Linda Caswell, Elizabeth. She can fill you in."

I had a thought about someone else who could fill me in—when I had time to call Mel in Chicago.

As Mike finished his sentence, Diana climbed into the passenger seat of my SUV.

"Filling in? Is Elizabeth filling you in on our conversation with Thurston last night?"

"She hasn't, but she better now," he said. "In half a second when Jen—Jennifer, hey there."

"Good. You're all here. I don't have any time to waste," she said. "Who's first?"

My hand went up. "I had quite the interesting conversation with Melissa's neighbor. And it's given us a lot to pursue. But first, we'll go over what Thurston said last night…"

I wrapped up that recap with, "The idiot, telling the sheriff's department—departments, plural—that he barely knew Melissa. They must have more than enough evidence of their connection. Melissa was obsessed. She wasn't going to be subtle about it."

"Lying was his best option, because he's guilty—"

"Wait, Jennifer. You haven't heard what Melissa's neighbor said. We have other people to talk to."

After warming up with the information about Melissa's last tutor, I hit the highlights from Faye Nafus—Melissa's fight with Fawn, previous encounters with Deputy Itson, and overnights from Thurston.

"…But Itson's the most suspicious one since he left out knowing Melissa."

"To us," Diana said. "We don't know if he told his sheriff or Shelton or anyone else."

Against my wishes, a single word came out. "True."

"Plus, it could be a matter of him knowing her about as well as I know him—a nodding acquaintance. It's common around here."

"True." I didn't like the taste of it any better the second time. "But he went to her house."

"Could have been some official something we don't know about. Or fund-raising for a charity. Or a church connection. Or dropping off something involving … I don't know, his wife? With not a lot of people living around here—"

"I know, I know. It's common." She was right. In addition to echoing what Needham had said. "You're a real buzz kill."

"I'm not saying we don't pursue it. Just to put it in perspective."

I narrowed my eyes at her and declared, "You've got something else."

"Just what I told you I'd ask around about. Magnus Boesch. First, he thought he'd inherit a lot more than he did from Barbara."

"Which would be a great motive if Barbara died under suspicious circumstances, but what about Melissa?" Mike demanded.

"He is being more circumspect than he was, perhaps having learned his lesson about counting his chickens before the will is read, but, yes, he is giving off a sunny-days-ahead vibe."

"Vibe," Mike repeated disparagingly. "Now, if he'd quit his job, bought a Ferrari…"

I agreed. "And you already gave Jennifer and me the gist of this before we went to his place."

Diana smiled at both of us. "He hasn't quit his job and no Ferrari on order. But, he did give notice Monday afternoon that he would not be renewing his apartment lease next month. He told his landlord he would be moving back *home*."

"*Nice*, Diana."

"Thank you. And now, I think it's Jennifer's turn, before she pops."

Chapter Thirty-Six

"**NOT POPPING,**" **SHE** said with dignity, "but I want to get back to what I was doing. So far, I've found two photos from that gap between when Melissa dropped Thurston off at the airport and when she picked him up. Here's the first one."

Thurston walking out of a hotel door, one hand raised in an apparent attempt to hold his hair in place against the wind.

"Got the hotel name," Jennifer said. "I could do a little, uh, snooping. Check phone records, credit cards—"

"Is snooping another word for hacking?" Diana asked.

"Not exactly."

"You're not doing it, not even inexactly," I said. "We'll pursue options that won't potentially get you kicked out of that special program before you start."

She sighed in mature acknowledgment of that wisdom. Also, possibly, at the passing of the wilder days of her youth.

"Anyway, here's the other one."

A man's pantleg, halfway down from the knee to the cuff, at an angle that indicated movement, extended past a suitcase that matched the ones we'd seen in Thurston's airport photos.

"Could be Thurston, but—"

"It's got to be. Matches what he was wearing leaving the hotel."

I checked the two photos. "Doesn't eliminate him," I conceded, "but this one's too blurry to be sure and—"

"Remember, she didn't take photos of anything but him. Besides, what's most interesting is the sign beside the door. And that's not blurry."

She was right. A small, polished plaque sharply in focus—because that's what Melissa meant to capture or by accident?—clearly read Chloe Vogt.

"Who is Chloe Vogt?"

"That might be what's most interesting. I'm having a hard time finding out."

She sounded more excited than distressed.

"No business name associated with the name. Personal address and phone number well hidden—although I did find her in a very nice part of town from tax records. But, still, no clue what she does. No professional license like a psychiatrist or therapist would have. No listing on a medical board or with a lawyer group. Definitely not a hair stylist. This person is way beyond discreet.

"I had to go way, way back in Internet history to find any other names associated with Chloe Vogt at all—well, except for people who were clearly other Chloe Vogts because they were all over publicly or not in Denver or both. So, these are the other names I found. I sent all you guys the list."

The fourth name was the key.

✧   ✧   ✧   ✧

FIRST, IT RATTLED in my head, echoing with a memory I couldn't pin down.

We searched the name and "Chloe Vogt." Nothing came up. I suggested we add "news." Still nothing. Jennifer asked if she should do her deeper dive into the historical Internet.

"Not yet. Let's try another search."

We added TV, took out news, and added scandal. That hit paydirt.

The name belonged to a former anchor in Alabama who first had a public dispute with his young girlfriend at a restaurant that included dumping salsa on her head, capped by being charged with DUI.

Another search, not using quote marks around his name, brought up someone with the same name, now with a middle name inserted, reporting in another part of the country.

Jennifer found photos that confirmed it was the same man, although his look had changed significantly.

With more digging, she found another of the names on the connected-to-Chloe Vogt list who had moved across the country after reinventing himself visually, although with no sign of the scandalous impetus of the first example.

With those hints, I found two references from more than a decade ago mentioning only "Chloe" on closed forums for discussion among TV news professionals.

"They're awfully vague." Jennifer didn't approve.

"They are being cautious and possibly self-protective." Reading between the lines, I suspected Chloe cleaned up scandals and other messes at that time.

"But why would Thurston go to her?" She sat up. "Unless, he was planning to kill Melissa and wanted to get his ducks in a row and—"

"Let's not jump ahead of ourselves. Evidence leads to theories. Let's concentrate on evidence. I'll see what I can find out with methods that do not involve the Internet."

Jennifer looked doubtful. She might have pursued a protest, but Mike sighed gustily enough to grab our attention.

"I'm feeling a little nostalgic after going through those KWMT newscasts Jennifer sent. That's the first of two things I have to tell you."

"That was fast. Plenty of laughs?" I asked.

"Not as many as I'd hoped for, but I did sleep well after. I'd fast-forward and didn't listen to him, so not as bad as watching him live. Anyway, most of the time he's definitely had his hair cut between the before-Denver and after-Denver dates. The weird thing is, I'd swear something else changed recently, but I can't put my finger on it. Clothes or… something. Maybe if you guys watch—"

"No," came a three-way chorus.

"Fine, but it does have me thinking about when will I ever get to work with someone like Thurston again?"

"When you're old and wrinkled and all your teeth fall out and you have to take whatever job you can get," Jennifer said, apparently cheered by that prospect.

"Maybe. But that's a long way off. In the meantime, I won't be on a newscast where the anchor calls the Baltimore Orioles the Oreos— multiple times. I told him during the break. But when we came back, he did it again, because he never listens to anyone. I broke in with unscripted cross talk to say it right on-air. Thought he'd have a stroke."

That part of the memory he liked.

Knowing it would annoy Mike, I said, "Oreos. I find that sweet."

"Oh, yeah? You didn't think it was so sweet when he had damage from a storm happening east of downtown Chicago and didn't listen when you told him his error put the event in Lake Michigan. Or," he continued, "how about when he said farmers are getting *wind* of a new kind of bean and he'd be right back with that *breaking* story?"

"He didn't."

"He did."

Diana confirmed, "He did. And never got it, even when Bruce tried—oh, so gently—to explain it. I can't decide if it's better or worse that he never recognizes his gaffes."

"Worse," I said. "Never learns, never improves. What's the second thing you have to tell us, Mike?"

"Yeah, hurry up. I want to get back to the photos," Jennifer said.

"The only other thing to tell you is I happen to have a transcript of the suicide recording found in Melissa Oxley's car."

"*What?* How—? No, I don't care how." It had to have been through his Aunt Gee. Though how he persuaded her to share it when she'd become a fan of Sheriff Russ Conrad, no longer revealing as much to us because she believed the Cottonwood County Sheriff's Department could and would thoroughly investigate—

Unless it was Horse Creek County's status as lead on the case that made the difference.

"I don't care how," I repeated. "How fast can you get it to us?"

"I've already sent it to Jennifer."

"Transcript you said, Mike?" Diana asked.

"Yeah. She'd recorded a message to Thurston. It cut off before she, you know. Never sent, but it was there on her phone."

"Got it," Jennifer announced. "Stashing a copy where it won't be found by any nosy officials, and now… yup, copies sent to Elizabeth and Diana."

With the replica of Melissa's note on our screens, silence settled in until Mike said, "Aren't you done yet?"

"Shh."

After another minute, he said, "Elizabeth, you're scowling at that like you want it to burst into flames."

"Wouldn't do any good. It's a copy."

His eyebrows hiked. "Why would you want to destroy it?"

"Because it totally misled people into thinking Melissa Oxley committed suicide."

Chapter Thirty-Seven

Jennifer hooted in triumph. "I knew it. *Not* suicide. He— Somebody killed her."

"Why do you think that, Elizabeth?" Mike asked.

"There's hope in this note. I did a story on a guy who studied the language of suicide notes, looking to head off attempts. The most frequent common denominator is the loss of hope. But Melissa hasn't lost hope. She's writing about the future.

"Another commonality in suicide notes are practical matters. Reminding the people they're addressing to pick up the necessary pieces of the life the person committing suicide is putting down. Things like get the furnace checked or don't forget to rotate the tires or you're due for a dental appointment. Ordinary, mundane, heart-breaking reminders.

"There's none of that in this, either. Read it again."

At the end, a frown tucked between Diana's brows.

"You see it, too," I said.

"What?" Jennifer demanded. "I mean, I see what you're saying about not having practical things in it. And she is talking about the future, because she's telling Thurston all the ways he needs to change."

Diana gave a soft *huh.*

"That's exactly it, Jennifer," I said. "She's not saying you did this and this and this to me, so I'm killing myself. She's saying that to get back in her good graces—and, by the way, to make up for what he's done in the past—he needs to do these things in the *future.*"

"Got it. Because she wouldn't have any future if she planned to commit suicide," Jennifer said.

"Why try to reform a man and have some other woman reap the rewards," Diana said. "Why didn't law enforcement recognize this?"

"They're men," Jennifer said.

So young to be so cynical. Although she had a point. "Partially. Also expectation bias. An apparent suicide and here's a note. And law enforcement wasn't alone. Magnus also pushed the suicide idea. Fawn, on the other hand, said she absolutely wouldn't have killed herself."

"I accept your point about Magnus, but when you include Fawn saying she couldn't possibly have committed suicide as one of the reasons, I'm not so sure," Diana said.

"Because Fawn didn't really know Melissa, right?" Jennifer said. "Because Melissa used Fawn as a stooge."

"That's harsh," I objected.

"Okay, maybe not a stooge, but, still, used her. Fawn was the only person around who'd listen to her praising Thurston. Anybody else would run the other direction. Fawn was so desperate for friendship, she'd pay the Thurston toll to get it."

"It was mutual—"

"Even if it was mutual," Diana interrupted me, "there's truth in what Jennifer said. Though there's always an element of each person getting something out of a friendship. In their case it's more obvious because they didn't have other friends.

"But what I was going to say is I'm not sure Fawn could admit—to herself or anyone else—that Melissa might have chosen to take her own life and leave her behind."

"Right. Because that would make her less important to Melissa, than Melissa was to her," Jennifer said.

"You do know," I said to her, "that you're now arguing *for* suicide and *against* murder. No murder, means no murderer."

She opened her mouth, then closed it. "Never mind. I'm with Elizabeth. It was murder."

Diana grimaced at both of us. "I'm not saying it definitely was, but I do think we have to look at Fawn's motives for saying it couldn't have been suicide. All her motives. Also Magnus'."

"And Greg Itson's. Him first. Yeah, I know their families' involvements in an old scam could be a coincidence and so could his going to her house. But they might not be, either."

◇ ◇ ◇ ◇

AN AUTOMATED MESSAGE informed me Deputy Itson was not available. I left a general, please call me back message.

I contacted the expert on suicide notes, asking if he'd look over one for me.

Next, I called Danielle Pruiting, Melissa Oxley's last tutor. She said she could meet me this afternoon at a park in town.

After a moment's consideration, I made another phone call, pursuing my non-online inquiries, as I'd told Jennifer.

I went right to the long-shot question, but Wardell Yardley knew a lot of people in a lot of places, especially related to the business. "Do you know anything about a woman named Chloe Vogt in Denver?"

"What about her?"

Nothing like a long shot hitting the target.

What about her? meant he knew a Chloe Vogt in Denver. It was still possible—barely—that it was a different one.

"She seems to be a consultant, but nothing else to be found."

"Of course. Discretion's vital. Why are you asking about her? Are you thinking about finally listening to me and coming back to civilization?"

"Hey, you've enjoyed your time in this *uncivilized* area."

"Some of it. If you're not looking to leave there, why ask about Chloe?"

"Her name came up in connection with an investigation."

"What kind of investigation?" This wasn't his usual reporter banter tone.

I told him some of it. Mostly what was public information.

"Thurston Fine has a fan?"

"See? That's what I said. In fact, more than one—"

"Have to have three for her to be his biggest fan."

"*Exactly.* Two would be *bigger.* Although so far, we've only found two. Or, really, one and a half. But the woman who's dead was a fan."

"Why would he have killed her? Decreased the population of his fandom."

"The theory seems to be there was a falling out, as yet unspecified, between idol and biggest fan. Law enforcement is not inclined to share."

If those two unrelated statements led him to think law enforcement was looking into what the falling out might be and if that triggered his thought that this might end up being a story big enough for him to care about and if that triggered his giving me more information… Well, sometimes people mislead themselves.

"And you're helping clear him?" His incredulity dropped a level from the reference to Thurston's fans, but still rode high.

"Clearing him is not the issue. Finding the truth is. We're gathering information. Right now, I'd like to know about Chloe Vogt."

"You're not that far out of the loop, Danny, that you don't know she's making a damned good living by filling a need."

Apparently, I *was* that far out until Jennifer's research gave me a glimpse of the loop. Which didn't bother me except I wanted to know about this woman.

If I asked too directly, he might well clam up. Because he hoarded information? Or did this touch closer to home?

"I know the networks want to have input into—"

Laughter drowned me out. "Please. The networks. Anyone relying on the network flunkies these days is left in the dust. You need an image strategy. Something that unifies all of it—hair, wardrobe, styling, presentation, makeup—into a distinctive whole. Someone loyal to you, only to you. Someone—"

"You, Dell? You have an *image* consultant?"

"Everybody has one." He was stating a fact as he knew it.

"But…"

"But what?"

My answer plunged past the edge in his question. "But you're a good reporter."

"I am a great reporter and an unequalled on-air presence. I also employ every method to stay that way. Every ethical method."

Have you ever thought you could hear people rolling over in their graves? Because the people I knew who'd hate this were not the kind to roll over quietly. Especially those still alive.

A duel to the death over the nuance of words, yes. Mano a mano on placement of a comma, of course. Bare knuckle brawls over the role of news in a free society, you bet.

What a journalist looked like? No way on earth.

The racket from noisy rolling-in-their-graves made me miss his next few words, but I told them to shut up when I heard, "…specifically *that* image consultant."

"*You* go to Chloe Vogt, Dell?"

His voice went frosty. "She comes to me."

Oops.

"Why her? Aren't image consultants thick on the ground in D.C.?"

"And in New York," he agreed. "Everybody flocks to the top two or three. And every anchor and reporter from Baton Rouge to Boston and Seattle to Saratoga gets the same advice from the same few people. Or worse for those who can only afford the second or third tier of consultants. Or—" His voice dropped in disdain. "—a local neophyte."

"She offers something new and different?"

"Just enough for an edge. And everyone does *not* know her name."

Ah.

Chloe Vogt was a secret club.

Two major questions.

How on earth had Thurston gotten in?

I wasn't asking Dell that. Not yet. I needed more information first.

The second question? Did this have anything to do with Melissa Oxley's death?

✧　✧　✧　✧

WITH NO RETURN call from Deputy Itson, I went to the library.

I liked librarian Ivy Short. I particularly liked Ivy's ability to put her hands on what I was after and faster than I could.

"I'm hoping for anything you have on the Shangri-La mine scam beyond the *Independence* series. I've read that. Anything else?"

"There's a book, although I think the writer took most of it from the *Independence*, but I'll get you that."

She brought it to a desk where I sat.

"Before I started working here, the library did a display on the scam and a librarian who's since retired pulled letters and such from the local history collection. They copied them and made a booklet. Let me see if I can find it."

She brought it as I finished skimming the book, which only added padding to Needham's series.

The booklet had no padding. Only the direct and distinct voices of about two dozen locals expressing themselves at the time of the Shangri-La mine.

Most disdained the get-rich scheme. A few referenced the main local loser—Terence Itson.

No one named him, but knowing enough of the background the reference was obvious.

Two of the snippets made clear that the elder Itson had been trying to get money to treat a daughter for what sounded like cancer.

I looked up local deaths. The girl had died at 15, two years after Itson sold off his cattle to get in on the Shangri-La mine.

That certainly was motive for bitterness about the scheme and the con men who ran it.

Was it enough, all these years later, for a descendant to take it out on the descendant of a man who might—or might not—have been involved in and/or profited from the scheme?

I returned the book and booklet to Ivy.

"Can I ask you, Elizabeth, are you looking into this because of Melissa Oxley's death?"

I put two and two together in an instant, possibly coming up with five. But opted to take the gamble.

"Yes. I know you're very careful about disclosing what patrons research, but considering her death, if she investigated the Shangri-La gold mine and saw more materials—"

"It's not that. She wanted original materials. But when she finished, she said she hadn't found anything that wasn't already in Needham's report or this booklet. I thought it would save you time."

I'm sure it did save me time. Although the basic tenet is to go for original sources, how much of a tangent was this? Was it worth the time to dig through original sources?

"Did you believe her that she didn't find anything else?"

Her mouth formed a surprised O, then relaxed before she said, "Yes, I did. She was disappointed, I think. But she also said she read the information with different eyes from when she'd studied the events as a student. She wasn't *upset*," she added earnestly. "More revisiting something that had interested her."

Like the other Cody apartments where Melissa lived, I tucked this away as something to revisit if needed.

Although I had a couple other sources I intended to revisit because a specific, unanswered aspect of the Shangri-La gold mine scam had struck me.

I thanked Ivy.

"You're welcome, Elizabeth. I wanted to say, I'm sorry for your colleague's difficulties." Embedded in her soft, pleasant voice was a big ol' *but*. "We kept saying there was no need for him to trouble himself, that another reporter could cover the library."

Thurston had done every story I remembered airing about the library. He liked events that were inside, clean, and might make him look like an important person in the community.

Her gaze met mine for an instant, then bounced away. "I cannot help but hope this might mean he won't be doing any further stories on the library."

Chapter Thirty-Eight

I MIGHT NOT have pursued the question of Val Heatherton making money off KWMT-TV if I hadn't run into Linda Caswell, walking into the library as I left.

"I know how busy you've been, but we need to have lunch soon," she said, drawing me down to a bench to the side of the entry. "In fact, I'd say right now, but I came from a business lunch."

"Lunch sounds great. Eventually. Tell me everything you know about Val Heatherton."

"Hello to you, too."

"Okay, okay. How are you? How's Grayson? How many civic organizations have you single-handedly—or with help from Mrs. Parens, Gisella Decker, and Tom Burrell—rescued since I last saw you?"

"I'm fine. Grayson is wonderful." As always, her smile at the mention of the rodeo cowboy transformed her face to beauty. "Mrs. Parens, Gee, Tom, and I have had conversations, what with the holiday season coming soon. As a matter of fact…"

"Yes, I'll donate."

"Actually, Tamantha suggested you bring your chocolate chip cookies to the Santa Tree celebration, when people take wishes off the tree they promise to fulfill. She says people will take double the number of wishes under the influence of your cookies."

"It's no big secret. Double the chocolate chips and increase the nuts. You're far better off asking Iris Undlin—"

"She always contributes generously. But Tamantha is adamant

about your cookies."

"I give. I'll make cookies." Craftily, I added, "If Tamantha will help and if you'll give me the low-down on Val Heatherton. Can't believe I haven't met the woman."

"That's not an accident." She slid me a side-eye look.

"What does that mean? I know you said she writes big enough checks to charities that not being sociable is considered acceptable."

"True, she doesn't mix in Cottonwood County society. Also, she's asked me about you."

"I hope you gave a glowing report."

"I told her you are an extraordinary journalist and KWMT is beyond fortunate to have you."

"Thanks, Linda." I grinned, but meant the words.

"Not sure it helped your cause. She does not like people knowing her business and you being nosy and all…"

"Ah. Well, if I've already got that reputation, I might as well live up to it. So, dish. Mike says she's making money on KWMT."

Her brows rose in a you-didn't-know? expression. "Mike's right. You've talked with him recently?"

"Sure. What with modern technology, we talk regularly. Especially with this woman found dead."

"Is that the only reason you and Mike talk?"

"No. We're friends."

She looked at me long enough that returning it strained—but didn't break—my resolve.

"And Tom?" she asked.

"Not enemies. Beyond that, you'll have to ask him."

Her mouth twisted. "Right."

For an instant, we were united on the prospect of asking Thomas David Burrell questions he didn't want to answer.

Then she asked, "Elizabeth…?" ending the unitedness.

"Linda."

She raised one hand. "Okay. For now." She sighed "You want to know about Val Heatherton? She makes money from the TV station. Not the bulk of her income, by any means, but a solid additional income stream. KWMT has no competition, costs are low."

I snorted. "Costs must be near zero. Equipment's ancient, staff is see-through thin, and salaries are abysmal."

"On the other side of the ledger, income per view is healthy. *Very* healthy." I was reminded that Linda was a proficient businesswoman herself.

Adjusting to this shifted view, I said, "She makes money on KWMT, but she and her son-in-law general manager leave it alone."

"She and Craig leave the news area alone. Not the same thing."

"Ah. They're active with the business side. Extrapolating from that, as long as we—the news operation—don't mess up her income stream, we're allowed to bump along on our own. Here I'd credited Mel's connection to her daughter Honey with negotiating me more autonomy than I'd ever expected."

"I'm sure that didn't hurt."

"Honey's the reason Craig's general manager, too? Only child and—No, she can't be an only child, because of Krista Seger." Her niece who owned the B&B.

"Val and her husband had three children. The other two went their own ways. Krista's dad and another daughter. Honey's the youngest."

She seemed to drift for a moment before sending me a look that clearly said *Off the Record.*

I nodded.

"Krista won't ask Val for money, much to her husband's displeasure. Dirk wants more upfront gravy from the Heathertons. Krista is smarter. She'll probably get more eventually and without strings."

"Val applies strings?"

"Ties, ropes, chains. Honey and Craig are completely wrapped up."

Which made me think of Les Haeburn and his *Ding-Dong! The Witch Is Dead* ringtone for Val Heatherton's calls. Could she be paying him enough to keep him in thrall to KWMT?

In TV news, nobody made much money at smaller stations. If he left KWMT-TV, he would have a long climb to reach markets where he'd earn a good living. If he did that here, it could be hard to break away.

And that was if he had the talent his earliest career hinted at.

As for Thurston, I couldn't imagine anyone hiring him.

Coming back to the Heathertons, I asked, "Do they resent Val's control or figure it's the cost of doing business?"

"It's complicated. I have a meeting inside now." Linda stood. "But at our lunch, we *will* talk."

MY PLANS TO go to the station to draft copy changed with a return phone call from Deputy Itson.

I said I wanted to talk.

"I'm not answering questions that—"

"I said I want to talk."

After a pause, he said, "I'll meet you at the county line for coffee."

I picked up lunch from Hamburger Heaven on the way out of town and drove one-handed except for two stretches when there was an oncoming vehicle.

ITSON WASN'T KIDDING.

He had his sheriff's department vehicle pulled off the road about a foot short of the county line, according to the sign. He poured from a thermos into a cup.

If it was a challenge to see if I'd come into his territory, hug the line, or insist he come in Cottonwood County, I mentally said the hell with that. I walked up to him and said, "You better have another cup."

He did.

"Good coffee. Thanks."

"You're welcome. My wife makes it."

I looked at him over the cup. "You were recognized."

That was my opening.

"You lost me."

"At Melissa's house Monday. Recognized and identified as someone who visited her multiple times in the months before her death."

He didn't even bother to go stiff. He'd been prepared to pass it off as nothing.

"You're relying on one of those nosy neighbors? What is that saying about consider the source?"

"Do you deny you were at Melissa Oxley's house?"

"Not answering the question at all."

"Then why did you agree to meet me?"

"Thought you might have something to tell me—"

"Tune in to KWMT."

"—and I have a question for you."

"What?"

"Why did you ask about what she was wearing?"

"Narrow down when she might have died. Also, possibly, when she met up with whoever killed her—if someone did. She was wearing jeans and a jacket, wasn't she?"

"Not bad."

I shrugged. "Didn't need the information after the news release gave the time you found her and approximate time of death."

"Suppose not."

"One of the things we've been wondering about is why Melissa Oxley would choose to go to your county to commit suicide. But if she were asked to go there, say, by someone she knew, that could explain why she ended up dead in Horse Creek County."

"We don't solicit folks to come here to commit suicide."

"Do you solicit people to come to your county for other reasons?"

"No. More coffee?"

"Yes, please."

He poured.

And then he shut up.

Murder, suicide, a good reason for him to have been seen at Melissa's house, or a lame excuse, he wasn't going to talk about any of it. I'd run into a few like him. Direct assault did not work. You had to plant seeds and hope one sprouted. To plant seeds, you had to work the soil.

"Tell me more about the stolen bike, Deputy."

"What about it?"

"You saw it there at the bar, then went to the owner's house to talk to him about it, and then driving back you saw Melissa's car, right? So why didn't you just take the bike and return it to its rightful owner?"

"To make Horse Creek County's roads a little safer for a little longer."

"Explain."

"You'd have to know that rightful owner. Only reason he has the bike is to pretend he rides it when his license is suspended after another DUI, like it is right now. Having to walk to the bar to get the bike slows him down and he knows I'm watching him." Without pausing, he added, "Quit fencing and say what you're thinking."

"You think Melissa Oxley committed suicide and I don't."

"Why don't you?" That jangled my antenna. Too calm. Too open.

But all I said was, "Her note." I used that word deliberately. I didn't have to tell him I knew it had been a recording.

After he spluttered about how did I see the note, which was highly gratifying, then abruptly went darkly suspicious and quiet—I believe he was thinking nasty thoughts about the Cottonwood County Sheriff's Department—he shut up and listened.

I told him about the expert I'd interviewed, even gave him the contact information and suggested he try to run Melissa's note past my expert. I didn't mention I'd put in a request, too. His might get faster action.

He wrote down the information on the expert.

I could like this guy.

He took the empty cup from me, wiped it out, wiped his own out, closed up the thermos and tucked all that away.

Finished, he said, "I'll tell you something just to get you to leave this alone and stop trying to prove Thurston Fine is innocent. His fingerprints were found in Melissa Oxley's home and vehicle."

My brain processed several facts at once.

We already knew Thurston's fingerprints would be expected in her home.

Fawn said Melissa drove him to and from the airport … in her car or his?

Shelton never would have told me these things, no matter how much he wanted to get rid of me.

"You said her fingerprints were found in her car. You said that at the news conference."

"They were. Didn't say there weren't more fingerprints found. So maybe your theory about her note not committing suicide is right after all."

He didn't think Melissa committed suicide. He thought Thurston killed her.

Or this was all to throw me off the scent that *he* had killed her.

I could hate this guy.

What I said was, "None of this will get me to leave this alone, because I'm not trying to prove Thurston Fine innocent. I'm trying to find out the truth."

I'D TURNED AROUND and gone maybe a quarter of a mile, heading for the Baxter place to find Fawn Raglettley when my phone rang.

I let it go to voice mail because the name on caller ID didn't click, but then called up voice mail immediately.

"You said to call if I thought of anything."

The voice did the trick, even though it was more awake than when I'd talked to her at her door. Kit, the waitress who lived a couple doors down from Melissa Oxley's apartment in Cody.

I called back immediately.

"Hi, Kit. Great to hear from you. Have you remembered something?"

"No. But I was talking to my boyfriend about it and he said he'd seen her—Melissa—recently in Cody."

"Where did he see her? When? Can you give me his information so I can talk to him directly?"

She ignored all but the first question. "That's the thing. She came into where he works. He said she didn't recognize him, but he remembered the name because it was on the parking space—M. Oxley—and he saw it every time he parked there."

I suppressed another run of questions. She was taking this at her pace.

"I suppose you'll want to talk to him—" Hell, yes, I wanted to talk to him. And she knew it. But she was making sure she was in this story, too. "—but you said I should call you, so…"

"I did. And I appreciate your calling to make sure that I'd like to talk to both of you, especially if your boyfriend seeing Melissa Oxley in Cody turns out to be significant."

"Significant. Yeah, I think it is. You see, the thing is, she bought a gun."

Chapter Thirty-Nine

THIS TIME, I spotted Fawn's pickup pulled off the side of the highway before I reached the turnoff to the home ranch. And blessed my good fortune that neither Shelley nor Glenn Baxter was in sight.

Also that no other vehicles had been on the road as I'd finished with Kit, then contacted Diana and arranged to meet her at KWMT later to talk to Kit and her boyfriend in Cody.

Fawn was fixing a section of fence that looked as if a vehicle had run into it. Perhaps someone on the phone.

She straightened, looking at me for several long seconds before putting her heavy gloves in a hip pocket and coming over.

She didn't say hello, but took a long drink from a thermos on the dropped-down tailgate of her old pickup.

Hers appeared to be lemonade. She didn't offer me any.

"You didn't tell me everything before, did you, Fawn?"

After a long moment, she shook her head once.

"About Melissa driving Thurston to the airport? Was it the most recent time?"

"She found something out. She didn't tell me what. But she said he was taking unnecessary risks. He said she had no right to go in his house. But I think he was really mad about her knowing whatever it was, not about her worrying about him."

"Something about what he was doing in Denver?"

"I don't know." But she wasn't done. I let the silence hold. "Maybe. It wasn't anything she said right out, but kind of what surrounded it that makes me think it could have to do with that, you know?"

"I do know. That's astute of you, Fawn."

She flushed.

"What their fight was about—that was her picking him up at the airport in her car, instead of his. Usually she drove to his house, they went to the airport, then she drove his car back to his house, because he wanted it in the garage."

Which meant Melissa had to be able to at least get into his garage and a good chance he simply gave her his keys, including to the house.

"But that last time, she drove him to the airport in her car. She said he was really, really angry. But she got to his house late—on purpose—and said they drove in her car or he'd have to find his own way to the airport and with it being so late he'd miss his flight.

"He told her she better bring his car when she picked him up at the airport. She told me that and about their fight when she called and said to be at the airport when he came back. She said she was going to use her car again and she told me where to stand to take pictures with my phone, so she'd have them of Thurston in her car. She even came over and made sure I would aim at the right spot, then got back in her car and was right there waiting for him when he came out.

"He was really angry. Said he was known for his car and people expected to see him in it. She said nobody could see into his car, couldn't see they were together. Then he said he liked it that way and that's when she got mad.

"She said it again about him taking unnecessary risks, only this time, she wasn't worried about him. She said she could take risks, too. And he'd see she wasn't the weak person he thought she was.

"And then she screamed at me, too. Because I was there, at the airport, and heard all this. Even though she'd told me to be there. So she drove off fast, even got dust on Thurston because he was still standing by the car and he was furious. I didn't want to hang around and try to talk to him or anything, so I left. And I didn't try to call Melissa, either. Not for two full days. And even then, she didn't call me back for another day because she was being ... weird."

"Fawn, between the day Melissa drove Thurston to the airport in her car and the day she was going to drive him home in her car, did you see her?"

"She called me. Like I said, she told me—"

"Yes, but did you see her?"

"No." She seemed unhappy about that.

"Do you know if she went to Denver, too, Fawn? Maybe left after Thurston did and came back before he did?"

"I don't know. I don't know. I don't know."

✧　✧　✧　✧

THE POSSIBILITY OF trying to track down Deputy Itson floated through my thoughts, to be immediately rejected.

First, I messaged Diana about a slight detour on our trip to Cody.

I called Jennifer to relay to Audrey that I wouldn't be in the newsroom for a while, but I would still write Leona's copy.

"Where are you going? That's me asking. I won't tell Audrey if you don't want me to."

"You can tell her. I have to go see Shelton, then to Cody, which might result in video."

"Shelton's not going to want to see you."

"Right back at him."

✧　✧　✧　✧

AFTER AN EXCHANGE with Deputy Ferrante that thoroughly covered the fact that neither Shelton nor I wanted to see the other, but my insistence that it was necessary or I'd air what I had to say tonight without any warning, I was granted access to the former supply closet that was Shelton's office.

He glared up at me from under his eyebrows without moving his head. "You have thirty seconds."

"That doesn't scare a broadcast journalist. You have no idea how much can be crammed into thirty seconds."

"Fifteen seconds."

"Hah. I only used up about ten. Your math's lousy."

"Five seconds."

"There's a legit reason Thurston's prints are in Melissa Oxley's vehicle that has nothing to do with murder."

I had the satisfaction of watching his head jerk up.

Also of having my internal timer inform me that everything I'd said totaled a fraction of a second less than thirty.

"What reason?" he demanded.

I noticed he left out legit, implying he'd decide that for himself. He thought it would hurt my feelings he didn't take my word for it. It didn't. I had the goods to back my statement.

"She drove him to and from the airport—"

"We know that."

"—the last time in her vehicle."

He didn't burst out in words that would betray his thoughts like any ordinary person, but his glare intensified.

"She usually drove him to and from in his car, but not this most recent time. She refused to use his car, insisted on taking hers, and he didn't have time—or the imagination—to figure out how else to get to the airport. When she picked him up, also in her car, there was a scene."

"Who's your witness?"

"That would be telling. Not to mention you'll want to confirm independently anyway—I'd start with security video, then search around for people most likely to be there when that Denver flight came in so they'd be on hand for the scene. Besides, we call them sources, Sergeant."

He growled. Music to my ears.

DIANA AND I made the drive to Cody in record time.

Diana makes just about every drive in record time when she's behind the wheel, as she was for this trip.

"Are you going to ride the whole way with your eyes closed?" she asked me. "Thought you'd use this time to work on copy for the Five."

"The lead will depend on if what Kit has to say is strong enough. Besides, I'm suffering from whiplash. That note is not suicidal. I know it's not. And Itson's fingerprint evidence doesn't point to Thurston the way he thinks it does. But Thurston was doing something in Denver—something risky according to Fawn, quoting Melissa. And presumably that was with this Chloe Vogt who's a former fixer turned image consultant. And among the images she consults on is my good friend Wardell Yardley."

"Well, when you put it like that, I'm sorry I don't have a cold compress for your throbbing forehead."

I thanked her for the thought in the spirit in which it had been delivered.

We met Kit outside the unprepossessing chain restaurant where she worked.

I hadn't asked Kit about bringing a cameraperson, but my instincts proved correct—she was thrilled. Her *boyfriend* less so, but I let her persuade him.

Kit and Frank provided a case against the terms *girlfriend* and *boyfriend* being used between the ages of thirty, up to which point they were possibly appropriate, and eighty, after which they were endearing.

Even dressed, made up, and with goo on her hair to partially mask the white roots, Kit clearly was farther from thirty than eighty.

The guy might have been a couple years younger, but not much.

"This is Frank," served as her entire introduction. We'd need more than that to use this on air, but I didn't want to scare him off before I knew if what he had to say was worth fighting to get and keep.

His stubble gave stubble a bad name, sprouting in patches of gray, brown, and muddy at odd angles from a round chin that folded itself in three. His flannel shirt strained over a belly that could have given Santa a run for the bowl full of jelly title. It overflowed the top of his dirty jeans.

He had the air of a skittish dog and a tendency to show the whites of his eyes.

"We want to hear what you saw first-hand, Frank."

"Just like you told me," Kit instructed him impatiently. "Go on, tell them."

I gave Diana a signal behind my back. I knew she'd have the camera rolling without making it a big deal to our whites-of-the-eyes interviewee.

"Let's start with when this was, Frank."

He frowned fiercely, jiggling his chins. "Might've been Tuesday, week before last, but I'd say it was Wednesday. Not this past Wednesday, but the one before that. Round about two p.m. Not long after lunch, anyway."

"Excellent. That's clear. Now, what happened?"

With his gaze pointing at the post of a nearby fence, he said, "Wasn't a whole lot to it. Like Kit told you, I used to park in her spot when she'd go weekends to Sherman. Happened a lot. So I saw her name on the spot a lot. Knew the name. When I heard Teddy—heard someone else say her name at the shop, I looked up and it was her. I hadn't seen her a whole lot, but I'd seen her, and I knew it was her, the woman who lived by Kit. The one whose spot I used there at the apartment."

He'd slid into a comfortable rhythm. I hated to interrupt it, but *she* wasn't going to cut it.

"What's this woman's name, Frank?"

"Melissa Oxley." He sounded surprised I hadn't kept up with him. "M. Oxley like it had on her parking spot by Kit's place. She was there at the counter with Teddy, finishing up a purchase. Couldn't see exactly what she got, because Teddy was already wrapping it up— securing it—for her to take. And then—"

"Wait. This was Melissa Oxley? At the counter, purchasing a gun?"

"Yeah."

"Did she have to get a background check?"

"Sure. Had to pass it, too, or Teddy wouldn't have sold to her otherwise. We don't mess around with that. Ever. And then she asked for ammunition. Teddy recommended a box that drops the price per bullet way down and would let her practice, but she said she didn't need practice and wanted the smallest box. He pushed a bit, and she said it would do the job she needed done, and no she wouldn't buy more ammunition."

He looked toward me.

"That's about it. She bought a handgun and ammunition. Said thank you, real polite to Teddy and left."

"Do you think she recognized you?"

"Didn't ever look my way. Sure didn't recognize me."

"And that's what he told me when I told him he had to talk to KWMT-TV," Kit inserted, making sure she was right next to him, in his shot.

Chapter Forty

I KEPT MY eyes open for the rest of the drive back to Sherman, drafting the lead story for the Five on my device.

With almost two hours to go, there was still plenty of time for events to squash every word I'd written.

Still, having it made me feel better. It—and even more, the video Diana delivered—eased Audrey's anxiety, too.

So I felt no compunction about switching from Diana's vehicle to mine in the parking lot without going inside. But I didn't linger in the parking lot, either. I drove a bit before finding someplace to pull over.

I had a few more minutes before I was to meet Danielle, the tutor, so I placed a call to a familiar number.

"Danny, how are you?"

The question was genuine. So was the hint of caution.

Mel Welch was among the people in my life that I knew with absolute certainty *always* wanted to know how I was and dearly hoped the answer was that I was great. I also knew he adored my mother and deeply feared her disapproval.

That combination put the man between a rock and a hard place at times. He generally wriggled out with no more than minor scrapes and bruises.

"I'm good. No, I'm tired. But beyond that, I'm good."

"Saw the special you ran over the weekend. Excellent, excellent work. As always."

Jennifer had been sending Mel copies of our specials all along. What I'd discovered recently was that he'd been sharing them with my parents, whom I had thought were ignorant of my murder investigating. So much for that.

"Thanks. What do you know about the current situation?"

He t'ched. "Jennifer sent me the relevant portions of the newscasts each of the past three days. Are you—?"

"I'm asking the questions, Mel. What do you know about Thurston Fine?"

"Nothing. Why would you—?"

"Have you talked with Val Heatherton or any of her family this week?"

"No. That's—?"

"Why didn't you tell me they make money on KWMT?"

From entirely innocent friend, his tone switched to careful lawyer. "I cannot confirm that as a fact. I am not privy to—"

"Forget it, Mel. I don't need you to confirm." Linda wouldn't have lied. But even if I'd needed confirmation, his change in tone provided it. "Tell me about the Heathertons."

"You mean the accident."

I had no idea what accident, but I remembered that side-eyed look from Linda as she said, *That's not an accident.*"

I immediately confirmed his assumption with "Yes."

He sighed. "I figured you'd find out about it eventually, no matter how well it was hidden. I told Val… But she was adamant to handle it her way and with it happening when and where it did, it was possible, while it wouldn't have been here or even there now. But thirty-five years ago, things were different.

"No question, it was Honey's fault—she'd been drinking heavily—but she's certainly paid for it. Val has, too, all those surgeries. Even Craig, with being tied to Val that way. They both are. Always will be. Looking back, I think that's what Val wanted from the start. Not to shield Honey, but to shackle her."

Lost?

Oh, heck, yeah, I was lost.

I'd been fishing for information on the ownership and management of a tiny TV station in Wyoming. On the end of my line I'd snagged ... something else.

Bit by careful bit, I kept the hook in Mel and pulled the story from him.

Honey Heatherton and Mel's wife, Peg, had been roommates and best friends in college. Gradually, he had come to be accepted by Honey's aging father and rules-the-roost mother. But Mel and Peg kept their distance. Peg loved Honey while recognizing her as a deeply troubled soul who made no effort to resolve her troubles.

Then came this accident in parts unnamed. Honey driving drunk with her parents as back seat passengers. Her father killed, her mother badly injured, Honey nearly unscathed.

They turned to Mel to negotiate the shoals.

"I did what I felt I could, but not everything Val wanted. Peg backed me completely, even when Honey begged us to do whatever Val said... I have no proof that Craig Morningside did what she wanted, but things did transpire as Val had dictated. The father became the driver. No charges for Honey. Everyone whisked back to the States with Val beginning the treatments that never have eradicated all her injuries...

"From that time, Honey acquiesced to Val making decisions for her, including the marriage to Craig Morningside." Mel skirted any direct statements, but I got the impression Val and Craig had been more than in-laws. And that Craig was far from the only one.

Peg tried to stay in touch with Honey, though that became erratic.

"Until I needed a job. And you came to my rescue." My shoulders suddenly hurt and I realized I'd slumped forward so far it felt as if they might touch in front of me. "Oh, Mel, I'm so sorry—"

"*No.* I know what you're thinking, Danny, and *no.* I never—*never*—asked them to give you a job or for any favor in any way. You owe them nothing. I owe them nothing. Do you understand me?"

"But—"

"I got Honey to get me the contact information for the person who does the work Craig Morningside is supposed to do. A name and phone number—that was all Honey did. A woman in Dallas, who oversees a lot of Heatherton business.

"Then I had an associate handle this end, so even if Morningside caught wind of it, he wouldn't connect the name. And the negotiation for your current contract was handled the same way. KWMT means something to the Heathertons because Honey's father started it with some guy named Artie, but to the woman in Dallas it's a dusty closet in the Heatherton complex. Still, she's not stupid. She saw what you do and she jumped on the opportunity to keep you there."

"But the request to do something on the B&B for Val's niece…"

"That came through the woman in Dallas to my associate to me. Maybe Val asked or maybe the woman initiated it herself. Either way, it wasn't connected to me. And nothing more came of it."

"Mel—"

"Stop worrying, Danny. I didn't compromise my ethics to help Peg's dear friend thirty-five years ago. I didn't compromise my ethics—or yours—to help you out. I am fairly good at this business, you know."

I chuckled. A little watery, but a chuckle nonetheless.

"I do know that. How can I ever thank you for—?"

"We're family. That's all. We're family."

My shoulders had returned to their rightful places.

I didn't cry until we'd ended the call.

✧   ✧   ✧   ✧

I PULLED MYSELF together—makeup and emotionally—before driving to the park Danielle Pruiting had named, which was connected to a middle school. Kids raced up and down a field with a soccer ball involved though I didn't know if it could be classified as a game.

A woman of the right age, sitting alone on the second row from the top of the small bleachers, stood and raised one arm over her head, looking right at me. She wore a denim jacket with black jeans. I made my way to her.

"Danielle?" Best to be sure.

"Yes, hello. Please, come join me." As we sat, she said, "We should be able to talk here. I was so sad to hear about Melissa's death."

"You got along well?"

She tipped her widespread hand side to side. "I was her tutor her senior year in high school. She was both looking forward to going away to college and terrified. She asked me all sorts of things about being away from Sherman and I think I came to represent being away. So when she was scared of that, she'd pull away completely."

"Did you stay in touch after?"

"Not really. She came to see me—to see my baby—" She smiled wryly, nodding toward a grubby boy near the close sideline, who was shouting to send him the ball. "—the summer after she graduated from college. I saw her a couple times at Legends Bookstore while she worked there.

"And then about three weeks ago, I saw her at the library." A tuck formed between her brows.

"Did you talk to her?"

"A little, yeah. She seemed fine. A little, um, intense, the way she'd get about a particular topic. She had a stack of books and magazines on relationships and more on cosmetic treatments and I said something vague about them, concerned she might be considering, you know, something drastic. But she was focused on the dangers, so I dropped it, especially since… Well, the year I worked with her, she was obsessed with a scam that happened in the next county over—"

"The Shangri-La gold mine."

"How did you—? Oh, I guess there aren't that many to choose from, huh? Anyway, she did papers on the events surrounding it. I mean, almost every research paper or essay I assigned, she'd find a way to include that nonexistent gold mine." She chuckled and tucked her light brown hair behind her ears. "And then there she was at a table at the library, going over information on the Shangri-La mine scandal with Ivy—you know Ivy Short?"

I confirmed I did.

"She was bringing Melissa material. I teased her a bit about being back on that hobbyhorse. She said time had a way of changing perspectives."

"Any specifics?"

"Nothing that stuck with me, I'm afraid."

I pushed a little more.

"Anything about the Itson family?"

"I don't think so, but… Why does that sound familiar?"

"Greg Itson?"

She shook her head. "Sorry, no. I was racing to get the kids to dental appointments and didn't pursue it. I so wish I'd spent more time with her that day. Maybe set up a time to get together… But there was nothing in the conversation that gave any hint she was depressed or…"

"I'm sure there was nothing you could have done that would have changed things."

I wasn't sure of that. No one could be. Whether Melissa died of suicide or murder.

Danielle struck me as someone wise enough to recognize that. Still, it seemed to make her feel better.

I WAS HIDING out in the studio after the Five.

It was, um, a bit of a rush at the end.

Frazzle off the charts. Things said that HR would probably classify as creating a hostile work environment for the creaking electronics repeatedly wished to hell. Everybody was so focused on holding up their strand of string that made up our tightrope that no one listened.

So, no harm, no foul, as my sports pal Mike Paycik said.

Except I needed a bit of a breather and cookies before returning to the fray.

As active as the place was if someone was filming in here or—especially—during newscasts, it could be the most peaceful place during down times.

The door opened and Jerry walked in.

He cocked his head at me.

"I'll go," I said.

This place belonged to him.

"No need. I'm going to re-set. Can go around you for a while. But you might want to get the cookie crumbs off the desk before Leona sees them."

"Yeah." I scooped them into my hand, closed up the package and headed for the door. But I turned back.

"Jerry, you might be the only person who hasn't told me about a Thurston screw-up from before my time. Yet you're right here, experiencing them in the moment and up close—the front lines, so to speak."

"That's why I block them out. If you never let the trauma in, you can't relive it. I got so I could hear the words I needed for the camera cues, but blocked his voice out entirely otherwise."

"That's an amazing skill."

"Self-preservation. Pure self-preservation. Did mean I had to check online to see what happened in the news, though, because even if Thurston said it, I didn't hear it. And since he hogged the big stories, I missed a lot until I could get home and find out what happened."

An employee of the station, needing to get news elsewhere. Did it get any worse?

"How *did* he survive all this time? Even Ivy Short at the library, one of the sweetest people on earth, said the staff tried to persuade him not to do stories on the library—when have you ever heard of public libraries not wanting coverage?"

He shook his head in commiseration. "Cottonwood County Public Library definitely took more than its share of Thurston blows. Before I perfected my technique, I remember he did an entire story about a library event using the past-tense pronunciation of read instead of the present-tense pronunciation.

"Bruce had just started being his producer then and hadn't abandoned all hope. He tried to tell Thurston what he'd done wrong, but he loftily ignored him. Bruce wimped out."

"No." I felt an overwhelming desire to laugh, the way you do at a funeral when someone has toilet paper on their shoe.

"A *few* of the sentences still made sense," Jerry continued, "though a lot of them sounded like the library was trying to turn the kids into communists. I heard the library got a lot of flak from a few people who took Thurston literally. That one episode could explain Ivy's attitude toward Thurston. But there were plenty more."

Chapter Forty-One

"SHE BOUGHT THE gun, she bought the ammunition. That pretty much seals it," Mike said. "Just when I was getting really curious about why this Chloe is connected to Thurston. But I guess that's a red herring. Sorry, Jennifer. I know you thought this was the opportunity to dispatch Thurston, but it looks like you're out of luck."

"Not necessarily," Jennifer argued.

She sat beside me on the floor outside the studio, our backs against the wall. Diana joined us from home by video call and Mike from Chicago.

"Melissa was in Denver for sure," Jennifer continued. "The guys confirmed that. *Public* video shows her there. But we can get receipts and stuff, too, if needed. And they had a big fight after."

"But why a gun and ammunition if she weren't planning to commit suicide?" Mike asked.

Without an answer to that, I said, "We can't prove it for sure—at least not yet—but it seems to me more likely than not that someone was out there with her. If it was suicide, why not come forward?"

"Afraid of getting in trouble for helping someone commit suicide," Mike said promptly. "Besides, how are you sure someone was out there with her?"

"Sure? I'm not. But…" I thought of Jenks' video of that location, of the feeling it gave me. "There's the bicycle."

"Because the bicycle was found the same morning Melissa Oxley was?"

"Because the bicycle was stolen the same night Melissa Oxley died.

It was left out all the time. Never taken. Then, the night she dies, it disappears. And reappears by the next morning in a spot less than a mile from Melissa's car by way of a rideable route."

"That seems like a stretch. Besides, you said yourself, you can't say it's suspicious that Thurston's prints were in her vehicle when there's a reasonable explanation. One that probably was observed by humans and almost certainly by airport security tape. Why *did* you tell Shelton about that?" Mike asked. "Could have held onto that info. In fact, could have waited and let the defense spring it on the prosecution at trial."

"With the result that Thurston would get off and couldn't be tried again."

"Ah-hah! And you wanted to make sure that didn't happen and he couldn't weasel out under double jeopardy. Now it makes sense." All was right in Jennifer's world again.

"That must mean you're sure Thurston's guilty," Mike said.

"I'm not sure of anything. Except that his fingerprints were already in that vehicle from the ride to the airport, so that is not evidence he killed Melissa."

"How can you be sure? You only have Fawn's word for it about the fingerprints," Diana said.

"Not anymore. Shelton must have confirmed it by now or he'd be in my ear gloating at my error and—Hold on. I've got a call." I swore. "It's Shelton. I'm going to take this. I'll be back."

I RETURNED TO them faster than I'd expected.

The call had been brief.

"Shelton gloating?" Diana asked sympathetically.

I didn't answer directly. "You want to know why I'm sure it's not suicide? Because Sergeant Wayne Shelton is boiling mad that we ran Frank from Cody telling us about Melissa Oxley buying a gun and ammunition. He did not want that info out there uncontrolled, because he's looking ahead to a trial. And muddying the waters with events indicating possible suicide is too much like reasonable doubt."

"But that deputy from Horse Creek County already said it was suicide," Mike objected.

"Yep. But no one from Cottonwood County did. I do believe our local sheriff's department is planning to co-opt the case of Melissa Oxley from their neighbors.

"Also, when I asked Shelton if they'd confirmed Thurston had been in Melissa's car and their tiff from airport video, he growled ferociously. So that's confirmed."

✧ ✧ ✧ ✧

"OH, GOD, IT'S you again," Thurston said when he opened his front door to me.

"I want to talk to you about Chloe Vogt." I didn't enter, even though he'd left enough room that I could have.

That was when Thurston surprised me.

"She won't take you on. She has a strict policy to represent only one client per station."

I thought he'd flat out deny, as he had about Melissa Oxley.

Instead, his need to one-up me overrode all other considerations.

"I'll have to live with the disappointment. What does she do for you?"

"The usual things."

"Be specific."

"It's consultant-client privilege."

"Image consultants do not have client privilege, Thurston. Especially when it comes to murder."

"I've told you, that woman committed—"

"Suicide. And even if she didn't, and it was murder, you didn't do it. That's your story."

"That's right."

"The hurdle is to *prove* any of that. Melissa was part of your life. You were part of hers. That makes you a suspect. She drove you to and picked you up from the airport each time you went to Denver. However, she also went to Denver the most recent time you went. With you? Af—"

"No."

"—ter you? Following you? We don't know. The sheriff's department doesn't know. That makes you an intriguing suspect. And when they find out Melissa Oxley was outside your image consultant's office while you had an appointment with her, that's going to make your relationship with your image consultant of great interest."

"I don't have a *relationship* with her. She's married."

He truly thought he'd scored a point.

"Do you realize Melissa drove you to the airport in her car because with her going to Denver, the vehicle would be left outside and she didn't want to do that to *your* car."

It took him a while to process. "Well, that makes sense. Why didn't she say so?"

I walked out.

✧ ✧ ✧ ✧

"WHAT WOULD YOU say if I said Chloe Vogt worked with Thurston Fine?"

Calling Dell from the car was my strategy for calming down enough to not go into Thurston's house and strangle him.

"I'd say no way in hell. She's very particular about her clients. You know Boyd Ridger from Philly?"

"I know of him. Up and comer."

"She turned him down flat last year. And then work with Thurston Fine? Absolutely no way. Or did you mean when she started out? Where was he before Sherman?"

I searched my memory for what Jennifer had found. "Zanesville, Ohio."

"Zanesville could explain everything. That's where she started, though she didn't stay there but a minute before jumping up the ranks of markets by chunks. Might have rivaled you—before your departure to Wyoming—if she hadn't decided to hone images for other broadcast journalists. Not just broadcast, either. She takes on print folks who're doing TV gigs as talking heads or the speaker circuit, though she's even pickier about them."

"Interesting. The information about Zanesville isn't in any of her online presence."

"No, it's not." He chuckled wickedly, reminding me to keep any secrets under lock and key around Wardell Yardley.

I DROVE PAST Linda Caswell's ranch on the way back from Thurston's house.

It is nobody's idea of a direct route, but I was rewarded by seeing lights still on in the small room on the side of the sprawling ranch house that Linda favors.

I called her from the driveway and she invited me in.

Without preliminaries, I said, "You know about the accident, don't you? Honey. Val. The Heathertons."

Without looking at me, she said, "Some. I've… I've tried to not know any more than I already do."

Got it.

I wouldn't have said anything that might have revealed Mel's knowledge, now I would say even less.

Linda released a breath through her lips. "I will say it changed Val. No, that's not right. It… *intensified* her. She'd always had a certain, uh, approach. Especially with men. She'd wanted what she wanted and went after it, if you know what I mean. But after the accident… It left her with a great many physical scars. Some think that's why she doesn't mix in society here. But she said to me once that they freed her from any need to pretend that any relationship was more than a transaction. The way she said it…"

She shook her head.

"She wasn't bitter. Not at all. She said it so matter of fact. She said her older two children had gone off, but she'd bought Honey's loyalty for life, with Craig as a buy-one-get-one-free—she actually used that phrase. And then she said she bought men, as well. That she found that rather than one-time or short-term leases, she preferred outright *purchases.* That there were sunk costs involved in *procuring* and securing a man and that it was better to amortize those over a longer period of time.

"I was... I couldn't say anything. I was so... And I think she thought that meant I agreed or approved or admired or ... something.

"Because then she said she'd learned that lesson when one of her *catches* escaped by striking it rich with a fake gold mine of all things."

For the first time she turned toward me and met my gaze.

"Dodd Oxley," I said. Then I had to explain.

DAY FIVE
FRIDAY

Chapter Forty-Two

AFTER YESTERDAY'S RAPID-FIRE events, I felt lethargic and slightly dizzy, as if I had whiplash.

In an effort to clear my mind, I played enough Free Cell last night to be utterly sick of it.

I walked Shadow three times between last night and this morning. He sat down partway through the third walk. Not that he couldn't keep going, but he clearly despaired for my mental health.

In the shower this morning, I realized I'd shampooed my hair at least three times before I moved on with the routine.

The situation didn't improve from a round of calls to Cottonwood County, Horse Creek County, and the newsroom. This wasn't a slow news day, it was a no news day.

Kicking myself for missing the basic, I called Dell back to get Chloe Vogt's contact information. He didn't answer. I asked Jennifer to see what she could find.

With nothing else jumping out at me, I went back to the end of my conversation the night before with Linda Caswell.

Dodd Oxley.

It was a stretch, but doing nothing slid me toward madness.

I decided to have my morning coffee at the offices of the *Independence.*

$\diamond \quad \diamond \quad \diamond \quad \diamond$

"**WHY DID THE** Shangri-La gold mine scam fall apart before the swindlers made their big score? If Dodd Oxley sold out early, did that spook investors?"

"Might have contributed, but not the spark that burned down the false front. Especially since Dodd didn't float the story that he'd sold out until after the lead guys disappeared."

Needham looked up at me from under his eyebrows. Yes, we agreed about the significance of that timing.

He continued. "For the series, I interviewed three locals who'd worked in the Shangri-La office. Every one of them swore there was a big uproar on a particular Monday morning. One of the women said she thought the two leads would kill each other right then, and she wasn't one to exaggerate.

"By Tuesday night, those two were gone, saying they had another mine to check on in Nevada. Except, one drove east and the other west. Never to be seen again. Bills unpaid, wages unpaid. Wednesday was the day Dodd Oxley said he sold his shares to an investor from Los Angeles. Handful of associates of the lead pair from out of town trickled away silently, all gone by the end of the week. News reached big investors after their independent engineers showed up in Horse Creek as scheduled and found the heads of the company skedaddled.

"The engineers sampled anyway and the fat was in the fire when they found way, way less gold than the first reports said. The big investors sent more engineers, who found almost nothing. In less than a month from that particular Monday morning, Shangri-La was left to the tumbleweeds."

"What set the two lead guys against each other?"

"Never known for sure. The engineers coming in from back East had been scheduled a while and the locals I interviewed said the two leaders were completely confident when they closed the office Friday night. Saw them out at Sunday dinner and they were as cool as ever. No sign at all that the upcoming sampling posed any problem."

"So what happened between Sunday night and Monday morning?" I watched him carefully as I asked, which led me to add, "Needham Bender, you think you know what happened."

"So do you," he shot back. "We have our logical suspicions, anyway."

"You said Dodd Oxley *said* he sold to an investor from Los Angeles."

"No such investor ever came forward."

"And the guys behind the con knew inspectors were coming, which meant they had to have samples that backed their claims in order to finalize the sale of the mine to the investors—in other words, their marks. That meant they had—or expected to have—the raw material with which to salt the mine. They had to have gold."

"Uh-huh. But if they somehow lost that gold, say between that Sunday night and Monday morning, with the sampling coming up the next week and with them being watched by agents of the big investors, they'd be hard-pressed to get a new supply of gold to match what had already been sampled."

"Ah. Couldn't just be any gold, could it? It needed to be the same. What form was the gold that got investors interested?"

"Nuggets."

"After Mrs. P's descriptions of mine salting, I expected something more exotic."

"Nuggets are plenty exotic when it comes to gold. Especially big ones, if you can even call them nuggets, that've been found in Alaska and Australia. Not so much here. But the dream never dies.

"As a matter of fact, the state of Wyoming's partnering with a mining company to explore an old copper mine on state land not far from Cheyenne. New technology and the price of copper make it economically feasible to check it out. Plus, they think there's gold along with the copper and there're ways to get to it that didn't exist a hundred years ago."

"I'm still back on nuggets from thirty years ago. They'd be more portable than other forms, right?" I asked.

"Absolutely."

"Easier to sell?"

"That, too."

Chapter Forty-Three

WHEN I CALLED Mrs. P to see if I could visit her in O'Hara Hill today, she informed me she was in Sherman.

Gee had driven her here for shopping and now was at the sheriff's department. Mrs. P was finishing up at the Sherman Western Frontier Life Museum, which was one of her projects. They had a meeting later to discuss plans for the Christmas Wish Tree.

To cut off more discussion of that, I said, "Linda's already got me signed up to bring cookies."

I asked if I could take her to coffee at the café—I'd float if I had much more coffee.

She consulted someone in the background—presumably Clara, the curator of the museum, then agreed.

"Mrs. Parens, do you know what happened to the two men who spearheaded the Shangri-La gold mine?" I asked once we settled at a table.

"I do not."

The succinctness of that tingled my antenna. As did the narrowness.

"Did you look for them?"

"I am not an investigative reporter with the tools to search for such people, nor was I one when the events transpired."

"You did look for them," I stated.

A shift of her shoulders indicated a twitch of impatience—with me? with her memories? with—?

"A fool's errand. It was abundantly clear that the names they used in that endeavor were neither the names they were born with nor the names they would use once they departed Wyoming. Yet I did do a modicum of research. Neither name appeared again in that research, although a man of approximately the right age with a name that reversed the names known here, with the first name as the last and the last as the first, did die in Richmond, Indiana, within the year and without family or resources, according to the short article."

"He warranted an article?"

"He was struck and killed by a train. The presumed pathos of such events can elicit an article."

Presumed pathos. So, death by train for this guy did not stir Mrs. P's sympathy.

"Were you affected by the scam?"

"I was not."

"But someone you cared about was?"

"Yes, although not, I believe, in the manner you imagine. My concern was for the confidence and faith of the community."

"Horse Creek County?"

She arched her brows. "Our neighbors are also part of our community."

"And it affected people from Cottonwood County. Like Melissa Oxley's family. Since Dodd Oxley left the Heathertons' employ to work for the Shangri-La mine, not to mention their fortunes *improved* when he sold his shares immediately before the scheme blew up."

"Their situation did improve financially. However, the change was not limited to monetary matters. In other aspects, the change was not beneficial."

"You told me you didn't have Melissa in class, yet you knew her as a girl?"

"I did not have her in class, however, a respected colleague did have her in class the year the Shangri-La mine scheme occurred. She became quite concerned for Melissa and by the changes in the girl. A happy child abruptly became a withdrawn child who exhibited distrust, anxiety, and unhappiness, all behaviors that intensified with the death of her father, an event which shortened the tether between mother and child as well as restricted Melissa's circle of trust, indeed, even of contact."

"Behaviors in the child could have been picked up from a father—or perhaps father *and* mother—who scared her about interacting with people. Or who served up that lesson by example. The interesting question is what might have prompted the change in the adults. From all accounts they were part of the community until that point ... and not afterward."

She returned my regard with a bland, unrevealing gaze.

That didn't stop me from reading things into it, including thoughts about unintended consequences and collateral damage.

"The timing is interesting," I continued. "Everyone knew Dodd Oxley said he sold his shares before the con's collapse, so that explains their improved financial standing. With locals not investing, they weren't taken, but was there still animosity toward the Oxleys over his great timing?"

"I did not observe animosity openly expressed. As you noted, few locals lost anything in the enterprise."

"Few, but not none. According to Needham, the office employees lost a paycheck, other bills weren't paid." I looked up quickly. "And the Itson family was left significantly worse off than when Shangri-La hit Wyoming, never restoring their ranch to what it had been."

She said nothing.

"Was there animosity from the Itsons toward the Oxleys?"

"I did not observe animosity openly expressed."

That phrase covered only what was openly expressed and she directly observed. Tip of the iceberg.

But trying to drill down from that tip into the bulk of the iceberg would get me nowhere with Emmaline Parens.

Better to come at it from a different angle.

"So if the Shangri-La con partner who headed east died penniless, then the partner who went west must have taken the stash."

"Elizabeth, if you believe you will goad me into saying more than I deem appropriate by positing a hypothesis riddled with fallacies, you have learned little in our acquaintanceship, even, I would assert, our friendship."

I put on a grin. "The guy who headed east wasn't necessarily the one who died in Indiana. That guy might not be connected at all. There might not have been a stash, since the payoff was expected after prospective investors forked over their money to buy the Shangri-La."

She raised one eyebrow slightly.

"On the other hand," I continued, "a logical supposition includes that they had the resources on hand to salt the mine before the investors' engineers' arrival the following week. That explains the jolly Sunday dinner. The sudden disappearance of those resources—also known as gold nuggets—by Monday morning explains subsequent attitudes and actions of Thing One and Thing Two."

"Indeed."

"The gold nuggets went into Dodd's pocket?"

"I do not know the answer to your question."

"But you have your suspicions."

"Suspicions are your realm, my dear Elizabeth."

JENNIFER CONVENED A video call that I attended in my car after delivering Mrs. P to Aunt Gee for their Christmas Wish Tree planning meeting.

"I found where Thurston and Chloe's paths crossed," Jennifer said. "Didn't take much imagination. Thurston only worked at one station before coming here—Zanesville, Ohio—so I focused there, even though it doesn't show up in the recent Chloe bios, which concentrate on a spattering of successful clients—she doesn't name many, citing confidentiality.

"I took that bio and started digging back. Collated all the results to work back deeper and deeper into her history, looking for Zanesville. I sent you each a copy." She waited impatiently for us to access what she'd sent. "There were a couple gaps, but I got most of it. She seemed to shed her past as she went along. But peeling back one job layer at a time, I got to a mention of Zanesville, Ohio. It definitely overlaps with Thurston's time there."

"Perfect, Jennifer."

"I also have a phone number for her."

"Beyond perfect. And you beat Dell."

She tried to look blasé. She failed. "Still don't know why Les hired Thurston."

"I wonder…" Diana's words faded. She would have let them drop.

"Wonder what?" I asked.

"I don't see how it could have anything to do with this situation and it's not nice to talk about co-workers or—"

"You mean like Thurston telling people I was kicked out of New York because of drug use?"

"I didn't believe him," Jennifer protested.

"Yes, you did. But it turned out for the best, because it got us talking."

"Well, that's true." She asked Diana, "Les is on drugs?"

"That's not—"

"You better tell us," Mike advised, "or we'll think something worse. Jennifer will, anyway."

"Hey—"

Diana exhaled. "When Les first came here, he drank."

"He still does," Jennifer said.

"A *lot*. Way more than now."

"You think that's why he moved so fast from station to station?"

"I have no idea."

"Moving from station to station isn't uncommon, although Chloe's attitude… Mike, I see it on your face. Go ahead and say what's striking you."

"I haven't been around TV news as long as you have, but—"

"Not the way to start," Diana said with a chuckle.

"—most people I've run into talk about their former shops all the time."

I loved him using the industry slang *shop* for stations. Although Diana was a little right about my not loving his prologue on my age.

"But not Chloe," Jennifer said. "Not only now, when discretion makes sense, but all along or my search would be a whole lot easier."

"Focusing on the next rung up the ladder?" Diana suggested.

"Or running away from something?" Mike said.

"I vote for Door Number Two," Jennifer said. "More possibilities. Maybe that's why she started fixing other people's messes. I'd have caught a big scandal, but could have missed something subtle because I was rushing. I'll go back over it."

"And, in hopes you find me a lever, I'll wait a bit longer before I talk to Chloe Vogt."

Despite waiting's deleterious effects on my mental health.

Chapter Forty-Four

I WAS HURTING.

My visits yesterday and today brought me to the theory that Dodd Oxley stole the gold nuggets the scammers planned to use to re-salt the Shangri-La mine, explaining the change in fortunes and the Oxleys' isolation.

Big deal.

What did I do with that?

I was back to whether Deputy Itson would have … what? … murdered Melissa Oxley because her father stole gold from the people who'd scammed his grandfather?

Stated like that, it was far-fetched.

I could say I'd wasted my time on this tangent, but did I have anything better to spend my time on?

Which brought me back to my pain point.

What to do next?

Besides wait.

MY PHONE RANG. I grabbed it before the second ring.

"Hi, Tom."

"Are you okay?"

"Why wouldn't I be?"

"The note you left on your counter was a little … cryptic."

"Oh. You're at my house, huh. I just said I didn't think Shadow would want a walk right now, but he'd love to visit with you and

Tamantha."

"Why no walk?"

"We, uh, took a few walks."

"Since yesterday?"

"Yeah."

"Hit a dead end on your inquiries?"

"Maybe."

"No more ideas?"

"Temporary lull."

"Uh-huh. What do you usually do when this happens?"

"It doesn't usually happen," I said loftily.

"What do you do on the rare occasions this happens. And—"

"That's better.

"—I think I know. Free Cell."

I didn't mention being sick of it. "It would not be politic to play endless games of Free Cell here in the newsroom, where other people who are working hard could see."

"What's your backup?"

I considered. "I noodle."

"Doodle?"

"Not *doodle*. Though I understand for people with an artistic bent, which I completely lack, that can free up the brain enough to unclog a jam. But for me, it's noodling—hopping around the Internet looking for tidbits of any shape, size, or texture that might spark some primordial version of thought. Something—anything—to put into my brain to get the sludge moving."

He said nothing.

"You think it's time for me to noodle."

"Sounds like," he said.

So, I noodled.

I looked up more on gold mine scams. And somehow got off onto a guy from Scotland who made up a whole country as part of his scam in the 1820s. Might be a stretch to use that in a "Helping Out!" segment.

I looked up Caroline Lockhart, the Huntington sisters, Bill Nye.

Needham and Mrs. Parens had told me the good stuff.

Now I was searching online for news from Horse Creek County with a vague hope it might turn over a rock with an answer of why Melissa Oxley went there.

What I found, instead, were a couple lines from the *Independence* citing Horse Creek County Sheriff's Department reports about a bicycle reported stolen and found at the Slake-ur-Thirst Bar in Colter.

The bike theft Deputy Itson talked about. There was even a photo of the bike leaning against a wall.

The name of the bar caught my attention. Unless the owner's last name was Slake, it was a fairly clever and original name.

I looked it up online.

No website. But there was a phone number and locator map.

More noodling by zooming in on the map while I called the number and got a recording with the hours. If I wanted to visit the Slake-ur-Thirst Bar, I'd have to noodle longer, because it was not a brunch kind of establishment.

I switched from the zoomed-in street view of the Slake-ur-Thirst Bar—it looked like a tumbleweed could knock it over—to the satellite view.

The first thing that struck me was how much could be seen.

Growing up in Illinois, then living in Dayton, St. Louis, and Washington, D.C., trees canopied much of a satellite view, providing privacy. In New York, the density of buildings masked many individual structures.

But in Wyoming, especially in Horse Creek County, the dun-colored earth and what rested on it was wide open to the spying eye from the sky.

The parking lot claimed prominence, fading into the earth at its edges. The roof of Slake-ur-Thirst presented a sturdier looking rectangle than the street view. It also showed a couple arms extending from the rectangle.

I focused on the one on the left. A bike leaned against the wall of the main part of the building would be blocked by that arm from the view of anyone in the parking lot. Interesting.

I zoomed out a bit to get a better grasp of the relationship to the highway.

I'd over zoomed out, leaving a strip of dun-colored earth across the bottom of the screen, then the darker tint of the highway, the parking lot, the building, then more expanse of nothing to the top.

My finger hovered, about to correct the zoom to show only the building, lot, and highway.

Almost nothing to the top. Not completely nothing to the top.

I pulled my finger back and squinted.

Above and to the left of the bar's building, ran an angled line.

It was much lighter and narrower than the highway. A pencil stroke compared to a paint brush swipe.

I shifted the center of focus to the line and zoomed in more.

A path of some kind.

It appeared to end at the highway, to the left of the building, not far from the indistinct edge of the Slake-ur-Thirst's parking lot.

But where did it come from?

I zoomed out slightly, recentering on the path, but keeping the building visible on the right to give me a landmark. The path disappeared off the top of the screen.

Letting go of the landmark, I scrolled up, still following the path.

A new line appeared. Horizontal, perpendicular with the path. This line wider than the path and narrower than the highway that now disappeared off the bottom of the screen. It was not as dark and precise as the highway, either, but just as straight.

I shifted to street-level, not sure there would be anything, since this wasn't a street. There was something. A shoddy rendition of the view Jenks' first video captured, with broken bluffs in the distance, a tumbleweed playground in the middle ground, and a broken-up road in the foreground.

A road.

The road. Shangri-La Mine Road.

But a closer look said this was not the same view as Jenks' video. The angle was off.

I backed off a bit on the zoom, remembering the video, squinting at the scenery.

Zeroed in on where I thought the VW Beetle was found. Then switched to the satellite view. Another tap to cut back on zoom.

And there was the highway. With the edge of Slake-ur-Thirst just showing up on the screen.

From my approximated location of Melissa's car to the bar was a little over a mile on an as-the-crow-flies trajectory—if the crow took no detours, which they tend to do, despite their reputation.

Adjusting the distance by following the path's route, it was about two miles.

But when I'd asked Jenks, he'd ticked off miles and miles—

Because I'd asked him about *driving* between that spot and Colter, not how far it was overland.

I called Mike. "How familiar are you with Horse Creek County?"

"Middling."

"There's a place called Slake-ur-Thirst—"

"*That* I know."

"Figures."

"Don't know how they did it and never asked, but when I was a kid, they used to get more NFL games pulled in than anywhere else around."

"A kid? At a bar?"

He chuckled. "They were stricter about my training than coach was. They already had an eye on me for UW." Playing football for the University of Wyoming was a communal affair.

"There's a path near the bar that connects to Shangri-La Mine Road."

"Oh, yeah. I sort of remember that. There was a bet one night and they settled it, running the path in the dark."

"How long to ride a bike?"

"It would be easier on horseback."

"No horses were stolen. A bike was. Wait, I'm sending you a screengrab."

"Was there a moon that night?"

"A moon—?" Light, of course. "It was a full moon. Or right after.

Also the bike…" I pulled up the photo from the *Independence*. "It has a headlight."

"Trouble is, as I recall the area, a bike light would be visible for miles. At least off and on with the ups and downs. Moonlight's a better bet."

"It was bright. No clouds. That's why it got so cold that night. I'm going to check out this path."

"Not by yourself."

I clicked my tongue. "You think Shangri-La Mine Road and Slake-ur-Thirst are dangerous?"

"Somebody's dead," he said solemnly, "and you're sure it wasn't suicide."

Chapter Forty-Five

I DROVE TO where Melissa Oxley had been found in her car.

The only sign of those events that remained was a foot-long ribbon of police tape flapping from a bare-branched bush.

I rolled slowly past it, keeping an eye on the left horizon for any glimpse of Colter or, especially, Slake-ur-Thirst.

Nothing.

Not until I spotted an unobtrusive indentation beyond a hillock.

Out of my SUV, I checked the indentation. It was the start of a path.

I'd changed into walking shoes before leaving KWMT and had two waters in my pockets. I was ready to go. Yet I looked back at the SUV, as if I'd forgotten something.

A few steps after the hillock blocked view of the SUV, I pulled out my phone. No connection.

I'm a great believer that knowing for sure is better than wondering. But this knowledge still wasn't cheery.

I tried not to keep my head down all the time, while still watching where I was walking. That was both because I didn't want to fall on my face on a path far from a paved sidewalk and because I now and then spotted bicycle tire tracks.

When I did, I took pictures of them with my phone.

At those spots, I also detoured off the path, which slowed me even more.

That might have been unnecessary caution.

I didn't doubt that top forensic scientists could match these tracks to specific bicycle tires. But there were two facts that diminished the value of that.

First, if it was the bike I suspected it was, identifying the bike didn't point to who had used it. Unless the thief kindly left his or her fingerprints and/or DNA or—what the heck, as long as I was being optimistic—a typed and signed confession with every detail of motive and method.

Second, the weather was rapidly eroding these tracks. And that was without the overhead clouds producing rain. Yet.

When I reached somewhere with connection, I'd have a bit of a dilemma about whether to share my finding of these tracks.

The sun slid down my back as the afternoon advanced.

If this was an antelope track as Needham said, I felt sorry for the antelope. Mike was right this would be easier on horseback. Most in Cottonwood and Horse Creek counties would know that and would have access to a horse.

Did that point to an outsider? An outsider with a bicycle, whether by fair means or foul?

At last, I spotted a corner of a building. Its ramshackle state matched what I'd seen online. I advanced more slowly, assessing if I'd be visible from the bar or its parking lot. I didn't think I would be.

Would someone on a bicycle be? Of course the fact the bike had a headlight didn't mean it had to be used.

Looking over my shoulder, I saw the sun had slipped behind a congregation of clouds rolling toward us from the west. Time for the return trip.

But, first, I tried my phone.

No connection.

That startled me momentarily. Until I thought that for visitors to Slake-ur-Thirst, the lack of connection might be a draw. No phone calls or messages from home or work telling you to get back where you belonged.

No connection anywhere along the track, though, did hurry me along.

Sidestepping the tire track segments, I wondered if this path and the bicycle could all be sideshow.

My SUV, glowing through a coating of dust thanks to sun streaking out of a break in the clouds, had never looked better.

Maybe I was getting imaginative from the setting and the knowledge of a woman's death nearby, but I almost felt like I could sense another presence.

I shivered.

But instead of hurrying to the SUV, I stopped at the last set of visible tire tracks, took photos, and did my best to cover the tracks— without touching—with the sparse brush options at hand.

I HESITATED ONLY a couple minutes when I reached the land of connection, just before turning onto the highway.

I pulled over and called the Cottonwood County Sheriff's Department.

Loyalty to my home county's law enforcement over Horse Creek's? Concern about Deputy Itson's role? Recognition that I'd have plenty of time for my next stop with the distance Cottonwood deputies needed to cover versus Horse Creek deputies?

I'm sure they each played a role.

Shelton wasn't available, I was told—with relish—by Deputy Ferrante.

I left a message, knowing the futility of it, but doing it anyway.

Then I sent three of the best photos—without explanation—to Deputy Richard Alvaro's personal phone, followed by a call.

If he hadn't seen the photos, he might not answer, but—

He answered with, "What *are* these, Elizabeth?"

I explained what and, possibly more important, where. Along with the fact that Deputy Greg Itson had returned a missing bicycle the morning he'd found Melissa Oxley's body.

"You shouldn't have disturbed—"

"If I hadn't, you wouldn't know anything about the existence of the bicycle tracks. Quit griping and do something about them."

✧ ✧ ✧ ✧

JENKS' INSTRUCTIONS TOOK me past the Slake-ur-Thirst, already open. I suppose it had to be happy hour somewhere.

I didn't stop. I went on into the town of Colter, which turned the highway into a wide main street with brick buildings on either side for two blocks, then more widely scattered buildings of less impressive construction.

Coming out the other side of town, where highway speed resumed, I spotted a beige rectangle of a house with a single window in front, a crumpled snowmobile on a trailer in the front yard, and toys, tools, and scrap wood jumbled near a set of tire tracks. The tiny house numbers matched what I'd found in the record for Harten Kuplenk, who'd reported his bike stolen.

As I walked to the door, I noted a bike resting against the snow-mobile trailer, on the side toward the house and within sight of the window. Wyoming dust covered it. I was no expert, but it looked like it held more than a one-time coat. Still, it looked solid—more solid than most of the other items in the yard.

My quick research into the owner before I left the station showed a number of arrests, most involving alcohol. No violence. That didn't turn off my cautionary instincts, however.

I knocked firmly, in spaced-out sets of three.

I heard movement and grumbling from the other side of the door.

The man who opened it wore a couple weeks of beard, pajama bottoms, and a t-shirt. He threw up an arm as the door opened, as if the cloudy day blinded him.

"Who are you?" He croaked.

The attire, the croaky voice, the watery eyes, the dark cave of a room behind him might add up to a man staying home from work with a cold. I didn't think so.

"Harten Kuplenk?" I took his quick blink as confirmation, not waiting for words, because that would give him time to engage his defense mechanisms. "Hello, I'm E.M. Danniher from KWMT-TV in Sherman. We're doing a series on bicycle thefts and I understand you were a victim recently."

"Damn right I was. Thieving scum taking a bike right out of my yard. Was right there with my other belongings."

His gesture took in the assembled junk.

"How long have you had the bike?"

"While. Sometimes I gotta ride it for transportation."

Like when his license was pulled and he wasn't feeling lucky.

"When did you notice it missing?"

"Told the sheriff's department all this when they made me go through a mountain of paperwork to tell them my bike was swiped. Went outside for somethin' about midnight and it was gone. Looked around, in case one of the kids moved it even though they know they're not to touch that or anything else of mine. It was gone. I called the sheriff. That's it. Got a call the next day—damned early, too—that it'd been found.

"That deputy—Uptight Itson, I call him. You'd think nobody'd ever had a baby before, the way he was last spring before his wife finally popped one out. A girl," he said dismissively. "He was so worked up about it he threw me in jail—all the way in Cottonwood County, too—for no good reason when I'd done the same thing a hundred times and only got warnings."

I coughed.

He looked at me suspiciously.

But I had my face under control.

"He hasn't gotten any better since the kid arrived. Asked about the bike, threw in a lecture about keeping it locked up free of charge, but did he bother bringing it back when it would've been easy for him? Oh, no. And he hasn't done a thing about following up on who took it."

I didn't think making the point that the Horse Creek County Sheriff's Department having found a dead body took precedence over his bike would penetrate. No sense wasting my breath.

"Was the bike in the same condition as before it was taken?"

His suspicion skyrocketed. "Why?" he barked.

"Anything broken? Or missing?"

Not bothering to answer, he elbowed past me, going outside to the bike, looking it over.

"You scared me. Like maybe I missed something. But it's in one piece."

"Was it this dusty the night it was taken?"

"Don't take it to no bike wash every Tuesday. Doesn't mean anybody else's got a right to take it off me."

"Absolutely. It's a shame that happened. A real shame. But you were fortunate you got your bike."

"Not so damned fortunate. I was going to use it that night. Stuck here all night with the kids screaming and the last beer gone."

"Have you used it since?"

"Of course I have. Last night and the night before."

Which meant there was little chance of useful forensics on the bike at this point.

Chapter Forty-Six

Rather to my surprise, Greg Itson agreed to meet me right away.

Even more to my surprise, he didn't balk at my suggestion of the Slake-ur-Thirst.

I arrived ahead of schedule and went inside.

It wasn't the worst I'd seen. And it certainly wasn't the worst I'd smelled.

A handful of customers already sat at the bar, with one sitting alone at a table.

I found a barstool widely separated from everyone else.

"What can I get you?" The bartender had a rat tail that would have indicated ill health in a rat, and even sparser patches of facial hair. But his eyes were unclouded and noticing.

"A mineral water on ice, please."

I put a bill on the counter that his eyes definitely noticed, while I contemplated how electronic means of payment made some transactions faster, but made others nearly impossible. Like getting information.

He placed a highball glass in front of me with lots of ice and mineral water, palming the bill smoothly.

"That's generous of you, E.M. Danniher," he said.

I grinned at him appreciatively—for recognizing me and for securing the bill first.

"What if I asked for change back?"

"You won't."

I chuckled. "You're right. I won't. You watch the news?"

"Yup. Read it, too. Diversity of sources. Only way to get a full picture. I like your specials."

"Thanks. It's teamwork."

"Never happened before you came. You here about that woman found dead back on the mine road?"

"Indirectly. I'm hoping for a couple answers about a regular customer."

Discretion settled around him thickly. "Who? And what questions?"

"Harten Kuplenk and his bike."

Discretion scattered with his low laugh. "Ask away."

"Did you see him here Sunday night?"

"No. Never came in."

"Did you see his bike here that night?"

"No. Wasn't there when I locked up."

"There?"

"Usual spot he parks it, around the side, behind where a bit of the front wall sticks out."

"Why does he leave his bike there?"

"His wife can't see it when she drives past on her way home from work. She'd have to pull in and get out of her vehicle. She usually just goes on home."

"When you say it's his usual spot, are other people aware it's his habit to leave it there?"

"Everybody? No. Most don't care enough to notice. But—" His gaze went to the door. I saw the movement of it opening in the age-dimmed mirror behind him. "—some that might have reason to pay attention? Absolutely."

The door swung back, revealing the new arrival visible in the mirror as Magnus Boesch. With his arm around a woman I could not imagine at the country club.

Odd how you can list jeans, V-neck top, cowboy boots, and be describing two entirely different outfits.

"A regular?" I asked the bartender.

"Semi."

"You seem surprised to see him."

"Last time he was in here—Sunday night—he was talking about how he'd be frequenting higher class establishments from then on. Said he was coming into money."

Counting on the agreement with Melissa he'd touted? Or something else?

Magnus recognized me and so abruptly changed his path to zag away from my vicinity that his companion stumbled sideways, nearly liberating part of her anatomy from the V of her top.

"Magnus, how are you?" I asked sweetly.

"Uh, fine, just fine." He bundled his friend to a table directly behind my barstool and as far away as he could get.

I gave the bartender a bland look, slid off the stool, and went to the table.

"I won't take up much of your time, Magnus, but I wanted to know if you'd made arrangements for the funeral yet?"

"Arrangements? Me?"

"Sure. As close as you said you are—were—to your stepdaughter. She died, you know." I directed that at the woman, who did not look impressed. "Just thirty-seven. Suspicious circumstances."

"No, no, not suspicious. Sad, absolutely, but not suspicious. Poor thing, she was real unhappy. Couldn't say she was stable, but losing her momma rocked her even worse. Depressed, you know."

Trying to persuade me or make sure I didn't persuade his friend. If he was worried about not getting lucky because talk of death disturbed this one, I think he was safe.

"Depressed? Had Melissa talked to a doctor or gotten a diagnosis?"

"Oh, well…"

"Did she ever talk about taking her own life?"

His fake startle response wouldn't have fooled a babe in arms. "Taking her own life?" He whistled softly. "That's a thought. Hadn't occurred to me, but I suppose with your experience with news and all, you'd think about something like that. Not that taking her own life is a crime—"

"Not anymore in this country, though it is in some countries. And it is illegal to assist a suicide in Wyoming."

"Assist? You think I—? No way."

"Your stepdaughter of more than a decade. Unhappy, as you said. Depressed, as you said."

"We weren't that close."

"Rocked by her mother's death, as you said. And which you certainly must understand, since your world, too was rocked by Barbara's death." I shook my head at all the rocking in the world. "Well, let me know when you know about the arrangements."

My bartender friend placed another mineral water on the bar as I returned to my spot.

"Whatever you said to him, it was a pleasure to watch that guy turn red, white, and blue."

I was already looking forward to the next time I talked to Magnus Boesch. He was nicely softened up, unlike the deputy who should arrive soon.

The bartender appeared about to share another observation when I lost out to his watching the door opening again.

This time, when he saw the newcomer heading for me, the bartender decamped to the other end without a farewell.

Greg Itson sat next to me.

✧　✧　✧　✧

"I UNDERSTAND YOU and your wife had a baby last spring."

Itson tried to look blank. But the glow seeped around the edges. Like an eclipse, all the more dazzling for the contrast.

"Congratulations. A girl? What's her name?"

"Isabel. Thanks."

Did he think clipped, single words blocked his reaction?

"You and your wife—?" I made the last word a question.

"Billie." He tamed the reluctance to share to mere deadpan.

"—must not be getting much sleep. That can be rough." When he didn't bite, I went another direction. "Anyway, that was Harten Kuplenk's theory about why you sent him to jail last spring instead of letting him off with another warning."

"Good—" He swallowed his first-choice word. "—grief. Is he still whining about that? It had nothing to do with Billie being pregnant or waiting for the baby to be born or anything other than his repeated boneheaded behavior. The magistrate finally had it with him and I say, great. Because Harten's been significantly less of a drain on our resources since then. Not that anybody expects him to straighten up and fly right forever, but at least we get a break."

"He didn't appreciate being told how to care for his bike, either."

For a second, his frown turned even more thunderous. Then it lifted.

"Sergeant Shelton and Deputy Alvaro told me about you."

"Did they tell you a group of us have helped solve—or outright solved—some of the county's murder cases?"

"They didn't mention that. But I've seen it on TV." He did not look impressed.

I'd pulled his chain. He'd responded with his own tug.

I reran what he'd said through my head, but nothing jumped out.

Sometimes when you chase something like that you catch it. Sometimes you shove it deeper in between the cushions in your mind and don't retrieve it until you get down there with a crevice tool.

Apparently, this would require a crevice tool.

Something I did not have at the moment.

Besides, I judged enough time had passed by now.

I did ask one more question. "Do you know the man sitting behind me in the corner?"

Points to Itson. He shifted as if reaching for a salt shaker down the bar and used the movement to check out Magnus.

"No. He's awfully interested in you."

I believed him about not knowing Magnus Boesch. That didn't prove he hadn't been to Melissa's house, since she'd kicked out her stepfather, but it was a little something.

"I can have that effect on people."

"I bet."

Chapter Forty-Seven

WE SAW THE clouds had piled in when we came out.

I noticed a blur of light bouncing off the cloud cover from the direction beyond the Slake-ur-Thirst.

Greg Itson noticed it, too. He frowned, checked his phone, then frowned more as he climbed into the cab of the requisite off-duty pickup.

As I prepared to leave, I saw him on his phone.

I pulled out and headed one direction. In my rear-view mirror, I saw Itson pull out of the Slake-ur-Thirst lot and head the opposite direction. The shortest drivable route to where I believed the Cottonwood County Sheriff's Department was looking at bicycle tire tracks from the Shangri-La Mine Road.

It started to rain.

✧ ✧ ✧ ✧

"I'VE GOT IT. I *think* I've got it. I've probably got it. No, I've got it."

Jennifer's outburst swamped the hellos as Diana and I arrived on the video call simultaneously. Mike was on assignment in Chicago and not reachable.

I'd pulled off the side of the road, with an accompaniment of rain on the SUV's roof and windshield.

"I bet you do," Diana said. "Now tell us what *it* is."

"The thing down the career ladder that she's trying to get away from. The consultant woman. Chloe."

"You see how what you said at the beginning was big news to you, but wasn't to us without context?" I asked. "Context is what *who, what, when, where, how* provide the listener. A government official has been arrested. Where? Who? Someone who governs us or halfway around the world? It's started to rain. Has it flooded recently? Or is there a drought. Context."

Jennifer protested, "You already know the context—"

"Not until you said it concerned Chloe."

"And now that Elizabeth has made her educational point, please tell us what you found out, Jennifer," Diana said.

"Yes, please," I added meekly.

"Chloe's old bios listed a station as the start of her career that came *after* Zanesville. But I found a piece about her joining that supposedly first station from a defunct weekly paper digitized by a local historical society. It said she'd been a reporter for the Zanesville station. And a quote from the news director said she'd impressed him with her tape from Zanesville.

"So I called the Zanesville station and said I was doing a report for my class at the local high school on the oral history of the station and who was the best person to talk to. *Bingo.* They connected me to Mary Tresser and she knew *everything* about everybody. For example, Chloe was Chloe Cosalini in Zanesville. The hard part was to get Mary to focus on the info I wanted.

"Boy, people complain about how much search has degraded on places like Google and Amazon—as if they ever were great—and they have. Because they shove what they want to sell at you instead of what you searched for. But trying to search a person's memory is even harder. I never realized how good you have to be to get as much information from someone as you do, Elizabeth."

Those words might be my favorite career accolade.

"Yes, Elizabeth is marvelous," Diana teased. "Now, get back to what Mary Tresser said about Chloe."

"She never was a reporter at the Zanesville station. She was a secretary. That's what Mary said—not even an assistant or admin—a secretary."

"But her audition tape that wowed the next news director… Was

Mary sure—?"

"Absolutely. Chloe was passed over for a reporter job. Got bitter. According to Mary, she up and left a couple months later, no notice, and no one heard from her again."

"She had to have submitted a fake audition tape. Stories that never aired," I said. "She could have done the video herself."

"Multimedia journalist," Jennifer said wisely. "The station was moving to MMJs—Mary called them one-man-bands, because they do video and standup and everything—and that would be the end of Thurston, since he can't play one instrument, much less the whole band. He left around the same time."

"He would know Chloe's first audition tape was fake, her first job as a journalist *wasn't* as a journalist. The lie at the foundation of her career. Pull that out and it all falls apart, including the consulting now," I said.

"She *could* be working with Thurston as a thank you for not giving her away." Diana hesitated a moment, then said, "On the other hand, would any of us put it past him to hold his knowledge over her head and insist she work with him?"

"Nope. I think it's time to talk to Chloe."

"If you go to Denver, Audrey will—"

"That's why we'll try the phone first. In the meantime, I have a little story about a bike."

I finished my account with the potential significance.

"Say the person who took the bike used it to ride out to meet Melissa. She thinks the bike-rider is going to help her fake her suicide to make Thurston sit up and take notice—based on the content of her note. Instead, he or she kills Melissa, rides the bike to the bar and leaves it there.

"Anyone who paid attention would know that's where the owner left it. Magnus is a semi-regular customer. Itson patrols there."

"Thurston? I can't imagine him on a bike," Jennifer said reluctantly. "Or in a place like Slake-ur-Thirst."

"Not ordinarily, but he's certainly strongly motivated by self-interest." That cheered her up.

"What about Fawn?" Diana asked.

"Possible. It's about a fifteen-minute drive from the Baxter ranch road."

Chapter Forty-Eight

CHLOE VOGT DID not answer the number Jennifer had found.

I'd keep trying as I drove into town. Also keep trying to reach Dell in case he had another number. The cloudburst had passed, trailing a rainbow for a short distance.

In the meantime, I went to Vegas again—Thurston's version in Sherman, Wyoming. This time in daylight, which did not help the décor or the host.

"Oh, God, you again."

He couldn't even be original with his greeting.

I decided I wouldn't be, either. "I want to talk to you about Chloe Vogt."

I did walk in today, but not past the foyer.

"You knew Chloe from Zanesville. Have you followed her all along or did you suddenly find her and realize the value of her information?"

"I don't know what you're—"

"Why do you take so much luggage to Denver to get your hair cut?"

"You are demented. Absolutely—"

"Large suitcases every trip. Are you taking your wardrobe for image consultant Chloe Vogt to go over? If you've hired her, show me the payments. That's all you have to do and I'll shut—"

"Image consultant? *Image* consultant? Thurston Fine does not need an image consultant."

He was right. An image consultant for him was the proverbial lipstick on the pig of his journalistic inability.

"We have photos of you going into Chloe Vogt's door with your suitcase." Not great photos, but Jennifer would keep searching.

"Nonsense." I hadn't dented his confidence.

You know how he doesn't see anything but his own wonderfulness. Leona had that right.

Remembering speculation about him being a really, really bad drug mule, I asked, "Thurston, have you noticed the contents of your suitcases not being exactly as you packed them when you reach your destination?"

He snorted. "You'd think baggage handlers couldn't possibly mishandle suitcases enough to disrupt my clothes so badly, time after time."

The sound I heard was me, trying not to laugh.

"I don't know what you're—" His mouth sagged open a second, then snapped closed. It jutted his chin out.

That twanged a recognition somewhere in my head where I stored non-essentials. No, several levels below non-essentials. Inconsequentials.

And then it combined with what Mike said about something changing with Thurston in the past couple months.

And I knew.

Thurston's chin was more of a chin than it used to be.

There are certain basic rules in life you follow because not following them can get you hurt. Basic rules, like putting your foot on the ground when you walk, rather than, oh, say, walking on a rope swaying in mid-air.

The basic rule about asking questions is to know what question is about to come out of your mouth.

Ideally to think it through first, to even have a strategy where the first question lays groundwork for a second question that takes you to a third, and eventually leads to a destination.

I broke that rule.

The one about questions. Not the one about walking a tightrope.

"Did you have surgery, Thurston?"

"What? Surgery? No. What are you talking about? What a question. Have no idea what you're talking about. Babbling. Utter nonsense."

The most naïve person on earth wouldn't buy that performance.

But knocking at that door again when he'd busied himself piling word furniture in front of it wouldn't work.

"You must have done something, because—" Here's the important part. "—something looks different."

"You think so?"

I latched onto his eagerness. "Absolutely. But if it wasn't surgery—and who could blame you if it was, because that's a permanent solution. One and done and forget about it. But if it wasn't…" I watched him closely for any sign of dismantling the barricade at the door. "…then you found an effective alternative. I'm impressed anything other than surgery could make such a difference."

"It *has* made a difference." No longer asking my opinion, but stating his own. "A fresher look."

"For sure."

"Not so tired."

"Exactly."

"More virile."

There was only so far I could go with this.

A stream of possibilities flowed through my head. Pills were marketed as adding, ahem, virility. Though I'd never heard them touted as firming other areas of the body and those late-night ads certainly would have mentioned that. "Injections?"

"Of course." His confirmation came with a side order of smug.

"For what?"

"You know for what."

"I don't. I mean, not precisely."

"Don't tell me you haven't had them."

"I still don't know what *them* is. You'll have to be clearer." Which is often what I thought when I heard his version of reporting.

Disbelief gave way to craftiness. "If you tell me what kind you've had, I'll tell you all about it."

"Okay."

C'mon, you would have made that deal, too.

"Tightening. That's all. A little tightening here and there. Nothing major at all. Around the eyes, in the forehead, under the chin. You know." He came *this* close to *wink-wink, nudge-nudge*. "Now, tell me. Have you had wrinkle ironing? I've heard the follow-up is extensive. And if you don't keep up with the regimen it can set you back even more than where you started."

"Wrinkle ironing?" I repeated.

"I knew it, I knew it, I knew it. I have to say—" He narrowed his eyes at me, like he was picking out a turkey for Thanksgiving. "—you are doing a fine job with the follow-up. I decided against it, at least for now because my schedule is so demanding."

Those daily naps, you know.

I suddenly thought of Fawn reporting Melissa being worried about Thurston taking risks.

"What about the dangers?" I asked.

"Greatly exaggerated. Especially for someone with my constitution. Why, the doctor told me the strands of my DNA might as well be composed of steel for how strong it is. As for the cost of the treatments, that's taken care of, too." He broke off his self-amused chuckle. "Where are you going?"

"The Sherman Supermarket."

I PEELED OUT of Thurston's neighborhood with Diana-like speed, but slowed to answer the phone.

"Mike, I'm on my way to the supermarket. I can't talk and risk losing this thread. Didn't even want to risk the phone IDing you, because it might have distracted me."

"From what?"

"They call them strands and give them fancy letters."

"What?"

"That's what Penny said. And Billie. It's i-e, not y. Actually, not the supermarket. I'm going to see Penny."

"I figured that." He sighed. "This is one of those things you're not going to tell me, isn't it?"

"I always tell you eventually."

"After tormenting me," said the martyr. "You could leave the phone on—"

"Not this time. Bye, Mike."

HALLELUJAH.

No one was in Penny's lane.

She stood at her register, blatantly listening to the chit-chat between the cashier three rows away and a customer with a month's worth of food.

That was remarkable—a customer chose another cashier over Penny when her line wasn't practically out the door. On the other hand, this customer and that cashier looked an awful lot alike. Sisters? That would explain it.

I swooped in so fast—and from the front of the store—I startled Penny.

She recovered quickly enough to start her routine greeting. "Well, hi there—"

"Penny, you said the other day that you told Billie that getting the test as a birthday present wasn't a good idea. That was Billie and Greg Itson?"

"—Elizabeth. You've been working so much, I got worried about your supply of cookies. Uh-huh. Told the boy—"

"Greg Itson, the deputy from Horse Creek County?" I needed to be sure. I knew *the boy* referred to the store's manager, who was at least forty.

She frowned down at the empty and unmoving track leading to her register.

"—to order more. If there aren't any on the shelves, I have some in back for you and there'll be a delivery next week. That's him. If that's not enough—"

Between the pointed look at her conveyer belt and the reference to the cookies, I got the hint. I grabbed a candy bar from the nearest rack and set it on the belt. She immediately started it down the track toward her. "A test about their baby? The paternity or—"

"—I'll get him to get some in from Cody or—The baby? No. Not Isabel's. No question there. Not with those two. Greg's. Opening that can of worms so it'd spill all over. Worms—"

"Why would Greg getting an ancestry test not be a good idea?"

With the candy bar rung up, I got another frown. I jerked a magazine out of the closest rack and added that.

"—that twist and tangle and you think you've got the end of one but turns out it's the middle of another. Old ways and shames holding on. And when there's love and pride—fierce love and fierce pride—mixed in and what you tried to do turns out the opposite of what you'd hoped and those who love you, no matter what the blood, carry on the burden—"

"Greg Itson was adopted."

"—of the ones before, trying to make things right. Of course. Didn't I just say so? If that's all, Elizabeth—"

"No, no. I'm getting more."

Cans of worms. Ancestry test not a good idea. Blood.

I tossed a pack of gum on the belt, as far from the register as I could. Why couldn't this darned thing go slower? Or backward. "But Greg didn't know his blood parents until—"

"Kept Terence Itson alive after his daughter died, having a grandson. Might've thought he'd be one not holding with adoption, but there was a tie between those two from the first second. Little bitty baby, but holding onto his Poppy's finger as strong as anything. But that's past. And now—"

"—the test results."

"—pop comes the top of the can off. Worms all over."

"So it had to be local people," I said, half to myself. Because Penny couldn't have predicted, nor witnessed the worms coming out of that particular can unless she already had an inkling…

"A good thing he's gone now—"

"Who? Who are the birth parents?"

"—the worm's out of the can. Might've been looking over his

shoulder, fearing he'd lose Greg. Isn't that always the question? Though even with a name, you can hardly know who the person really was, especially when they're gone. Well, bye—"

"No. *No!* Not this time. You're going to finish telling me."

She frowned at the empty belt again.

I grabbed a variety of candy bars—she wasn't going to ring up multiples on me this time—dropped one to start its path to Penny, then loaded my crooked arm with as many as it could hold. Peripherally aware of someone moving from Penny's lane to the other checker with a number of backward glances toward me.

Didn't care.

"Give me a name. I don't care about a person not really being who you thought they were."

"No chance to know who they really were then."

I tossed a candy bar back to the start of the belt. Penny watched it coming toward her with a slightly puzzled expression, as if she didn't know how to deal with this situation … except by ringing them up one by one.

"Those that knew thought it would go the other way, so they must not have known her. Went right along with it all, quiet as a mouse. Never seemed to mind or wonder and now she's gone for good and the past—"

She's gone for good.

Dead. But who?

I kept feeding candy bars onto the belt, like feeding coins into one of those fortune-telling machines to keep it talking.

"—can't be changed. Be a mess if it could be changed if you asked—"

Melissa was dead, obviously. But she was around Itson's age. Younger if I had to guess. How could she possibly—?

"Her mother," I said. Maybe louder than necessary. I dropped my voice. "Melissa's *mother.* Barbara Boesch. She was Greg's mother."

Our wait for the next of kin had been useless. The distant cousin in Aliquippa, Pa., was not the next of kin. The next of kin was the first to know, since her half-brother found Melissa's body.

Another candy bar toss. This one didn't make it all the way to the beginning of the belt, so it wouldn't buy me as much time as my good tosses.

"—me. Just have different problems from the ones they've got now. Barbara Fyall when that all happened. Before she met Dodd Oxley. Then Barbara Oxley. Then Barbara Boesch. Though Fyall was what mattered to her. The family and that's why—"

"Greg Itson found out Barbara Fyall was his birth mother from an ancestry test, but not until after she'd died. So he—"

"—she went along so meek. Left it all to her parents. Like she left the mess with Magnus Boesch to her daughter.

"—went to Melissa, his half-sister. And, what? Did they get along? Fight? Was she shocked? Frightened? Did she—?"

"Well, bye now."

I'd run out of candy bars.

Chapter Forty-Nine

DIANA LOOKED AT the bags I'd dumped on the chair next to her in the editing booth. "You do know Halloween's past, don't you? Not to mention this could keep a dentist in business for several years."

Audrey had barely noticed me walking through the newsroom. The death of Melissa Oxley would not lead the Five today, beaten out by a local non-profit training dogs for veterans becoming a finalist for national funding.

Dogs, veterans, money, and Sherman being on the national stage. It was a no-brainer.

Unless someone was charged with murder very quickly, it let me off the hook except to write a brief up-dater for Leona, which is even less newsy than a second-day story.

"There's a pack of gum that's supposed to be good for teeth somewhere down in there. A magazine, too."

Diana pulled it out. "Are you trying to bond with Joanne Sheidenstricker by reading about celebrities?"

Jennifer joined me in the doorway as I answered. "No. I was trying to keep Penny talking. Any way I could. Greg Itson was adopted. His birth mother was Barbara Boesch, Barbara Fyall when she gave birth to him. Making him Melissa Oxley's half-brother."

Diana whistled.

Jennifer said, "Holy—"

"Exactly." I answered their questions, giving them some, but not all of what Penny said. I backtracked a bit to give them the rest of the day, too. "This changes everything. I need to talk to Itson again as soon as possible."

"How are you going to get him to come here?" Jennifer asked.

"I'm not. I have to go find him." I grimaced. "Somewhere in Horse Creek County. I checked on the way here. He's on patrol."

"You are not talking to him alone," Diana said. "I can't leave and neither can Jennifer."

"I could get Dale to—"

"And neither can Jennifer," Diana repeated more strongly, taking her phone out.

"I'll be fine. I'll just take a few candy bars and—"

"Sit." She moved the bags to the floor with the hand not holding the phone. "Tom? It's Diana. You said you'd help and—"

How did she know that? Must have been Jennifer. I sure hadn't mentioned it. Oh. Or Mrs. P or Aunt Gee. Or Mike via Aunt Gee.

Were there no secrets in this place?

I sat.

"—we need someone to go with Elizabeth to talk to a possible murderer. … Yes… Uh-huh. … In Horse Creek County. …I'll tell her."

She clicked off.

"Really, Diana."

"Tom's meeting you by the Baxter's ranch road in fifty-five minutes."

"An hour? I should strike now—"

"You think Penny's going to warn him? Relax."

"I have to get back to work, unless there's something else you can think of," Jennifer said hopefully.

"Get back to work," I said, "but if you can message Mike an update without interfering with your work, that would be great."

"If you got rid of Jennifer to yell at me about calling Tom, forget it. I'm right."

"I have already adapted. I'll write the up-dater and make phone calls before I head back to Horse Creek County." I started to stand.

"Sit."

I sat.

"Elizabeth Margaret Danniher, you are afraid to reach out for what you want. I know the symptoms—heck, I know the disease—because I've been there. It's scary. Especially if you've been drifting for a long time. But when you want something and acknowledge that to yourself, you have to start rowing hard toward it. Despite the scary."

"You and Russ," I said.

"Yeah. And the kids. And how that would work for all of us."

"You'll do it. He loves you. They love you. You love them. And you're all good people. It will work."

"As I believe you said to me about empty nesting not so long ago, right back atcha."

"Difference being, I don't know what I want."

"Yes, you do, Elizabeth."

"Oh, great, if you know, please tell me."

"I didn't say I know. I said you know. If you stop fighting it, it will come to the surface. I also didn't say it's easy," Diana continued. "It takes soul-searching. And nerves of steel."

THE ASSISTANT SAID Chloe Vogt would take my call in just a moment.

That was after I used a phrase about working on a story and wanting to give her a chance to comment.

The assistant got the last laugh when she said it would be a video call.

I'll admit it, I kicked myself for not tending to hair and makeup before trying the number again. I combed through my hair with my fingers, sat up straight, and ran my tongue over my teeth. That would have to do.

"Hello. Thank you for taking my call," I told the well-put-together woman with a discreetly softened focus on her screen. "I'm E.M. Danniher. May I call you Chloe? I've heard of you, of course. Including from my friend, Wardell Yardley."

She declined her head in gracious acknowledgement. "I know." She didn't say it, but the implication being that was her reason for taking the call. "And I can say the same of you, that I've heard of you. I'm flattered you thought to use your connections to reach me."

That had a slight edge. She was letting me know she recognized I'd applied a bit of pressure to the thumbscrews through the message via the assistant, but she could take it.

"And," she continued, "excited by the prospect of employing my professional expertise with someone of your caliber."

That was disingenuous, since I'd mentioned working on a story, not seeking her advice.

But it delighted me.

I'd be repeating the line to Dell at my earliest opportunity. If he interpreted it as her saying he wasn't equal to my caliber he would be out of her clutches immediately.

"Do I need your professional expertise?" I asked.

She jousted back. "It's essential in our profession—."

Our profession my eye. As if she were a journalist.

"—to present a credible image."

"The information presented needs to be credible."

She wasn't stupid. She got the implication that image and credible were not synonymous in my dictionary. She might have heard the argument before. Anyhow, she had a set speech to counter it.

"To best deliver information, you—anyone delivering it—must not allow any distractions to interfere. It's a matter of presenting a consistent and, yes, credible image so the audience receives the information. If the presentation isn't adequate, the information never reaches its target."

"I bow to your expertise."

She smiled. Not entirely pleasantly. "Thank you."

"Wardell Yardley speaks highly of you." That thawed her a bit. "As does Thurston Fine."

Her gaze sharpened. "Ah. Thurston. I thought his situation might be the reason for this call. I'm afraid you've wasted your time—and mine. I have nothing to tell you."

"Please don't concern yourself on my account. It's already been a fruitful call. And I'm certain it will be even more fruitful. The woman who was killed—"

"She wasn't stable. She committed suicide."

"I'd think you'd recognize the dangers of relying on Thurston as a source. Law enforcement is operating on the assumption she was murdered."

If she'd given in to her automatic reaction, her gaze would have jerked to me. But she'd squelched *automatic* ages ago. Still, the twitch of her eyes remained. Even when she closed her lids, the movement underneath revealed the impulse.

"Having worked with him at the beginning of your journalistic career, I mean," I added blandly.

She looked back at me through the screen. She did not like me at that moment.

"Will Thurston be arrested?"

"I don't think you can rely on that, do you?"

She expelled a huff of exasperation, though it didn't seem to dent her supply. "What do you want?"

"The truth."

"It sounds to me like you think you already know it."

Okay. She was not going to spill. At least to the extent of spelling out the situation.

"He insisted you work with him," I stated, taking the pressure off her saying it.

"If it were only that. You must know what he's capable of, of the threat he could pose to the protections I've created for the assets I offer my clients."

In other words, her reputation. Or a house of mirrors, based on a lie.

But I wasn't after her. Yet.

"Thurston brings options for you to choose what he will wear on-air."

Her exhalation scoffed. "Options. It's like starting from scratch every time. The man learns nothing. Not in wardrobe or presentation."

"And you have guided him toward ... treatments."

"What he chooses to receive from other professionals—"

"Melissa Oxley was worried about potential dangers of those treatments when she came to see you last month, wasn't she?"

"Melissa—? Now wait a minute. I never talked to that woman. Never."

"Did she persuade Thurston to stop them? To cut your income or—?"

"Cut it? It would save me paying out of my own pocket for him. I'd be happy if she'd persuaded him to stop. I'd be ecstatic if she'd persuaded him to go away completely. But she did not. Yes, she came to my office and was not allowed entry. She was told to talk to Thurston if she had an issue. My assistant called him and told him we could not have such disruptions."

Chapter Fifty

"YOU AGAIN? HOW did you find me?"

"It's my job to find people, Deputy."

Besides, that had been my other phone call.

My bartender friend at the Slake-ur-Thirst said, sure, he could get Deputy Itson there. He had a fake ID he'd confiscated off a kid just the night before—a three-time offender. He didn't mind putting Itson on the kid's tail at all.

When we pulled into the Slake-ur-Thirst parking lot and spotted the Horse Creek Sheriff's Department vehicle, Tom gave me a look, but said nothing.

He'd been mostly silent since climbing into the passenger seat at our rendezvous. I appreciated that, because I was thinking hard.

Itson came out of the bar. I got out and intercepted him, aware of Tom's presence nearby.

"Let's talk awhile over there." I nodded toward a deteriorating picnic table that had the advantage of being in the sun where it had already dried out, protected from the wind, and not in the direct line of sight of anyone coming or going from the main door.

"Why not. And this time you brought Tom Burrell." Itson smirked as he shifted focus to Tom. "You here for security?"

"You could say that."

"Hers or mine?"

"Maybe both. But if I have to choose, hers."

Itson sat. Before I could sit across from him, Tom took that seat, shunting me down the bench a bit.

Didn't matter. I could ask questions at an angle.

"Deputy Itson, you dismissed being identified as someone who visited Melissa Oxley's house multiple times in the past few months and said I should consider the source. Not only do I consider that source reliable, but now I have an additional source. Penny Czylinski."

"Penny—? At the supermarket?" He chuckled, sounding at ease. "She's been after our department ever since Horse Creek upset Cottonwood, kept them out of the football playoffs and our sheriff paid her back in kind for a few things she'd said before the game. Proud to say I was on that team."

"And I bet you played defense."

He waited half a beat too long to say, "Don't know what you mean."

"I mean you're playing defense now. Because I'm confident you took a genetic test your wife, Billie, gave you as a present. It led you to the knowledge that Melissa was your half-sister. And then you found her body, worked the crime scene, and questioned Thurston Fine and others. That's got to be against policy."

"Policy can't stop a deputy from finding the body of someone they're related to. I'm not the first, won't be the last."

I raised my eyebrows. He plowed ahead.

"You're wrong about the rest. First, I called it in. Second call was to the sheriff. Told him the outlines. He asked if I was okay staying on the case. I said I was. He said as soon as I was relieved at the scene, to take a couple other deputies and go to Cottonwood County to go to the victim's house, because we don't have staff to spare."

With each word, he'd grown steadier, more certain of his ground. By the end he sounded as if he were testifying.

"We discovered material that made it prudent to talk to Thurston Fine immediately. I headed that effort, while leaving others in charge at the house."

"Why?" Zeroed in on him, I saw a flicker of confusion. Good. He could still be rocked off that certain ground. "Why question Fine instead of staying at the house?"

"I'd think that would make you happier, me not staying at the house. Tampering with evidence is what you're accusing me of, right? Harder to do in a recorded interview."

Not rising to the *accusing* bait, I said, "I recognize the opportunity and the motive."

"Talk to your Sergeant Shelton if you think I had opportunity."

Which almost certainly meant he hadn't.

I'd still check.

Especially considering he didn't deny having motive.

"**YEAH, MY WIFE** gave me one of those kits where you send in DNA and they're supposed to send you possible matches in your family tree."

Give Greg Itson points for brains. It would be easy to confirm he'd submitted the test. No sense denying it.

"We'd talked about it, Billie and me," he continued. "Whether to do it. It's more complicated for me. I was adopted. Always knew that. Always fine with it. My parents are—" He swallowed. "—the best. Never felt any inclination to look beyond them, even when they encouraged me by saying curiosity was natural.

"I wasn't interested. Not until my wife came up pregnant. After twelve years of marriage, we didn't think it would happen. We'd accepted it. Started getting on lists to adopt, but hadn't advanced much. Then she started having symptoms. Neither of us said anything because we'd been there before. Eventually, her doctor said, look, we can't keep ignoring this… That's when I started wondering about what my half might be handing over to a baby."

I got it. It was all for his baby.

At least that's what he wanted us to believe.

"Anyway, there's a box you can check to find close relatives. I did it and sent it in. And when it came back… I'd been so focused on biological parents, I hadn't thought about other relatives. But it said I had a biological half-sister in their database. We had the same mother.

"We connected through the website, and met not long after. Melissa had done the test with several companies, got into databases. She said I deserved to know the whole story."

And then he stopped.

I held my tongue—with the help of my teeth clamping it from above and below—and waited.

"Melissa told me when her—our—Listen, I can't call her my mother. Barbara. When Barbara was in college, she worked summers as a cook at a ranch around here. The last summer there was a new hand hired. They hit it off." His mouth twisted. "Real well. She got pregnant. He wanted to marry her. Her family said no. Sent her back to school. Had the baby there. That was me. She put me up for adoption."

She let her parents decide? Or was it what she'd wanted, too?

Leona's words echoed in my head.

Barbara Fyall Oxley Boesch …one of those women who thought she deserved to be taken care of.

How had that set up her daughter's expectations for life and relationships?

"Barbara never looked for me. Had no interest. Melissa said her mother only told her because she was so upset about her mother being terminal and she'd have no relatives left."

"Your father?"

"Don't know. After what Melissa said, I took more tests, to see if he might be in one of the other databases—same reason, to get Isabel's history. Nothing. Barbara told Melissa she never talked to him again. Melissa said the way she said it, she didn't believe it. But that could have been Melissa's imagination. She built up this whole romantic *thing*—said Barbara never got over it. Not even with Melissa's father, Dodd Oxley.

"Still, Melissa thought it was a great story—romantic, she said. Should be a movie, she said. Didn't feel like that from my side.

"She said her mother—our mother—was born a Fyall and raised in that house in Sherman, but the family didn't have money. When she was little, her family, her grandparents, all lived there. By the time Melissa was old enough to really remember, they'd all died except her mother, and the family fortunes had turned around. You know about that?"

"I know the story of the gold, the Shangri-La, and the suspicion that Dodd Oxley benefited off the scheme that broke your grandfather and—"

"My grandfather—" He caught his words, tempered them. "My grandfather tried his damnedest to save his daughter. He grabbed at the only chance he had."

"Must have caused a lot of tension in the family."

"Yeah. Right. My dad was pissed at losing the family ranch, because he would have made a different choice. He would've said screw it to trying to save his sister's life, would've kept the ranch intact, even if he had to ride across his sister's grave to do it."

"Passing it off with sarcasm doesn't make it not true. In fact, it sounds like it didn't end with your father's generation."

"What does any of this history have to do with—?"

"You've got to be kidding. Your family history—the family history of your biological family—is, at the least, the backdrop to Melissa's death."

His tight jaw went tighter—Thurston would turn green. "The Itsons are my family."

"It doesn't change that Barbara Fyall was your biological mother and Melissa was your half-sister."

"It doesn't connect this to the Itsons."

"Except through you."

"DID YOU TELL anyone you were related to Melissa Oxley?"

"No."

"Even your wife?"

"With the baby and not sleeping, her emotions are all over the place. Wanted to see how things went before I told her. If we met once and never saw each other again…" Abruptly, he asked, "Why are you so sure she didn't commit suicide? She left a note—"

"Because she wanted Thurston's attention, not to leave this earth. That note was written to change him. Because she got in the back seat.

Because she oh-so-publicly bought the gun and the ammunition—"

"That points to suicide."

"No. Not unless she wanted to be stopped. She didn't care how public her purchase was because she knew she wasn't going to use it. It was play-acting. Because her dealings with Thurston say she didn't. Because her best friend and only confidant says she didn't. Maybe even because her stepfather says she did and that's darned convenient for him.

"But perhaps most of all because she went to that particular spot. Isolated, but within view of the highway in the daylight and not that far from the Slake-ur-Thirst, even in the dark on foot. Or on a bicycle."

His head jerked up. He shifted his eyes to Tom, then back to me.

"You think I did this. You think I lured her to territory I'm familiar with, where I could be sure to be the one who found her to cover up any forensic trace I might have missed."

"It makes sense. And your sheriff sure helped by leaving you on the case. Hell, you might even have had opportunities to plant things to make Thurston look more guilty."

Although Thurston did a good job of that himself.

Chapter Fifty-One

TOM WAS QUIET on the way back to his truck.

But then he didn't get out of my SUV right away.

"That wasn't easy," he said.

"No, it wasn't."

"You're good at this, Elizabeth. Really good. Tough, but never cruel. I… Well. I better go now."

"Okay. Say hi to Tamantha for me."

"I will."

"And, thanks, Tom."

He dipped his cowboy hat at me.

THE FIVE HAD just started when I came in the newsroom with takeout bags. I hadn't had lunch and Diana and Jennifer took me up on the offer to pick up for them, too.

We could talk while we ate and waited for Mike to call, because everyone else was on assignment, gone for the day, or in the studio for the newscast.

We had the Five on, but with the volume low.

"Nice job, Leona," I murmured as she wrapped the dogs-for-veterans story. "If that non-profit only knew how fortunate they are to have her instead of Thurston."

"At least it would be dogs and not whales." A smile tugged at Diana's mouth.

"Another Thurston story?"

"Oh, yes. It was the year before you arrived. We had less local news then than we do now."

"Fewer dead bodies," Jennifer noted. "Not that you've caused the dead bodies, Elizabeth, but you've found more. Along with finding out more of the dead bodies were murdered than they used to."

Diana, not doing a very good job of hiding a grin, said, "There was a story about a whale washed up on a beach and people tried to help it. Except Thurston read the entire story without the word *whale*. According to Thurston, *sperm* washed up on the beach and people banded together to send the *sperm* back out into the water.

"Phones started before his last reference to *sperm*. But nobody could answer because everyone was laughing so hard." Her expressions shifted. "He never realized it. Never asked why people were laughing. Never showed any interest."

"You know," I said thoughtfully, "a week ago, I'd have said that was the worst indictment of Thurston—a complete lack of journalistic curiosity—but considering he's blackmailing Chloe Vogt and…"

Jennifer completed what I hadn't. "Might have murdered Melissa, sperm doesn't seem so bad. I was thinking, since he blackmailed Chloe Vogt, that makes it more likely he could blackmail someone else, right?"

"Logical. Although if you're thinking that makes him look more guilty of killing Melissa, it falls apart. Blackmailers tend not to kill people. Cuts down their business."

"What if someone he blackmailed killed Melissa thinking they really were a couple and that would punish Thurston enough that he'd stop blackmailing them."

"They couldn't know Thurston very well. But what if Chloe Vogt killed Melissa because she threatened to go public about Chloe and what she's doing out of concern for Thurston."

"But we have no evidence Melissa knew about Chloe's original lie. Without that would it be enough to make Chloe kill her?" Diana asked.

"Chloe wouldn't have known what Melissa did or didn't know. Besides, if Melissa started a stink and people started looking into Chloe—."

"They'd find out about her past and she wouldn't want to risk it. That's good, Elizabeth."

"What about this? Melissa telling people about Chloe threatened Thurston getting her services and other stuff for free, so he silenced Melissa."

"Back to Thurston? Jennifer, you need to widen—."

Mike came on then, having caught the very end of what Jennifer said.

That required explanation, so we caught him up—mostly.

"There's one more big thing," I said, referring to Greg Itson's birth mother. "But before we tell you that, Mike, I have something to tell all of you. I'm telling you up front I'm not going to tell you all of it. I'm never going to tell you my sources. And each of you must swear you will never tell anyone else. Also that you'll never try to find out more about this—because I know each of you is good at investigating and could use what I tell you to dig up more. If you can't accept those terms, you have to get off the call right now."

A silence descended.

I appreciated that because each was considering what I'd said.

"I swear," Diana said.

"I can't not know now," Mike admitted. "And I respect your judgment. I swear."

We all looked at Jennifer. She pulled her bottom lip with her teeth. "Never to even look into whatever it is a little?"

"Never," I confirmed.

It would be toughest on her. At some level she still believed everything could be known and she could find it out.

"There's no shame in saying you don't want to make this promise," Diana said. "But you should also recognize the trust Elizabeth is putting in you to offer you the choice."

She nodded, her lip back in place and a fierce frown drawing down her brows. "You're saying that never knowing more is the only way to know some."

"That's right."

After three more beats, Jennifer looked up. "I swear."

I told them a carefully expurgated account of Val Heatherton, blended from Mel and Linda.

At the end, Mike whistled.

"Holy—" Diana stopped with that single word, apparently feeling *moley* didn't match the circumstances.

Again, we all looked at Jennifer.

Her frown had returned. "But if she had Dodd Oxley as one of her bought men and he got away, what does that tell us about somebody killing Melissa?"

I was so proud of Jennifer Lawton—for her logic and for not asking how it helped us pin a murder on Thurston—that it took an extra beat to absorb the truth of her point.

"It doesn't." At the shoulder-slumping exhales—including my own—I added, "But all information is good. We just don't see how it helps us in this moment."

"How about whatever else went on today. You said something big…"

I took up Mike's invitation and told him the story of Melissa and Greg Itson discovering they had the same mother.

"Huh."

The rest of us peered at the screen at Mike's syllable of reaction.

"That's all you have to say?" Jennifer asked.

"This might be a tangent and no guarantee it's connected to anything we're looking at. Plus, considering this might have to do with murder—"

"For Pete's sake, tell us."

While the head in my voice agreed with Jennifer, I also recognized Mike's quandary. "If it isn't necessary to catching a murderer or explaining a murder to our viewers, it's off the record."

He breathed out. "It has to do with Jack. Jack Delahunt."

Chapter Fifty-Two

"LET ME TELL it from the start. It was the summer after I graduated high school. Four of us worked a fence line way out from the home ranch. Could only get so close with the horse trailers, that's how far out it was. So we camped overnight to finish up in the morning, instead of burning daylight coming and going.

"One of the guys pulled out a bottle—Isaac Raglettley, as a matter of fact—and we all had some. Then more. Then Isaac, who'd worked there before, started needling Jack. Something about when Jack was young and foolish, and the past didn't always stay in the past and stuff like that.

"We went to sleep and it was pretty much forgotten after. But the last night of my working that summer, we were out at the same spot and stayed overnight again, this time just Jack and me.

"He got quiet, then he pulled out a bottle. Never saw him do that before or since. He offered me some, then he started drinking pretty steady. Tell the truth, it rattled me. Maybe even more when he started talking. You know Jack, he doesn't talk all that much, so that was weird.

"As he talked, I realized he was back on what Isaac brought up earlier in the summer. In bits and pieces, it came out Jack fell for a girl working at the ranch one summer and she fell for him. Her parents didn't approve. When they found out she was having a baby, they really didn't approve."

Not sure who sucked in the audible breath as we made the connection. It could have been me.

"Yeah," Mike said. "Barbara Fyall was the girl."

I remembered feeling Greg Itson was familiar when I'd met him. He was no carbon copy, but he *did* resemble Jack Delahunt.

"Barbara came back to town as a married woman. She and Jack hadn't done more than nod hello until they ran into each other after Melissa's father died and Jack said he was sorry about her bereavement and she lit into him. Said at least she'd married a man who provided for her, not a saddle tramp like him—which Jack never was—and their baby was better off not having him as a father. Then she burst into tears.

"He got her off the street to where they could talk and she said she was pregnant after that summer, but her parents took care of everything. She didn't know what happened to the boy, and didn't want to. It was done. Past. She had nothing else to tell him, except her parents had done right and she'd appreciate it if he never talked to her again. He didn't. Jack said it was like she was a different person from the girl he'd loved.

"But it ate at him, wondering about the baby. What I remember clearest was him saying, *You can get over a girl, but not sure you can ever get over having a kid out there in the world and having no idea where.*

"He never lectured, never tied it to me. But looking back, I think he might not have been as drunk as I thought. For sure those words made me a heck of a lot more careful at times when it could have been real easy to be stupid."

Had Jack Delahunt seen in the teenage Mike a son he'd never known? Mike had always said Jack had been good to him—tough, but scrupulously fair, and taught him a lot.

I sat back, exhaling deeply as my back connected with the chair. "It's not our job to tell Jack about Itson or Itson about Jack. Not to mention—."

Jennifer swung around to me. "You can't be serious. They have to know."

"Ease up, Jennifer," Mike said. "Elizabeth has an idea."

"Do you?" she demanded.

"Itson said he signed up for all the DNA testing companies and checked to find family members on them, but never found anyone else."

"Because Jack Delahunt hasn't taken any of those tests," Diana picked up. "But if he did now, say, because somebody he knows and trusts tells him he should…"

"Oh," Jennifer's voice squeaked. "You have to do that, Mike."

"I can do better. I can send him all the tests and tell him I'll bust his butt if he doesn't."

"The true language of love," Diana said.

"Except you might be telling him his son is a murderer," I said.

"I think… Jack would want to know."

"What about Greg Itson?" Diana asked.

"If he's a murderer, I don't care." I shifted in the chair. "I've been thinking about Itson saying in that first interview that Melissa wasn't going to cause anyone a problem ever again."

"Like she was a problem to him? But," Diana reminded me, "you thought his sympathy for her was genuine."

"Maybe. Or he's a good actor. Awfully convenient he found her body."

"Why would he kill her when he just found her?" Jennifer asked.

"He considers the Itsons his true family. It was only because of wanting the medical background for his daughter he started searching for his birth parents. He wasn't looking for the kind of family Melissa represented," Diana said. "We only have his word for it that they got along. Or that she wanted to find him, that she welcomed him."

"And now he's next of kin, right? That's motive," Mike said. "He's got that financial pressure you talked about, Diana, needing funds to keep his mother in that nice place in Cody. With the way he feels about the Itsons, that's a motive. And it could have seemed like justice that his family got the money from the Oxleys. Whether Dodd Oxley directly participated in misleading Terence Itson or not, he benefited while the Itsons suffered."

I became aware of the others focusing on me.

"You're quiet, Elizabeth," Diana said. "What are you thinking about?"

"Cross talk. Not Thurston's version, but the way it's *supposed* to be done. Questions and answers that provide more information."

"Like what?" Jennifer asked.

But I wasn't quite ready.

I thought I had pieces, but the right pieces?

"I'm thinking about going back to the beginning. If we take what Fawn said as the truth, Melissa wasn't going to kill herself. She saw what she planned to do Sunday night as a solution that would make her relationship with Thurston better and that she would then tell Fawn all about.

"If we go right back to the beginning, clearing out the idea of suicide, looking at all of it through the lens of murder…"

As I said the words, I did that myself, went back to the beginning, hearing phrases again, weighing what was said, what was not said during cross talk.

"I'm thinking about…"

Puzzle pieces.

Puzzle pieces in that all black, round jigsaw puzzle my brother Rob bought. We'd stopped trying to put the puzzle together the way we did other ones. We started looking at each piece individually, turning them, this way, then that.

Putting aside expectations.

Shifting and settling. Sorting and re-ordering.

"I'm thinking…" I looked up. "We have to make phone calls. I'll do it. Get Itson here. The others. And, Jennifer? That phone number you have for Les, it's time to use it. We're going to deal with everything at once. Also, can you get into Thurston's office? I know he locked—"

"Yes."

"Good. We'll set this up for an hour, say."

"An hour? So soon? But—."

"I don't want to drag this out." And I needed to know if I was right. No delaying.

✧ ✧ ✧ ✧

THURSTON'S OFFICE SMELLED musty, but opening the window

briefly, along with leaving the door open dealt with that.

So that wasn't the reason one of our invited attendees—Les Haeburn—reacted to being escorted there with a slight recoil. "In here? No, my office."

Diana herded him in ahead of her. "We'll be more comfortable here. Everyone can sit. Can't do that in your office."

"Thurston will—" He looked around. "When he gets here, he'll—"

"Deputy Itson, I don't believe you know Les Haeburn, the news director for KWMT-TV." I didn't move out of the way, which kept them too far apart to shake hands. They nodded to each other. "Deputy Itson is Melissa Oxley's half-brother."

The eyebrows of both men popped up. Les at the information, Itson at my sharing it.

"Won't you have a seat, please."

I gestured Haeburn to take the open middle cushion of the couch, between Dale on one side and Diana on the other, then nodded Itson to the chair sitting directly across from the couch.

I sat in a chair positioned at the head of the coffee table, with the couch to my right.

As arranged, Jennifer moved three empty chairs up on the same side as Itson, all out of his reach. In preparation for taking the desk chair by the door herself, she shifted it slightly.

"We'll be joined by, ah, other interested parties shortly."

"Thurston is going to—"

I cut across Les. "Not anymore. That's why—"

What cut across my words was not a voice, but a surprise entrance, as Jennifer went to close the door.

Tom Burrell.

His gaze flicked over the setup before coming to me. "Mike invited me."

Dale, who'd turned pale with the arrival of Les and Itson, flushed red and popped up. "If you'd like my seat, sir."

"No, you stay right there, son. I'll …" He closed the door, looked at the three empty chairs, then snagged the back of another one, swinging it into position at the opposite end of the coffee table, but well back from it.

He looked relaxed and at ease.

Bull.

He now had a view of the entire room, an easy path to any corner of it, and an angle so the door opening would catch his eye immediately. If he'd been truly relaxed and at ease, he'd have hooked his hat on his knee, not tossed it on the table—as he did now—out of his way.

Jennifer gave me a questioning look, as if I might tell her to eject the intruder. As if she could.

"Have a seat, Jennifer. This isn't one of the interested parties I mentioned, but I think you're all acquainted."

The three men nodded to each other.

"Thurston Fine and Magnus Boesch among your interested parties?" Itson asked.

"Of course. Fawn Raglettley, too. While we wait, I'll fill you in a little. Melissa Oxley did not commit suicide."

Neither man reacted to that bald statement.

"She intended to pretend to commit suicide to impress on Thurston that their relationship was changing. She'd been his fan, loyal and beyond, but she had reached the point where she wanted more from him, and she intended to get it.

"Did Thurston kill her because of that? To prevent being *caught* in a relationship with her?

"Did Fawn kill her because of that? Jealous at the thought of losing her friendship … or more?

"Did Magnus Boesch kill her because a deeper relationship with Thurston threatened what Magnus expected by way of inheritance eventually? Or—forget eventually—because he wanted to inherit immediately.

"Did Greg Itson kill her because he wanted to inherit immediately from his half-sister?"

Les gaped at the deputy, caught himself and looked away. Tom looked at him with interest. Itson never took his eyes off me.

"Before we address those possibilities in more detail and before the others get here, there's something you should know. We have a witness that Thurston was blackmailing them. Extracting, ah, services under threat that Thurston would reveal a secret that would ruin the witness."

Not that Chloe would willingly admit that.

"And that got us thinking. Could Melissa's death have been a way for someone else being blackmailed to deal with Thurston—to scare him off, or frame him, or both? That would be awfully insidious. On the other hand, murderers aren't exactly known for their sense of justice.

"That theory tied in with a couple questions rattling around in my head. The kind of questions that would be great for cross talk. One was something I said to Jerry—you won't know him, Deputy Itson, but he's our studio cameraman. Been around forever. He told me a story about a Thurston on-air screwup—I've been hearing a lot of those—and I said to him, *How* did *he survive all this time?*

"Interesting question, isn't it? Brought into sharper focus by a journalist friend who said to me, *Why did he hire Thurston? And why give him free rein?*

"I passed it off at the time. I shouldn't have. Because that is the question, isn't it? There had to be a reason. Not a fluke. A real reason. Why *did* you hire Thurston and give him free rein, Les?"

Chapter Fifty-Three

EVERY EYE SHOULD have been on Les Haeburn.

They weren't.

Tom kept a general view that would let him react to anything or everything.

Jennifer focused on the computer on Thurston's desk.

Dale, who'd been roped in as our lame aim at muscle, looked adoringly at Jennifer. Maybe Mike had been right to invite Tom.

Itson looked at me. Not adoringly.

Diana looked at Les.

After my quick survey of the others, so did I.

"You think I don't know it's over." Now every eye was on Les. "You think I didn't know it when you called me to come tonight? Though I've got to admit having the half-brother here, I thought… But not for long. You've always thought of me as an idiot, Danniher, but I'm not. I'm a victim of circumstances. Circumstances, Thurston Fine, and now of you and your damned investigating. From the time you started here… I'll tell you, damn you. I'll tell all of you. But first—"

He reached into his shirt pocket.

Several of us flinched, myself included, despite the impossibility of that pocket holding much more than the folded papers sticking out the top of it.

He saw our reaction and smirked.

"I'm not going to off myself. But I have two final official acts."

He pulled out papers. He signed and dated the first sheet, checking the time then adding a notation after the date. He repeated the routine with the second.

"This—" He held up the first. "—fires Thurston Fine. This—" He held up the second. "—is my resignation. You're all witnesses that I fired him while still news director."

He put the sheets on the coffee table.

Without looking up, he said, "Jennifer, in the bottom right drawer of that desk, there's a bottle and a glass. Get them."

She looked at me. I nodded. She brought them partway, but Tom took them from her, keeping her well back. He placed them on the table.

Les Haeburn wasn't the first journalist I'd seen with a reliance on alcohol, but I'd never seen any look at a bottle the way he did.

As he poured himself an unhealthy slug, he said, "I've dreamed of firing Thurston forever. Firing him, quitting, and going someplace better. Hell, any place would be better."

I bit my tongue against saying this place could be better if he'd put any effort into it.

When a murderer was confessing, it wasn't good to stop their flow with a critique of their work ethic.

"*Quit?* I couldn't ever quit. I was caught. No escape. And as long as I couldn't quit, I couldn't fire Thurston.

"And then that woman—Melissa Oxley—came to me with her idiotic plan and I thought even if I couldn't get out completely, I'd finally get rid of that horse's ass. Maybe even turn this piss-ant station into something resembling a news operation."

"What was Melissa's plan?"

He snorted out a harsh sound. "She thought if she pretended to commit suicide and Thurston saw a video of it, he'd regret *being mean to her*." He mimicked with a falsetto whine. "She planned that I would record it, take the recording to Thurston, then rush him back to her side to discover she hadn't killed herself and all would be light and joy."

"Why you?" Jennifer's confusion slid in without interrupting.

"She thought since Thurston could call the shots with me, she could, too. She'd picked up that he had something on me. When he tried to pull away from her, she dug up what it was. She and Thurston deserved each other."

"What proof?"

"Audio. Bastard taped me. She'd copied it. I will say this for her. She promised to give me her copy after we taped her fake suicide and she did bring it with her. Found it right there in her bag … after."

"But how did you get her to put a gun to her head?" Under Diana's calm, I heard horror.

"That was her scenario. She told me the whole thing when she came to blackmail me, like I couldn't help being impressed. She would record a message to Thurston about how he'd driven her to this desperate act, pretend to shoot herself in the head, then put on fake blood and stuff she'd bought. She said she could count on me to make it look realistic.

"It's when she was going on and on about her preparations that the idea came to me. Just enough of a glimmer to ask what she was doing about a gun. She had a starter's pistol. I said she needed a real gun with blanks to make it believable."

"She bought real ammunition." Itson's voice was calm, but strained.

"Yeah. Told her she needed to do that. Said if Thurston looked into it, it would ruin everything if she bought blanks or had no ammunition. She accepted that, but ordered me to buy blanks. No way was I leaving that trail. I had some from a stunt in Michigan a million years ago. Didn't tell her that. Though she wasn't entirely stupid. She insisted on checking the box and comparing the bullets. She'd read somewhere that blanks and bullets are different.

"But all I had to do was distract her about how she should be situated, palm the blanks, slip in a couple bullets. Pretended to check the whole setup through her phone camera, then came back to her and said, *Here, hold the gun like this. It'll look more realistic.* Positioned her hand with the finger on the trigger. Told her I was ready and she pulled the trigger."

Someone drew in a sharp breath. It might have been me.

It was so bland, so unconnected to the fact he'd taken a life.

He—and Thurston—griped me from the moment I started here with how they subverted journalism. I'd thought—probably said—I hated them.

But this… This was so far beyond that.

"Why was she in the back seat?"

He breathed out through his nose. "That was all her. She'd done a dry run and she couldn't get the angle she wanted in the front seat. She decided the back seat worked better. Idiot woman."

Horribly, tragically misguided, but not an idiot.

"Then it was a matter of following my plan. Wiped the phone and put her fingers on it—I'd worn gloves, natural with the cold that night. Brushed out footprints, though there weren't many. But I hadn't risked taking my car in there in case tire prints could be lifted.

"Simple matter of backtracking. Walked down the middle of the pavement to where I'd left a bike. Rode it to that bar's parking lot where I'd left my car among all the drunks' pickups. Stowed the bike in the trunk, drove a way out to wipe down the bike, then went back and left it at the bar, figuring it would be gone by morning.

"Dumping the bike was the end of my plan and I didn't expect…" He poured more and took it in one swallow. "It shouldn't have mattered. I should have had time. That road doesn't go anywhere. Nobody drives it. There was no reason for that deputy—You—"

His head jerked, but he didn't meet Itson's gaze.

"—to find it so fast. I thought I'd have time. Even though that meant putting up with Thurston days or even weeks longer, while the cops figured out the connection, his motive.

"That next day, when you told me the sheriff's department had taken Thurston in for questioning, I almost burst out laughing. Even locked in my office, I wasn't sure I could contain it."

"But you were shocked. You looked shocked."

"Maybe I was. Shocked something went right in my life for the first time since I met Val Heatherton."

✧   ✧   ✧   ✧

"THAT WAS AT the national broadcaster's conference. When she hired you."

"Yeah. After I *auditioned*." His mouth twisted. "It wasn't so bad then. She was old and the scars from some accident… But she knew things and it seemed a fair trade. It was only supposed to be a short time. Get news director on my resume, a couple accolades, then up and out.

"A few months here, she made it clear what my job really was. Whenever she wanted and never to let anybody know. Ever. There'd be no quitting for another job in journalism. I made, uh, transactions on the station accounts those first few months. She had proof. She'd also tracked a source for a story I'd done that got awards. Had the source saying I'd faked the story."

Had he? This did not seem the moment to demand he edit for clarity.

"That was the choice. No job, no reputation, no future. Or stick here, keep my mouth shut, and make decent money. I figured I could make it work. Make it better. Make KWMT something."

"Until Thurston blackmailed you into hiring him," I said.

"Hell, yes, he blackmailed me. You think I hired that walking, talking, brainless mannequin voluntarily?" He poured and drank.

"How'd he find out about you and Val?"

"I went back to a Midwest regional conference to collect an award—a damned award. Didn't even care about it because I expected to have a million more, but it wasn't long after Val made the terms of employment clear and it was an excuse to get away awhile. Maybe I even thought I could make a connection, get a lead on a job…

"It was a shitshow from the start. Weather delayed me. Hotel gave away my room. Nearby hotels filled because of the storm. And then this guy I didn't know said his room had two beds and I could bunk with him.

"I knew he was on the hunt for a job from the way he looked at my news director badge. But how bad could it be for a couple nights?" The volume of bitter rose on that question.

"You got drunk."

"On my ass. Made it to the room—barely—and there was

Thurston, waiting to congratulate me, listen to every word. If I'd been drinking normally, the amount I had that night wouldn't have made a dent. But I'd backed way off for a while. I wasn't used to it. That's why I ran my mouth off."

Yeah, that was the problem. He hadn't been drinking enough.

"To keep my job—my life—I had to keep Fine quiet. Hire him, let him do whatever the hell he wanted. And he was never going to leave. God knows I tried, writing him recs that made me want to puke. But no news director who saw his tape, much less talked to him, would ever take him off my hands."

THIS TIME THE KWMT-TV staffer escorted out of Thurston's office by deputies was handcuffed.

Thurston, Magnus, and Fawn never showed up, because they had not been invited.

Sergeant Wayne Shelton and other members of the Cottonwood County Sheriff's Department did, entering from the studio, where Jennifer had piped audio and visual for their viewing pleasure, with an assist from the control room guys.

Tom cocked one eyebrow at me. I echoed his expression as a placeholder for reminding both him and Mike that I'd learned my lesson from another confrontation when a suspect pulled a gun from his desk. I hadn't been about to give Les that opportunity.

Besides, Itson hadn't been solely a misdirection to keep Les from clenching into self-protection. I'd figured that even unwarned, his law enforcement instincts would kick in long enough for the Cottonwood guys to get to the room if absolutely necessary.

"You knew about this?" Itson asked Shelton, then didn't give him time to answer. "Never would have believed a guy would spill his guts like that with as little on him as she had."

"Worth a try," Shelton said.

I grimaced at him.

He hadn't believed it, either. And he'd been clear that none of his people or recording equipment would be involved.

At some point, Itson would probably realize the setup could have left him in an *awkward* position, which was unlikely to help inter-county cooperation. But for now, he was caught up in the answers to his half-sister's death.

"Why did he talk?" Itson asked.

Because somewhere deep in Les Haeburn's heart remained a core of a journalist. Unfortunately, a bigger part was murderous. And all the rest was self-centered.

I said it more simply.

"He needed to tell the story."

And he did it in time for the Ten.

Chapter Fifty-Four

WE HAD CLEARED Thurston Fine of murder.

That night, he stepped in front of me in the hallway at the sheriff's office where we'd all given statements. He didn't look at me.

"I have thought about the situation with Melissa, uh, dying."

As if referring to it as *dying* wiped away the truth.

"I'm taking the rest of the week off. Then—" He sucked in a breath. "—I have decided you can anchor. Sometimes. I could use more days off."

Beneath instant irritation that his main goal was to get more time off—because he worked so hard—and he thought he could still make decisions at KWMT-TV, something deeper twanged inside me.

I hadn't refused Audrey's request to anchor because it would have driven Thurston into a frenzy—a perk—or because Leona would be a more familiar presence for viewers.

I didn't want the job.

I liked my professional life as it was. I wasn't working toward a promotion or the next bigger market. I wasn't striving for external markers of success.

I'd had them. I'd lost them—or had them stolen, depending on how I was feeling about my ex at the moment. Either way, they were gone and … I didn't care.

"No, thanks. Not to mention it's not your job to bestow on anybody, Thurston."

"We'll see about that."

Time was, I would have argued. Now, I decided to let events take their course.

We had cleared Thurston Fine of murder. Not of anything else.

Epilogue

WE'D DONE SPECIALS for KWMT-TV after other murder cases.

We'd never done one with the news director's office turned over to detectives and scientists, searching for evidence to buttress a confession. In case Les recanted, they said.

I suppose they had to do their jobs. Especially with the case officially transferred from Horse Creek County to Cottonwood County to resolve any conflict of interest for Deputy Greg Itson.

It was pure bonus for Shelton that doing their jobs distracted from us doing our jobs.

Turns out, Les was wrong about the bicycle.

He'd thought it would be taken from the bar, obscuring all connection to him. Instead, it remained at the bar, waiting for its rightful owner. No fingerprints were found, except a few from the owner in odd places on the frame … and one of Les Haeburn's on a pedal, in keeping with someone adjusting it to close the trunk of a car, after he removed the gloves he'd worn earlier.

The Slake-ur-Thirst bartender identified Les as coming in every month or so for years, with a tendency to drink deep and fast. Had he chosen that spot because Val Heatherton couldn't reach him in its black hole of connection?

It was where he spent Monday, which made it possible he'd told the truth when he said he hadn't heard about events until we told him at KWMT-TV Monday night.

Except we told him a Sherman woman was dead. He said a woman was killed in Horse Creek County.

Something he couldn't have known about ... if he was telling the truth.

The fingerprint and bartenders' IDs were—pardon the expression—overkill. Haeburn confessed again in a Cottonwood County Sheriff's Department interview room while they recorded.

The county attorney and James Longbaugh were in discussions of what KWMT-TV could run of our recordings.

In the newsroom, brief but spirited debate ensued about whether we should skip a special this time, considering how close to home it hit.

That, my argument went, was precisely why we had to do one—to treat this murderer the same as we had others. The opposing argument was we didn't have the time, staff, or resources.

Both things being true, we worked like crazy to keep the daily newscasts up to their recent, improved, standard while also producing a special.

Audrey aired another of my stockpiled "Helping Out!" segments. Two in under two weeks. At this rate, I'd run out in a couple years.

It reminded me I'd done a "Helping Out!" piece earlier in the year on negotiating the bureaucracy to get help for sufferers of early onset Alzheimer's and their families.

Somehow a copy of that show and a printout of resources got sent to Deputy Greg Itson.

I know it was received because Deputy Richard Alvaro stopped me in the cookie aisle of the Sherman Supermarket while I was on an emergency run and—after clearing his throat three times—told me Itson's mother's position in the good facility in Cody was secured and it was a real decent thing I'd done.

The second piece of news about Greg Itson came in pieces via Mike.

First, that Jack Delahunt had received, taken, and returned tests from all the major family DNA companies. Mike used some connections to get those tests to the front of the line.

Next, Jack got several hits that turned out to be distant cousins. That was a blow.

Finally, the day of our special on the murder of Melissa Oxley, Mike called with the update we'd been hoping for. Jack had a hit. A son.

He sent a message.

A response came back immediately.

They talked on the phone.

That's when they realized how close they were geographically.

They've set up a meeting, with the blessing of Greg Itson's parents.

Magnus Boesch renewed his apartment lease. He continues to work in the back office of the country club.

Fawn Raglettley has started helping teach little kids basketball. Mike and Mrs. P worked together to bring this about, thanks to an old coach of Mike's and Mrs. P's connection in the school system.

The report is she is greatly enjoying interacting with the kids in addition to her ranch work for the Baxters.

That couple has had a meeting with James Longbaugh about setting up their estate to take care of them if they're no longer able to work on the ranch, and to help provide for Fawn after they're gone.

They were delighted to hear of a special program available to them through Fawn's work with the kids to cover the cost of James advising them and drawing up necessary documents.

James has said he will not outright lie, but agreed that if they don't ask, he won't reveal exactly who's funding this special program.

On that same emergency run to Sherman Supermarket, I saw Fawn with Shelley.

We all said hello, a few pleasantries, then parted ways. A couple aisles later, Fawn hurried up to me.

"I looked up that word you said before. Astute. Took a while. I didn't know how it was spelled or anything. But I found it. That was real nice of you."

"I reported the fact, Fawn. Recognizing that what's said around another statement gives us additional information is truly astute."

She smiled widely, raised her hand in farewell, and trotted off to find Shelley.

✧ ✧ ✧ ✧

THE DAILY NEWSCAST folks and those of us working on the special all took time out when Dale brought in the dinner order.

KWMT kept Hamburger Heaven in business.

With the worst of the hunger pangs sated, I said, "I've heard Thurston screw-up stories about Oreos and in absentia and sperm whales and finger-sucking. But nothing from you, Leona."

She grinned.

"Those are all good. But not the best one."

We all quieted, acknowledging she had our full attention.

"He was doing a teaser for the next block, including a medical story."

We groaned. Thurston's renditions of scientific terms—even with the pronouncers supplied by the wires—defied logic or description. Remembering Jerry's account about the story on the library, he wasn't foolproof with ordinary English, either.

"It was about researchers discovering a deadly organism. But Thurston announced that after the break, he'd reveal details behind researchers discovering—"

"Oh, no," Diana and I said together.

"—a deadly *orgasm*."

"*No!*" came a chorus nearly as loud as the laughter.

"And with nobody willing to face the wrath of Fine," Leona continued, "that's what he said throughout the story."

After the laughter eased, she added, "I've had that recording transferred to new media every couple years so I don't lose it. Institutional memory."

Late that night, when the two of us walked out together, I said to Leona, "I've been thinking about institutional memory."

She waited.

"Your voice when you said Les didn't have *the same kind of sway* with the ownership Artie had. You knew. About Val Heatherton."

"Knew? Like with proof? No. Suspect? Yes. Artie had enough on her to keep her away from the newsroom, but he told me never to get on the wrong side of her. She'd had a string of men she controlled, mostly working for the company."

"Dodd Oxley."

"Dodd?" Her eyes went wide, which let me see her brain putting together pieces. "Huh. His father-in-law, too? That would explain why he hated Dodd. Protective of Barbara or angry at being pushed out by his son-in-law or both. Also, probably pissed Dodd escaped… My, my, my."

And she'd scoffed at Jennifer for a soap opera plot.

She added thoughtfully, "Bet Dodd Oxley surprised the heck out of her when he sprung loose."

"Explains why he was willing to take the risk of stealing from those con men."

"All this explains why Val, Honey, Craig, and staff have decamped for a home in Spain. No sign of an imminent return."

I WATCHED THE special at home, with a making-up-for-lost-time cuddle with Shadow.

Though, in fact, my dog might not have felt the lack of my company, with Iris and Zeb Undlin caring for him, plus visits from Tamantha and Tom, which I'd heard averaged out to more than daily.

I needed to thank them for their Shadow missions of mercy.

Tamantha would be easy.

Watching the special, I saw more I'd like to change than any of our previous ones. We'd covered the bases, but areas that would have benefited from another edit or a re-ordering of information to make it easier to follow. I suppose if we ever produced the perfect one there'd be no point in doing more.

My phone rang as the credits ran.

Mike.

His face appeared and a smile welled up from my heart.

"I only have a minute, because I'm the sports guy tonight, but you all did great on this," he said.

"How did you get it so fast?"

"Jennifer."

Of course.

"You don't look as pleased with yourself as you should, Elizabeth. The special or—?"

"I thought… I thought maybe I didn't want to look into this at the beginning because part of me hoped Thurston was guilty."

"*All* of Jennifer hoped that."

"I know. But there was an innocence about her hope—her belief."

"So you wondered for, what? A day? After that, you didn't. You found out who did it. You found out the truth."

The truth.

I looked at him on the screen. "Mike, it was awful. He… It was so awful."

"You didn't make it awful, Elizabeth. He did." He swore under his breath. "I know this isn't the time, but I need to talk to you about something. Something big. Something that could change both of our futures."

My heartbeat stumbled like a tripped-up runner. "Mike—"

"Don't say anything. I can't get into it now, here." He dropped his voice, reminding me he was in a newsroom. "And you can't really know until I tell you all of it. But I've been doing a lot of thinking. Soul-searching."

Soul-searching.

I gulped in air. "Of course. We should set up a time when we can talk without interruption. If you want to video chat—"

"In person. I'm coming there. Soon. Elizabeth—" He swore again. "I've gotta go. I'm sorry, but—"

"Go, go. I know the strident call of deadline. We'll talk."

He chuckled lightly as we hung up.

I didn't.

✧ ✧ ✧ ✧

THE NEXT AFTERNOON, Tom Burrell and I stood at the bottom of my back steps, watching my dog and his daughter adore each other.

Apparently, the Burrells had not been prepared to quit visiting

Shadow cold turkey. I knew he wasn't, either, and welcomed them happily.

Tom and I had already dealt with his showing up for the scene at KWMT. I expressed my independence and self-reliance. He listened carefully and said he'd do it again and to get over myself.

Not quite in those words.

He shared that Leona and Linda Caswell individually had conversations with Val Heatherton before her departure for Spain.

No word on specifics or even what aspect they talked about. But take your pick—it couldn't have been comfortable.

Without ever going back on the air, Thurston Fine resigned from KWMT-TV, refusing to acknowledge that Les fired him.

Either way, he was gone.

Needham had the best line: "Oh-ho, so this is playing out with a hush, not a bang."

Dale had been tasked with packing Thurston's office belongings and taking them to his home. He said the house was dark and no one answered the door.

Penny said Thurston was seen at the airport within hours of leaving the Heatherton house the day after Les' arrest.

The release put out by the station's owners—in other words written by news aide Jennifer Lawton and approved by Craig Morningside via email—said he'd left to explore other pursuits.

He's in Denver, working for a corporation headquartered there, in their PR department—excuse me, Communications Department. I suspected Chloe helped get him the job. After all, she wouldn't want a failure besmirching her stats. Not to mention any other besmirching.

The best part is Thurston's writing news releases. I expect he's decent at it, considering his familiarity with the genre from reading so many on-air as his version of news.

Could Les do anything about Thurston's thumbscrew-turning? Considering his own legal issues, he probably has other priorities.

Nothing has been said publicly about the relationship between Val and Les, but even if it doesn't figure during the investigation or court case, enough of the newsroom knows that it could sift into the public realm like mist across a mountain.

Perhaps with the upheaval in so many lives and the memory our previous backyard chat on my mind, I said to Tom. "I did want the truth. I needed to find it."

"I know."

"*Hah!* That's not what you said Monday night."

"Elizabeth—"

"No. Wait. I shouldn't have said it that way, like I was outraged or even mock outraged, because I needed to hear it. Yes, keeping KWMT from rolling off the tracks was the priority the first day, but I needed to be brought up short. To be reminded about—"

"No, you didn't. You were always going to look into it. You were tired. You'd wrapped up that other murder and with Jennifer here for only part of it and Mike gone—"

"And you."

"—and me. You carried a lot. After a breath, you were always going to pick this up and look into what happened to Melissa Oxley. And I knew that. That's what Diana said when I called her on my way here Monday night. That I already knew what you would do and I was making excuses."

Excuses? But that wasn't the real question. "Why did you come, then?"

He swallowed.

"I couldn't stay away from you."

He turned to me and stroked the back of his knuckles down my cheek.

"I can't stay away from you."

Timing is everything.

Like the sound of someone at my gate.

We turned together to see Krista Seger standing there.

"Mind if I come in?" She looked uncomfortable enough to have witnessed that moment between Tom and me.

There was nothing to say except, "Of course not, come in."

I thought she might want to discuss the news that broke yesterday and led both the Five and Ten newscasts.

A lawyer from Cody, who'd been away when Melissa died, came forward with her will, drawn up in September.

Melissa left a few bequests, including a modest trust for Fawn and money to the library. Everything else went to Greg Itson.

The neighbors were so thrilled Magnus Boesch did not inherit the house, that I hadn't heard even one wondering why Melissa made a Horse Creek County deputy her heir. Yet. That connection was sure to come out. Not from me, however.

So even if Krista was interested in that aspect, I would not be spilling…

She had an entirely different topic in mind.

"Elizabeth, you know I've appreciated how you handled that, uh, situation at the B&B last year and I wanted you to hear this before it goes public. Aunt Val is selling KWMT."

"To whom?"

"Nothing's final, but she's talking with a group that owns other stations. They broadcast old sitcoms and religious services." She inhaled quickly, then exhaled slowly. "They don't consider news wholesome. They've dropped it from all their stations."

The End

For news about upcoming books, as well as other titles and news, join Patricia McLinn's ReadHeads and receive her twice-monthly free newsletter.

patriciamclinn.com/readers-list

You can buy this book and all my others, including print editions and audiobooks, from my online store. I've added direct-to-you buying options to better control how my books reach you, while having lots more elbow room to give you special bundles, early offers, and exclusive bonuses.

Patricia's Bookstore

shop.patriciamclinn.com

Thank you for reading Elizabeth and her KWMT colleagues' story! Team Tom? Team Mike? You're finally going to find out the answer … and so is Elizabeth. After investigating a series of murders, Elizabeth is drawn to both the enigmatic rancher and the journalist/home-town sports hero. But Mike has TV career aspirations of his own, and Tom has a feisty daughter who's definitely Team Dad.

Will crime in Sherman go on hiatus so that Elizabeth can sort out her next moves? Not on your life.

Air Ready

Enjoy **Cross Talk**? (Hope so)

Elizabeth and friends ask if you'll help spread the word about them and the Caught Dead in Wyoming series. You have the power to do that in two quick ways:

Recommend the book and the series to your friends and/or the whole wide world on social media. Shouting from rooftops is particularly appreciated.

Review the book. Take a few minutes to write an honest review and it can make a huge difference. As you likely know, it's the single best way for your fellow readers to find books they'll enjoy, too.

To me—as an author and a reader—the goal is always to find a good author-reader match. By sharing your reading experience through recommendations and reviews, you become a vital matchmaker. ☺

The Caught Dead in Wyoming series

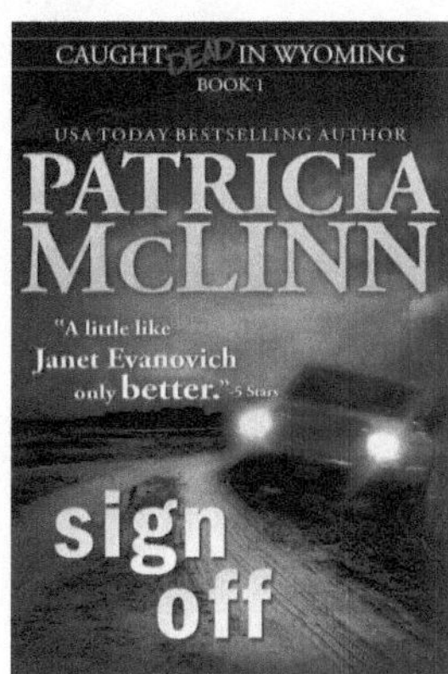

SIGN OFF

Divorce a husband, lose a career … grapple with a murder.

LEFT HANGING

Trampled by bulls — an accident? Elizabeth, Mike and friends dig into the world of rodeo.

SHOOT FIRST

For Elizabeth, death hits close to home. She and friends delve into old Wyoming treasures and secrets to save lives.

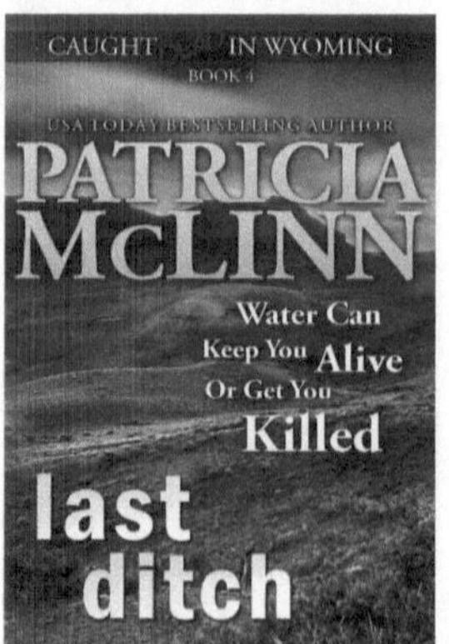

LAST DITCH

Elizabeth and Mike search after a man in a wheelchair goes missing in dangerous, desolate country.

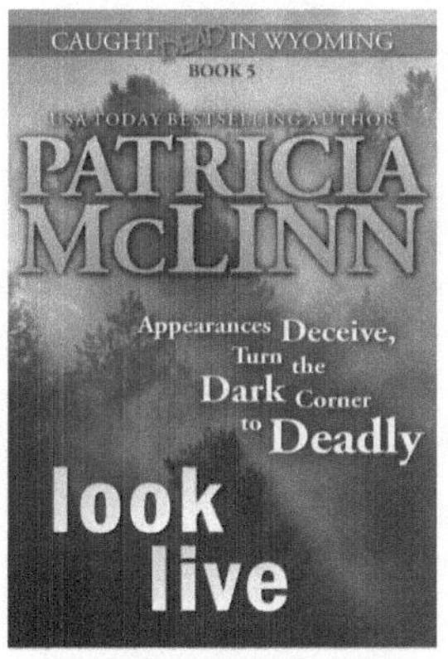

LOOK LIVE

Elizabeth and friends take on misleading murder with help — and hindrance — from intriguing out-of-towners.

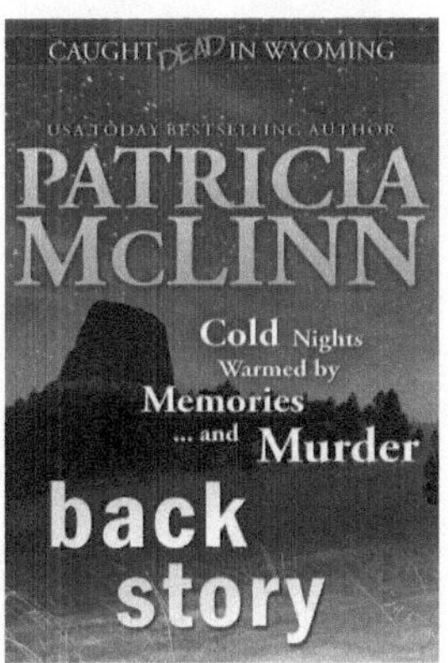

BACK STORY

Murder never dies, but comes back to threaten Elizabeth and team of investigators.

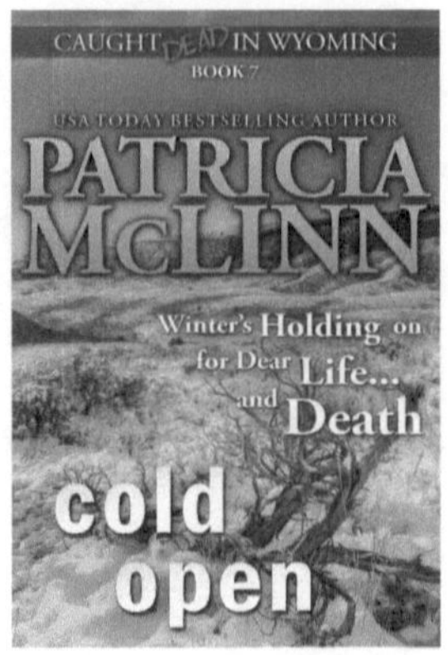

COLD OPEN

Elizabeth's search for a place of her own becomes an open house
for murder.

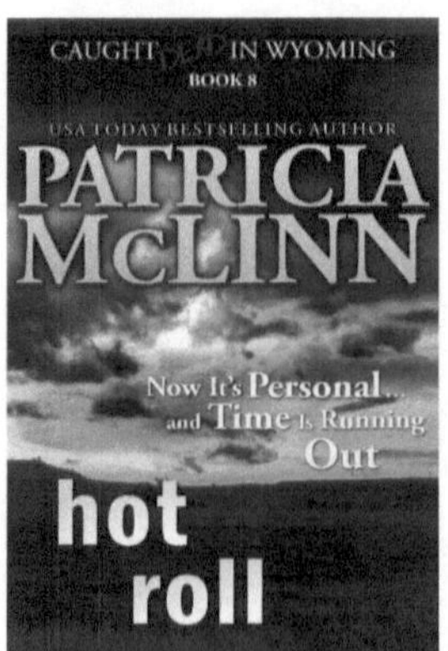

HOT ROLL

One of their own becomes a target — and time is running out.

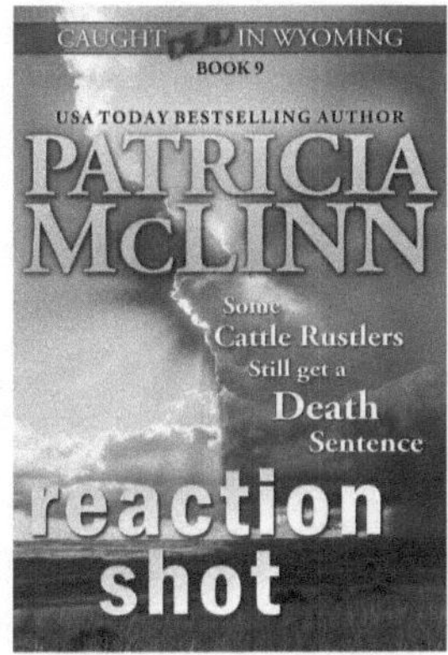

REACTION SHOT

Sometimes cattle rustlers still get a death sentence.

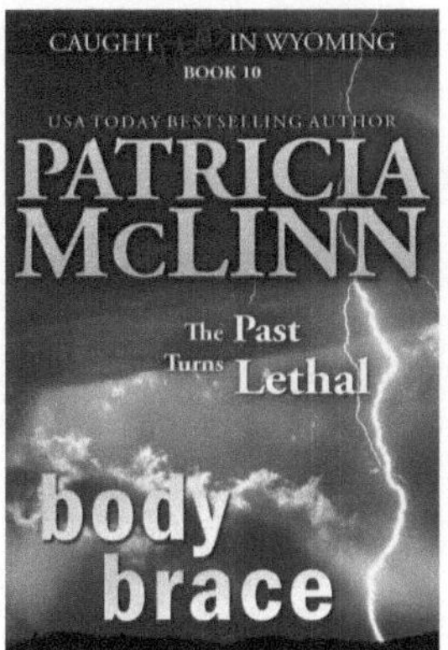

BODY BRACE

Everything can change, but murder still comes calling.

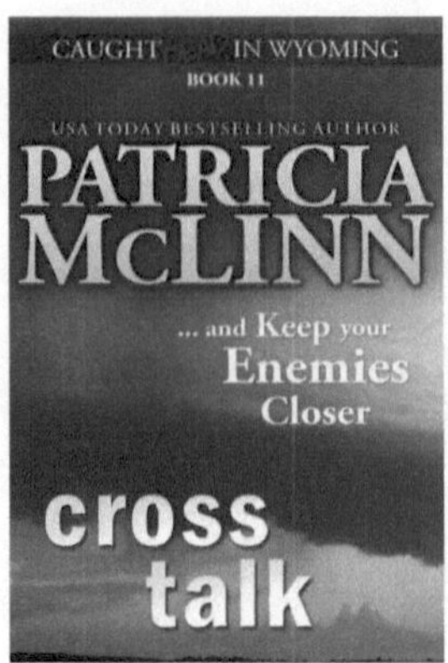

CROSS TALK

Prime suspect: The most annoying man in Sherman.

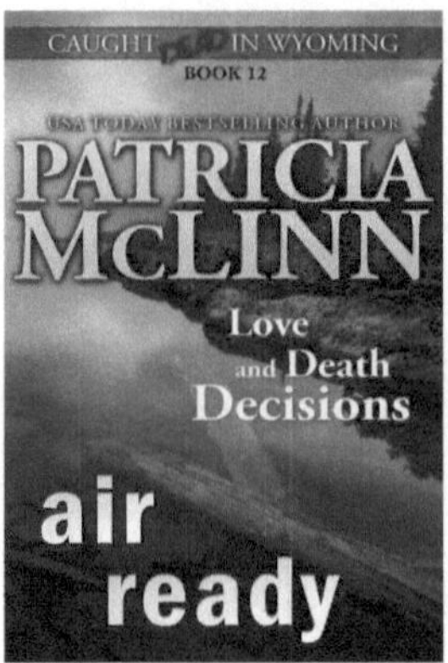

AIR READY

Love and death decisions.

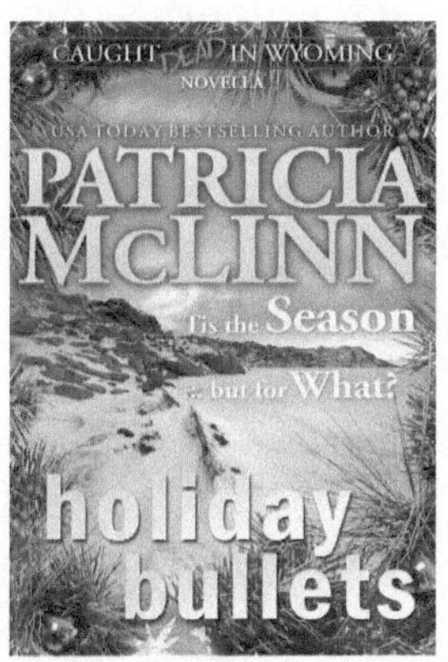

HOLIDAY BULLETS

A Christmas wish with Elizabeth's name on it.

CUE UP

On the trail of murder.

DEATH ON BEGUILING WAY

No zen in sight as Sheila untangles a yoga instructor's murder.

DEATH ON COVERT CIRCLE

A supermarket CEO meets his expiration date.

DEATH ON SHADY BRIDGE

A homicide cold case heats up.

DEATH ON CARRION LANE

A reunion for murder in Haines Tavern.

DEATH ON ZIGZAG TRAIL

A spooky legend twists grave matters.

DEATH ON PUZZLE PLACE

Season's greetings: Whodunit?

PREMISE OF INNOCENCE

The last woman Detective Landis is prepared to see is the one he
must save.

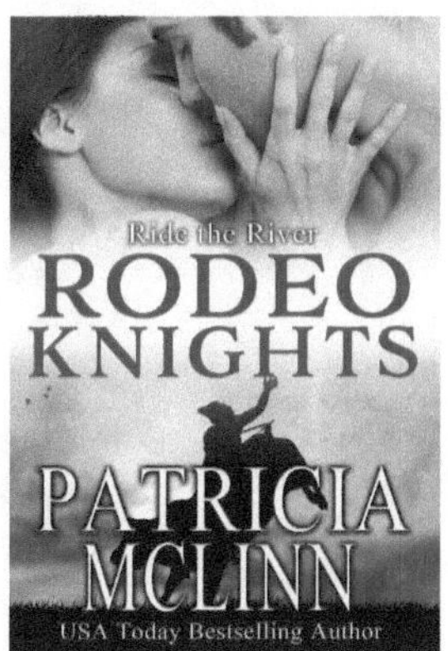

RIDE THE RIVER: RODEO KNIGHTS

Her rodeo cowboy ex is back … as her prime suspect.

Explore a complete list of all Patricia's books
patriciamclinn.com/patricias-books

Or get a printable booklist
patriciamclinn.com/patricias-books/printable-booklist

Patricia's Bookstore (buy online directly from Patricia)
shop.patriciamclinn.com

About the Author

Patricia McLinn is the USA Today bestselling author of more than 60 published novels cited by readers and reviewers for their wit and vivid characterization. Her books include mysteries, romantic suspense, contemporary romance, historical romance, and women's fiction. They have topped bestseller lists and won numerous awards.

She has spoken about writing from London to Melbourne, Australia, to Washington, D.C., including being a guest speaker at the Smithsonian Institution.

McLinn spent more than 20 years as an editor at The Washington Post after stints as a sports writer (Rockford, Ill.) and assistant sports editor (Charlotte, N.C.). She received BA and MSJ degrees from Northwestern University.

Now living in northern Kentucky, McLinn loves to hear from readers through her website and social media.

Visit with Patricia:

Website: patriciamclinn.com

Facebook: facebook.com/PatriciaMcLinn

Pinterest: pinterest.com/patriciamclinn

Instagram: instagram.com/patriciamclinnauthor

9 781954 478046